WESTERN

Rugged men looking for love...

Recapturing Her Heart
Jennifer Slattery

The Cowboy's Return
Danica Favorite

MILLS & BOON

RECAPTURING HER HEART
© 2024 by Jennifer Slattery
Philippine Copyright 2024
Australian Copyright 2024
New Zealand Copyright 2024

First Published 2024
First Australian Paperback Edition 2024
ISBN 978 1 038 90579 6

THE COWBOY'S RETURN
© 2024 by Danica Favorite
Philippine Copyright 2024
Australian Copyright 2024
New Zealand Copyright 2024

First Published 2024
First Australian Paperback Edition 2024
ISBN 978 1 038 90579 6

MIX
Paper | Supporting
responsible forestry
FSC® C001695

Published by
Harlequin Mills & Boon
An imprint of Harlequin Enterprises (Australia) Pty Limited
(ABN 47 001 180 918), a subsidiary of HarperCollins
Publishers Australia Pty Limited
(ABN 36 009 913 517)
Level 19, 201 Elizabeth Street
SYDNEY NSW 2000 AUSTRALIA

Cover art used by arrangement with Harlequin Books S.A.. All rights reserved.

Printed and bound in Australia by McPherson's Printing Group

Recapturing Her Heart
Jennifer Slattery

MILLS & BOON

Jennifer Slattery is a writer and speaker who has addressed women's and church groups across the nation. As the founder of Wholly Loved Ministries, she and her team help women rest in their true worth and live with maximum impact. When not writing, Jennifer loves spending time with her adult daughter and hilarious husband. Visit her online at jenniferslatterylivesoutloud.com to learn more or to book her for your next women's event.

And now abideth faith, hope, charity, these three; but the greatest of these is charity.
—*1 Corinthians* 13:13

DEDICATION

To my father-in-law John Slattery.
I was blessed to know you.

CHAPTER ONE

CLAMMY HANDS GRIPPING her steering wheel, Harper Moore forced herself to park in front of the one place in Sage Creek, Texas, she had determined to avoid. The name painted on the dusty window—Nuts, Bolts and Boards—seemed to mock her, reminding her of the words she'd spoken the night she and CJ Jenkins broke up.

She'd never intended to hurt him. She'd simply wanted more than this town and, by association, CJ could offer.

Yet here she was, back home, living with her mom, no less, and needing help from the people least likely to give it to her. But only for a season. God willing, in two months, she'd move with her daughter and return to the world of professional dance.

But first, she needed to muster the courage to get out of her car, march into the Jenkinses' hardware store and apply for a job.

Her baby's paternal grandmother, Cynthia Rhodam, Managing Director of South East Repertory, had promised to use her connections to land Harper a prestigious choreographer position. As if that could rectify the injustice Harper suffered when the woman forced her to resign to avoid tarnishing her son's name. Nor could a job, however needed, heal the wound caused when Chaz denied paternity.

Harper could've fought the matter. She'd certainly had every right. But standing up to someone with such influence could've killed any future opportunities in the dance world.

Lost child support, she could handle. The death of her dream, she could not. So, she'd conceded to "lie low" until lawyers resolved a sexual harassment suit against Emaline's father that didn't directly involve Harper but affected her nonetheless.

Needing a dose of encouragement, she called her best friend.

Trisha answered on the first ring. "Hey, girl. Been praying for you. How'd it go?"

She released a sigh. "Haven't done the deed yet."

"Okay. What do you need from me?"

"A reminder that I can do hard things? If only

I'd been able to make ends meet in Seattle." Unfortunately, childcare fees and the skyrocketed cost of living had forced her home.

"But then you wouldn't get to see me."

Harper laughed. "You do remember this is temporary, right? Just until I save funds for first and last on an apartment and a month's worth of childcare fees."

"And assuming Chaz's mother holds true to her word?"

"And that." Emaline's paternal grandmother hadn't exactly demonstrated high integrity. But she did hold a lot of influence in the dance industry. "If only the library would give me more hours, I wouldn't have to be here, about to eat the biggest slice of humble pie imaginable."

"You've got nothing to feel insecure about. March in there with your head high. And remember, you look amazing, by the way."

Sitting taller, Harper eyed her reflection in the rearview mirror, more thankful than ever that her beautician friend had treated her to a free hair makeover. "I do love the burgundy highlights."

"I knew they'd look great with your sable-toned locks. Like I said yesterday, the color combo really makes your blue eyes pop."

"Thanks." The curl cream she'd purchased, which emitted a faint pineapple-coconut scent, countered the Texas humidity that normally turned her wavy hair to frizz.

Regardless, she couldn't help but view herself through CJ's eyes, certain she'd find nothing but bitterness and contempt staring back at her.

"You want to celebrate with milkshakes at Wilma's after?" Trisha asked.

"Can't. Promised Mom I'd clean the kitchen in exchange for her watching Emaline."

While her mother hadn't always been the best source of support, and often offered it with contempt, Harper was grateful for her help now.

Unfortunately, her father hadn't been a part of her life since he bailed on her and her mom fifteen years prior.

She released a heavy breath that did little to ease her churning gut. "Guess I best get this over with." Ending the call, she grabbed her printed résumé and stepped out and into the pleasant spring sun. The soft scent of geraniums and petunias wafted toward her from pots hanging from either side of the lamppost streetlight. The faint twang of a country song emanated from the hardware store, merging with the eighties' rock drifting from the adjacent pawnshop.

Harper paused on the sidewalk to center herself, watching through the window as Nancy, CJ's mom, spoke with a potbellied man wearing a stretched-out navy T-shirt. Harper scanned the store's interior for a glimpse of CJ's dad, John Michael. She'd much prefer to deal with him. With his relatively even-keeled personality, he was less likely to respond to Harper's job inquiry with venom.

Nancy, however, epitomized the mama-bear sweatshirt she used to wear. Hopefully time had overcome any residual anger. CJ's mom was an adult, after all. And a business owner, one who, if that Help Wanted sign tacked to the window still held true, needed an employee.

"Are you going in?" The deep voice startled her.

She turned toward the tall, lanky man who held the door open for her. "Yes, thank you." Her legs and fingers felt tingly as she stepped inside, and not from the gush of air-conditioning blowing overhead.

Nancy shifted in their direction. "Welcome to—" Her instant smile faltered before returning, taut, below stony eyes. Her gaze remained locked on Harper.

"Ma'am." Her lungs felt tight as she fought

for the courage to say why she'd come. Instead, Harper stared, mouth dry, at the woman who'd once encouraged her to call her Mama, while Nancy stared back.

An approaching customer wanting a particular color of paint interrupted the heavy silence that stretched between them. Watching Nancy disappear down a nearby aisle, Harper released the breath she'd been holding.

Everything within her urged her to exit the store as quickly as possible. Instead, she squared her shoulders and walked, stiff-legged, toward the long, pine checkout counter.

What would she do if, once Nancy returned, she kicked her out? At least the store was nearly empty; any public humiliation wouldn't gather much of an audience. Not that she expected Nancy to respond with such unprofessional behavior. She could, however, see the woman avoiding her until Harper's growing anxiety overpowered the last of her resolve.

"Yes, ma'am. We've got two-wheel dollies next to our moving boxes."

Harper froze, a jolt shooting through her, at the sound of CJ's approaching voice. She darted behind a steel pillar barely wider than her five-foot-four frame.

What was he doing here? Her friend Trisha had seen him scraping paint off somebody's shed not long ago. They'd assumed he was working construction, but he may have been helping a friend. Or, maybe, like her, he needed to piece together the hours from two jobs to make ends meet.

Harper focused on his conversation with his customer to gauge which direction they were heading.

"My friends keep pestering me to hire a moving company to come in and pack all my things." The woman huffed. "As if I've got money for that." Her footsteps halted. "Oh. Spackle. Is this what I need to fill in the holes in my walls? From hanging picture frames and such?"

It sounded as if she and CJ had stopped a few feet away. Unfortunately, they appeared in no hurry to leave. Harper held her breath as the woman went on to talk about her various collections and other items she hoped to sell at a garage sale. Apparently, she was moving into an assisted-living facility near her oldest son.

"That sounds like a big transition." Compassion softened CJ's tone, his words unhurried, as if prepared to listen for as long as the lady needed.

He'd always been kind, a trait that had initially caught her off guard. She'd expected him, the high school quarterback, to act cocky and self-obsessed. Instead, he'd been the first to reach out to the new kid or the teen lingering on the fringe. Although she'd initially felt drawn to his striking good looks, it was his heart that had captured hers.

She could still envision his easy grin and the way his greenish-gray eyes lit whenever they landed on hers.

Had he changed much over the years?

Harper waited until CJ and his customer's conversation and footfalls receded, then slipped out from behind the pillar. Curiosity and something she couldn't name drew her in the direction of their voices. Second to the last aisle to the end, she paused, pulse quickened, and slowly peered around the corner.

CJ stood with his back to her, talking to a short lady with long silver hair and a boxy torso. His faded blue jeans complemented his muscular frame, and his broad shoulders seemed to strain against the cotton of his teal T-shirt. He wore his hair shorter than he had in high school. The blond locks that used to curl up from under his cowboy hat were not presently visible.

He laughed at something the woman said—Harper couldn't quite make it out.

"Well, now, we can't let that happen." He handed his customer a roll of Bubble Wrap and a stack of large flattened boxes. "My folks would never let me hear the end of it. Anything else you need?"

She shook her head and the two turned in Harper's direction—CJ's widening eyes landing on her before she could dart out of sight. Thick brows pinched together, he frowned, seeming at a loss for words. But then he gave a quick firm nod she'd seen him greet others with numerous times before.

The steady thud of his boots matched the loud pounding of her heart as, expression tense, he strolled toward her. "Harper."

"Hey, CJ." Her voice came out squeaky.

The customer followed his eyes, and a look of curiosity flashed across her face. She offered Harper a smile and thanked CJ for his help. "I best get back home to wrap those gnomes I told you about."

His chuckle sounded forced. "You do that. And don't forget to call Pastor Roger to ask about borrowing Trinity Faith's cargo trailer. He'd be thrilled to know it was being put to good use, as long as he hasn't already promised it to someone else that day."

"I'll do that." The woman walked away with a wiggly fingered wave.

CJ's jaw muscle twitched as he faced Harper, his cedar-citrus aroma scenting the space between them. "You need help with something?" His tone carried an edge.

Although they'd seen one another around town about half a dozen times since she'd returned to Sage Creek, they'd managed to avoid each other until now. The downward slant of his flattened lips verified he wasn't any happier to break that trend than she was.

She rubbed the back of her arm. Clearly, Nancy wasn't the most challenging Jenkins family member to have this conversation with. "Do you work here?" If so, they'd be spending a great deal of time together.

Just how badly did she need this job?

Unfortunately, very.

The crevice between his brows deepened. Jutting his chin, he nodded. "No surprise there, huh?"

She winced inwardly, thinking about the words she'd spoken the night they broke up—how she'd told him that she wanted more, thereby implying that he, and the life he'd offered her, wasn't enough.

He studied her, a shadow of sorrow softening his glare. "I need to get back to work." He turned to leave.

"Wait." She grabbed his wrist, and a familiar shiver shot through her.

His frown returned. "What do you need, Harper?"

She couldn't remember him ever having spoken to her so harshly. Much had changed—because of her.

"I…" She pushed at her thumb cuticle. "Are your parents still hiring?"

"Why? You know of someone looking for a job?"

"Yeah. Me." She spoke quickly, before she could chicken out.

His eyebrows shot up, and he gave his head a slight shake, as if he wasn't sure he'd heard her correctly. "Aren't you working at the library?"

"I am, but they cut my hours." She'd been part-time since Christmas.

He sighed and scrubbed a hand over his face, probably contemplating the most professional way to brush her off. "Applications are in the office. Come on." He made a sweeping motion with his arm.

Sucking in a breath to still her jittery stomach, she followed him past a bin of screws, a ladder attached to a ceiling rail, like one might see in old libraries, and a large yellow barrel filled with rakes, prongs up.

At the back of the store, she lingered in the short hallway, beside a corkboard covered with community event posters and various flyers. Someone had German shepherd puppies for sale. Someone else was offering housecleaning services. Tomorrow, the church was hosting a craft bazaar and family carnival event to fund a youth-group mission trip. According to the thumbtacked page, the activities included face painting, a clown making balloon animals, a petting zoo and a bounce house, among other things.

CJ nudged a plastic cooler out of his way to reach a metal filing cabinet. The top drawer opened with a screech. He handed her a printed application. "You can fill this out now or take it home and bring it back."

Focused on the paper, she nodded. "Thank you." The question was, if she left, would she have the courage to return?

CHRISTOPHER JAMES JENKINS'S steps felt stiff as he walked Harper to the break room. His gut was filled with the same ache he'd experienced the night she'd shattered his heart. Apparently, he hadn't healed as much as he'd thought in the five years since. That also meant her working here was a bad idea.

But he couldn't just turn her away without at least glancing at her application. He wasn't an expert in civil law, but it seemed that would qualify as job discrimination or something.

He motioned for her to sit at the scratched and wobbly table centering the space. "Can I get you a water or cup of coffee?"

She perched on the edge of a folding chair. "I'm fine, but thank you."

Lingering a few feet away, he watched as she leaned over the page. Her dark, wavy hair spilled forward, exposing the gentle curve of her slender neck. Her trim dancer's build from high school had filled out and softened in all the right ways.

He still caught his breath when her blue eyes, framed by thick, dark lashes, latched on to his. The vulnerability her nervous posture and heart-shaped face had displayed moments ago stirred emotions within him he'd thought had long died.

That she triggered a reaction at all, especially since she'd made it clear how little she'd thought of him, caused his teeth to clench.

Why was she here? Clearly, the life in the big city she'd left him for hadn't been enough to keep her attention, either.

Was it wrong that the thought gave him a measure of satisfaction?

With a mental shake, he crossed to the counter, gathered three days' worth of dirty mugs and tidied up the napkins and creamers. He picked up a damp rag next to the sink and wiped a splotch of ketchup from the countertop.

He cast a glance over his shoulder. "My folks can't pay much more than minimum wage. And they're looking for someone able to work evenings and weekends." He figured that alone would deter her.

She met his gaze. "I understand."

Hadn't that been one of her biggest fears? That she'd end up chained to this place—the store and town—forever? At least, that's how Trisha had later relayed it. She'd said Harper couldn't marry a man with zero ambition.

"CJ?" His mom's voice preceded her.

"Harper." She stood in the doorway, her tone as cold as her expression. She moved to the table and glanced at the application. Her eyebrows plummeted. "You're looking for work?"

Harper's pen paused midstroke. "Yes, ma'am. If you and Mr. Jenkins will have me." Her voice trembled slightly.

His mom's gaze shot to CJ, her expression clouded, before landing back on Harper. "I see." She hesitated, as if contemplating saying more.

Remembering how stirred up his mother had been when he'd told her of the breakup, he hoped she wouldn't. His mom was anything but even-tempered, especially when someone hurt those she loved. And her stony expression suggested bitterness from that day still lingered.

He understood that. Whoever'd said time healed all wounds had never loved, and lost, a woman like Harper. The years had merely tamed the ache—a hurt he had no intentions of experiencing again.

Making eye contact, his mom tilted her head toward the door.

He nodded and followed her into the hall.

Arms crossed, Nancy stood with her back to the long plastic PVC sheets from the loading area entrance. "What's this about?"

"Don't know. Maybe she saw the Help Wanted sign in the window."

"We don't need help that badly."

"I agree."

Her gaze flicked back to the break room, and she frowned. "But she must be really struggling financially to come in here. And she does have a kid. That matters, regardless of how we all feel about her."

CJ's gut sank. "What are you saying?"

"That we need to pray on this some."

He didn't want to hear any talk about loving his enemies or giving them the shirt off his back. Harper had already taken too much.

His mom's phone chimed a text, and she glanced at the screen then at CJ. "Dad's asking for more information on those website plug-ins you told us about."

"Meant to work on that this morning." He'd poked around on a few websites but preferred to speak with an actual person. "I got sidetracked helping a gal find a tool for her father's birthday." If they wanted the store to survive this internet era, where folks were used to doing most of their shopping with a click, they'd need to provide online ordering options.

His folks disagreed, but they were willing to

hear him out. They probably understood that he had additional reasons for wanting to expand their online presence. He needed to find a way to increase his exposure as an artist if he wanted to turn what his father called a "hobby" into a viable career. He wouldn't abandon his parents to run this place on their own. But adding another worker would allow him to reduce his hours since they hadn't yet been able to convince their part-time guy to increase his.

A steady crew would help his parents to maintain a more reasonable schedule as well. Their aging bodies wouldn't keep up with their seventy-plus-hour, highly physical workweeks forever. The way CJ saw it, every win for the store was a win for him, and vice versa.

But he'd much rather hire someone—anyone—other than Harper.

"I best go water our spring flowers." His mom bit off a hangnail. "When the ballerina princess is finished with her application, place it on my desk. Then walk her out."

"Okay."

He returned to the break room to find Harper waiting where he'd left her, typing on her phone.

She sprang to her feet when he entered. "Here." She handed him her completed paper.

He skimmed her work history with a raised brow. So, she had found her big break, after all. She'd worked for some Seattle-based dance company for just under a year. Why had she left? Had they cut her loose once she became pregnant? He doubted that was legal.

"Everything look okay?"

CJ glanced up to find her watching him with a wrinkled brow. "Yeah. This is great." He motioned to the door then followed her out.

"When do you think y'all will make a decision?" Her tone conveyed a hint of anxiety.

"Soon. We're heading into our busy season." The uptick should have started with the coming of spring. But while their sales numbers had increased, it had not been by as much as his parents had hoped. They feared they were losing people to a new chain that had popped up in the next county. CJ doubted locals would drive that far for lumber and nails. Contractors, however, were another matter. Still, he had to believe the fact that they'd always charged fair prices would count for something.

"Oh, wow." Harper stopped in front of a section his dad had allowed CJ to use to display some of his chain-saw carvings. He'd marked off the corner area using a wooden arch made of two thick trunks, bark shining with finishing wax. She gazed up at his name burned into the sign attached to the tops by adjacent chains. "Are these yours?"

Did he detect a note of admiration in her voice? Standing a mite taller, he nodded. "It relaxes me."

"Do you mind?" She stepped toward his designs.

"Not at all." He followed as she approached a carving of three bear cubs climbing a stripped branch.

"This is amazing."

CJ hated that her praise still affected him. "Thank you." He lingered in the center of the circular rug bearing a red Texas star as she moved from one carving to the next.

"I had no idea you were so creative." She paused in front of a baby fox standing in the center of a hollowed-out stump. "How long have you been doing this?"

About a year after Harper had left, CJ had learned from Trisha that his supposed lack of ambition had played a significant role in their breakup. Seeing him now, working in the same place that he always had, as she'd predicted, had probably confirmed her assessment.

She'd be wrong.

But…would Harper view his newfound passion for carving as him chasing a fantasy or an attainable dream?

Her opinion shouldn't matter.

He shifted his weight to his other foot. "A while."

He straightened a stack of promotional cards printed on glossy card stock. "Got into it a couple years ago after watching a demonstration in Branson."

He'd gone camping with some buddies shortly after his and Harper's breakup, devasted and forced to rethink how he'd envisioned the rest of his life playing out. For a while, he'd floundered without motivation for much of anything. When he'd learned how Harper had felt regarding his so-called lack of drive, his low aspirations had felt like a personal defect.

He now knew he simply hadn't yet discovered the thing that made him feel most alive.

CJ rested a hand on his belt buckle. "The town was hosting a Timber festival, with activities, live music, and various artists and craftsmen, chain-saw carvers included."

"Interesting."

"It was." He chuckled, remembering one man

in particular dressed in jeans and a plaid flannel, his long, black hair pulled into one of those messy man-buns folks used to make social media memes out of. "About half the guys looked like they'd come from a remote mountain somewhere—with their wild eyebrows curling every which way and their mouths hidden behind bushy mustaches and beards."

"Not exactly the standard image of an artist, huh?"

"True." That was probably why those men had made such an impact. They'd helped him see that a guy could be creative and masculine. In this, they'd given him permission to explore an outlet he'd never previously considered. That experience had awakened a part of him he hadn't known existed. A love that felt so inherent to his being, he'd found himself wanting to downplay its intensity to shield himself from further rejection.

Shoulders stiff, he watched Harper peruse each item, a hint of a smile emerging as she paused over some of his most complex pieces.

And if her estimation of him had changed?

His heart squeezed, threatening to unleash emotions he'd spent the past five years fighting against. What was that saying about falling into the same trap twice?

But what if the sense of adventure that attracted her to Seattle had left her disappointed? What if she'd realized all that was lost the day she'd left, with the wisdom that can only come from shattered expectations, and had returned for good?

CHAPTER TWO

THE NEXT MORNING, Harper woke early and was showered and ready to go by nine thirty. Behind her, Emaline, also dressed and ready, lay on her Noah's ark baby blanket, playing contentedly with the brightly colored animal rings dangling from the arch of her floor mat "gym." Considering Emaline's disrupted sleep the night before, she'd likely need a nap in an hour or two.

That could be a good thing, if it caused her to sleep through church. Not so much, if it made her fussy.

Harper, on the other hand, would need to fight to stay awake.

She scrutinized her reflection in the mirror, trying to remember what the women had been wearing the last time she'd attended Trinity Faith.

Business casual was probably the safest choice. She'd selected a peach dress with a gathered neckline decorated with buttons down the front. For shoes, she chose cream ankle-strap wedges.

She added a hint of gloss to her lips, fluffed her hair, then turned to her happily cooing daughter. "All right, sweet girl." She eased Emaline out from under her hanging mobile and kissed her cheek. "You ready to see how most people in this town spend their Sunday mornings? And hopefully show Mrs. Jenkins I'm not a terrible person?"

If she wanted to land that hardware store job, she needed to find a way to soften the woman's opinion of her. Hopefully, her seeing Harper sitting in the pews would help.

She cast a nervous glance to the ceiling. Was that a wrong reason to attend church?

With Emaline cradled close to her chest, Harper exited her room.

Her mom's voice drifted toward her. It sounded like she was on the phone.

Hearing her name, Harper stopped midstep to listen.

"I mean, I'm not exactly raking in the money, as you well know. Things have been tight. I had to call out quite a bit the past few months due to my back. Now my boss is threatening to fire me. Not that he's ever given me enough work to actually make a decent living." She huffed.

Who was her mom talking to?

"I'm going to talk to Harper. Tell her she needs to start paying rent. Maybe pitch in for food, too. The good Lord knows I could use the extra cash."

Harper's stomach dropped. How had she not realized how much her mother struggled?

But what could she do? She'd put in applications at about every business in Sage Creek, even those that said they weren't hiring on the chance that they might soon.

Regardless, she needed to contribute more financially. That was another reason she desperately needed Nancy to hire her. And, God willing, give her enough hours to allow her to pay rent, help with groceries and save up for a move to the city.

What if nothing came of the choreographer's job? Emaline's paternal grandmother—or father, for that matter—wasn't exactly a person of honor who kept her word.

Then she'd find something else—teaching private lessons or something.

For now, at least she received free babysitting.

If that were to change, it'd probably cost more to work than she earned.

With a quick glance to her mother, who sat with her back to her in the living room, Harper dashed into the kitchen for a bagel and cup of coffee. Not that her jittery nerves needed the caffeine, but her sleep-deprived brain did.

She took a sip and winced. Lukewarm. Not the most appetizing, but it'd do.

Rounding the corner, she ran smack into her mom, dying the front of Harper's dress in a lovely shade of brown.

"Oh." Her mom stepped back. "Sorry about that."

"No big deal." She glanced at the carpet, thankful her clothes had absorbed the spill— for her and her mom's relationship.

As to Harper's wardrobe, however, that was another story.

Lovely. Now she was going to be late, especially considering this was her only wrinkle-free dress.

Did her mom even own an iron?

By the time she finally left, she felt more than a little frazzled and debated heading back inside. But she really needed that hardware store job. Now more than ever.

At the church, the parking lot was nearly full. The sun streaked through the clouds drifting past the bell tower and steeple. A stained-glass Gothic window, vibrant against the white siding, stood on either side of the door. Bordering the stone foundation, bluebonnets, pink buttercups and red poppies grew between neatly trimmed bushes.

Locking her car, she pressed her lips to the side of her daughter's soft head and inhaled her sweet baby scent. "We've got this, right, baby girl?"

Why did she feel so nervous?

Because she hadn't stepped inside a church in five years and wasn't sure what to expect? Or because she was apprehensive about potentially running into Nancy, the woman she hoped to see but would also rather avoid?

Or because she might run into CJ?

Probably all three.

Squaring her shoulders, Harper strode across the asphalt, up the concrete stairs and through the heavy wooden doors. The air, cooler than outside but more humid nonetheless, emitted a musty aroma mixed with lemon-scented wood polish and an undercurrent of dust. Rich notes from an organ flowed over her as she stepped into the short foyer separating the entrance from the visible sanctuary beyond.

Great. As she feared, service had already started.

A few heads turned, surveying her as she stood, stiffly, beneath the archway. Others swayed to the music, led in song by a robed choir up front.

Wiping a sweaty hand on her skirt, Harper scanned the rows of heads in front of her. A balding man was fighting with a toddler determined to climb over the pew back.

Movement in her peripheral view caught her attention. She turned, inhaling sharply to see CJ walking toward her, a look of surprise in his eyes.

He was clean-shaven and dressed in a navy-and-white plaid collared shirt with pearl buttons and a silver buckle centered with a turquoise stone. It felt odd to see him without his cowboy hat, but then she remembered where they were. Back in high school, one of her friends used to joke that, with his strong jaw, blond hair, now spiked, and chiseled build, he belonged on the cover of one of those outdoorsman magazines.

If that was true then, it was triply so now.

He smelled like a mixture between leather,

sage and apple. "Morning." His hoarse whisper made her feel as if she were disrupting the service.

Harper nodded with a shaky smile. "Hello." Why did her stomach feel so unsettled whenever he was around? Whereas he always seemed ultraconfident and completely unfazed.

As if she no longer meant anything to him.

And why would she? They hadn't dated in over five years.

His eyes softened as he looked briefly at Emaline, who'd shoved her fist into her mouth and was blowing raspberries. "Hey, cutie," he whispered, then looked at Harper. "Would you like me to walk you to the nursery?"

That was kind of him to offer. To notice she'd come in, period, and make an effort to see that she felt comfortable.

She bit her lip and scanned the sanctuary. Had anyone else brought in their baby?

Although she didn't see any infants, she noted a handful or so of children squirming about. A round-faced boy maybe nine years old was alternating between bouncing in his seat and staring awkwardly at a couple behind him. Harper was half expecting the child to start making silly faces.

Harper bit the inside of her lip to stifle her laugh before turning back to CJ. "Would it be okay if I kept her with me?"

"Whatever makes you most comfortable." He handed her a bulletin from the stack on top of his Bible.

Ah. He served as an usher. That's why he was acting so helpful, not because he actually cared that she felt as out of place as a hip-hop dancer tossed onstage at *The Nutcracker.*

He guided her to an empty seat next to an older couple near the back right and pulled a thick green book from the pocket in front of her. "Page three seventy-eight." He opened it for her then handed it over as she slid into the row. "'I Surrender All.'"

She blinked. "You what?"

"The song." He tapped the title on the left-hand side.

"Oh. Right." Warmth climbed up her neck. "Thank you."

He nodded, studied her a moment, then walked away.

Spine straight, legs crossed at the ankles, she focused on the printed lyrics while casting furtive glances at the people singing around her. Nancy and her husband sat halfway up to the right, a family of four on one side and a younger couple on the other.

Swiveling slightly, she slid a look behind her. CJ occupied a wooden chair placed against the back wall. Was he seeing anyone? Considering the size of Sage Creek, seems she would've heard if he was.

Not that this was any of her business, except that she wanted to know he was happy.

His gaze landed on hers. Face hot once again, Harper turned back around, gently swaying Emaline to sleep while frantically scanning the printed lyrics to catch up. By the time she figured out that the congregation had moved to another song entirely, the pastor was walking onto the stage while the choir streamed off.

His message was on identity, and he repeated the phrase, "You got to know who you are and whose you are," about half a dozen times. "Ain't no one else has the right to define you or tell you what you're worth."

"That's right!" a male voice from the right boomed, startling Harper.

She scanned the parishioners, unsettled to find Nancy watching her with an unreadable expression. Upon eye contact, the woman straightened and turned back around.

Was she as surprised as CJ had clearly been to see Harper there? And if so, was that a good thing?

If it got her the job, yes.

Maybe Harper should try to talk to her after church. Not about the job, by any means. That would be all sorts of impolite. She'd simply say hi and hopefully create some positive interactions to counter whatever negative emotions the woman felt toward her.

When the service ended, she held Emaline close and filed out behind an older man with a black comb-over and protruding ears. The line bottlenecked at the archway as people chatted with one another. Someone's overpowering floral perfume and the increased noise combined with her growing sleepiness, threatening to give Harper a headache.

She glanced from the chair CJ had been sitting in to behind her to catch a glimpse of Nancy through the throng. She stood at the end of her row talking to a larger woman wearing a fuchsia blouse.

"Harper!"

Recognizing the enthusiastic voice, she turned toward her friend with a smile. "Trisha, hi."

"Why didn't you tell me you were coming? I would've saved you a seat."

Because Harper had reserved the right, up until she'd ascended the church steps, to change her mind. But she blamed her lack of communication on her daughter. "I wasn't sure how Emaline would do. If we'd actually be able to stay." That wasn't entirely false.

They stepped aside so as not to block traffic.

"Boy, do I hear that." Trisha tucked her bulletin into her Bible. "Come with me to get my munchkins?"

"Uh…" She looked back at Nancy, still engaged in conversation. Oh, well. At least she'd seen Harper there. That had to count for something.

Harper still felt guilty over her motivations for attending. She glanced at the ceiling. *I'll come again—to learn more about You next time.*

And if You help me get that job at Nuts, Bolts and Boards, I'll be here every Sunday.

AFTER SERVICE, CJ's friend Oliver snagged him to offer a business proposition. "My landlord wants to sell my building. Asked if I wanted to buy it. Said he's giving me first dibs before listing it."

"And?"

"I would if he was willing to divide it up and let me purchase the area I run my antique store in. But I don't need, nor can I afford, the whole space. You still wanting to open a gallery of sorts to sell your chain-saw carvings?"

"Eventually."

"Any way I can get you to move the needle in the sooner rather than later direction?" He relayed the price and about how much they'd need to put down.

CJ whistled. "That's a lot. A good deal, I'm sure. But more than I've got."

"Think you can wrangle up some funds, maybe liquidate some of your bigger pieces?"

"The idea's appealing. It's the doing that'll be the challenge. So far, I haven't done a great job of getting my work to sell with any kind of consistency."

"This might-could give you the motivation you need." Oliver clamped a hand on his shoulder. "Just think about it."

"Will do."

His friend helped him gather dropped bulletins to be tossed and return Bibles to the back of pews.

"I saw you talking to Harper earlier." Oliver

picked up a pacifier lying on the floor. "Y'all patch things up?"

CJ tensed. "We don't hate each other, if that's what you mean."

"That's progress."

"And about as far as things will progress."

Oliver laughed then left CJ to finish up and turn off the sanctuary lights.

The sun streamed through the stained glass, decorating the wood flooring in beams of red, blue and green. Nearing the heavy double doors that, now closed, separated the large open space from the foyer, he paused midstep at the sound of Harper's familiar laugh.

He closed his eyes as a wave of sorrow swept over him, followed by a rush of anger at the fact that, after all these years, his heart still felt so bruised. It'd be so easy to talk his mom out of hiring her, if only to retain the distance he and Harper had managed to keep between one another since her return. But he also wanted to do right by God.

The Bible said not to withhold good when a fella had the power to act. As much as he'd like to believe otherwise, he figured the prov-erb applied in this instance. Besides, as his mom had said, Harper had a kid. The baby certainly wasn't to blame for his pain any more than she was for the circumstances that had brought her mama back. Didn't seem right for the cutie to bear the consequences, either.

Someone's phone chimed a notification. A voice, sounded like Trisha St. James's, followed. "I better get back to my poor, sick husband, who clearly has the worst head cold in the history of all mankind." Sarcasm deepened her tone.

With a deep breath, he strode forward, reaching the concrete steps moments after Harper and her friend, now in the parking lot, had separated, each to their respective vehicles.

Once at his truck, he was surprised to see Harper's car still in the lot. Seeing her with her baby this morning, the tender way she'd spoken to her, and the way Emaline had smiled and babbled in return, caused a wave of grief to swell within him. He'd always thought Harper would make a great mom. Seemed his hunch had been right. He'd also assumed he'd be able to see the nurturing side of her bloom, day in and day out, as they'd raised children together.

Giving himself a mental shake, he slid into his driver's seat, slipped on his sunglasses and turned his key in the ignition. One of his favorite country music songs poured through his radio, and the scent of stale coffee wafted from the half-filled mug he'd left in his cup holder.

About to turn onto B Street, he cast one last glance at Harper through his rearview mirror. She was still sitting, parked, in her vehicle. Based on the way she smacked her steering wheel, she was *not* happy. Engine problems? Not exactly something a single mom on a part-time, and likely minimum wage, salary needed. On the most inconvenient day to boot, considering Sage Creek's lone mechanic didn't work or answer his phone most Sundays.

Then again, she could always call someone else.

Although everything within him longed to pretend he hadn't seen her, manners dictated he at least check that she was okay, especially considering he served on the church's greeting team. With a heavy exhale, he shifted into Reverse and looped back around.

Her blush was evident as, window down, he idled his vehicle beside hers. "You all right?"

Her thin eyebrows pinched together, and her gaze seemed to falter, as if she were debating how to answer. She never had liked asking for help. That probably made her current predicament, finance-wise, all the more challenging.

It must have taken a great deal of courage and humility for her to walk into his parents' store. Jolted by her presence or not, he respected that.

She looked at her baby, who'd begun to fuss, then back at him with a sheepish smile. "My car won't start."

He nodded, parked and got out. A faint floral scent wafted toward him as he neared her car. "Give it a try so I can hear it."

She did. The engine made one click and nothing more.

The lights in the car were on, so it wasn't the battery. Didn't look like an issue with her anti-theft immobilizer; the vehicle's computer seemed to be working. "Probably an issue with your starter."

She now stood outside her vehicle, gently swaying, daughter clutched to her chest. "Is that expensive to fix?"

He shrugged. "Maybe three hundred fifty?"

"Okay, thanks. Guess I better call a tow truck, huh?"

"Doubt you'll reach anyone today."

"Right." Either the sun was making her eyes water, or she was fighting tears. "Thank you for your help." She grabbed her phone from the seat in her car, probably to call her folks.

"Hop in my truck and I'll give you a ride home."

"Are you sure?"

Having Harper sitting close beside him, her vulnerability making her even more beautiful than the day she broke his heart? That was the last thing he wanted. Regardless of their past, he wasn't jerk enough to walk away.

"It's no problem." He opened her back passenger door, unhooked the car seat, and grabbed it and the diaper bag from the floorboard. "I was heading that way. Promised my mom I'd swing by the grocery for milk and butter on the way to Sunday supper."

"Thanks."

He nodded. "The baby's car seat okay, the pickup not having a back seat and all?"

"Yeah. So long as it's rear facing."

Minding his manners, he waited until both mother and child were securely settled inside the cab. Then he closed her door, rounded the front of his truck and slid behind the wheel.

With how her nearness sent his heart thudding, he was grateful for the barrier the infant and her bulky car seat formed between them. Seemed his heart was forgetting what his mind refused to let go—Harper had left him years ago, without so much as a backward glance.

He eased his truck onto the quiet residential street lined with well-manicured lawns and brick homes tucked behind cheery flower beds. Most of the houses had covered porches, some with rockers, others with wooden swings. The road dimmed as thick white clouds moved across the sun, then brightened again.

He stopped at a four-way. "What'd you think of the service?" He'd not seen her in church since they were kids and figured she hadn't been in some time.

"It wasn't nearly as long as I remembered. Guess that's a sign of age, huh? When an hour actually feels like an hour?"

An elementary-aged boy in jeans and a baseball cap rode his bike down the sidewalk while two preschoolers raced big-wheels up and down a nearby driveway.

He gave a slight nod. "Guess so." A woman in all pink, from her shorts to her ball cap, jogged by. "And the sermon?" The pastor's message had been a bit mushier than he preferred—more "assurance" than action-focused. Yet he could see how the content might have encouraged Harper.

"It gave me some things to think about."

He wanted to ask her what, but they no longer had the type of relationship that allowed for such conversations. There'd been a time when they'd talked about pretty much everything.

Everything except her decision to leave Sage Creek. She'd obviously been contemplating that action for some time, at least long enough to send out college applications and secure housing. Yet she hadn't said a thing to him—the person she'd supposedly loved "more than anyone in the world"—until her bags were packed.

If she had told him, how would he have responded?

He would've begged her to stay. That was probably why she'd kept so quiet. While that realization helped ease the bite of the bitterness that remained, it didn't excuse her behavior.

"I saw in the bulletin that the youth are still doing their annual talent show." She pulled a tube of lotion from her purse and squirted some on her hands, releasing the scent of cherry blossoms. "Made me think of that 'synchronized swimming' routine you and your buddies performed."

He shook his head. "We were such dorks."

"The skit was hilarious—your facial expressions especially. I still can't believe you lost to that Mick Jagger impersonation."

Her easy banter suggested their interaction

wasn't as hard for her as it was for him—yet one
more reminder of how easily she'd walked away
all those years ago.

"We still got our pizza." He tried to match
her casual tone. "Ricky's mom bought us two
large Supremes—so we were good."

"I'd forgotten how food-motivated you were."

Harper had always been great at making small
talk. The part of him that had worried their
drive would feel awkward was grateful for this.
The part of him trying to forget how much fun
they used to have together, not so much.

But maybe this was good—the beginning of a
new normal. Could they rebuild the friendship
they'd once shared without him losing his heart?

Was that even something he wanted? To open
himself for future hurt? No, thank you.

He at least needed to reach a place where he
didn't feel like he was holding his breath whenever she was around.

He pulled into her mom's cracked driveway,
feeling a sense of déjà vu as he surveyed the
peeling paint and dandelion-infested yard. A
layer of dust covered the windows, and weeds
sprouted up from the sun-bleached mulch lining the walk. A partially broken flowerpot sat
on the porch next to a pair of old tennis shoes.

He was struck by how much hadn't changed, and yet, how much had.

Engine idling, he shifted into Park, got out and hurried to open the door for her, waiting as she unfastened her daughter's car seat.

He took it, with the child secure, and the diaper bag from her. "I got it."

"Thank you."

"No problem."

He followed her up the sagging steps. They'd barely reached the stoop when the door swung open to reveal Harper's mom, her hair mussed and showing two-inch gray roots.

"Well, I'll be." She wore a stained T-shirt with remnants of screen-printed words too faded to make out. Eyebrows raised about as high as they could go, she looked from CJ to Harper then back to him. "Christopher James. I thought I recognized that truck."

"Ma'am." He tipped his hat at her.

"Come in, darlin'." She moved aside and motioned to her home's dim interior. "I was just about to make a batch of sweet tea."

"I appreciate the offer, ma'am, but I can't stay. My mama's got Sunday supper waiting."

Mrs. Moore's face fell. "Another time then."

He shifted toward Harper. "Hope Mike's able

to get your car up and running no problem." He handed Harper the car seat, started to leave, then stopped. He could fix her vehicle easily enough, and for the cost of parts. Matter of fact, he probably would've already offered had she been any other single mom he'd encountered at the church.

Seemed hypocritical for him not to do the same for her.

He turned back around. "Listen. I can come work on your car tomorrow."

"Are you sure?" Thin lines etched across her delicate forehead.

"I've got a bit of time around midmorning."

"Thank you!" Her eyes lit up, adding to her beauty.

With a nod, he hurried back to his truck before the vise squeezing his chest showed on his face.

CHAPTER THREE

THE NEXT MORNING, CJ stayed busy dealing with contractors. For a Monday, he was surprised at the steady flow of business. Was the uptick due to the advertising campaign he'd pushed for? He'd finally talked his parents into stepping into the twenty-first century to utilize social media. A few quick videos with remodeling ideas, followed by a series of related discounts, had brought in folks they hadn't seen for a while.

Unfortunately, only a handful of them had ventured far enough into the store to see his carvings. No one had purchased anything.

He'd never support himself as an artist this way.

With a sigh, he made his usual rounds to check what items they needed to reorder and what shelves needed tidying. Afterward, he popped into the office to ask his mom what she wanted him to prioritize—and to once again broach the conversation regarding Harper.

Alert to the irony of advocating for the woman who'd abandoned him, a twinge of bitterness contracted his muscles. But he refused to travel down that all-too-familiar road yet again. He'd fought much too hard to reclaim his joy and peace to forfeit it over a past offense.

He closed his eyes, asking God to cleanse his heart—a practice he'd learned from Pastor Roger.

Would this always be such a struggle?

"Hey, kiddo." His mom smiled as he stepped into the small, cluttered space.

Scribbled notes on random scraps of paper, various knickknacks, three mugs and a container of store-bought cookies covered most of her desktop. Family photos and framed drawings he'd made as a kid decorated the wall behind her.

"Hi." Slipping a hand in his pocket, he relayed the morning orders. "Our shipment of drywall arrived wet. We're going to have to scrap several pieces. Manufacturer's going to resend what we lost."

"Who was this for?"

"JK Interior Finishers." He rubbed the back of his neck.

"They're the ones working with that high-maintenance homeowner? The fella turning his garage into his man cave?"

"The guy who wanted it completed by yesterday. Unfortunately."

"Lovely." She typed on her computer keyboard.

Shifting his weight, he lingered then cleared his throat. "Have you and Dad made any decisions regarding Harper's application?"

"I don't want to talk about that now." Her typing became more forceful. She wiggled the mouse, clicked through a few things and paused. Her gaze landed on a flip-calendar to the right of her screen.

He followed her line of sight to the day's verse bordered with vines and flowers. It was from Proverbs 19:17, and read, "He that hath pity upon the poor lendeth unto the Lord; and that which he hath given will he pay him again."

That felt like a hard nugget to accept. "I've got to head out for a bit. Need me to do anything first?"

She looked at the clock above him and shook her head.

Ten minutes later, he found himself at Harper's house, fighting to suppress memories from all the nights, years ago, he'd dropped her off. He should've snagged Harper's number from her application to let her know he was coming. Better yet, had he asked for her car keys the day before, he could've fixed the thing with little interaction.

Yet here he was, parked in her driveway—which was empty.

If no one was home and the trip over had been a waste? Wouldn't hurt his feelings none. He could leave knowing he'd tried to do the right thing. A man couldn't do much more than that.

CJ stepped out, pocketed his keys and ambled up the walk to her stoop. He pressed the doorbell, waited, peered through slats caused by bends in the blinds and rang again. He turned to leave then stopped. He glanced about. Was that Harper—singing?

Seemed he'd be spending the rest of his morning turning a wrench, after all—a fact he'd feel good about if he were doing it for anyone else. It wasn't that he didn't want to help Harper. He did. At least, he *wanted* to want to help her.

Apparently, he had yet to conquer the resentment triggered by her leaving.

He followed the rise and fall of Harper's voice around the side of the house to the rusted chain-link fence bordering her backyard. The image of her dancing about while holding Emaline jolted him. Hair bouncing against her slender shoulders, Harper's face radiated joy as she gazed, completely enamored, at her daughter—who was equally enthralled with her mother.

"We shall go a-frolicking, up the hill and down again. Round and round and round again. Until we go to town again, on a spring sunshiny morning."

It sounded like one of the spontaneous songs she'd made up for the neighbor kids she used to babysit. When she'd thought no one else was within earshot. Once she'd caught him watching her. The blush in her cheeks and shy drop of her gaze had stirred something deep inside him.

She'd stolen his heart that night and stomped on it four years later. Seeing her tenderness with her daughter now felt like an elbow jab to the ribs—a vivid example of what could have been.

Yet she was here now. Did that change anything?

No. He hadn't been enough for her before. He had no desire to become her plan B now.

His phone rang, startling him.

Harper turned around, eyes wide, her face bearing the same expression and tinge of pink that had halted his breath years ago. Straightening, she smoothed back her breeze-stirred hair and walked toward him. "Hi."

He swallowed. "Hey."

His phone rang again.

"You going to get that?" she asked.

"Huh? Yeah." He glanced at the screen. It was his mom. Had he walked off with the forklift keys again? He patted his pockets. Nope. He answered. "Yes, ma'am?"

"About Harper… As much as I hate this, I know your father and I need to do the hard right thing. We want to set the example of how a person should act—to put feet to all those lessons we've given you over the years."

"You both have done nothing but demonstrate integrity."

"I appreciate you saying that, but I know I could've handled this situation better. My attitude has downright stunk. She needs a job, and she's got a little one to support. While she did you wrong, she was just a kid. As were you. Two teenagers caught up in a high school crush that, for a while, felt like the world. Clearly, the years have matured you both. Figure it's about time I start acting like a grown-up, too."

"Meaning?"

His mom ran hot at times, but she was always quick to admit when she'd been wrong. He admired that about her—even if her honorable choices negatively affected him.

Harper shot him periodic glances, listening but acting like she wasn't. She'd probably guessed why he'd come and was waiting to give him her keys.

His mom's breath vibrated through the phone. "I've decided to invite her in for an interview. Just wanted you to know."

"Okay." Oliver's offer to go in on that building, and therefore reduce the time spent at the store with Harper, was looking more appealing. It struck CJ as comical. They were hiring help, in part, so that he could focus on establishing himself as an artist, and if they hired Harper, she'd push him out even faster. He just needed to figure out how to earn his part of the down payment. "When were you thinking?"

"Soon as she can come in. We need the help, and obviously, she could use the money. I'll call her now and will text you whatever time we land on."

"I can ask. I'm with her now."

Harper's furtive glances became more direct. Watching him, she meandered over and lingered on the other side of the fence, carrying a faint scent of cinnamon with her.

"You're where?" Surprise hiked his mom's tone.

He rubbed a hand over his face and explained why he'd come. "Didn't feel right leaving her to pay for a tow and whatnot, when I can get it working." Prior to carving, he'd fiddled some with engine rebuilding. "Seems this morning might be as good a time as any, seeing how I'm already over here and all."

His mom didn't respond right away. When she did, her voice sounded flat. "I'm available now."

"I'll shoot you a text in a few."

He ended the call and slipped his phone into his back pocket. "You free for the next hour or so? For a job interview?"

Her eyes widened and then brightened with her smile. "Really? That would be great!" She glanced at her daughter and her face fell. "Except my mom won't be back to watch Emaline until this afternoon."

He scratched his jaw. "You can always bring her. If you want."

"You sure?"

He nodded. It wasn't like she was applying at some fancy big-city law firm or anything. They were a family-owned business, after all. He'd spent a good chunk of his childhood in his parents' office, from as early as he could remember. Besides, like his mom had said, they needed the help and Harper needed employment.

"Okay." She eyed her T-shirt and jeans. "Give me a minute to change." Smoothing a hand over her baby's head, she kissed her temple then dashed inside.

CJ meandered back to his truck and waited, leaning against the passenger side. When Harper reemerged, he hurried to carry her car seat and diaper bag. With one under his arm, the other draped over his shoulder, he opened her door for her.

"Thank you."

He nodded. He cast her a sideways glance, his chest aching at the memory of her expression the day she'd walked away. Eyes cold, chin raised. As if he'd meant nothing to her.

With Emaline secured in her car seat, he shifted into Drive, and he gave himself a mental shake. Rehashing the past would only stir up seeds of bitterness it'd taken years to kill.

AFTER SUCCESSFULLY AVOIDING interacting with CJ for nearly six months, not an easy task in a town Sage Creek's size, here she sat in his truck, for the second day in a row. Based on his stiff posture, he wasn't too thrilled with this arrangement, either.

She wouldn't blame him if he hated her. Yet, tense body language aside, he was going out of his way to help her.

That had always been his way.

He cast her a sideways glance. "Any chance you brought your car keys with you? I can tinker with your engine some this afternoon."

She nodded, dug through her diaper bag and handed them over. "Want my debit card? In case you need to buy parts?"

Staring through the windshield, he dragged the back of his hand under his jaw. Then he shook his head. "I can catch you on the back end, if need be."

She had a feeling he planned to cover whatever expenses arose. While she appreciated his generosity, she bristled at what felt like pity. The state of her bank account, and her love for Emaline, pushed her to swallow her pride. For now. She could revisit the conversation later. The air in his cab was thick enough.

He drummed his fingers on the steering wheel. "How are your parents? Your dad still driving semis?"

"Sort of, but for a moving company based in Houston."

Unfortunately, her father had never been one to stay at the same job for long, and his inconsistent employment history had finally caught up with him. If only her mom had finished her teaching degree when she'd had the chance, they wouldn't be in such a financial mess now. But she'd been so "head over heels in love" that she'd withdrawn to follow Harper's dad doing feed delivery to Sage Creek. The hourly pay had looked good in the classifieds, but not so much when bills had come due.

He'd spent the years since bouncing from one hiring bonus to the next.

Facing the rear, Emaline started to coo and kick her feet.

Amusement lit CJ's eyes. "Really, now?" He slipped his index finger into her fisted hand and gave a gentle tug. "Sounds like you're telling tales to me."

Harper thought back to the evenings when he used to hop the fence between his place and the children she babysat for's. It had never taken him long to pull the kids into a game, and always one in which he'd found some way to display his agility. She'd been flattered to think such a popular, good-looking upperclassman wanted to show off for her.

When they reached the hardware store, he dropped her and Emaline at the front entrance, parked, then met them inside.

He nodded to an older gentleman with a large protruding gut and crooked nose. Typing into his phone, CJ led her to the break room. She let her gaze linger over his carved statues as they passed that area once again, impressed by his talent. Had he always been this creative? If so, he'd never mentioned anything.

What else didn't she know about him?

"Have a seat." He motioned to the same table she'd sat at to fill out her application.

Palms sweaty, she chose the chair facing the door. The space smelled like a mixture of coffee, popcorn and pizza—an odd combination for ten in the morning. Then again, the Jenkinses probably started their day at dawn's first glow.

CJ strode to the counter lining the opposite

wall and opened the cupboard above the sink. "Can I get you a cup of coffee or some water?"

"I'm good, but thank you." Her daughter reached for her earrings.

Harper faced her outward and bounced her on her knee. What if CJ's mom wasn't as keen on her bringing Emaline with her as CJ had thought? Harper probably should've insisted they schedule the interview for another time, but he'd caught her off guard, showing up like he had. As had the phone call he'd received from his mom.

With the way Nancy had scowled at her twice—first when she'd come to apply then again at church—Harper had assumed the Jenkinses had slammed this door shut. Upon seeing it inch open, she knew she needed to jam her foot in before the woman changed her mind.

Footsteps approached moments before CJ's mom entered. "Thank you for coming in." Nancy's stiff smile softened slightly as her gaze pinged from Harper to her daughter making raspberry noises around the fist shoved into her mouth. "And this sugarplum is?"

"Emaline."

"Beautiful name for a beautiful girl." She caressed the baby's cheek with the back of her hand, glanced at CJ, then took the seat directly across from Harper.

He chose the one kitty-corner to them both. "I told her she could bring the little one, this being so last minute and all."

"That's fine." She placed Harper's application on the table, backside up, and scanned her references. "I see you've been working at the library for going on six months now."

"Yes, ma'am."

"Seems a fitting employment. You always were quite the reader." She rested folded hands in front of her. "I must say, I am a bit surprised you'd want to work at a hardware store. We make a point to treat our employees well and pay a fair wage, but this isn't a cakewalk. You'll work up a sweat. Get your hands dirty. Might even break a nail."

Harper flinched inwardly at the sarcastic remark but did her best to keep her expression pleasant. "I'm prepared to work hard, ma'am."

"You'd be working under CJ. Would that be a problem?"

Her gaze shot to him, her face warm. "No, ma'am." She had to believe their interactions wouldn't always feel so strained and awkward. They were adults, after all.

Nancy asked a few more standard questions, such as the days and hours she could work, then indicated for her son to take over.

He shifted his chair closer. "I noticed on your résumé you worked with a traveling dance company. I know that was always your dream. Congrats."

She almost believed he meant that. "Thank you."

"Then, after, as a waitress in Seattle for a few months. Why'd you leave?"

She dropped her gaze before forcing herself to make eye contact. Her answer would only prove she hadn't achieved the success she'd so confidently predicted upon receiving her college acceptance letter. Not that he and the rest of Sage Creek hadn't figured that out already. She was living with her mom, working a part-time, minimum-wage job, after all.

Did that give him some level of satisfaction? A sense of vindication?

No. He'd never been the spiteful type. His gentle nature had surprised her, as had his down-to-earth personality, especially considering his muscular build and striking good looks.

Over half the girls at school had openly pined after him. She could still picture the chain reaction he'd initiated whenever he walked down the halls. Heavily hair-sprayed heads would turn, conversations growing more animated, high-pitched giggles following one after another like toppling dominoes.

Awaiting her answer, CJ rolled a pencil back and forth on the table.

She exhaled and wiped a sweaty palm on her leg. "Cost of living was high, and with my student loan payments, I just couldn't make ends meet."

He nodded. "Understandable. We're especially looking for someone with management potential."

The look his mom shot him suggested his statement surprised her.

He continued, "What do you see yourself doing five years from now?"

Another question to which she lacked a flattering answer. "Do I see myself in a leadership role, you mean? I suppose that's always a possibility." That was true enough, especially if she were able to become self-employed as a dance choreographer. But the twinge in her gut indicated her vagueness ventured on deception.

"Let me rephrase that for him." Nancy

brought fisted hands beneath her chin. "If hired, how long do you anticipate staying on?"

If she told them the truth, they'd never hire her and, without this job, she'd never save enough to get out of Sage Creek. The epitome of an ironic catch-22. But neither could she lie to them. That didn't mean, however, that she needed to divulge everything. While she hated being so disingenuous, she wasn't just thinking about her dreams. She needed to consider Emaline, too, and raising a child was expensive.

Harper squared her shoulders and kept her gaze leveled on Nancy. "I plan to be a hardworking, faithful employee focused on helping the store thrive."

Feeling the intensity of their eyes on her, she sensed her breathing shallow and quicken.

The ticking of the clock sounded loud in the tense silence that stretched between them.

Muted voices drifted toward them, then passed by.

Emaline started to fuss. With the baby leaning back against her stomach, Harper wiggled her thumbs in front of her, then jostled her arms once she clamped on. It didn't help.

This was far from a successful interview.

"I'll take the munchkin so you can focus."
Nancy extended her hands.

Harper bit the inside of her cheek. "Are you
sure?" Maybe holding a baby would soften Nancy's coarse demeanor, not that her obvious hostility was unreasonable.

"I've soothed an unhappy little one a time
or two." Pushing back from the table, she took
Emaline and rose. "Any other information we
should know or that you'd like us to consider?"

Seemed Nancy had already made her decision, and that it would not go in Harper's favor.
"Just that I'm a quick learner and a hard worker."

CJ studied her. "This isn't agricultural sci-
ence, obviously, and none of us expect you to
stay on the rest of your life." The look his mom
shot him suggested she felt differently. "But we
don't want to waste employee hours, either, and
training takes time."

"I know how to use the cash register."

Gently bouncing Emaline, Nancy scoffed.
"Honey, we don't do that sort of specialization
here. We're all-hands-on-deck. Expect everyone
to pull their weight. Back to my question. If we
hire and train you, how long are you planning
on sticking around?"

"I really need this job." She forced the words out and fought the urge to break eye contact.

CJ observed her a moment longer. When he said nothing more, his mom returned Emaline. "Thank you for coming in." She walked to the door, clearly intending for Harper to do the same.

No "We'll get back to you"?

"Yes, ma'am."

Obviously, she did not get the job, which, her sad bank account aside, wasn't entirely terrible. At least now she and CJ could return to avoiding one another.

CHAPTER FOUR

CJ's MOM WATCHED Harper leave then turned back around. "That was a train wreck."

He shrugged. "I'm not too surprised. Now what?"

She raked her fingers through her hair. "You asking me what I want to do or what I think we should do?"

"The baby?"

She gave a one-shouldered shrug. "That and…well, we do need help."

"But what if we give her the job and she high-tails it out of town by summer's end?"

"Wouldn't be much different than hiring a high school student, except that she'd be spending her paycheck on diapers instead of junk food and whatnot."

He sighed. "I guess."

She looped an arm around his waist and gave

a squeeze. "You think you could handle having her around?"

He scoffed. "Of course."

She regarded him with a raised brow.

"Seriously. I'm over her."

Then why did he still feel that ache in his gut whenever she was around?

Memories of a painful season, nothing more.

Nancy's phone chimed and she glanced at the screen and frowned. "Your dad needs help in lumber with a disgruntled customer."

"Want me to come?" Why did he feel the need to insert himself into yet another encounter that would only set his nerves on edge?

"Nah." She waved a hand. "I'm sure it's nothing a smile and some extra attention can't fix. Most likely something's just gotten lost in translation." She hurried out to do one of the things she did best—make sure people knew they were more than dollar signs.

He poured himself a cup of coffee then paused, mug in hand, to scan his email inbox. Most of the messages were spam. The Williamses had sent out a request for childcare volunteers for their midweek recovery group meeting held at the church. A buddy's kid was selling overpriced candy bars to raise money for peewee soccer uniforms.

A subject line halfway down caught his attention. A woodworking club he'd joined a while back had forwarded information on an upcoming chain-saw carving festival held in San Angelo. Some called that city the art capital of Texas.

He opened the message and scanned the information. A live contest where people were given a set amount of time to create their best work. Winner receives five thousand dollars, a feature in a nationally known craftsman magazine, and all contestants would have the opportunity to sell their items on consignment.

He scrolled back to the top. They were hosting the event in two weeks. That wouldn't give him much time to practice. Too bad he couldn't submit something he'd already made. There were a bunch of his items gathering dust in the far corner of the store.

Still, it was worth a try. If he did well, he'd walk away with a chunk of change to put toward his buddy's building.

Hurried footsteps approached moments before Harper appeared in the open doorway. "I hate to be a pain, but I sort of need a ride home."

"Oh. Right. I parked in the back." He led her out to his truck and opened her door for her. "I'll go work on your vehicle after I drop you off."

"Want me to come?"

A jolt shot through him, clearly from emotional memory rather than anything related to how he felt now, because that was most certainly what he *didn't* want. If he had his choice, he'd spend as little time with her and her adorable baby as possible since, based on his gut reaction, every moment they spent together was sure to lead him down dangerous ground.

"Nope." He turned the ignition. "It could take a while."

She observed him with a furrowed brow, and he feared she might insist. But then she nodded. "If you're sure."

"Yep. I'll come get you when I'm done so you can drive it home."

"You think you'll be able to fix it today?"

"Should."

"Just let me know what it costs."

He wasn't sure how to respond, so he simply offered one quick noncommittal nod.

If she had money to spare, she never would've applied at the hardware store. But he also remembered how prideful she could be, especially when it came to money. He figured this stemmed from hanging out with the rich kids while growing up without funds for the latest clothing styles and other petty things the popular kids used to separate themselves from everyone else.

He veered onto a residential street beneath a canopy of intertwined tree branches. A gentle breeze stirred the leaves, causing splashes of light to dance on the asphalt. Ahead, two teenagers on skateboards, both wearing hoodies, zigged diagonally back and forth across the road. A runner passed from the opposite direction.

Her mom stepped outside as he pulled into her driveway, her toothy grin and energetic wave suggesting she'd sprung to false conclusions upon seeing Harper in his pickup. He'd barely shifted into Park before she was standing outside the passenger's-side door.

He stepped out and rounded the truck to help Harper with Emaline. "Ma'am." He tipped his hat at Harper's mom.

Patricia's wide grin revealed crooked, coffee-stained teeth. "CJ. So good to see you again."

He winced inwardly, knowing she attached too much meaning to his being at their place two days in a row. "You, too, ma'am." She had to know about Harper's application and broken-down vehicle. Although a person could still misread between the lines, making too much of something as simple as a kind gesture.

He carried the now-empty car seat to the stoop and set it to the right of the door.

Harper followed and placed her daughter in her mom's open arms.

Facing CJ, she lingered as the two went inside. "I really appreciate your help. With the car, taking the time to interview me." Her expression suggested his kindness had caught her off guard, and maybe even filled her with a twinge of remorse for how she'd ended things.

Now who was the one attaching deeper meaning to what was nothing more than a normal display of gratitude? And why? Because he wanted her to know how much she'd hurt him? That wouldn't change anything.

He hooked a thumb through his belt loop. "That's the Sage Creek way. We help one another when we've got the means." Had she missed that when she'd lived in Seattle?

Two boys barreled out of the adjacent house, hooping and hollering. A moment later, a pregnant woman with spiked black hair and combat boots emerged and sat on the top step. She was talking to someone on the phone.

Harper's mom reappeared without the baby.

Partially facing Harper and partially facing the street, CJ slid her a sideways glance. "Guess I best get."

"Girl, where are your manners?" Mrs. Moore crossed her arms. "Show the man some appreciation."

Harper's eyes widened and she stammered. "I don't get paid until—" She looked at her mom. "Do you have any money I can borrow until Friday?"

CJ raised his hands, palms out. "No need to pay me. Elbow grease is free."

And as to whatever parts he might need to buy, Pastor Roger often talked about how a person's checkbook tended to reflect their heart. Seemed if he couldn't help a single mom working part-time for minimum wage, he needed to rethink his convictions.

"Well, then, the least we can do is send you off with a full belly." Patricia Moore smiled.

"That's mighty kind of you, ma'am, but I've already had breakfast. Plus, I should really get moving on your daughter's car."

If his mom were here, she'd find his refusal

of Southern hospitality rude. Then again, she might make exceptions, considering who'd made the offer.

"There's always room for a nice, fat piece of chocolate cake." She took his arm and tugged him inside.

"Mama!" Voice tight, Harper dashed in after them.

Patricia pulled CJ, stunned, into the kitchen, despite her daughter's protests. "Park yourself, sugar." She motioned to one of four mismatched chairs positioned around a slightly lopsided table covered with a blue-and-green plastic tablecloth. Frog-shaped salt and pepper shakers, a bottle of hot sauce and a small cactus with fuzz-like spikes centered the space.

"Go on, now." She gestured once again for him to take a seat. "Otherwise, I'll think you don't like my baking."

If only he had a pressing meeting to attend, then he could provide a legitimate reason to leave. Without a polite reason to decline, he soon found himself sitting across from his ex-girlfriend, who suddenly appeared reluctant to meet his gaze. She'd placed Emaline at her feet in one of those bouncy contraptions with something resembling a colorful abacus forming two crisscrossing arches from one side of the doo-hickey to the other. The baby seemed fascinated with a plush sunshine sprouting from an empty food tray.

The room hadn't changed much in the five years since he'd sat in this kitchen. Fake ivy dulled by a layer of dust stretched across the tops of the cupboards, draping down at the dish-filled sink. Numerous business card magnets held a mass of pictures, pizza coupons and newspaper clippings to the fridge door, and two stained towels hung from the handle on the oven door. The room itself smelled like a mixture of vinegar, cinnamon and burned food.

"How're your folks doing?" Mrs. Moore sliced three pieces of cake, set them on saucers and distributed one to each of them. "Things picking up at the store, now that it's spring?"

"Yes, ma'am. A lot of folks are fixing to garden, take care of their lawn and whatnot. We also tend to see more of our contractors this time of year through the summer."

"So, you could use Harper's help." She shot her daughter a wink and dropped into an open chair. "My girl was a smidgeon nervous about applying, but I told her she had nothing to fret about. You've always done the hard right thing.

I admire that about you, and I'm grateful that you've got my daughter's back. Everyone needs someone with influence in their corner, right?"

Her question felt like a veiled way to pressure CJ to leverage his relationship with his parents to play favorites—with a woman who wasn't exactly high on any of their most-esteemed list.

He searched his brain for the best way to answer. "We're thankful for the increased business."

Her mother scoffed. "You sound like a politician. But I get it. Can't exactly go talking—"

"Mom!" Cheeks flushed, Harper narrowed her eyes. She shifted her attention to CJ. "Do you still restore car engines?"

He shook his head. "Haven't done much of that since my old school buddy Crosby and I tinkered with the beast." That's what they'd called the 1950 peacock blue pickup his friend had purchased dirt cheap at a salvage lot. Their initial plans to fix it up and sell it to fund a camping trip had turned into a mutual hobby. "His parents got tired of having a messy garage and a couple of clumsy teenagers spilling oil all over the place."

"I remember how cluttered your workplace had been." Her strained chuckle suggested she didn't enjoy this forced gathering any more than he did. Yet Southern manners kept them both there, responding politely to her mother's conversation.

"Speaking of memories." Patricia gave one clap and sprang to her feet. "I'll be right back." She darted out and soon returned with a light pink photo album with a cover bordered by interloping flowers. "Do you remember when you first came over for supper?"

He swallowed. "A bit." What did the woman want? She hadn't been this talkative since the time she'd come into the store looking for free plumbing help if she bought the material.

She laid a hand on his arm. "Believe that was Harper's freshman year. That would've made you, what? A junior?"

"Yes, ma'am."

"He doesn't want to look at these." Based on Harper's strained expression, she felt even more uncomfortable than he did.

"Oh, hush now." Patricia waved a hand and refocused on CJ. "That evening, you were so nervous, you were visibly shaking."

He'd had no intention of coming then any more than he had today. Yet he'd found himself sinking into their sagging sofa, concerned her mom had no intention of letting him leave.

"Ah, here we are." Album on the table, she angled it so everyone could see the pictures taken at a makeshift photo booth set up by the local library. On one section of wall, they'd hung a background of heavily knotted wood paneling painted on butcher paper and had gathered several props—hats, comically large glasses, feather boas and various cutouts sold in party stores.

He and Harper had stayed long enough to put on nearly every item and probably used up way too much of the library's Polaroid film. In the end, they'd only kept three photos—the two in Mrs. Moore's album and another tossed in the trash a few months after Harper had ditched him to move to Seattle.

Forearm on the table, Harper leaned forward. "You saved that?" Her voice carried a note of nostalgia that clenched his jaw.

"Of course," Patricia said. "It was your first real date, after all. Before I'd given you permission to start dating, I might add."

Harper's laugh sounded strained. "Well, you hadn't said no, either. Just that you'd think about it."

Her mom scraped frosting off the top of her

cake. "Which you took advantage of." She made eye contact with CJ. "Had a mind to toss you out."

That wasn't how CJ remembered things. Matter of fact, Mrs. Moore had been about as friendly as when she'd pulled him inside today.

"That was an expensive little outing." Harper quirked an eyebrow at CJ. "How much money did you spend on that coin toss game?"

He chuckled. "Considering I never did win the panda bear I promised you, at least ten dollars too many."

It was comical, looking back on it now, how competitive he'd become. Seemed whether on the football field or at a small-town carnival, his drive to win rose up—that and his desire to please Harper.

A goal that had ultimately ended in failure.

"But you did get me that big hand with the pointing finger."

"I redeemed myself then." Their jaunt down memory lane roused conflicting emotions within him. A latently bitter part of him he'd thought he'd overcome stirred him to end this conversation and leave. But there was also a tiny part of him that wanted to stay. To hear her laugh and drift back, even for a moment, to the time when he'd felt profoundly happy.

Only to feel as if someone had literally ripped his heart from his chest four years later.

He finished the last bite of his cake then pushed up from the table. "Thank you for your hospitality, ma'am."

Her mother sprang to her feet. "I'll see you out." She led the way to the door, Harper following. "Now, don't be a stranger, you hear?"

With a polite but noncommittal nod, he descended the steps, pausing when Harper called out to him.

"I really appreciate this."

The vulnerability in her eyes left him feeling off kilter. It evoked too many memories from their past when she'd sought strength in his embrace. "I'll text you once I know for sure what the problem is and about how long it'll take me to fix it."

"Do you have my number?"

"Not on me."

"Give me your cell and I'll add my contact info."

He hesitated, reluctant to create yet one more connection between them.

It felt like the invisible barriers they'd managed to maintain between them were crumbling. Worse, there was a small rebellious part of him that felt okay with that. A part of him that could easily hope for more, if he let himself.

That, he refused to do.

HARPER RETURNED TO the kitchen to clean up their cake plates.

Her mom entered a few moments later, humming a familiar tune and carrying her basket of yarn and knitting needles. "That sure was a pleasant and unexpected little visit." She set her craft items on the table, next to the still-open photo album. "I take it your interview this morning went well?"

Harper frowned, thinking back to the expression on CJ's face when he'd asked about her long-term plans. It was almost as if he'd known she didn't intend to stay.

She was probably being paranoid.

"Not exactly." She relayed the discussion.

Her mom's brow creased. "Guess you best apply somewhere else."

"I know."

"Look, I don't want to tear down your rainbow or nothing, but it might be time to change directions. You've told me how competitive the dance industry is."

She regretted telling her mom that, but, at the time, she'd felt it necessary to explain why she'd needed to move back home. It had felt less like a failure. "I've never shied away from a challenge, and with hard work and perseverance—"

"As I told you before when you were hemming and hawing about applying at the hardware store, your circumstances have changed. You've got a baby to think of now."

Her mom's words picked at an old wound. Tears stung her eyes at the reminder of just how little her parents had truly believed in her. Growing up, while they'd never outright discouraged her from pursuing dance, neither had they offered much support.

She'd been the one to pay for her lessons and summer camps through babysitting, washing people's cars, tutoring younger students and whatever other means she could find. She'd even had to find and secure her own rides once she'd progressed beyond Sage Creek Dance Academy to a more advanced program in Houston. Thankfully, she'd learned about a girl taking weekend classes at one of the city's community colleges. She'd driven her to and from. She'd also allowed Harper, with permission from the family the girl rented a basement bedroom from, to crash on an air mattress in her room.

"I don't mean to sound harsh." Her mom's needles clicked and clacked. "And I know how it feels to change your plans and have to give something up. I just want you to be realistic, is all."

"By that you mean trading my dreams to spend the rest of my life working piecemeal minimum-wage jobs?" Her tone came out harsher than she'd expected.

"There are worse things."

She knew her mom spoke from experience. She'd gotten married the week after she'd finished her freshman year in college. Prior, she'd been struggling to work and go to school, and spending a bit too much time in extracurricular activities. Then she'd met Harper's dad, and the two had fallen hard for each other. When he'd learned about the feed driver job with a large hire-on bonus, he convinced her mom to drop out of school and move with him to Sage Creek, Texas.

From Harper's perspective, the rest of their story was far from happily-ever-after. Her dad was rarely around, money was always tight and, when he was around, her parents spent most of that time arguing. She suspected her mom harbored resentment for choosing his career over hers.

Harper wouldn't follow in her footsteps.

She kissed her mother on the cheek, breathing in her strawberry-scented shampoo. "I appreciate your concern, and I greatly appreciate you allowing me and Emaline to stay while I get my feet back under me."

Her mom set her knitting down. "About that. I wanted to talk to you about something." She repeated what Harper had overheard that morning, adding, "Starting next month."

"Okay."

"I hope you know, I'm doing this for your own good. This might even help you realize what you could've had, and maybe even still can, with CJ."

Her jaw went slack. "You're not seriously suggesting we get back together for financial reasons. You should know me better than that."

"Motherhood changes things. And I saw his expression when I flipped to that photo booth picture of the two of you—and the way he looked at you. I don't know what all happened between you both. Figured you must've bushwhacked him good, with how he and his mom acted once you left. Still, after what I've seen today—if given the chance, he'd take you back. No doubt in my mind."

Harper's heart gave a lurch. Sucking in her breath, she shook her head. "Even if that were true—which it absolutely isn't—did you not notice his reluctance to come in today, or his hurry to leave?"

Patricia flicked a hand. "That don't mean nothing. He's fixing your car, isn't he?"

"You're misreading his kindly nature. Pretty sure he's done the same for numerous other people in this town." Back in high school, he used to mow the lawn for an older couple who lived next door. "Regardless, he and I are not getting back together because I'm not staying in Sage Creek."

Nor would he ever leave. He'd always been content to live in this town—and work for his parents—for the rest of his life. While she didn't fault him for that, she wanted more. For herself and Emaline.

CHAPTER FIVE

HARPER HAD JUST put Emaline down for a late-afternoon nap when CJ returned to let her know that he'd fixed her vehicle.

"Wow, that was fast." She grabbed her purse from the tall, wobbly accent table just inside the door. "How much do I owe you?"

"Nothing. Now a good time for me to take you to your car?"

"Sure. Just give me a sec to let my mom know where I'm going." She dashed into the kitchen, told her mom she was leaving, then hurried outside.

CJ stood waiting at his truck and opened the passenger's-side door as she approached.

"Thank you." She dipped beneath his arm, her senses all too aware of his closeness. Averting her gaze, she busied herself with settling into her seat. Once he slid in beside her and pulled away from the curb, she returned to the safer

topic—for her emotions, not her pocketbook—
of reimbursement.

"It's all good. Really." His firm tone said drop
the subject.

Considering she was still waiting to hear back
on her job application, she didn't want to do or
say anything to potentially hinder his sense of
good will. Yet letting the issue drop felt rude.
But she also worried, should she push the matter further, it'd come off as nagging, and maybe
even stubborn. Men in the South were trained
in chivalry from the time they could string a
sentence together—in Sage Creek especially.

He cast her a sideways glance. "Tell me more
about your time dancing with that organization
from Seattle. You do much traveling?"

"I did."

"Ever out of the country?"

She shook her head. "I wasn't that good."

"But you could've been, right?"

"That was my goal." Although she hadn't
given up on that dream entirely, now that she
had Emaline, she understood that she'd need to
compromise. She wasn't an Anca Cojocaru or
Céline Dupont, two of the highest paid dancers in the industry. No amount of frugal living

would allow her to pay for a sitter to accompany her on tour.

However, she fully intended to earn enough to cover local daycare and cost of living. If only that wasn't increasing in nearly every city throughout the United States. Seattle especially. Yet others made it work.

He stopped at a four-way intersection. "What was your favorite place to visit?"

She angled her head, thinking back on what felt like a whirlwind career, however short. "Probably Denver. They've got great restaurants, museums, shopping districts with fun, independent boutiques, some 850 miles of paved bike trails. You can enjoy all the benefits of the city while living within thirty minutes of incredibly beautiful hiking."

A frown flashed across his face before smoothing into his previous casual expression. "Sounds like a fun place to visit. Did you get to do much exploring?"

"Sometimes, especially when we stayed in one location for a few weeks."

"That must've been quite the adventure. I imagine that felt good, to achieve something you worked so hard for."

Focusing on her hands, Harper gave a slight

nod. The experience had changed and matured her. She'd loved every moment she'd danced on-stage, the preshow rehearsals, the bright lights, and the sound of applause that swirled throughout the auditorium. But her time with the company had also been tough. Hours spent on the bus, checking in and out of hotels, the increased intensity in the rehearsals. Mostly, however, she'd felt lonely—like the annoying little sister who was always hanging around, hoping she'd be included.

The competitive, cutthroat culture that had permeated the organization had left her feeling unsettled and insecure. She'd been so desperate for a friend. That was probably why she'd been so blinded by the charm displayed by Emaline's father.

"You okay?" CJ studied her with a furrowed brow.

She forced a smile. "Yeah. Just thinking."

"About?"

She took a breath and gave herself a mental shake. "Finishing our conversation regarding how I can reimburse you for your time and money spent fixing my car."

"I already told you—"

"I'm not a charity case, CJ." Although, she

didn't exactly have money to spare, a fact her application had probably broadcasted. But neither was she a leech, which is how his random acts of kindness were beginning to make her feel. "If you won't let me pay you back financially, at least let me return the favor in some way."

He quirked an eyebrow and turned into the church parking lot. "What're you thinking?"

Great question. "Do you need any yard work done?"

His lips inched toward a smile. "You do landscaping now?"

She picked at a hangnail. "No, but I can mow."

"Four acres?"

She swallowed. "How much is that?"

"Three football fields."

"Oh." She studied him. "Your yard is seriously that big?"

"My property, yeah—the cleared portion. With trees, it's just shy of six. Horse pasture takes up two of those acres."

She released a breath. "Okay. So that leaves… what?" She calculated the number in her head and frowned. "An acre. Your lawn's that big?"

"Uphill both ways."

She laughed. "You're messing with me."

He shrugged. "Some. My yard truly is a full acre. A bit more, actually, and behind the house, it is pretty hilly. But I don't need any help with it. I purchased a riding lawn mower for super cheap a few years back. One of the perks of working in a hardware store."

She rubbed the back of her arm, trying to think of another option. "I could make you dinner."

He seemed surprised. "Since when did you learn to cook? Because I distinctly remember you burning instant mashed potatoes."

She laughed, thinking back to the time she'd tried to cook him a meal. "I've grown up a bit since my high school days.".

"And learned to boil water?"

"Quit being a stink."

He raised a hand, palm out. "Hey, if you want to throw a couple chicken breasts on the stove, I'm game."

A couple? Did that mean he expected them to eat together? Would it seem odd for her to leave without doing so?

Regardless, she'd promised something she didn't have the skills to deliver, as much as she wished otherwise. She highly doubted boxed macaroni and bagged salad would constitute a fair exchange.

She released a breath. "Maybe me in the kitchen isn't such a great idea, unless you point me to a sink full of dishes." She brightened. "Housework!" She snapped her fingers. "I bet you don't like scrubbing floors and bathrooms."

The skin crinkled around his eyes. "Can't say that's my favorite way to spend an off day."

"Perfect. I'll come clean your place then." She was off the next day, as was her mom, which meant she could tend to Emaline. "How about tomorrow?"

Stopping beside her compact, he cut the engine. Someone driving by on the adjacent street honked. The wind blew a garbage sack across the asphalt. The afternoon sun dimmed behind drifting clouds, then brightened again.

She huffed. "Come on, CJ. Don't be so stubborn. Actually, *elitist* is a better word."

He scoffed. "What?"

"You can give it out but can't take it. Seriously, how would you respond if our roles were switched?"

"I'd be worried about my car."

She rolled her eyes. "You know what I mean.

If I were the one helping you out with something like this."

"That's different."

"Why? Because I'm a woman or because I have a kid? What makes me inherently inferior?"

He opened his mouth then closed it. He swiped a hand over his face. "I get it. You're right."

She reached for her purse, stopped and fell against her seat back. "Look, I'm broke, okay, which you obviously assumed." *Way to fight for something only to backpedal once you got it.* Regardless, she would not lose her sense of human dignity to someone with a hero complex. "But I'm not helpless, nor do I want your handout." Her eyes stung. Blinking, she turned and reached for the door handle before he could see her building tears.

"I'm sorry. I was acting like a clueless jerk." He placed a gentle hand on her shoulder. "I would love for you to come and clean my house. Although you should know, it's a mite messy."

She grinned. "Perfect. When would you like me to stop by?"

He drummed his fingers on the steering

wheel. "I'm off most any night this week—after six or so."

"I mostly work afternoons, but I'm off tomorrow. Is that too soon?"

"That'll work. I'll text you my address."

Wait a minute. Had she really just invited herself to his house? Now that their plans were set, the notion of her spending time in his home, with him there, felt much too intimate.

THE NEXT AFTERNOON, CJ put misplaced plumbing parts in the right places, educated a woman on what tools to buy to retile her bathroom and made some calls to schedule upcoming deliveries. Then, after a quick visit to the storage area to ensure all their shipments had gone out for the day, he looked for his mom to let her know he was leaving.

He found her in electrical, working through an inventory sheet attached to a clipboard. She turned to him with a warm smile. "You finished for the day?"

"Yep." He relayed what he'd done and what he'd communicated with Ken, a retired schoolteacher who worked for his parents.

She studied him with a furrowed brow. "You in a hurry?"

Her expression suggested she was concerned about something. "Not hugely." He could always shoot Harper a text saying he'd be late, if need be. "What's up?"

"Your father and I have decided to hire Harper. We know, based on past experience, this could come back to bite us. But we're trusting that she's grown up since her high school days. If not...well, I guess that's a risk we're willing to take." She exhaled. "Back when y'all were kids, I told her I loved her like a daughter."

"I remember." Along with every word he'd ever told Harper, as well, and all the promises she'd made in return.

"This morning, as I read my Bible about the kind of love we receive from Christ, I sensed Him asking me to show that same love to Harper. The kind that reaches out, even when a person isn't acting all that loveable. Because that's what God has called us to do."

"Okay." He hated to admit it, but he agreed. As challenging as it would be working alongside Harper each day, his mom had always raised him to do the hard right thing.

She took his hand in hers. "But I don't want to hurt you, or make this a miserable place for you to work."

"I'm good. I promise."

She gave one quick nod. "I'll call her in the morning."

CJ shifted. "I can tell her. I'll see her tonight, anyway."

Her lips flattened into a firm line. "What do you mean?"

He explained their arrangement. "I understood where she was coming from."

"I'm worried that you might be finding reasons, subconsciously, to spend more time with her."

He snorted. "What? Of course not. I'm simply trying to help a single mom who appears to be down on her luck."

His mother studied him. "Be careful, CJ."

"Not sure what danger there could be in pushing a vacuum around, but okay."

"You know what I mean."

"If you're worried about me falling for her again, I can assure you that won't happen. I'm not that foolish. Experience taught me she'll bail as soon as something more exciting comes along."

"You may be right. Just make sure she doesn't take a piece of your heart with her."

"Hardly." He kissed her cheek. "Seriously. You've got nothing to fret about."

"But I'm a mom. Pretty sure worrying is part of my job description." She glanced past him toward the end of the aisle. "That, and figuring out where all of our fifty-two-inch distressed wood ceiling fans went, because my records show we should have fifteen, but I only see eleven on the shelves."

"A lot of those boxes do look alike. Someone probably got in a hurry and put a bunch of them in the wrong place. Want me to stick around to sort them all out?"

"No. You've been here long enough, especially with it being your off day and all."

CJ hadn't had much of those since they'd lost Albert, an older farmer who'd worked part-time to supplement his income. A few months ago, he'd decided to sell it all and move to Florida, near his daughter, son-in-law and grandkids. Since he'd left at the beginning of winter, when sales were beginning to dip, Nuts, Bolts and Boards had managed well.

When spring hit and folks started coming out of figurative hibernation, however, they'd realized just how shorthanded they were. With Albert's work ethic and over ten years of store experience, they'd about need to hire two people to take his place.

The more Harper worked, the less CJ would need to. Then maybe he could cut his hours here and devote more time to his carvings.

"See you in the morning." He let his mom give him a sideways squeeze then strolled to the back of the store, through the lumber and to his truck sitting near their overflowing dumpster.

Once behind the wheel, he shot Harper a text to let her know he was heading home, along with a You can still back out.

She responded with an almost immediate Nice try. Leaving soon.

She arrived at his place moments after him and parked alongside the storage shed where he kept all his tools. She seemed to hesitate, almost as if fortifying herself, before stepping out of her vehicle.

He found himself doing the same thing, though perhaps for different reasons. Even in her gym shorts and an old softball jersey, her hair pulled back in one of those messy buns, she looked beautiful. Her erect posture, toned legs and overall fit frame testified to her years of dancing. The early evening sun glimmered on her glossy pink lips and highlighted the mahogany streaks in her hair.

She gazed across the land. "It's so beautiful out here."

He tried to view his property through her eyes. Directly in front of them, an old maroon barn centered a section of pasture with taller grass dotted with purple, yellow and red flowers. Beyond that, clouds drifted above gently sloping hills hemmed in by a grove of trees on either side.

His house itself, a single-story painted white with sage trim, wasn't much to look at. He'd built the simple covered porch and had added lattice beneath it, placing limestone and sandstone boulders surrounded by river rocks. He'd also carved the three Texas stars decorating the gable.

Harper rotated toward the corral and two-stall stable and gasped. "You have horses?"

"I do. A Morgan and quarter horse, both in their early teens and adopted from the horse rescue."

"That's awesome." Her gaze turned wistful. "I miss riding. I didn't do a whole lot of it as a kid. Only chance I got, really, was when I spent the night with Abigail. Her parents own a hobby farm close to the Owen place."

"I remember." He rubbed the back of his

neck, feeling a nudge to invite her back to come riding. Seemed the kind thing to do.

He thought of his mom's statement prior to his leaving the store. *You might be finding reasons... to spend more time with her.*

While that was far from true, he agreed with the implication beneath her words. He and Harper would already be spending way too much time together without him adding cause for more.

"Well." Hands on her hips, Harper faced her car. "Guess I best get busy." She strode to her trunk. From it, she produced a large overstuffed tote with a fat roll of paper towels poking out the top.

"What's all this?" He led the way up his steps, the wooden boards sagging beneath them.

"I wasn't sure what all you had in terms of cleaning supplies."

Holding open the door, he motioned for her to enter. "In case I'm the stereotypical bachelor slob?"

She laughed. "I didn't say that." She stepped inside and made a visual sweep of the interior. Light streamed through the blinds, casting horizontal lines across the wooden floor. On the coffee table, made from a slab of wood with retained live edges, sat a pile of unopened mail, coasters formed from branch slices and a hobbit house carved from cottonwood bark.

She eyed some sketches he'd made in preparation for the chain-saw carving contest. "What are these? Do you mind?"

"Go ahead."

She picked up the pages, moving to the event details he'd printed from online. "You doing this?"

He shrugged and told her what he'd learned and his tentative plans. "Not sure how I'll do as I've never created anything with a timer ticking." He could easily spend months on a project, envisioning the final piece then allowing that image to change and evolve with every cut. "But figured there's no harm in trying."

"I'm sure you'll do great." She set the papers down. "You're super talented."

"Thanks."

It felt good to hear her affirmation and to know, based on the admiration in her eyes, that she meant it. Helped lessen the sting her words had left when he'd learned what she'd said about his lack of ambition. Maybe if she'd said that to him personally, in the heat of an argument or something, it wouldn't have cut so deeply. But the accusation had trickled back to him from one of her friends, which meant she'd been complaining about him, and thinking of leaving, while he'd thought all was good between them.

"Back to your slobby bachelor statement." Lips twitching toward a smile, she shot him a pointed look. "I did block off a full two hours for this endeavor."

"Ouch. Hopefully, it won't take that long." He wasn't exactly a neat freak, but he wasn't a careless frat boy, either.

She gave a simple shrug. "It's not like I have a jam-packed schedule or anything. I have quite a bit of extra time on my hands, actually." Her voice conveyed a trace of discouragement.

"Speaking of…my folks decided to give you the job."

Her face brightened. "Really? That's fantastic." Her enthusiasm revealed how much she needed additional work.

"When can you start?"

"Now?" Humor danced in her eyes.

"What? And leave me with a sink full of dirty dishes?"

"You're right. That would be heartless. Tomorrow?"

"That works." Their easy banter reminded

him of the fun they used to have together. Back then, her simple presence had always added color to an otherwise dreary day. "How does 8:00 a.m. sound?"

"I'll need to make sure my mom can watch Emaline, but yeah. I should be able to do that."

She ran her hand across an oak chair with a curved seat and two-tone twisted legs, her gaze sweeping from it to his other furniture pieces positioned around the room. "Did you carve all this?"

The note of amazement in her voice made him stand taller. "I did."

"It's all so beautiful, although…" She frowned. "I have to admit, I was expecting more of a mess."

"You sound disappointed." Between working on his carvings, tending to his horses and the extra hours he'd been spending at the store, he hadn't had a lot of time to make much of a mess.

She shrugged and deposited her bag along the wall next to the accent table formed from cedar roots. "Just want to make sure I'm actually being helpful, is all."

"You haven't seen the kitchen or bathroom."

"Should I be nervous?"

He chuckled. "Terrified."

"Challenge accepted." The way her smile brightened her eyes only added to her beauty, threatening to undo his resolve to maintain a safe emotional distance.

He cleared his throat. "Need anything from me?"

She glanced around. "Not that I can think of."

"All right." He backed toward the still-open door, increasing the distance between them. "I'll be outside."

"Okay. Thanks, CJ. Really. This might not seem like a big deal to you, letting me scrub your floors and all. But it means a lot to me." Her eyes carried a hint of vulnerability he found unnerving.

"No problem."

Stepping onto the porch, he took in a deep breath. That simple conversation should not have caused his pulse to increase the way it had.

His mom's warning was feeling more justified by the minute.

CHAPTER SIX

THE NEXT MORNING, Harper arrived at Nuts, Bolts and Boards fifteen minutes early dressed in jeans and a navy V-necked T-shirt Trisha had said made her eyes pop. Wearing the earrings that always helped increase her confidence, she'd pulled her hair back in a loose ponytail. A few tendrils had slipped out and tickled her neck.

An older man with a white-and-brown-streaked beard and thinning hair approached. "Can I help you find something, ma'am?" The name tag attached to his coarse gray vest displayed the store name and logo.

She donned a wide smile and, initiating a handshake, introduced herself.

He nodded and brought a walkie-talkie from his belt to his mouth. "Got a gal here ready to work. Says her name's Harper."

The walkie crackled, then Nancy's voice followed. "Take her to the break room to clock in. CJ will be there shortly."

"Yes, ma'am." He returned the device to his belt and, with a tilt of his head, motioned for her to follow him.

Harper nodded and complied, breathing deep to calm her first-day jitters as they marched down the paint aisle, past CJ's amazing carvings and to where, she'd felt only days before, she had completely blown any chance of getting hired.

The man ambled to a metal time card cabinet attached to the far wall. "I'm Ken Palensky. I work Wednesdays, Fridays and Saturdays, 6:00 a.m. to 2:00 p.m." He pulled out one of the cards and a permanent marker from his vest pocket and handed her both. "Just add your name. Mr. or Mrs. Jenkins will fill in the rest."

"Okay, thank you."

Once done, she sat at the table to wait for CJ. He strolled in a moment later, cheeks slightly flushed, likely from some sort of strenuous activity on the store floor.

He offered a stiff smile. "Hey. Sorry to keep you waiting." He was dressed in his signature cowboy hat, sprinkled with a layer of sawdust, and appeared out of breath.

Because he'd hurried to see her? The thought sent a rush of warmth through her, doused by the reality check that followed. If he had hurried to the break room, that was only out of a supervisor-to-employee type of respect, and nothing more.

Besides, their relationship had ended years ago, and she had no intention of rekindling it.

Harper stood. "I haven't been here long." She handed him her time card, and he glanced at the clock on the machine.

"When did you get here?"

"Seven fifty," Ken answered for her.

CJ gave one quick nod. "Early. I like it."

Did she seem too eager? Then again, she was. She was broke, nearly out of gas, and Emaline was quickly outgrowing all of her clothes. Her desperate state sent a wave of shyness washing over her.

"We'll start you with the exciting stuff." Mirth lit his eyes. "Reading our training material."

"That's my cue to leave." Ken chuckled, then faced Harper. "Good to meet you, and welcome to the Nuts, Bolts and Boards family."

"Thank you."

Upon CJ's direction, she sat at the table and

waited while he dashed out. He returned with a stack of papers stapled together, which he deposited in front of her. Typed in bold letters, the words "Volunteer Handbook and Safety Manual" dominated the front page.

He glanced at the clock on the wall above her. "I'll be back about eight thirty."

She nodded and settled in to read what she expected would be the most boring content since high school biology class. Her immediate goal? Finish without falling asleep. The fact that Emaline had woken her three times during the previous night would make that challenging.

Harper scanned the first page with a yawn. She could already feel her focus waning. Hopefully, there wouldn't be a test over this material. Midway through the second page, her eyelids began to droop. She sat back, shook out her arms, slapped her cheeks, then started again. She'd repeated the cycle three times and was contemplating splashing cold water on her face when CJ returned.

He stood beside her. "What'd I tell you? Fascinating stuff, right?"

His nearness sent a wave of heat through her. "Absolutely enthralling. What's next?"

"I'll give you a tour of the store. After that, you'll shadow me."

She'd assumed that would be the case when his mom had said she'd be working under him. But hearing him say it now caused her stomach to flutter in much the same way as it had back when they'd been dating.

Not a good sign.

Seattle. Dance choreographer and coach. She needed to focus on her dreams, of which working at a hardware store in Sage Creek, Texas, was not. If she wanted to be a teacher or hairdresser, or even barrel racing queen, maybe. But the one studio in the entire county only had classes through fifth grade. That meant there wasn't enough business to support her doing what she loved. If the studio owner decided to sell, maybe, but Harper wouldn't detour for a maybe.

CJ's voice cut through her thoughts. "For now, just give me, Ken or my parents a holler, and we'll get down whatever you need."

She followed his line of sight to the display of doors and trim lining the back wall. "What?"

"Just until we can get you forklift certified."

She nodded, as if his statement made perfect sense and she hadn't been completely zoned out.

She really needed to catch up on her sleep soon, especially if he planned to train her to use some sort of powered apparatus to retrieve heavy items from uncomfortably high places. Were she to drop or break something, they'd fire her for sure. Maybe even take the breakage from her pay. Could they do that?

After a tour of the store, including of the lumber and customer pickup areas in the back, she shadowed CJ while he dealt with local contractors. A younger couple came in next, asking questions about tiling a bathroom. As CJ explained the process along with the tools they'd need to complete the project, Harper could see their enthusiasm fizzle. She wasn't surprised when they left without buying anything other than a gardening magazine displayed near the register.

Things remained slow but steady all day, although not busy enough for Mr. and Mrs. Jenkins to need additional help. Matter of fact, Harper couldn't remember when she'd ever seen more than a few customers in the store at a time. Then again, the Jenkinses were getting older. They hadn't had CJ until their forties. That put them in their sixties or so. Regardless, she hoped they wouldn't change their mind about hiring her. At least, not until she'd earned at least two months' worth of living expenses—a cushion to allow her to work toward her career goals.

If they gave her enough hours and she managed her money well, she could return to Seattle by summer's end, if not sooner. At least, that was the plan.

"Hey, CJ." They turned to see Ken approaching. "Got a gal asking questions about your carvings."

"Really?" His tone sounded hopeful. He glanced past him, then to Harper. "You mind?"

"Not at all. I'd enjoy hearing more about your work."

He studied her for a moment, his expression hovering between distrust and…appreciation? Then he turned and headed in the direction from which they'd come.

At CJ's nook, or department, or whatever he called it, a short woman stood waiting next to a carving of a mother bear with two cubs crawling across a log behind her.

"Ma'am." CJ tipped his hat. "How can I help you?"

She had wiry gray hair, large orange earrings and wine-toned lipstick that bled into the fine lines around her mouth. "Are you the genius behind all of these wonderful pieces?"

He seemed to struggle for words. "More like a fella with too much time on his hands, but these are mine, yes."

The slight color to his cheeks suggested he wasn't any more comfortable receiving praise now than he had been back in high school. His humility had been one of the first things she'd noticed—an almost shocking characteristic for such a talented athlete.

"They are simply fabulous." The woman rotated, making a visual sweep of the space. "My granddaddy was a carver. Small stuff. Santas, ornaments, that sort of thing. Of course, never for money. Mostly made gifts for people.

"When did you start selling your items?"

CJ slid a hand into his pocket. "A few years ago."

"Really? How long has your work been displayed here?"

"About since I started."

She frowned and angled her head. "You serious?"

He nodded, looking confused.

"Sure wish I'd known. I would've purchased something for my son. He recently retired from the military, and he and his wife purchased the most adorable little cabin out on the lake in Tool. Would've loved to buy him that carving of that Sasquatch peeking around that tree trunk." She pointed. "He and the kids had a game they used to play when they went camping. Not sure how it started, but they'd grab binoculars and go searching for the big, hairy beast, as he called it."

Harper raised her eyebrows. "That didn't scare them?"

"Nah." The woman flicked a hand. "My son made the creature sound harmless. Said he lurked in the bushes, hoping to steal their chocolate bars."

CJ laughed. "Sounds like a fun dad. Tool's what? Three hours from here?"

"Thereabouts."

"If you still want to buy it, I could drive it to him for a reasonable delivery fee."

"Don't I wish. Unfortunately, we already busted the bank on his gift. But I'll certainly keep you in mind for the next time one of my men celebrate a major life event and I want to buy them something unexpected. You do special orders, if I want something particular?"

"Sure."

"I'll be back."

His posture slumped slightly. "Sounds good."

Harper watched the woman leave then turned to CJ. "That must have been encouraging."

"How so?"

"To have someone express such appreciation for your stuff."

"People can say a lot of things when their checkbooks aren't involved."

"You look disappointed."

"A bit surprised, maybe. That woman wasn't our most frequent customer, but she'd been in here enough that I would've expected her to have seen my work by now."

"I guess that just goes to show how people tend to have tunnel vision."

"And that I need to do a better job of promoting my carvings. Hopefully, the chain-saw contest will help with that. Assuming I do well enough to generate a buzz."

"Might not be that hard in a town the size of Sage Creek." She smiled. "People love to support their own."

He looked at her a moment, a teasing glint in his eyes. "You saying that's the only reason I'll get people talking? That I'll fall flat on my face?"

"What? No, of course not. You'll do great.

You're obviously super talented, to create all this." She made a wide sweeping motion with her arm. "You're very talented."

"Thank you." Still eyeing the Sasquatch, he scratched his jaw. "Although, I'd be happy just to make it into the Final Cut." He explained how almost anyone could participate as an amateur. "Artists competing in the televised portion, the only category with money attached, need a personal invite from the judges."

"How do you get that?"

"You send in a portfolio, which I need to work on, and footage in action. I don't expect to win. Not by a long shot. But that kind of exposure could launch me as an artist."

"I can help."

He stared at her a moment. "With what?"

"All of it." She grinned. "Taking pictures of your work, videotaping while you carve the stump. I can help you stretch your creativity muscles, too. I can share some tips designed to increase your divergent thinking skills."

"My what?"

"Basically, your ability to dream up innovative ideas."

"I see." His amused expression suggested he didn't find her suggestion all that plausible.

"Seriously. I can send you articles to back this up, but scientists call it neuroplasticity, which essentially refers to how our brain is constantly changing and adapting. Just give it a try. The way I figure it, you don't have anything to lose."

"Except time."

In other words, he viewed an afternoon or evening spent with her, outside of work, a loss. She'd been fooling herself to think he'd feel otherwise. Yes, he'd showed her kindness at the church event, in fixing her car, in helping her get this job and in patiently training her. But he'd clearly drawn the line when it came to step-ping into this area of his life—the space where dreams live.

Looking away, she clicked her pinkie and thumb nails together. "It was just an idea."

"I appreciate it. I really do." Slipping a hand in his pocket, he studied her. "You know what? I'll try it." He paused. "So long as you don't ask me to do anything too goofy."

She laughed. "No promises."

"Oh, man. What have I gotten myself into?"

She could ask herself the same question be-cause the more time they spent together, the more her heart threatened to tumble back into the old emotions that could've easily doused her dreams, had she let them.

But she hadn't, nor would she now, no matter how charming and handsome he could be.

WHAT AM I DOING? A smart man would've declined Harper's invitation, and he still could. He could give her a reason why she couldn't help him after all, except that he did need her help.

Right?

His mom was too busy and leaned more to the logical, analytical side. He didn't want to bother his buddies Noah and Drake, although, if asked, they'd probably do about anything for him, taking random pictures and video recordings included.

He was way overthinking things.

With a mental shake, he refocused on his present responsibilities—familiarizing Harper with Nuts, Bolts and Boards.

"As you can see—" he motioned toward the shelves and the end of the aisle beyond "—we have numerous products. It'll take time for you to learn where everything is, but one of the best ways to do that is to work on returns. This is part of your job description anyway."

He led the way past the shelves with trim,

doors and stairs to the customer returns area. Numerous items, from two-by-fours to lamps and tools, filled the large bins positioned behind a long, cluttered Formica counter. All the material clogging the small space was proof of their need for Harper.

Harper eyed a container of tools supporting a stack of lattice. "Do people ever buy something, use it, then bring it back for a refund?"

He followed her line of sight to a Spackle with a drop of paint on the handle. "Unfortunately, yeah. That happens quite a bit."

"Can you still resell them?"

"Unless it's broken or defective in some way. We just repackage it and put it back on the shelves." He picked up a gallon of paint in one hand and wood sealant in the other. "Saves time and steps to gather stuff stored in the same basic location. Grab that flat cart, will you?"

She complied and helped him stack primer, sealant, brushes, rollers and trays onto the cart. "Remember when you helped me paint my room?"

He chuckled. "Aqua and rose with a big ol' purple stripe? That I spilled on your carpet? Yeah." He'd knocked the entire can over, creating a puddle her cat had stepped in as they'd scrambled to clean up what they could. Thankfully, Harper had picked the cat up and placed him outside before he'd reached the hallway—but not before he'd left a trail of paw prints from the splotch to about a few feet from the door.

"I can still picture my mom's face when she saw it. I thought she was about to have a heart attack."

"And I remember yours when she told you that you were going to have to replace the carpet."

"I don't know what I would've done if your parents hadn't sold me the materials at cost. And if you and your dad hadn't done the tearing up and laying down free of charge."

"Well, it was my fault." At the time, he'd been frustrated his folks hadn't comped the entire cost, or let him cover it all himself. But they'd felt strongly that both he and Harper needed to take responsibility for their mistakes. Now he understood and respected their decision.

She smiled. "The blame was mutual. And the situation wasn't a total loss. I did end up with new carpet, after all, which was much better than the stained and sun-bleached maroon I'd had before."

"Guess that's one way to get a remodel."

Cart loaded, he rolled it toward the paint aisle.

Someone called out to him as he passed the cash register. He turned to see a middle-aged woman approaching with a glossy book in one hand and a large quilted tote draped over her shoulder. She had shoulder-length blond hair and bangs that reached just below penciled-on eyebrows.

He recognized her from church, although he couldn't remember her name. "Yes, ma'am."

"My grandson will be staying with me over spring break. He's ten and gets bored playing cards or dominoes or whatnot. I don't want him watching televisions or playing video games all the time, although he'd probably love that." She laughed. "I found this at a garage sale." She held up her book. "I thought maybe he and I could make something together, only I'm not sure what project would be best, with his age and all."

"Let's see what you've got." He glanced over her shoulder as she began turning pages, then looked at Harper. Her shift would be ending soon. "Can you give me one moment?"

"Of course."

He turned to Harper. "Do you think you

can find where these go?" He motioned to the items in the cart.

She gave a slight laugh. "Eventually."

"You can clock out when you're done. See you at eight tomorrow? To shadow me again?"

Her smile was dangerously captivating him. "Sounds great."

He focused on the customer once again. "I love your desire to connect with your grandson. What a wonderful way to build lasting memories."

"I hope so. He is such a lovely child, and so imaginative. He spends hours building this three-dimensional virtual world, with detailed oceans, forests, bridges and castles. Of course, all while focused on a screen of some sort." She shook her head. "He's asked me to join him, but it feels so… I don't know. I guess this just shows that we're from completely different generations. I want to tap into some of that creativity—without the need for a remote control." She smiled. "Then I found this." She raised the book.

"It has some great options." He once again scanned each project as she resumed turning pages, and then tapped one of the diagrams. "That boat wouldn't be too difficult. Then, after the two of you build it, you could take him to the lake to see if it floats."

"What a wonderful idea. We could make a day of it. I could bring some kites and pack a picnic with strawberries and cookies. I always bake batches of oatmeal raisin whenever he comes."

"That sounds delicious."

"Do you have a sweet tooth?"

He chuckled. "A bit."

"Well, then, I'll bring you some one of these days."

"Oh, no. You don't have to do that."

"I want to." She patted his arm. "Consider it my way of expressing my gratitude." She raised an eyebrow. "You will help me find everything I need, won't you?"

"Absolutely. Let's go get you some wood."

"I'll need tools, too. I'm not sure I even own a screwdriver."

Oh, boy. Maybe the boat project wasn't the best idea. "Have you seen any of our kits?"

"I didn't know you carried such a thing."

"I'll show you."

Numerous questions and short stories later— of her grandson and his father when he was the same age—she selected a monster truck kit and a one-by-eight board for him to roll it down. CJ checked her out then headed to the office to gather his things.

His mom and Ken were talking just outside the break room. Based on the man's tense expression, it was about something unpleasant.

CJ stopped at their side. "Everything okay?"

Ken started popping his knuckles like he often did when nervous. "I messed up."

"How so?" Hopefully, he hadn't ordered something incorrectly for one of their contractors. Those guys often worked on a tight schedule.

"Crystal Simpson stopped in today, saw you training Harper and asked when y'all hired her on."

"Okay?" He looked between him and his mom. Had Harper done something concerning?

Ken squeezed the bill of his ball cap. "Wanted to know why no one called her son in for an interview."

CJ frowned. "Gael?" That guy would've been a great asset. Strong, hardworking, personable and, as far as CJ could tell, a person with integrity. "He was wanting to work here?"

Ken nodded. "He came in a couple of weeks ago. I was busy dealing with an upset customer, making a key for another gal, the phone was ringing and someone else was waiting for me to mix paint. You and your mama were off that morning, and your daddy was helping a builder in lumber. With all that going on, guess I didn't pay much attention when Gael handed me his application. I just set it with some other papers, my clipboard on top of it, then forgot all about it."

CJ released a breath and nodded. "Stuff happens."

The crevice between Ken's brows deepened. "I feel like I cost him his job. One, according to his mama, that he really needed. She didn't give specifics, but I got the sense the kid's in a bad place financially."

He placed a hand on Ken's shoulder. "I appreciate your compassion." The man had a big heart. "But there's not much we can do about that now." Although, they could bring the guy on, once CJ started devoting more time to his chain-saw carvings. Once his art earned the funds to allow for that.

Ken's hardened expression suggested he didn't much care for CJ's response. "Then I'll let you explain to Crystal, and her son, if he comes in asking, why we've got a ballerina working here rather than a fit young man with years of construction experience."

He stomped off before CJ could respond.

He turned to his mom. "Now what?"

She shrugged. "Do our best to soothe tempers?"

And if Ken, a man with an underdeveloped filter, drove Harper away?

CJ should find that prospect encouraging. Instead, it left a hollow feeling in his gut.

CHAPTER SEVEN

THE NEXT MORNING, Harper spent the first few hours shadowing CJ once again while he straightened up shelves, cleared aisles of clutter and dealt with customers. She enjoyed watching how he interacted with people and how easily he pulled them into conversation. Granted, that was what they were paid to do. Nancy had stressed, numerous times, the importance of prioritizing patrons. But she got the sense that, to CJ, this was more than a job. He had such a genuine love for people.

She admired that about him.

CJ laughed about something, and she refocused on him and the older gentleman he was helping. The man had a thick white beard with a center streak of black, eyes the color of coal and a large, slightly crooked nose.

"I hear you." CJ pulled a plastic-wrapped air

filter from the shelf. "These gas prices have me seriously considering buying a motorcycle."

The man chuckled. "Doubt you'll find a better excuse to tell the missus."

CJ's gaze pinged to Harper's, a hint of sadness shadowing his eyes. But then his easy smile returned. "Want to ring Mr. Huxley up for me?"

"Sure."

The three of them walked to the front and CJ placed the man's item on the counter, him standing in front of the cash register while she and CJ moved behind it.

"Did you find everything okay?" Her cheeks heated at the absurdity of her question, considering she and CJ had been helping the gentleman only moments prior. "I mean, is there anything else you need?"

"Nope." He pulled a tattered wallet from his back pocket and flipped it open. "I'm right as rain and wouldn't have it any other way."

She laughed. "All right then." She rang him up, swiped his card and handed him his receipt. "Have a great day, sir."

"It already has been, little lady." He winked and, with his purchase under his arm, strolled out whistling a tune she didn't recognize.

CJ turned to her with a smile. "You're a pro."

He glanced at his phone. "I've got to leave soon to meet a buddy who'll be doing some church repairs. We shouldn't be too busy. Think you can finish up shelving our returns while I'm gone?"

"Sure." Hopefully, he didn't expect her to work quickly without him there to direct her. She still wasn't all that familiar with where they kept things, especially when it came to the tools section. She didn't even know what half of them were.

Harper spent the next couple of hours walking up and down the aisles, searching the pictures displayed on various items and their specifications with what was printed on the shelf stickers. There'd been a few times when she'd finally given up and asked Ken for help, only to learn the light bulbs or extension cord or whatever she'd been searching for had been in plain view the entire time.

She sensed Ken was beginning to get frustrated, which is why she was trying so hard to lift an eighty-pound bag of cement, one of four piled along the wall, onto the rolling cart. But no amount of pushing and grunting budged the thing.

With a huff, she went, once again, in search

of her irritated coworker. She found him helping a customer in plumbing. He glanced up as she approached, frowned and then refocused on the short, broad-shouldered man standing in front of him. Apparently, the guy had a clogged main drain that was causing backup in his sink and bathrooms.

Ken crossed one arm over his chest and widened his stance. "Before you do anything, make sure to shut off your water and let it all drain out overnight. Otherwise, you're going to have a mess on your hands. If your nut's corners have been rounded off, file it square, so you can grip it with a pipe wrench. You got one of those?"

The man nodded.

Ken tipped up the bill of his cap. "'Cause if not, we've got a bunch of our tools on sale for 15 percent off."

This launched a discussion on other discounts, current and upcoming, which then morphed into a conversation on rising inflation and its negative effect on farmers. She contemplated leaving to find a more productive use of her time, but she'd put away everything she could lift on her own and CJ hadn't given her any other tasks before he'd left. Instead, she occupied herself by scanning the contraptions displayed on either side of her in an attempt to remember the location for each.

She felt like she was back in anatomy class, only swapping studying bones, muscles and veins for faucet stems, cartridges and steel repair clamps.

Her hopes of gaining Ken's attention once he and the man finished talking clogs and poorly installed plumbing were dashed when he led the man to the cash register without a sideways glance her way. By the time the guy left, she felt even more like an inconvenience, thanks in part to Ken's tense expression.

"You need something?" His tone revealed his irritation.

"Yes, if you have a minute." She told him about the heavy bags she'd been unable to lift.

He released a breath and marched over to where they temporarily stored returns.

She hurried after him, confused by his sudden change in behavior. He hadn't been this prickly the day before. Had something happened? She told herself his mood wasn't about her, but he'd acted pleasant enough to the man with the plumbing issue. Then again, he'd been a customer. It made sense Ken would don a helpful persona.

He tossed the bags, one after the other, onto the rolling cart as if they were little more than overstuffed pillows.

"Thank you." She grabbed the cart's handles.

Dusting off his hands, he gave a quick nod and started to leave.

"Excuse me?"

He turned back around, eyebrow quirked.

"Can you help me place these back on the shelves, please?"

He eyed her for a moment. "This is a physical job. You sure you're up for it?"

She swallowed and, picking at her pinkie nail, dropped her gaze. Then, taking a deep breath, looked up once again only to see him pushing the cart toward the garden department.

She caught up with him at the seed display.

Ken glanced over his shoulder. "I got this. You go do whatever else you've got to do."

Had she done something to upset him? This was the last place to start creating enemies. CJ and his mom had just started warming up to her. She didn't need Ken, a man who probably carried a great deal of influence here, to start poking at recently settled emotions.

Harper spent the next hour roaming the store, straightening and doing her best to familiarize

herself with all the products. But she couldn't
help but feel as if she was wasting the hourly
wage Nancy paid her. What if she determined
Harper wasn't useful enough and cut her loose?

Then she'd find something else and remain
focused on her goal. She'd risen above numerous challenges over the years. She could certainly overcome whatever present hurdles stood
between her and her dreams.

CJ walked in at a quarter to three, carrying
a grocery bag in one hand and a leftover container in the other. "Hey." His grin gave Harper's heart a slight lurch. "How'd things go while
I was gone? The walls still standing?" He looked
about. "Ceiling didn't fall. That's a good sign."

Anxiety tempered her laugh, her interaction
with Ken and the hour of inefficiency that had
followed still fresh on her mind. "If that's your
definition of a great workday, I'd say I rocked
it."

He pulled his phone from his back pocket
and glanced at his screen. "You ready to clock
out for the day?"

"Okay."

As she followed him to the break room, he
asked questions about her afternoon while he
was away. Had she had any difficulties? Had

they been busy? Did she get any time on the cash register?

Taking her time card, she shook her head. "Ken rang everybody up." Not knowing the answers to anyone's questions, she'd mainly hung back and let him tend to whoever had come in. Hopefully, she'd become more useful once her understanding of Nuts, Bolts and Boards grew. Yet she'd never gain the experience and knowledge that he, CJ and CJ's parents had. Nor would she be able to lift eighty-pound bags of cement like Ken.

His question replayed through her mind. *This is a physical job. You sure you're up for it?* A physical job where people wanted to know everything from how to regrout tile to how to build a deck, activities she hadn't a clue about.

Maybe she wasn't the best person for this position, but she was here, and she needed the paycheck. She'd do her best for as long as the Jenkinses allowed. If they ended up cutting her loose, she'd move to plan B.

More accurately, she'd create a plan to move on to.

CJ crossed to the fridge, opened it, then glanced at his to-go. "Might as well take this home with me and leave my lunch for tomorrow." He closed the door and turned to her.

"You're leaving now?" She had somehow assumed he'd work through the evening. Understanding how demanding small business ownership could be, she liked thinking that maybe he was able to catch some free time.

"Yep. I try to watch my hours."

Apparently, he'd learned how to set boundaries, something he'd struggled with in the past. They'd both grown up since their high school days.

She retrieved her purse from one of the lockers. "You free tonight?"

His eyes widened and he simply stared at her for an extended moment.

Heat rushed to her face. Did he think she was asking him on a date? She spoke quickly on an exhale. "To practice for the chain-saw carving event."

His face relaxed. "Oh. Sure." He hesitated. "You don't work at the library?"

"Not until 4:00 p.m. tomorrow. Although, I might need to bring Emaline with me." Her mom had talked about wanting to make candles to sell with her other home-crafted items at the farmers market—her way of "supplementing her sporadic employment." An endeavor that, from Harper's perspective, didn't bring in enough to justify the time and expense, not that this was any of her concern. She had enough to worry about keeping herself employed.

"Then, yeah, I can do that." He grinned. "I really appreciate the help, and you can bring your daughter, no problem. I could use a dash of cuteness in my day."

She laughed, grateful for his acceptance. "What time should I come over?" She accompanied him as he strolled down the hall and toward the front of the store. She sensed Ken watching her from where he stood near the cash register. She offered a slight smile and wave, receiving a quick nod in return.

CJ raised a hand in goodbye then opened and held the door for her. "Come on by whenever. I'll be there."

As she stepped past him, a gentle breeze carried his sage, leather and apple scent toward her, alerting her to his nearness. It reminded her of the sense of comfort, safety and acceptance she'd always felt whenever they'd been together.

Harper had missed that connection. She'd never found a replacement, and not for lack of trying. She'd dated a few people in Seattle, some healthier and more mature than others, before finally falling for Emaline's biological dad. He'd seemed so attentive, so charming, and he had been. But, unfortunately, not just to her.

She adjusted her purse strap draped over her shoulder, suddenly feeling shy and uncertain. "I need to run home and grab Emaline. Give me thirty minutes?"

A spark lit his eyes then faded behind the professional expression she'd seen him don for customers. "Sounds great."

Once in her car, she sat with both hands on the steering wheel and released a heavy breath. *Harper Moore, what are you doing?*

She could not, would not, fall for CJ again. Their lives were headed in completely different directions, and she'd already sacrificed way too much for her dream for her to abandon it now. Otherwise, all her hard work, the hours of rehearsals, bruised feet, sprained ankles and sleepless nights spent stressing over that last open slot would be wasted.

Shifting her thoughts to her daughter, she clicked on her car radio and eased onto Main Street.

She entered her house to the smell of melted wax, cinnamon, and the sound of eighties' rock.

Emaline was in the baby swing, which had stopped swinging.

Harper dropped her purse on the ground and hurried across the room. "Hey, sweet girl." She unfastened her daughter's straps, picked her up and pulled her close to her chest. "How long have you been in there?"

"Are you implying I'm neglecting my granddaughter?" her mom said from the kitchen entrance.

She sounded frustrated. Had she had a bad day?

Her mom wore a red floral T-shirt and her hair pulled back with a wide cotton headband. Her eyes still carried the smudges from yesterday's mascara.

"I didn't mean to sound ungrateful." Harper did, however, worry that Emaline might be spending too much time occupying herself. But she was probably just being an overprotective, nervous mother.

Hand acting as a seat, she faced her daughter outward, back to her chest, and bounced her way into the kitchen. Blue hobnail glass jars and bags of wax lined the counter next to a stack of wicks. On the stove, her mom's metal candle pitcher centered a large steaming pot.

"You've been busy." She glanced around, craving something citrusy. Not finding anything, she pulled a box of crackers from the cupboard and poured some into a mug.

"Building up my merchandise. Folks didn't seem to like the sage much, so I decided to try foodie scents."

For her sake, Harper hoped she was right. Otherwise, her mom would soon be adding to the boxes of unsold goods clogging the garage.

She suspected there'd soon come a time when her mom would be forced to admit the obvious—Sage Creek had more crafters, and many of them quite talented, than purchasers.

That seemed to be CJ's struggle as well. Although he was incredibly talented, not everyone appreciated the time and skill that went into creating a piece of art. If his desire to make it as a carver felt anything like hers for dancing, then she could understand how important this upcoming contest must feel.

After the pain she'd cost him chasing after her dream, it felt somewhat redemptive to think she could play a part in him reaching his. That was the only reason she'd volunteered to help—not because she'd wanted to spend more time with him. She was already doing enough of that as it was. She could feel her emotional resolve to remain detached from the man who had once been her entire world weaken.

WHEN CJ GOT HOME, he checked on his horses then jumped in the shower. He was in the middle of tidying up his house when he heard a car approach. He took his morning dishes from the coffee table to the sink, along with his plate and silverware from supper, and returned a bag of chips and half a loaf of bread to the cupboard.

Glancing at the overfilled garbage can that he should have emptied the day before, he grabbed the papers with contest information and pictures printed off the internet and hustled outside.

Harper was removing Emaline from her car seat. She wore the same formfitting jeans and V-necked T-shirt she'd worn to work, only without the vest. She'd also let her hair down, and her wavy locks, streaked with a hint of red, stirred in the breeze.

A memory resurfaced of him sifting his hands through her silky hair, releasing the soft scent of her shampoo. Back then, she'd smelled like jasmine. Now she smelled like an enticing mixture of pineapple and coconut. It reminded him of lazy summer afternoons sitting on a gently swaying porch swing, the wind stirring his mama's flowers extending from the stairs both ways for the length of the house.

He came to her side with a smile that felt much too big. "Hey. Thanks for coming."

"Of course."

"You, too, little one." He held out an index finger and wiggled it when she grabbed it. "You come to help your mama toss out impossible challenges?"

The child's face lit up.

He chuckled. "You are, huh? That's why you came?" What was it about babies that could turn a man's voice singsongy? He looked at Harper once again. "I have a feeling your little cutie will be a mite distracting."

She laughed. "I have that problem on occasion." She kissed her daughter's neck, triggering a delighted squeal. "Emaline is by far the best thing to happen to me."

She'd once said the same thing about him.

Why did his thoughts keep drifting to the past? Those days were over and, had you asked him a month ago, he would've said forgotten. Well, mostly forgotten, except for those unexpected memories that reminded him of the love they'd once shared.

Back then, he'd felt certain nothing would come between them.

"Would you like to hold her?" Harper asked.

"Huh?" He swallowed. He hadn't held a little one since Harper's babysitting days, and he'd made the baby cry.

"She won't break. Promise."

"Um…okay." He set his pages on the ground and extended his arms, hands up. Muscles tensing, he waited for her to place Emaline in the crook of his bent elbows.

"Relax and hold her to you."

He did, warmth and an odd paternal pull washing over him as he cradled her soft little body against his chest. She smelled like strawberry, milk and fresh bread.

Making a gurgling noise, she bounced, her chubby arm smacking him in the face before her fist found her mouth.

Peering down on her, he laughed. "That must taste awfully good. Think I can get a nibble?" He brought her other hand to his lips and mouthed it, eliciting a contagious giggle. "Just one more bite?" He did it again, unable to contain his grin. He glanced at Harper, his attention snagged by the intensity in her eyes.

She was looking at him with the same expression, the same focus, as she often had back when they'd been dating.

He cleared his throat, returned her daughter and picked up his papers. "So, how should we do this?" He handed her the top page—a copy of various carving challenges he'd ferreted out online.

She scanned the sheet and shrugged. "I'm guessing during the competition, the judges give you a certain amount of time to create something that fits particular themes?"

"Yep."

"How about I do something similar. Might help prepare you to think and carve in a high-pressure situation."

"Sounds effectively stressful." He chuckled and led the way to his shop. As he muscled open the wide sliding door and flicked on the light, the scent of cedar, shellac and lacquer wafted to him.

Harper came up behind him. "What's this going to be?" She stepped up to a partially finished—then abandoned—statue of an octopus.

"A mistake." He laughed and explained his intentions. "A tentacle broke off and I need to mend it."

"What about these?" She pointed to three eagles mounted on stumps.

"Need to do the detail feather work on those." He pointed out other pieces, some awaiting wax or paint, others with cracks he needed to repair. "And those little jewels growing cobwebs in that corner—" he pointed "—are bursts of inspiration I haven't finished."

"How many hours a week do you spend carving?"

He shrugged. "Depends on the week and what all I've got going on." In some ways, this space was evidence of his largely nonexistent social life. His closest friends were all married with kids, and there wasn't anyone he'd felt interested in dating.

Until now.

But that wasn't why she was here—in Sage Creek or his workshop.

Shucking the thought, he grabbed his chain saw, the partially filled gasoline can, and slipped back outside. "So, what's my first challenge?"

"Hmm…" She tapped a finger against her lips. The lips he'd kissed countless times. "I know. Ocean meets land."

"What does that mean?"

She smiled. "You tell me."

"Right." He crossed one arm over his chest, clasped his elbow in one hand and scratched his jaw with the other. "First thought is waves, maybe a dolphin with rocky cliffs behind, but I doubt that's unique enough to get much traction."

"How about we do some word associations." She sat on a thick section of trunk lying on the ground. "I'll say something, like water, then you say the next object that pops into your head, then I will, then you, and so forth."

"Okay."

"Water."

"Waves."

"Mermaid."

"Coral."

"Sunken treasure."

"Pirates."

They continued for a few minutes before she said, "What if you put a few of those together?"

He sifted through a series of ideas, some more plausible than others, but at least a handful with plenty of grabability. "I'll have to try this exercise more often."

Regardless of how he did in the contest, or if the judges even invited him to compete in the master's class, he could come up with highly original pieces to sell collectors. And one day, he *would* have collectors seeking out his stuff. Even if it took him decades to reach that level of notoriety.

Her grin lit up her face. "Yeah? You found it helpful?"

"I did. In fact, I think I know what I want to make."

"Awesome." She held out Emaline. "Can you take her for a minute?"

"Um, sure? Although, I might create better results if I kept my hands infant-free."

She rolled her eyes. "Hilarious. Just give me a second to get her set up."

He rested his chain saw against the outside of his shed and took the baby, then waited while Harper unloaded numerous items from her vehicle, including a playpen, toys and a video camera. "Wow. You came prepared."

"Just hoping to bring her home with all of her fingers and toes intact."

"Smart."

One hand on her hip, she glanced back toward her car. "I brought my ring light. They're easier to transport than those big LEDs photographers use and usually get the job done. But with the sun being out and all, I don't think we'll need it."

He raised an eyebrow. "You one of those social media influencers or something?"

She laughed. "Hardly. I take clips of me dancing. When companies want video auditions."

He frowned at the reminder of her plans to leave Sage Creek. "I see."

He spent the next hour carving while she alternated between taking photos and video clips with her phone and entertaining her daughter. Had Harper not been there, he probably would've kept at it until dusk, but he was probably starting to bore her.

Starting? She'd probably reached that state long ago. Not to mention, it was getting near suppertime.

He set his chain saw aside and brushed dust from his hands and hair. "You hungry?"

Her eyebrows shot up and, for a moment, she seemed unsure how to respond. But then her expression relaxed into a soft smile. "I am, actually."

"How about I grill us some steaks?"

"That sounds wonderful."

And just like that, he'd extended their evening

and turned it from something obviously platonic into what could easily become romantic.

If they let it. But he had no intention of doing that, and she hadn't showed anything other than a casual, friendly interest in him, if that.

In fact, Harper was probably only here out of obligation, still feeling like she had to pay him back in some way, first for him fixing her car, then for the job. And maybe, if he reminded himself of how uninterested she was, he wouldn't fall in love with her all over again. Although he was beginning to fear it was too late for that.

CHAPTER EIGHT

HARPER CENTERED HERSELF with a deep breath. The prospect of sitting across a table from CJ spiked her pulse. She couldn't think of anything more romantic than sharing a meal with the man she'd once loved so deeply, except perhaps to be sharing one that he himself had cooked. Had he always been this thoughtful?

Holding Emaline, he glanced over his shoulder at her playpen. "Need me to help you with anything?"

The fact that he didn't immediately try to return her daughter, and the way his eyes softened whenever he glanced down at her, made Harper think perhaps he felt reluctant to do so.

"I've got it." Gathering her daughter's blanket, diaper bag and toys would give her time to manage her emotions.

What had she just agreed to? Accepting his dinner invite might not have been such a horrible idea, if her insides didn't practically melt to mush whenever he turned his green eyes her way. Or, if she wasn't growing increasingly attached to him, her internal reactions creeping toward pre-breakup intensity. Or, if seeing him holding his chain saw, his thick brows pinched in concentration, his biceps flexing, hadn't almost made her regret walking away five years ago.

Almost. She'd made the right decision, for them both. Regardless of how things had turned out for her—temporarily—she'd been able to tour with a professional dance company. And in her absence, CJ had birthed a dream. She could tell by watching him that carving made him feel alive in much the same way dance did her. Had she stayed, his constant focus on her could've kept him from discovering his passion for carving.

And now? They both kept moving—him toward becoming a successful artist and her toward returning to the stage. Saying goodbye, again, would hurt. But they'd healed before and would do so again.

With a sigh, she placed a handful of Emaline's sensory toys back into her diaper bag alongside her folded Noah's ark blanket, draped the strap over her shoulder and climbed CJ's steps. He'd left the front door open and his deep voice drifting through the screen caused her heart to stutter.

He was singing! Stepping inside, she paused to make out the song, then suppressed a giggle.

Harper smiled and leaned a shoulder against the door frame separating the living room from the kitchen. "That's a lullaby I've not heard before. What's it called?"

A hint of pink settled into his face. "It's *The Green Berets* movie theme song."

She quirked an eyebrow at him. "Quite soothing and whimsical, I'm sure."

He laughed. "She looked like she was about to fuss, and those were the only lyrics I could think of."

"*About* to fuss, huh? Must have been terrifying." How easily she was falling back into their old teasing banter. Was that a sign of friendship or further indication that her heart was inching in a forbidden direction?

He gave a one-shoulder shrug and turned toward his cupboards, her daughter looking quite content tucked between his chest and arm.

Either Harper had hurt him or he, too, had sensed their precarious footing—an indication that he'd closed his heart to her as firmly as she was trying to close hers to him.

She came up beside him and placed a hand on his shoulder, a surge of warmth shooting through her upon contact. "I was just teasing. Would you like me to take her?"

He glanced at Emaline with a look of wonder in his eyes. "I don't mind."

Maybe she was reading too much into this, but she sensed he wanted to say no. Funny, he'd always been great with kids—the way he used to get the children she babysat laughing! But she never remembered him looking at them with the almost paternal fondness with which she'd caught him gazing at Emaline.

Thinking this way would only make it harder when it came time for her to leave.

Gently bouncing the little one, cradled one-handedly against his opposite shoulder, he moved to the fridge, opened it and stared inside for a moment. "Although… I probably shouldn't get raw meat juice on her." He rotated to reveal his adorable easy grin, made all the more charming by the disarming display of both strength and tenderness.

Unable to contain the smile that seemed to erupt from somewhere deep in her soul, Harper extended her arms. "Come here, sweet pea." She kissed her temple, then her nose and, after swaying with her for a few moments, retrieved her blanket from her diaper bag.

Midway through spreading it across the floor, she glanced back at the archway leading to the tidy but not babyproof living room, thankful Emaline hadn't yet learned to crawl. But she wouldn't remain occupied on her back long.

"Excuse me for a sec." She darted back outside and returned with her daughter's stroller, placed a few animal-shaped teething rings on the tray and clipped the activity toy to the raised handle. Emaline loved batting at the hanging rattle.

CJ watched with an amused glint in his eye as she fastened Emaline in. "Transportable confinement. Smart."

"She actually loves this thing, probably because it lets her see what's going on."

"And allows you a quick getaway, should I botch the meal?"

Although she knew he spoke in jest, his words felt a bit too apropos. Only, not because of any outcome in relation to the steaks, but rather the inner resolve his grilling, and this evening in general, threatened to weaken.

Covering her vulnerability with a laugh that

came out too high-pitched, Harper lifted her chin and strode to his cupboards. "Want me to make a side?"

"You can try. But I must warn you, I don't have much. I'd say I need to hit the grocery, which technically would be accurate. The truth of the matter is, I tend to survive on frozen meals and snack items." He pulled out a package of meat wrapped in butcher paper, unwrapped it and placed it on a flat baking sheet.

"Typical bachelor." She rolled her eyes with feigned annoyance. "Yet you have steak."

"Always." He chuckled. "Well, almost. Buy half a cow from a rancher buddy every now and again. Best beef I've tasted."

"I'm in for a treat then." She grabbed a can of mushrooms and a couple packages of Top Ramen from his cupboards then moved to the fridge, which was heavy on condiments and light on most everything else. Harper picked up a rather large bunch of kale and turned to him, amused. "Why do I feel like there's a story behind this?"

He laughed. "An older lady brought that into the store as a way to thank us for repairing a few of her windows."

"For free?" She carried the vegetable to his sink.

CJ gave a slight shrug and set a handful of spices, some brown sugar and vinegar on the counter. "Her husband was one of our most loyal—and friendly—customers. I remember him coming in as far back as my kindergarten year, and always with a sucker or piece of gum for me. On Christmas, he and his wife always brought us a pie of some sort, and often a small gift for me. A few years ago, he suddenly stopped coming in. After a while, my folks got worried, so went out to his place."

"Do you have a cutting board I can use?"

He nodded, rummaged through a bottom shelf near his knee and handed one over, made, not surprisingly, from two shades of wood, along with a chef's knife.

"Thanks." She started slicing the stems from the kale. "Regarding the couple—how'd your parents know where they lived?"

"Phone book, an old delivery invoice? Asking around?"

"Right. Sometimes I forget how close-knit this town is."

"One of the things I love about it."

He covered the steaks with the spice-brown-sugar mixture he'd stirred together with a dash of vinegar and oil.

"You made your own marinade?" she asked. "I'm impressed."

"Stole the recipe from my dad. Anyway, back to your question, my parents arrived at that couple's place to find the lawn overgrown, the house dark, and Mrs. Shaw was just sort of... I don't remember how my parents described it, but their basic interpretation was that she'd given up."

"Did they have kids?"

He shook his head. "That was probably why Mr. Shaw took such interest in me."

"Poor thing. She must have felt so alone."

"And hopeless. Least, that was my mom's fear. So, she convinced my dad to convince her that her husband had purchased lifetime handyman service. The way they figured it, this wasn't dishonest, because he'd spent enough of his hard-earned dollars at Nuts, Bolts and Boards to qualify him for such a thing, had it existed. Plus, it just seemed the right thing to do."

Harper had heard him and his parents use that phrase countless times back when they'd been dating. While she'd always admired their sense of town member loyalty, she could now see this was obviously a core family trait, perhaps one passed down for generations.

What moral characteristics was she actively instilling in Emaline?

Maybe her need for church extended beyond making good on her promise to God.

"I better go fire up the grill." CJ moved to the sink to wash his hands. "Probably should've done that first thing."

While he dashed out through the kitchen door she assumed led to his back porch or yard, she chopped the kale, turned it, then began chopping again. He returned, a hint of charcoal merging with his familiar sage, apple and leather scent.

He came up behind her, his breath warm on the back of her neck. "Need any help?"

"No." Did her strong, rapid response disclose her nervousness? She took in a deep breath and released it slowly. "But thank you."

Behind them, Emaline cooed and babbled.

He chuckled and turned around. "Well, then, if you don't need me, how about I spend some time with this little nugget?" He pivoted a chair to face her, sat and pulled her stroller closer. "What do you think, princess? Does that sound okay to you?"

She was touched by the slight lilt in his voice

whenever he addressed Emaline. "You can pick her up, if you want."

"Did you hear that?" He leaned forward to unbuckle her safety straps. "I'm about to break you free." He extended the last word in a whimsical tone. Settling her onto his lap, back resting against his chest, he glanced up. "You don't happen to have any of those thick books made from cloth or cardboard, do you?"

She paused midsauté to look at him. "You want to read to her?"

"Is that okay?"

"Of course. I'm just surprised."

"A couple years ago, I visited one of my cousins and her family up in Woodinville, Washington. She and her husband hadn't lived there long and hadn't found a sitter they felt comfortable with."

"I can relate to that!" She laughed. "Let me guess, you quickly found yourself filling that role."

"I did. A bunch of their friends were going out to celebrate one of their birthdays. My cousin had originally declined, but then the kids all crashed while watching television."

"After you wore them out all day?"

He smiled. "Maybe. And myself, which is

why it made sense to us all for them to slip out for a bit. For the first hour or so, everything was fine. I didn't hear a peep out of them. But then their toddler had a nightmare and started hollering loud enough to wake the neighbors—and the baby."

She covered a giggle with her hand. "Oh, no."

"Oh, yes. And it gets worse. I hurried to comfort the two-year-old, but that only made him cry harder, demanding his mom. By this point, their youngest was wailing and the oldest—she was six—was asking me over and over where her parents were. So, here I am, holding a screaming infant, trying to comfort a toddler who was looking at me like I was the monster from his dreams, hoping their daughter, who had started to whimper, didn't lose it as well."

"Did you call the parents?"

"I tried, but their phones—both of them—kept ringing until they went to voice mail. I learned later, with a football game playing, people talking and laughing, their surroundings were pretty noisy."

"What'd you do?"

"At first, I just stood there, phone in one hand, screeching infant held in the other. But then I saw a pile of books on the floor in the living room. So, I walked over, sat on the ground, grabbed one and started to read."

"And they listened?"

"Not at first. Pretty sure they couldn't hear me above all their carrying on. They were near burst-your-eardrums loud."

"I can imagine!"

"Eventually, they grew curious, or maybe their voices grew tired, I don't know. The two older ones started inching toward me, the sister first. Pretty soon, she was close enough to rub the back of her littlest brother's head. 'He likes this one,' she said, picking up a thick, cardboard-type book with colorful animals on the cover."

"That's so precious."

"This gave the toddler the courage to nestle in. By the time my cousin and her husband arrived home an hour and a half later, they were all back asleep—on me, because I was *not* moving!"

She laughed. "I imagine not." She turned the temperature on the stove burner down and faced him with a fist on her hip in mock irritation. "In regard to your question, are you worried Emaline's about to start bawling?"

"No, not at all." He spoke quickly, adorable when concerned. "I just figured—"

"I'm just teasing." She crossed the room to the diaper bag and located one cloth book and another made from plastic for the bath and brought them both to CJ. "She especially loves it when I make the animal sounds."

He blushed, his gaze dropping first to the cover then to Emaline. Clearing his throat, he straightened. "Uh, okay."

Harper watched him for a moment longer as his almost shy demeanor turned more animated with each new page. Chest warm, she returned to her stir-fry to add pepper. "The library has children's story and craft time on Tuesdays and Thursdays. I look forward to the day when I can take Emaline to those types of things."

She'd love for her daughter to have a kind, strong yet tender father figure like CJ in her life one day, as well. Too bad he'd always remain so tied to Sage Creek, and that she couldn't do what she loved most, should she stay.

CJ POKED HIS head through the back door, the aroma of apple, garlic and mesquite wafting over him and causing his stomach to rumble. "Want to eat out here on the deck? It's shaded, and there's a nice breeze blowing, so it's not suffocatingly hot." Not to mention, mail, rough sketches, a chunk of wood and various hand-carving tools cluttered his kitchen table.

From the stove, Harper glanced over her shoulder. First at him and then at Emaline, who babbled in her stroller, then back to him. "That sounds lovely." She opened a couple cupboards in front of her. "Do you have a serving dish?"

"How about we dish ourselves up in here." He closed the air vents and lid to his grill and stepped inside.

"Efficient." She smiled and scooped a spoonful of ramen stir-fry onto two plates.

"I'll take those so you can grab little miss."

"Thanks." She handed over the dishes then followed him out, pushing Emaline's stroller, which she rolled to the wooden picnic table. "This was one of the best investments I've made as a mom. Stroller, car seat, grocery cart when needed." She motioned to the basket underneath Emaline's seat. "And a portable high chair."

"Brilliant." Steaming steaks distributed, he darted back inside to make a pitcher of lemonade from a powder mix, then returned with it and two glasses. "Hope you're not craving sweet tea."

She sat kitty-corner to her daughter. "Nope. I'm just happy for the food." She laughed.

Her response concerned him. "This probably isn't any of my business, but are you doing all right?"

"I'm not starving or anything, although I am learning to stretch my buck, as they say." She explained an upcoming change in her living arrangement with her parents. "I found a website where you can type in a list of whatever you have on hand, and they'll pull up a series of recipes." She handed Emaline a glittery pink sippy cup.

He swallowed a mouthful of surprisingly good noodles. "Is that how you came up with the idea for this?" He pointed at the stir-fry. "Because it's amazing."

"Really?"

About to take a drink, he nodded. "Might need to send me a link." Although what he'd love even more would be for her to come over again so they could cook—and eat—together. He knew his thoughts, and his heart, were treading on shaky turf, but he wasn't sure he cared.

"You do know you actually need some groceries to work with, right? Besides ketchup packets, I mean."

"Ouch." He placed a fist to his chest in mock offense. "You wound me."

"Oh, I'm sure." She plopped a slice of steak into her mouth, closed her eyes and gave a soft moan. "This is seriously amazing."

"Got more in my freezer just waiting to get fired up. Come over anytime."

Her eyes widened slightly, as if she'd read the deeper invitation beneath his casual words. But then she pulled a small jar filled with something orange from her diaper bag and shifted toward her daughter. "I almost feel mean feeding you mushy squash now." She turned to CJ. "Except that she loves it—along with pureed peas, turkey and carrots."

"Delicious, I'm sure." Memories swept over him as he watched her interact with her daughter. "Do you remember the day you were babysitting for the Morenos and you thought someone had snuck into their basement?"

She giggled. "And how you turned all knight-in-shining-armor, creeping down the stairs wielding a frying pan? I do."

"I admit, I may have overreacted a bit."

"You think?" Amusement danced in her eyes. "Either that or you'd watched too many slapstick cartoons."

"But I also seem to remember someone telling the kids y'all were playing hide-and-seek so that you could convince them to cram into the cupboards above the washing machine and dryer."

"Hey, now. I was just trying to keep them safe."

"From a stray cat." Their shared laughter reminded him of all the times they'd connected over humor. Harper could be serious and determined, especially when pursuing a goal. But she could be loads of fun as well. The type of person able to brighten even the most frustrating or discouraging days.

He'd missed this. Missed her.

CJ hated thinking that she was having a difficult time financially and hoped working at the hardware store helped. But a little struggle wasn't all bad, if it kept her from saving up whatever she needed to return to Seattle.

If it kept her here, in Sage Creek, with him.

The longer she stayed, the more time he had to win her heart—for good.

CHAPTER NINE

THE NEXT DAY, with extra time before she needed to leave for the library, Harper sat at the kitchen table with her laptop open before her. The whiff of hazelnut rising from her heavily doctored coffee merged with the lingering aroma of barbecued chicken and melted Swiss from lunch. She smiled at her mom's off-key voice as she rocked and sang to Emaline in the living room.

Moving back home, and all that had precipitated it, had cut deeply, and living under her mom's roof once again certainly wasn't easy. But it did come with priceless benefits, like the fact that her daughter was getting so much time with her grandmother.

If only Sage Creek had more of a dance community, then maybe Harper could stay. But she couldn't let go of her dream.

What if she found a choreographer's job in Houston? Then she could see CJ on the weekends.

She frowned. Obviously, she was falling for the man; the one thing she'd determined *not* to do. Their lives were heading in completely different directions.

Right?

Could he, would he, follow her, whether to Seattle, Houston or whatever city offered her the career she'd spent her life working toward?

Highly unlikely. He may have found his passion, but he remained precisely where she'd left him—tied to this place and his parents' store.

Was that the root of her frustration? The reason she'd not been able to commit to him, to promise the rest of her life to him, years ago? Because she'd known, if it came down to it, he'd choose his parents' business over her. Just as her dad had chosen his job and, ultimately, whatever had appealed to him most in the moment, over her mom—only to leave her scrambling to make ends meet, raising her daughter alone, with a half-earned college degree?

With a huff, Harper refocused on her internet job search. Forty-five minutes later, she'd sent her résumé and some video clips to five companies. Later, she'd need to record some new videos for her Instagram account. Although a lot of places still conducted live auditions, they often spent time checking out applicants on-line. Social media was quickly becoming a vital dance portfolio.

She eyed the clock and stood with a moan. "Apparently, time flies when you're trying to plan your life."

Her mom glanced around Emaline, who stood, bouncing in her lap. "You heading to work?"

She nodded, grabbed her sacked dinner from the fridge and, entering the living room, her purse and water bottle from the coffee table. "Thank you for watching Miss Princess for me. Again." She ran a hand over her daughter's silky-fine hair and kissed her cheek.

"You know I love it."

"I do, and I'm really grateful for all of your help." Lack of dependable and affordable childcare had been her biggest challenge in Seattle. Next time she signed with a dance company, in any capacity, she'd make sure they paid enough for her and Emaline to live on. Maybe even spring for a movie or lunch out occasionally.

Until then, she'd juggle her job schedules and save every possible penny.

Harper arrived at the library to find each parking space in front and in the small lot behind full. Inside, children of varied ages darted about while moms, some dressed in exercise pants, others in trendy outfits, chatted with one another. One woman wearing a purple T-shirt and jeans, her frizzy red hair barely contained in a messy bun, scampered after a toddler pulling books from the shelves.

At the checkout desk, Harper paused and made eye contact with Ruby. "I take it Dynamo the Dragon was a hit?" That character, and the books and now cartoons from which he'd come, had become quite popular, which was why their boss had planned today's event—a craft, dress up, sing songs deal—themed after the program.

"If by hit, you mean crazy and chaotic, then yes." Ruby laughed. "But don't worry, the rest of the night should be pretty quiet. Saltwater Taffy is playing at the lake."

Harper groaned. "Live music, and we're stuck here?"

"You could've requested tonight off."

Except that she really needed the money. "I doubt Elise would've given it to me."

"Considering she's not here and we are, you're probably right."

Harper laughed. "Any other fun social stuff

coming up I should know about?" She spent way too many of her off hours at home. Except for the times she'd gone to CJ's—something she could easily get used to. She smiled as an image of him singing *The Green Berets* song to Emaline came to mind. Then she reminded herself of their ultimate trajectories— him here, her not.

"Check the community board." Ruby crumpled a sticky note and tossed it into the nearby wastebasket. "People are always pinning stuff up. Spaghetti feeds. Charity functions. Lost pets. Horses for sale…"

"Well, now, that sounds useful. For that stable sitting empty in my mother's massive backyard."

"Pretty sure CJ would take you riding, if you asked." Ruby wiggled her brows.

"Stop." She turned and marched toward the employee break room before her coworker could see the heat flooding her face.

Although, the idea was appealing. Too appealing for her, or her goal's, good.

With a sigh, she set her dinner in the fridge and walked out, pausing to scan the corkboard she'd walked by dozens of times. She'd never paid much attention to the numerous flyers, posters and note cards attached to it. Most of what she read didn't interest her. She didn't need a Realtor or lawyer, and couldn't afford a house-keeper or a babysitter for that matter. Nor did she have a place to board a broodmare.

Harper started to leave when a burst of color caught her eye. Refocusing on the glossy pages in front of her, she read the bold letters printed in blue, red, yellow and orange. Little Tykes, a place she'd always wanted to check out but had never had the funds to visit, was offering a two-for-one special. While that would certainly stretch her finances, it seemed too good a deal to pass up. And if the claims made by the ad were true, the activities would help stimulate Emaline's brain development.

Regardless of what those classes entailed, they would give her something to do other than binge-watch rom-coms.

Maybe she'd even find an in with the local moms, a group that seemed so connected with one another but not exactly open to her. Probably, in part, because of her over-the-top bragging when she'd received admittance into one of the most prestigious dance universities in Seattle. But that had been over five years ago. She'd grown a lot since then.

Humility had a way of maturing a person.

Maybe the Little Tykes deal would provide her an opportunity to demonstrate how much she'd changed. The next class was tomorrow morning. She checked her phone calendar, equally relieved and nervous to discover she was off. Considering Trisha was practically her only friend, unless one counted those in her former dance community with whom she shared social media "likes," she absolutely needed to go. But she wasn't looking forward to encountering any of the ladies who seemed to exchange raised-eyebrow whispers whenever she came around.

Regardless, Harper had never allowed the "keepers of the cliques" to intimidate her in high school, nor did she intend to start doing so now.

She took a picture of the advertisement and traipsed back up front, feeling considerably cheered to tackle the ever-full return carts.

"What's got you all smiley today?"

She turned to find Lucy, someone of whom she'd grown quite fond, standing before her, wearing a blue-and-white-striped cotton dress and large sunshine earrings.

Harper smiled. "Hello, ma'am."

"How's your sweet baby? Growing like a weed, I imagine?"

"About."

"Figured she's due for another one of these." She pulled out a knit beanie that looked like a ladybug with two twisted strings poking up from the top. "And these." She handed over a matching bib and booties.

"They're adorable!" And must have taken her hours. "You didn't have to do this."

"Fiddling with yarn soothes me." She winked. "And making stuff for your little one reminds me to return my horrifically overdue books. If I'm not careful, Elise will soon confiscate my card." She nodded a greeting to a short plump woman who walked past carrying a squirming, grunting toddler who clearly wanted down. Probably to join that other little guy tossing books from the shelves and onto the floor. "Speaking of reading material, do you happen to have any more copies of this book club's selection?"

"Not sure, but I can find out." She walked Lucy to the desk and repeated her question to Ruby.

When the two women launched into a conversation about the most swoonworthy heroes in print, Harper politely excused herself to tackle the filled return carts. Meandering toward the arts and recreation section, she tried to focus on

the Dewey decimal system, but her thoughts
kept drifting to CJ. The boyish glint in his eyes
when she'd tried to pull out his creative side, followed by his intense, single-focused gaze as he'd
sized up his chunk of wood, chain saw in hand.

He stood a chance at winning the carving
contest. She'd love to be there when he did, and
to see the look on his face when they called his
name. Maybe it was because she'd helped him
prepare for the competition, but she felt invested
in his success.

In him.

Because she cared for him—as a friend, and
nothing more.

As she slipped a how-to on abstract painting onto the shelf, another title caught her eye.
Spoon carving. Interesting. Probably not something CJ would find fascinating, but he might
the one next to it with patterns from the top
carvers worldwide. She snapped a picture of the
cover and sent it to him via text. Then waited,
checking her phone obsessively for his reply.

When a customer ambled down the aisle,
Harper straightened, smiled and returned to the
duties her boss was paying her for. If she lingered much longer, she'd appear derelict, and
she could *not* afford to get fired.

Her notifications pinged when she reached the biographies. In her hurry to respond, she nearly dropped her phone.

What in the world was wrong with her? She was acting like she'd never texted a man—who happened to be her boss, a fact she'd do well to remember—before.

With a deep breath to slow her spiked pulse, she read his text. That looks great. Check it out for me?

An image of her stopping by his place, book in hand, flashed through her mind. Frowning, she once again chastised herself for her almost comical reaction. She and CJ were friends, nothing more.

Then why had her pulse spiked at the thought of standing on his stoop, close enough to see the gray specks in his green eyes?

THE NEXT MORNING, having arrived at Little Tykes intentionally early, she spent nearly ten minutes driving up and down the street, debating whether she wanted to be one of the first to enter the building or to stroll in fashionably late. Unfortunately, every time she looped back around, some of her courage seeped out.

So much for leading with confidence. Seemed

she'd decreased in that department since her awkward teenage years. Then again, back then, she'd felt judged because of her mom, not for what she'd feared people might be saying about her personally.

With a deep breath, Harper repeated a statement that had helped her show up to dance rehearsal, knowing she'd have to interact with her baby-denying ex. *I can do hard things.*

She parked, cut the engine and glanced at her reflection in the rearview mirror, then at her daughter, who was blowing raspberries around her fist shoved into her mouth. "Guess it's time I quit wasting gas, put on a winning smile and march in that place like the adult I am."

Grabbing the diaper bag that doubled as a purse, she stepped out and to the rear passenger's-side door. "Girl, your hair, all half an inch of it, is on point." She tapped her daughter's nose and unhooked her carrier.

Walking toward Little Tykes's single-door entrance, she made a visual sweep of the lot, trying to ignore how sharply her dilapidated vehicle stood out among its newer neighbors. She'd hoped, these classes being discounted and all, that she'd encounter a different demographic than the more affluent women who typically took their children to these types of things.

Clearly, she'd been wrong. But this was good. She'd been wanting to find a way to break into Sage Creek's mommy circle. Hopefully, this class would provide the opportunity.

With a deep breath, she burst inside with the same feigned confidence that had propelled her onto countless dance stages. A bell above her chimed, and numerous heads turned her direction, most expressions ranging from friendly to surprised. A tall brunette with mousy, shoulder-length hair parted down the middle regarded her with a scowl.

Only one out of ten openly hostile. Harper could handle that.

She made eye contact with the owner, Julia Nieves, who came into the library looking for picture books on occasion. "Sorry I'm late."

Sleek, blond hair tapered around her face, the green-eyed woman flicked a hand with a wide smile. "You're right on time." Fingertips pressed together at her waist, she addressed them all. "Welcome to Little Tykes, everyone. How many of you are first-time moms?"

A few of them, Harper included, raised their hands.

"Congrats and welcome to the beautiful world of motherhood. How many of you are taking a Mommy-Baby Little Tykes class for the first time?"

More raised hands.

"I'm grateful to have the opportunity to introduce you to our rich, memorable, multisensory experience scientifically proven to enhance brain development." She explained how, interspersed with icebreaker questions, then directed everyone to form a circle on the polka-dotted carpet.

Harper quickly sat, her back to the long window, before her friendless status in a room full of besties became awkward. The others soon joined her on either side, legs crisscrossed, their babies in their laps.

"We'll start with some tactile tempo fun." Dressed in a jungle-print T-shirt that fit with the bright walls, Julia glided to a console on a raised shelf and upped the volume of the song playing in the background. "Grab hold of your baby's ankles and raise and lower their legs to the beat." She sashayed from person to person, arms extended and fluid, matching the lyrics about a roly-poly, rickety-pickety, silly-willy, squiggly-wiggly squirrel.

The wall to her right was painted orange with large black musical notes with smiling faces. Adjacent to that, someone had painted a mural of rolling hills, a blue sky and thick yellow beams radiating from a half-circle sun. Across from the mural, someone had painted a city made from purple, red, green and coral rectangles topped with contrasting triangles. A mess of mats, cylinder or wedged, filled the far back corner, behind which peeked a plastic wading pool filled with balls of various colors.

After they'd engaged their infants' arms and torsos in time to the music, Julia motioned for them all to stand. "Now turn your kiddo so that they face out, their back to your chest." She glanced around. "That's right. Use one hand as their seat, and with the other, hug them nice and tight around their chest. Then gently bounce as you walk about the room."

Lily, a woman who'd graduated a year after Harper, took a few lunges. "If I go deep like this, does it count as cardio training for the day?"

Her friend, a short woman with the top half of her black hair pulled back in a knot, laughed. "Girl, if you're looking to raise your heart rate, you can borrow my kindergartner anytime. I get enough steps chasing after him to last me through middle age."

"No joke." Lily huffed. "With all the running around I do, upstairs and downstairs, and everywhere in between, you'd think I'd have lost my gut by now."

Harper eyed her, noting the woman's beautiful, wavy hair, vibrant skin and infectious smile. "You look great."

Lily halted midbounce, as if momentarily caught off guard by the compliment. Then, a look of kindness filled her expression. "Thank you. That encouraged me." She angled her head. "I'd say the same about you. No one could tell that you'd ever had a watermelon-sized critter stretching your stomach."

"Right?" Her friend regarded Harper with raised eyebrows. "You a runner?"

Harper shook her head. "But I do dance, although not as much as I used to." Nor as much as she should or wanted.

She needed to stay fit in case the companies with the choreographer jobs asked for live auditions. She'd also find it easier to gain dancers' respect, and therefore cooperation, if she was able to perform the moves she prescribed.

Mauve, a former classmate who'd been silently brooding since she'd walked in, shot Harper a pointed look. "Seems you didn't turn out to be the successful ballerina you thought."

Harper fought to keep her gaze level. "I was actually into hip-hop. But yes, my plans did change. Temporarily." She could only imagine the stories about her circulating Sage Creek.

Let them talk. She'd be gone, steadily progressing toward her dream, soon enough. While Mauve and other gossips spent the rest of their lives gabbing about how others lived theirs, Harper intended to end her days with something worth talking about.

Lily gave a slight cough and switched hands beneath her son. "My sister—she lives in Corpus Christi—she goes to one of those barre fitness classes."

Creative exercise experiences seemed to be growing in popularity. A momentary fad or ongoing trend? What did it take to run one of those establishments, anyway? Maybe, once she started her choreographer job, assuming it actually came through, Harper could work part-time at one of those fitness facilities, to gain some experience. While still devoting sufficient time with Emaline, of course.

Laughter drew her attention to three moms gathered to her left. A sense of longing welled within her as she watched the ladies interact with one another's babies. Those were the types of friends she needed. She needed to make sure to find such a community when she moved, even if it meant taking expensive mommy-baby classes.

"What's that?" Her friend bounced alongside her.

Everyone followed Lily's gaze to Harper.

She raised her chin a notch, no longer feeling like the outcast trying to muscle her way in. "It's a type of workout that combines ballet, Pilates, stretching and breathing."

Lily nodded. "My sister's super toned. Has long, lean legs and an amazing posture. After three kids."

"You know what I'd love to do?" asked a lady who'd been quiet up until then. "I'd like to try one of those ribbon classes—I think that's what they're called. Where people loop themselves around those massively long strips of fabric hanging from the ceiling."

Harper followed her gaze to the thick, exposed wooden beams above her. She loved old buildings like this one. "I did some aerial acrobatics in college."

Lily's son became fussy, so she kissed the fat folds in his neck until he began to giggle. "Was it fun?"

"It was. A great stress reliever, too." She'd chosen her first class as one of her electives then continued during open gym times for her remaining years.

Lily sighed. "Too bad we don't have anything like that here."

Harper's cell rang. Repositioning Emaline to free a hand, she pulled her phone from her back pocket and glanced at the screen.

Her breath caught and she glanced up. "Excuse me." She backed away from the group and answered. "Hey."

"Hey." His tentative tone intrigued her. "You at the library?"

"Actually, I have the day off." She told him where she was.

"That's right." He paused. "Listen, I know this is last minute, and not exactly the most exciting way to spend a Saturday night…"

Clearly, he didn't know how she spent most of her off hours. Anything he suggested would be more entertaining than ending her evening with rom-coms and a giant bowl of chocolate-mint ice cream.

The music changed to a quick-tempo song about a mother duck leading her brood over rolling hills and a stream.

She leaned a shoulder against the beam between two long windows. "What's up?"

"My parents bought tickets for the Cattle Baron's Ball."

"A fundraiser for cancer research, right?"

"Yeah. They planned on going, but then my mom got sick and my dad… He's just not the social type. Doesn't like to attend these deals alone."

"Can't say I blame him."

"Me, either. Which is sort of why I'm calling. They asked me to go, but I'd rather not show up solo…"

Her pulse spiked. Was he asking her out? "Okay?"

"Any chance you're free and up for some prime rib, live music and helping me not appear socially awkward?"

She forced a nervous laugh. "Um, as to that last part…" Hopefully her teasing tone masked her sudden breathlessness. "I'm not sure that's possible."

He went silent. Had he taken her banter as a brush-off? "What time is the event?"

"Refreshments, meet and greet starts at six thirty."

"Will I need boots and a hat?" She didn't have anything even remotely cowgirl. Thankfully, Trisha did and would be more than happy to lend a few pieces out. Unfortunately, she'd probably also bombard Harper with a plethora of questions all centered around one—were she and CJ getting back together?

Harper was beginning to wonder the same thing and wasn't sure how she felt about that.

"Does that mean you'll go?" CJ sounded pleasantly surprised, with an almost giddy undercurrent.

Harper inhaled and exhaled slowly so as not to match his tone. This wasn't a date, after all. "I'll need to make sure my mom can watch Emaline, but sure. I don't have anything better to do."

"Okay." Had her response deflated him, or was she simply detecting a relaxed, post-anxiety state?

Regardless, she would not allow this function to become more than it was—one friend supporting the other.

Both of whom once loved one another.

Why did she feel like she was tiptoeing toward the proverbial point of no return—at least, if she wanted to leave Sage Creek with her heart intact?

CHAPTER TEN

NOT WANTING TO appear overly eager, CJ pulled into Harper's driveway at a quarter after six, dressed in dark jeans, a checked button-down shirt and a black vest. He'd even dusted and polished his boots, not that anyone would pay much attention to his feet.

They would be spending their night in a barn, after all. A mite fancied up, but an old farm building just the same.

Who was he kidding? Tonight was a big deal and potentially the most romantic time he'd spend with Harper since high school prom.

He feared he was falling for her all over again.

In high school, he'd loved her for her looks, determination, her wit and the fun they'd had together.

Now watching her with her daughter hit him in a deeper place.

The place where his longing for a family of his own resided.

Her front door opened. Harper emerged wearing a jean skirt that hugged her curves and hit midknee, a white cowgirl hat and a pink blouse that highlighted the beginning of a tan.

Her beauty stalled his thoughts.

But then manners shot him from his truck. He met her on the sidewalk.

Did she think he'd been sitting out here, waiting on her? He'd seen some of his more immature high school buddies acting that way, laying on their horns to "fetch" their girls. That had never been his way, not even when doing so seemed cool.

He beat her to her door and opened it for her. "You look beautiful."

With a slight blush, she fingered the pendant resting in the dimple between her collarbones. "Thanks."

She slid past him and into the seat, a faint pineapple-coconut scent floating on the air.

Clearing his throat to jolt some common sense into his muddled brain, he rounded his truck and eased in behind the wheel. He'd left the engine running, and a country music song about a lost love poured from the speakers.

He clicked it off and backed out into the road. "You been to an event at Angus Village before?"

Originally a ranch, the family had turned most of their property into a bookable venue generations ago. As the only place he knew of, apart from churches, folks could rent for parties and whatnot, it'd become a popular location for charity events, weddings and other celebrations.

She nodded. "For Haven's thirteenth birthday party." They'd both gone to school with her.

"I remember that. Wasn't that when you were dating Paul?"

"Don't remind me. I have no idea what I saw in him."

"I heard your next boyfriend was quite a step up."

She blinked as if his comment unnerved her, and he wished he could take it back.

But then she laughed. "He wasn't terrible."

He didn't know how to read her statement or whether to continue their banter or switch directions. Seemed wise to lean toward caution and not do or say anything that might make the rest of their evening painfully awkward.

And hope there'd come a day when they could speak about their emotions, past and present, more freely.

Did she even have feelings to discuss, or was she simply treating him like a friend?

What then? Could he handle being her "buddy"? Spending time with her, at this event, at work, at church—wherever they interacted now that they weren't actively avoiding one another—as little more than a pleasant companion?

Suppressing a sigh, he drove out of town and onto the two-lane highway dissecting fields and pastures.

Harper pulled a pack of gum from her purse and offered him some.

He declined.

She shrugged and popped a piece into her mouth. "I was talking to my mom about your chain-saw contest. She was impressed."

"Yeah?"

She nodded. "She even suggested we go watch. Make a girls' weekend out of it."

"Really? That's awesome."

That had to mean a lot to Harper. Back when they'd been dating, she'd cried on his shoulder numerous times about how her mom didn't seem to like her. Mrs. Moore hadn't been a terrible mom, just not always that engaged.

"Only problem, I have to work." Her tone carried a note of disappointment.

He could understand why. This might've been the first time her mother had suggested she and her daughter spend such quality time together.

Drumming his fingers on the steering wheel, he mentally reviewed the schedule. "Bet my folks could make do without you."

"You sure? On this short of notice."

"Next weekend's Principal Nguyen's retirement party."

"Meaning?"

"S'pect that'll keep most people occupied."

"You're probably right. He's a great man. Worth celebrating."

He nodded. "I'll talk with my parents."

She smiled. "Thanks."

The possibility of her coming to his event triggered a sense of giddy anticipation and anxiety.

CJ thought back to when they were teens and all the times he'd scanned the bleachers, mid football game, to catch sight of her. Each time, he'd found her standing, eyes locked on him, waving with both arms raised.

She'd never missed a game.

But back then, he'd also rarely fumbled. By the time they'd started dating, he'd felt confident in his ability to impress her on the field.

He'd felt equally sure of their relationship. He'd trusted in their love so fully, he'd never considered she might leave.

Now?

Now he realized if he wanted to reestablish what they'd once shared, he'd have to work for it. Knowing she could bail at any time.

Could this time be different? Could he somehow figure out how to hold on to her for good?

Did the fact that he was even asking himself these questions make him foolish?

Nearing the location for the ball, he followed a line of cars onto a winding gravel road lined with blooming myrtle trees growing in a long stretch of wildflowers. Beyond, fields of tall, waving grass grew in each direction.

This soon gave way to a vehicle-covered field on the right, the decked-out venue on the left and a simple farmhouse with a wraparound porch some four hundred yards ahead.

Once parked, he fell into step beside Harper, hand instinctively touching the small of her back. She started and looked at him with inquisitive eyes that gave no indication as to whether she welcomed the touch.

Not that he'd intended to cross whatever invisible boundaries they'd placed between themselves. It was just that being here, in this place with Harper, felt all too familiar. So familiar, his body seemed to be reacting to her presence as he had so easily before.

Except, things had changed.

But that didn't mean they couldn't change things back. Maybe tonight could be their first step in that direction.

She paused to gaze up at the entrance, swathed with cream and sheer curtains, white potted flowers on each side of the frame. "Beautiful."

He followed her line of sight to the barn's interior, lit by strings of lights encircling and draping from the rafters.

White linens covered long rectangular tables lined end to end, side to side, with walking space between. Every three or so place settings stood trios of glass vases of varying heights, banded with silver, matching cloth napkins placed on the plates.

Seeing the decorations, which were much fancier than he'd expected, he worried he'd told her to underdress. But while a few of the ladies were blitzed out, most of them wore outfits similar to Harper's.

Although none of them looked nearly as beautiful.

She'd always been unrivaled in that area. That was the main reason so many of the girls in their social circle had acted so ugly to her. They'd been jealous and afraid she might grow tired of CJ and try to steal their boyfriends.

She glanced about. "I'm guessing your parents want you to hobnob?"

He groaned. "I hope not, because I am so not that guy."

She laughed. "I remember the year you were voted homecoming king and everyone tried to pressure you into giving a speech."

"Only because they knew how much I'd hate it."

"I also seem to remember that you used me as your excuse not to."

"I truly was a little worried. I hadn't seen you for some time."

"I'm still upset with Maya Ward for telling you I was, and I quote, 'hiding in the bathroom.'"

"I'm sorry you felt you had to. If I'd known Sally Jo and her annoying echo were being so ugly, I would've done something."

"And made things worse. Besides, they got what was coming to them when someone found, copied and distributed the notes they'd been sending one another."

He chuckled. "Wow. I'd completely forgotten

about that. Those were some of the most hilarious pages I've ever read."

He glanced toward a flash of red in his peripheral vision. *Perfect.* It was Sally Jo, the drama queen herself and, unfortunately, she hadn't grown up much since their teenage days. Based on the gossip folks attributed to her, the woman's contempt for Harper hadn't chilled much, either.

He touched Harper's elbow, her skin as soft as her strands of hair he used to run his fingers through. "Hate to say it, but look who decided to make an appearance."

She followed his line of sight. "And based on how tight, short and revealing her sequined dress is, hoping to snag herself a man."

"Guess some things never change."

"Seems not."

"I hope she won't make you feel uncomfortable."

That was the opposite of what he wanted. He was hoping this evening could be a big step toward winning back Harper's heart.

Before she and her adorable daughter returned to Seattle, potentially never to return.

Harper scoffed. "I seriously couldn't care less

what that woman and her childish posse think of me, or say about me, for that matter."

So she'd heard the rumors. That had to sting, although her response indicated she took them for what they were—nothing more than the immature antics of people who'd peaked at sixteen and had yet to enter the world of adult decency.

"I would, however, love to try one of those." She pointed to an appetizer someone walking by was eating. It looked like a bite of steak wrapped in bacon.

"Let's get some." He led the way to one of numerous high-tops laden with veggie platters, hush puppies, some kind of cheesy pastry and numerous other items. "If this is what they call refreshments, I can't wait to see what they serve for dinner."

At the drink station, they ran into a woman Harper had interacted with at the mother-baby class she'd taken that morning. The two seemed engaged in a humorous conversation.

This was good. Every relationship she formed would make it harder for her to leave Sage Creek.

And him.

He was about to excuse himself when the ladies started talking about some ribbon acrobatics.

But then the band started playing one of Harper's favorite songs.

She turned to him with a grin. "Join us." She tugged him toward the dance floor, where a group of people, almost all female, were forming a line.

CJ resisted and shook his head. "I'm not really into those line dance deals. I'd just stumble all over the place and end up hurting a person."

"Or your ego?" She quirked a brow at him. "Seriously, it's the electric slide. No one could grow up in Texas without knowing how to do that one."

"Apparently, someone could have." He pointed at himself.

"I don't believe you."

"It's the truth. When y'all go left, I go right, and when you slide, toe-tap right, I fall backward."

"That's not how I remember things."

He swallowed as an image rushed to his mind from homecoming night. A slow song had come on that had reminded him of her. Something about a strong-willed, smart-witted woman who wasn't afraid to do things her own way, even if that meant going it alone.

At first, she'd been stiff in his arms, her gaze

darting from him to the others swaying around them. But then he'd leaned close enough that his lips had brushed her ear and said, "I could've written these lyrics about you. If I could write, I mean."

She'd laughed, then locked hopeful eyes on his and asked, "You mean it?"

He'd nodded and spent the rest of the dance singing to her words she'd come to live out. A woman so unafraid to live independently, she'd left him behind.

But now Harper was back and asking him to dance in a space similar to the one in which they'd first begun to fall in love. He could keep resisting and spend the evening sitting bored at a table, wondering what might have happened had he said yes. Or he could embrace the moment.

And if doing so led to another heartbreak?

He needed to stop overthinking everything.

He turned back to Harper. "It's been a long time since I've done any kind of line dancing. Pretty sure I forget when to step where."

"I'll teach you." Her grin widened, and she looked so incredibly beautiful, so happy, he couldn't disappoint her.

He laughed and fell beside her at the end of the line. "Don't say I didn't warn you."

"Slide, close, slide, tap."

He did his best to follow as she spoke out each step.

"Great job. When you go forward, swing your arm like this." She demonstrated.

He soon caught the rhythm and his moves felt more natural. While his steps weren't nearly as smooth as hers or her friend's, he no longer felt like he was about to stomp on somebody.

Then a slow song came on, and the crowd started to thin.

He took her hand. "You up for one more?"

Harper studied him a moment, her breath heavy and her cheeks red.

She bit her lip as if sensing the weight of this moment, same as him. "Okay."

CJ's heart gave a lurch as he pulled her to him, his hands resting on the small of her back as hers landed softly on his shoulders. Her eyes locked on his, her face so close, he could feel the warmth of her breath. Feeling her relax in his embrace, he leaned closer, inhaling the coconut-pineapple scent of her shampoo, and began to sing with the lyrics.

Just as he had when holding her, just like this, on a dance floor many years prior—feeling again as if he could've penned the words for her. "'The first time I saw you, hair wild, eyes blue, you took my breath away. I fell in love that day.'"

"CJ." She pulled back to look into his eyes, a hint of uncertainty in her expression.

"Don't overthink this, Harper." He told her the same thing he'd been telling himself since they'd entered this space. Because, for now, he just wanted to enjoy the moment, knowing that it could easily be the last time he held her this close.

Did she feel the same? He couldn't be certain, but she once again relaxed against him, this time with her cheek on his chest, her face turned into his neck. Her breath tickled his skin, sending goose bumps up his arm.

He could've stayed like that for the rest of the night—feeling her soft warmth as the past and present merged in his mind and the dreams they'd once formed together reignited. He was in a dangerous place. He knew that. But he didn't have the strength to leave.

But then the tempo picked up, and the floor became crowded once again, and the moment was broken. When everyone started doing the Cotton Eye Joe, he slid out of the throng to an open chair at a nearby table. By then, Harper had gotten caught up helping two older women learn the complicated dance steps.

CJ couldn't keep his eyes off her. The way her face lit up when she laughed. Her wavy hair, shimmering beneath the lights above her, bouncing on her slender shoulders. How she noticed those who lingered on the edge, inhibited, and gently drew them in. Or came alongside those struggling to keep up.

Harper dominated the dance floor, only not in an obnoxious look-at-me kind of way. The music made her come alive with a joy that was contagious.

He'd always known this was her thing.

What did that mean for the two of them? Could she find what made her heart sing in Sage Creek?

If not, could he let her go a second time?

"I wondered how long it'd take her to get her hooks in you."

CJ turned to see Paul, the guy Harper had dated prior to him, standing beside him. He wore a charcoal-gray cowboy hat that looked fresh out of the box, and a plaid shirt with pearl buttons. A green-and-blue tattoo of a howling wolf stretched from his wrist to his elbow.

Shaking his head, Paul sat in the recently vacated chair to CJ's right. "Don't blame her none. I mean, a mama's got to do what a mama's got to do, right? Not surprised she'd target you, either."

He tensed. "What're you talking about?"

"You haven't figured it out yet? That ex-girlfriend of yours is hunting for a baby daddy."

CJ sat upright. "Dude. It's been…what, ten years? And you haven't gotten over her yet?"

"Oh, I'm long over that one, believe me. You, on the other hand." He shook his head. "Just can't let that one go, no matter how clear the lettering is on the wall. You realize she's playing you, right? That's what she does."

"You know nothing about her."

"And you do? History says otherwise, my man. If memory serves, you were about the last person to learn about her grand Seattle University Dance plans."

Jaw tight, CJ stood before he said or did anything he'd regret.

"Truth hurts, huh, Jenkins."

That guy didn't have a clue. Harper may have blindsided him that night, and completely broken his heart, but she'd never manipulated or used him. That had never been her way.

And if her time in the city and with that fancy dance company had changed her?

No. He refused to believe that.

CHAPTER ELEVEN

NANCY MET HARPER in the break room when she arrived at work Monday morning to ask if she wanted the weekend off.

Harper picked at her pinkie nail. "I really want to support CJ." The gleam in Nancy's eye suggested this response pleased her. "But I also need the money."

Nancy tapped a finger to her chin. "Let me talk with Ken."

She darted out and returned a moment later with a grin. "You up for pulling a double today and tomorrow?"

Harper mentally reviewed her library schedule. With their latest children's program ended and a brief lull before they launched the next, she wasn't due there until Wednesday afternoon.

"I need to check with my mom to make sure she can watch Emaline." Her response would show just how important this "girls' weekend," as she'd called it, was to her. It was one thing to suggest an idea—her mom was great at coming up with grand plans. Follow-through was another matter entirely.

"How about you give her a call? And if your mom's busy, you can always bring the pumpkin in."

"Are you sure?"

Nancy shrugged. "Don't see why not. I practically raised CJ here. As long as you don't go trying to lift eighty-pound cement bags off the shelves—which you shouldn't be doing anyway." She gave her a stern gaze.

"No, ma'am." Harper smiled, enjoying the renewed sense of camaraderie she'd started to experience with CJ's mom. They'd once been close.

She'd filled numerous maternal holes during Harper's teen years. Taught her to cook and bake, to treat others with kindness and respect and to expect them to do the same. But most importantly, whereas her mother often made her feel tolerated, Nancy had always acted as if the time spent with Harper had been the best part of her day.

After lunch, she found Nancy talking with CJ in her office.

She poked her head inside. "Hi. I spoke with my mom."

Nancy swiveled her chair to face her more directly. "And?"

"She's good to watch Emaline for however long I need."

"Yes!" CJ shot a fist in the air, making her laugh.

Nancy seemed equally pleased, making Harper more alert to the impact of her actions. CJ hadn't been the only one hurt when she'd left the last time, nor would he be the only one affected when it came time for her to move once again.

Maybe she shouldn't go to San Angelo after all.

But how could she decline, now that every plausible obstacle had been removed?

Besides, she was really looking forward to connecting with her mom. It'd be their first ever vacation together, unless you counted the time they drove, nonstop, to Cincinnati, Ohio, to take care of her grandmother recovering from knee surgery. They'd made the trip there in one day, barely left the house their entire time there, and Harper had been battling an intense stomach virus on the drive back.

As to watching CJ do his thing—Harper was simply going to show her support, like he had done for her countless times.

And she would do so while keeping her rogue emotions in check, a steadily decreasing skill, it seemed. It didn't help that CJ had started looking at her the same way he had not that long ago. But neither of them needed to repeat their breakup from five years prior. His pained expression the day she'd ended things had haunted her dreams for months.

Yet, despite the ache of knowing how deeply she'd hurt him, and her grief over the loss itself, she knew she'd made the right decision. Had she stayed, she would've always wondered whether or not she could succeed in the dance industry.

And if he'd tried to talk her out of going, or offered to join her?

Regardless, he hadn't. She'd chosen dance; he'd chosen the store. Neither of them chose each other. Seemed that meant something.

Over the next couple days, Harper tried to be exceptionally helpful, in part to thank Nancy for all the kindness she'd displayed, but also to keep herself from overanalyzing things between her and CJ.

The night before the event, she tossed and

turned over her feelings for CJ and her difficulty shutting them down. She awoke with purplish bags under her bloodshot eyes and hair that refused to cooperate.

CJ stopped by before heading out, to offer her a ride. She felt a strong urge to accept but, thankfully, her brain stepped up before her mouth.

Standing at her open door, she glanced from his truck and trailer filled with his tools and carvings to the pile of luggage behind her—admittedly more than they needed for a three-day trip. This was technically a mother-daughter-granddaughter trip.

She turned back to CJ. "I should probably ride with my mom, this technically being a girls' trip and all."

"Right." His smile faltered momentarily. He pulled his phone from his back pocket and glanced at the screen. "You ever try roulade?"

"Is that a game?"

He shook his head. "Melt in your mouth German beef pastry."

Odd question. "Can't say that I have."

"There's a restaurant in Fredericksburg that serves it. We could stop. It's on our way."

"San Angelo's only a few hours' drive, right?"

Again, his face fell. "Yeah."

She seemed to be shooting down all his ideas, not exactly a bad thing, considering they needed to spend less time together, not more.

Yet she found herself scrambling to reverse her words. "But I'm sure Emaline could use a midway break from her car seat." That was true. Her daughter tended to get bored and fussy after about forty-five minutes.

Her mom's patience for Harper's attempts to keep the baby entertained didn't last much longer.

He shot her the boyish grin that used to turn her insides to mush, and maybe still did. "Great. I'll text you the location."

She thanked him then stepped back inside, hand lingering on the doorknob.

"Don't know why y'all keep playing games with one another."

She turned to find her mom standing behind her with a burned piece of toast in one hand and a steaming mug of coffee in the other. Beyond her, Emaline bounced and chattered in her door jumper, thankfully wearing herself out some.

Harper frowned. "What are you talking about?" She picked up her packed duffel and Emaline's diaper bag, draping each from a shoulder.

"Don't act coy. I've seen how googly-eyed y'all are for each other."

Harper opened her mouth to respond, but her mom raised a hand.

"I ain't judging you none. Far from it. Dumbest move you made was letting that boy go." She took a bite of her toast, crumbs cascading from her mouth. "But I'll tell you this—you're going to lose him, for good this time, if you don't stop toying with his emotions. Then where will you be? I'll tell you where. In a pool of regret so big, it'll take a lifetime to climb out of."

Harper winced as fear pinged deep inside her. What if her mom was right?

Then again, she didn't exactly have a wealth of positive relationship experience to draw from.

Not wanting to say anything that might unleash more of her mother's sage advice, Harper squared her shoulders and once again opened the front door. "I'll load up the car."

Fastening her seat belt ten minutes later, she mentally prepared herself for more of her mother's lessons. Thankfully, her mom immediately started to sing to eighties' rock instead.

By the time they pulled into the Old German Bakery and Restaurant in Fredericksburg, the tension she'd entered her mom's vehicle with had turned to laughter. Lunch was pleasant and, thankfully, minimally awkward, even with her mother's not-so-veiled "What are your intentions with my daughter?" questions.

The remaining drive to San Angelo was uneventful.

Once they arrived, Harper smoothed a hand over Emaline's soft head. "I'd suggest we do some sightseeing before the contest starts, but if this peanut doesn't nap soon, she's bound to throw a fit." That wouldn't help CJ mentally prepare for his competition.

"I still can't believe she didn't fall asleep on the drive." Harper's mom handed her a spare hotel key. "Tell you what. Once we get all of our stuff to the room, why don't you leave the peanut with Grandma and go help CJ get checked in to the contest and whatnot?"

"You sure?"

"Yep." She eyed CJ, who stood at the counter, getting his room, which, from the sounds of it, was right next door to theirs. "She and I will grab a quick nap then mosey around to see if we can't scope out the lumberjack scene."

Harper rolled her eyes. "You're insufferable. Please tell me that wasn't why you were so excited to come to this event." She hated to think that way, but her mom had once joined her for one of CJ's football banquets to flirt with his coach.

"Don't be ridiculous." She gave the back of Emaline's ruffle-hem blouse a tug. "But I'm certainly not going to waste this experience."

Harper couldn't shake the sense that she shouldn't, either. It was obvious, with how CJ kept jingling the change in his pocket, how much hope he was putting into the next three days. This contest could easily launch him as an artist, which meant that this weekend could be the most important of his life so far.

She'd get to share that moment with him.

As to the countless moments after, and knowing that should he reach his dream, it practically guaranteed he wouldn't follow her as she chased after hers?

She wouldn't think about that now. There'd be time for hard goodbyes later.

This weekend, she planned to show the most handsome, talented and honorable man in Texas the same support he'd showed her all those years ago.

CJ FOLLOWED THE map the hotel clerk gave him to San Angelo's vehicle-clogged downtown area then joined a line of half a dozen trucks and trailers similar to his waiting to drop their salable items at the consignment store.

He drummed his fingers on his steering wheel, trying not to fret about the competition. "Guess we're going to be here awhile."

"I'm in no hurry." She watched a potbellied man wearing large sunglasses and an American flag bandana around his head pulling a rolling cooler with one hand, holding a dog leash in the other, with two folding lawn chairs sandwiched between his arm and ribs. She turned back to CJ. "You nervous?"

He gave a slight shrug. "I've never worked in front of an audience—or been filmed—before."

"You'll do great. I have no doubt." She shot him a smile he felt all the way to his toes. "And like you said before, regardless how you place, this type of publicity will definitely put your name, and our town, on the map. Holy cow, can you imagine what the hardware store will be like come Monday morning? With folks clamoring in to see the new celebrity. It'll be like high school football all over again."

He laughed and placed his hand over hers. "Thanks for your support. This means a lot."

"Of course. Although you do know what'll

happen if—*when*—you win, right, and get the money you need to buy that building with your friend?"

"What?"

"I'll be stuck at the hardware store with my biggest fan." The sarcasm was thick.

"Ken doesn't have anything against you. He can just be gruff at times."

Although, she was right about one thing. If CJ walked away with that prize check, his time at Nuts, Bolts and Boards, and therefore, with Harper, would be drastically reduced.

When they were just beginning to rebuild things.

What if the affection that had started to reform between them dwindled with less time spent together and she once again decided to leave?

Did he really believe she could leave the dance world behind? They both knew she'd only returned out of necessity, which meant she could leave just as quickly.

Unless he gave her reason to stay.

"Hey, now." She gave him a playful shove. "Don't get so knotted up inside that you forget to have fun."

He shot her a grin. "Don't plan on it." That

was, in fact, the last thing he planned to do—especially since this could be his best shot of winning her heart.

Once he and Harper, with the help of contest staff, got his consignment items loaded into their store and he'd signed all the necessary forms, they checked out the carvings by the other competitors.

He paused in front of a large stump with raccoons peeking between the thick, knobbed-off branches. "Some of these are really phenomenal."

"As are yours." She placed her hand, her skin warm and soft, in the crook of his elbow. "Besides, for all you know, this one could've taken decades. Whoever made it might not even be in the master competition."

"Not helpful."

She bit her bottom lip. "Sorry. What I—"

He smiled. "I know what you meant, and I appreciate it."

"I'm really proud of you for going after your dreams like this."

"Thank you." He probably should've said the same to her, the night she'd told him about her college plans. But in that moment, all he could think of was how her decision had affected him.

Did that make him less of a person?

The bigger question was how would he act if he found himself in that situation again?

He cast her a sideways glance. "You thirsty? Because I'm pretty sure someone just walked by with frozen lemonade."

"Let's go."

They strolled toward a long line of pop-up tents housing food and craft vendors. Numerous scents and noises swirled all around them. Hot dogs, funnel cakes, sunscreen. Laughter, people talking, music from two different directions. One came from a passing bicyclist who, apparently, had yet to discover headphones—and quality tunes. Another came from a local radio station that had sent hosts to cover the event.

Their van, black with their logo painted in thick, red lettering, stood behind a matching pop-up tent with two speakers anchored on either end. A man in plaid and a tan cowboy hat sat behind a table holding window clings, bumper stickers and other paraphernalia.

CJ cast Harper a sideways glance. If he grabbed her hand, would she pull away?

She paused at one of half a dozen tool companies' booths to look at an electric power cap. "What's this for?"

"To keep dust and whatnot from your lungs and eyes. It's got a fan that sucks in air from the top and filters out wood chips. Plus, it's air-conditioned."

"Seriously?"

"So I've heard."

"You don't have one?"

"I wish. Maybe once I start bringing in some green. These little jewels cost a pretty penny." He turned it over so she could see the price on the bottom.

"Wow. Although I'm guessing the other tools don't come cheap, either."

"Not exactly, but at least I can justify buying them for other things. A man always needs a good chain saw and grinder."

She laughed and moved on to a display of handcrafted jewelry. She picked up a teal-and-peach pair of earrings made from wood and resin. "My mom would love these."

"How'd the drive over go?"

"Better than I'd expected." She fingered wooden beads on a necklace. "I worried about how she and I would get along, with me living under her roof again. I know I annoy her sometimes. But I can also tell that she likes spending time with her first grandchild. And it's good for

Emaline. I like that she's had so much one-on-one attention."

It was nice to hear Harper talk this way regarding her time in Sage Creek. Hopefully, all these positive experiences would motivate her to stay put.

They continued past a man selling customized charcuterie boards, another display of hand-crafted jewelry and an older couple offering samples of homemade honeys and jams.

Harper eyed an opened jar of mint jalapeño jelly. "Interesting."

The vendor standing behind the table lifted a cup of pretzel sticks. "Would you like to sample some?"

Harper held out her hand. "No, thank you." She walked beside CJ as they continued on. "My dad used to love strange combinations like that. Popcorn and ketchup. Tortilla chips and peanut butter. Fries dipped in a chocolate milkshake."

"That last one I could do."

She scrunched her nose. "Remind me never to let you cook for me."

"Except, I already have. And if memory serves, you liked it."

She laughed. "I have to admit, you grill a mean steak."

"Your father. You talk to him much?"

She frowned and dropped her gaze. "I try. But he's never been that interested in me."

"I'm sorry." He remembered how much that had hurt her. She'd once told him that she knew in her head that he'd left her mom and that his abandonment wasn't about her. But that it was hard to believe that when he'd so easily walked away from her as well.

"I called him the day I got hired on with that touring dance company, so certain he'd be proud of me. Caught him while he was at a bar. I could hear how noisy it was on his end. Only, instead of stepping outside for even five minutes, he said it was too loud for him to hear me and could he call me back later."

"Did he?"

"Of course not. Probably forgot about it, and me, as soon as he hung up."

"I'm sorry," he repeated, not knowing what else to say. "Does he know about Emaline?"

"Yeah, and that I'm back home living with Mom." She snorted. "Doubt that surprised him any. He always said I was just like her."

Now CJ understood why that statement had hurt her so deeply. Most likely, her dad hadn't meant it in the way she'd taken it. Although, he might have. He'd never been high on the nurturing side. But that must've been how she'd made sense of his rejection. Her father hadn't walked away from her, as much as the part of her that resembled her mother.

He took Harper's hand and studied her expression, so much making sense. "Is that why you tried so hard not to be like her?"

"It's more complicated than that."

"Okay?"

"If you're asking why I moved to Seattle—" She shook her head. "Dancing is who I am."

"You're so much more than that."

"I get what you're saying. And obviously things didn't work out as I'd hoped. I know I need to course correct. It's just... I've spent years—hours upon hours—training. I don't want my hard work to be for nothing."

They'd stopped in the middle of the walking path, the jostle of people pushing past them alerting him to the fact that they were blocking traffic.

He pulled her aside and turned her to face him. He searched her eyes, struggling to speak. "You know I never asked you not to dance." His words came out as a hoarse whisper. "I just asked you to stay."

"Essentially, to give up my dream for you."

"It wasn't like that."

Tears brimmed in her eyes. "But it was. And we both know, if the shoe were on the other foot, you would've done the same."

"That's not true."

"Really?" Her tone held bite. "If you win this contest and someone offers you a shiny deal in New York or somewhere, you seriously believe you'd turn them down? For me? I mean, sure, I get that you can carve in Sage Creek. But you get my point. Do you really think, if forced, that you'd choose me over carving?"

"I would."

"Then why didn't you five years ago?"

"You never let me." His chest squeezed. "By the time I could breathe again, you were gone."

"You still could have come after me."

He dragged a hand across his jaw, frustrated with how their conversation had turned, and terrified one wrong word would shatter their relationship for good. "How would that have worked? I was a broke kid whose only job experience involved working for his parents."

That, according to Harper's friend, had been precisely what she'd said about him, and that was the reason he'd let her go. Because he'd believed he wasn't good enough for her. That she deserved, and would find, someone better than a pickup-driving, country-music-listening guy from the sticks.

"Besides," he said, "you'd made it clear you didn't want me."

"I don't want to talk about the past anymore." She gave his hand a squeeze. "We were nothing but a couple of stupid kids thinking we were ready to be grown. Which, obviously, we weren't." She started walking once again.

He sensed there was something deeper going on.

As they merged back onto the crowded sidewalk, he fell into step beside her.

Then it hit him. "You wanted me to fight for you. Because your dad never did."

Her steps halted as her gaze shot to him, the vulnerability in her eyes giving her an almost childlike appearance.

CHAPTER TWELVE

THE NEXT MORNING, Harper hurried to get ready, not wanting to miss any of CJ's big day. Running her fingers through her still-damp hair, she glanced through the mirror to Emaline. She was sitting in her playpen, babbling and batting at a glittery spinning drum raised on a wooden stand.

Harper smiled and grabbed her mascara wand. "You making music, sweet girl?"

She squealed, and Harper laughed. "You carry a key about as well as CJ does, little one." Her heart warmed as she thought back to the evening she'd caught him singing that army theme song to Emaline in his kitchen. Such a sap.

Then she frowned, remembering their spat from the day before—if you could call it that, which she didn't. They'd simply...been rehashing junk they needed to let lie. Correction.

She'd been rehashing things, and on the day of his big competition.

Some support she was.

Lord, help him to do well today. To think and carve quickly. Without losing any fingers.

The judges had given him and the others their challenge the night before. They had one day to carve out a sculpture that in some way symbolized passing time. Sunday, they'd receive scores for creativity, skill and artistic ability.

Her mom sat on the edge of the hotel bed, eating a bowl of dry cereal. "I was impressed with how quickly CJ landed on an idea last night. Guess all that brainstorming practice the two of you did gave him a head start on the competition, huh?"

"I hope so." Whereas some of the others had spent nearly half of their allotted "sketching" time staring at a blank page, or starting one idea then shifting to another, CJ had gotten straight to drawing. "He said the hardest part was balancing complexity with speed. Said a plan was only as great as its final execution."

"I s'pect so. You get a chance to talk to him once they finished for the night?"

She nodded. "Thanks for bringing Emaline back to the room."

Her mom shrugged. "I was ready to head back anyway. Can do the same tonight, if you'd like."

"I appreciate it." She turned around to face her. "Really. You've been great."

"Figure I wasn't always there for you like I should've been when you were growing up. Grateful for the chance of a do-over."

Tears stung Harper's eyes as the words she hadn't known she'd so desperately needed to hear washed over her. "Thank you for saying that."

Her mom nodded then stood and tossed her empty paper bowl in the trash. "Guess I best jump in the shower."

Harper was still processing her words, and CJ's from the night before, when she arrived at the contest site twenty minutes later. A steady hum and the spicy-sweet scent of cedar shavings filled the air.

The television crew was back with two cameramen, each shooting from different angles, and the crowd of spectators had nearly doubled. She worried both would only add to CJ's nervousness. If they did, he didn't show it.

She tried to make out his design from the blocked shape. He'd refused to tell her last night. Said he wanted to keep it a secret. She could tell how much he wanted to impress her, and that touched her.

Lifting Emaline from her stroller, she surveyed the competition arena, a large circular space encased by thick, five-foot logs standing on end side by side. The ground within was nearly covered with sawdust, with larger mounds accumulated beneath each carver's project secured on top of wooden pallets. Numerous electric cords snaked from somewhere outside the marked area.

A nasally voiced man behind her gave constant commentary on each of the competitors, loudly proclaiming their "obvious" errors and risky moves. "That kid's got guts," he said, clearly indicating CJ, the youngest of the group. "The guys he's up against have probably been carving about as long as he's been alive."

Harper resisted the urge to turn around and fire off a retort. So what that CJ was relatively new to all this? Whatever he lacked in experience, he more than made up for in creativity, of that she was certain.

She'd hoped to catch his eye, to offer him an encouraging smile, but he'd remained focused on his project from the time she'd arrived through now. The only brief pauses she'd seen him take had been for a swig of water or to switch tools.

To think, this weekend could be his big break—the event that piqued the attention of some of this nation's most affluent and influential art collectors.

Harper remembered how it felt, knowing you stood on the cusp of a dream. The excitement, anxiety and giddy anticipation. The realization that you could soon see the fruit of countless hours of hard work and sacrifice.

She thought back to what he'd said the day before, about her not giving him a chance to choose her. Would he now?

Did she want him to?

She shifted her weight, gazing toward wispy clouds drifting across the horizon. Could she be happy in Sage Creek? Considering she still hadn't heard anything about that choreographer's job she'd been waiting on, she might have to be. She was beginning to think her ex's mom had been feeding her a line to make Harper go away. Either that, or she didn't have the power she claimed and the position had been filled by someone else.

Now what? The longer Harper stayed out

of the dance world, the harder it would be to break back in.

Could she find a way to do what made her soul sing in the town she was beginning to grow fond of—if it meant experiencing the type of love CJ had once promised her?

When the contest officiator signaled it was time to break for lunch, CJ set down the smaller chain saw he'd been using and shucked off his protective gear. He glanced up, his gaze sweeping the crowd. Upon seeing her, he grinned and headed her direction.

A few spectators, one a chubby kid with thick glasses and jet-black hair, another an older lady wearing a floppy green hat, intercepted him. Others stood nearby, waiting to catch a word, to ask a question, or maybe to congratulate him on his work.

She watched with a smile, amused to see he didn't seem any more comfortable being the center of attention now than he had back in high school.

His humility was one of his most endearing traits.

CJ caught her eye, and the look of exasperation displayed on his face was enough to motivate her to do the one thing every mom in the history of motherhood termed an atrocity—risk waking a sleeping baby. But then he slipped free and jogged toward her.

He released a heavy breath. "I thought I'd never break free."

"Guess it's tough being a celebrity, huh?"

"Yeah, right."

"You won't find that statement so absurd come Monday when everyone comes clamoring into the store to get their chain saws signed by the national carving champion."

"You think so, huh?" He glanced down at Emaline, tenderness radiating in his eyes. "Looks like someone's down for the count. She hot? Her cheeks look flushed."

"Probably just from all her fussing. I don't think she's thrilled that I'm making her wear noise-canceling headphones."

"Need to bring her back to the room?"

Harper bit her lip. She didn't want to miss the final segment of the competition. That's when CJ would most need her support, but she also worried Emaline could be becoming overstimulated. Most days, her world was rather quiet.

She shifted to extend her left leg, which was starting to cramp. "If she's still acting uncomfortable after her nap, I'll ask my mom to take her."

"You hungry?" He glanced at his phone then at the rows of booths stretching in either direction. "How about if I go grab us something to eat and a couple of iced lemonades?"

"I'm sorry. I meant to do that. I knew you wouldn't have much time for lunch, but then she fell asleep, and—"

"Hey, it's no big deal. I could use the movement, believe me."

"I can imagine." She reached for the diaper bag in the bottom of the nearby stroller. "Let me give—"

"Nope."

"At least let me—"

He'd jogged off before she could finish, and returned balancing a tray with three walking tacos, two drinks, chili fries and a large funnel cake.

She stared at it as he eased to the ground, nearly spilling it all. "Hungry much?"

He laughed. "Always." He poked a straw into one of the drink tops and handed it over. "Hope you don't mind, but I got us watermelon slushies. Just couldn't brave the line for the frozen lemonades."

"That bad?"

"You have no idea."

They ate in comfortable silence awhile, him gazing toward the contest arena, probably planning out his remaining hours, while she eavesdropped on conversations drifting by. A teenage boy was furious his parents wouldn't buy him a chain saw for his birthday and didn't think it fair that they held some "skateboard fiasco" against him. A group of men, dressed in nearly identical muscle shirts, was cracking "dad jokes." A middle-aged couple was fighting over who contributed most to their credit card debt.

CJ took a long pull on his drink. "You ever think about opening your own dance studio in Sage Creek?"

"A studio, yes. As to Sage Creek, it's crossed my mind. I just don't think there'd be enough business to sustain it." Otherwise, someone else already would've opened one.

"Doesn't every mom sign their little girl up for ballet?"

"That might be overestimating things a bit. But even if that were true, most parents and children lose interest once the kids reach fourth or fifth grade. I feel, to support Emaline and myself, I'd need more business than that."

"So find a way to appeal to the adults."

"What do you mean?"

"I once saw this place, like a bar but without alcohol, that had fifties' dancing. Folks came in, took a lesson, then spent the rest of the night doing their thing."

"Interesting." She took a drink of her slushy and told him about the fitness classes the ladies had talked about when she'd taken Emaline to Little Tykes.

"That something you're interested in?"

"I wouldn't know how to get started."

"Seems for the ballerina-style one, all you need is a wooden floor, a long bar attached to the wall and a floor-to-ceiling mirror. That acrobatics deal might be trickier. You'll want a building with strong support beams in the ceiling. And a business license and permits and whatnot."

She watched a ladybug crawl up a nearby blade of grass. "That sounds complicated."

"I could help with the legal stuff, and probably most of the remodel, too. Got a friend who'd tackle whatever I couldn't for cheap. He'd make sure everything was done right. Safe for your customers."

"That sounds expensive, even if your friend offers a hugely discounted rate. Finding a building, remodeling the place…"

"Maybe you could find a building that wouldn't need much of an overhaul. Like the community theater or something. Pretty sure they've got a wooden stage."

This discussion created mixed emotions. On the one hand, CJ was expanding her thinking. Could she find a workable facility close enough to prove feasible, and at a location people would actually visit? Whereas people in Seattle thought nothing of a thirty-minute drive, Sage Creek folks tended to stay close to Main Street.

The contestants around them started to migrate toward the competition area.

CJ looked around, glanced at his phone, grabbed their lunch garbage and stood. "Guess I best get back to it." He popped a few of his knuckles, a nervous tell. "Got to make the last four hours count."

She struggled to stand with minimal jostling to Emaline, who'd been sleeping much more soundly than expected, considering the noisy environment.

She smiled and, holding her daughter to her chest, cheek against her shoulder, gave CJ's hand a gentle squeeze. "You'll do great."

His gaze intensified as his eyes latched on to hers. "Thanks." Emaline stirred and made a few whimpering sounds. "Hey, there, cutie." He skimmed her cheek with his knuckles. Concern lines etched across his forehead. "She seems warm."

Harper frowned and pressed her wrist to Emaline's temple, then glanced at the cloud-streaked sky. "I'd hoped she'd do okay so long as we stayed in the shade."

"Think you should take her back to the hotel?"

Harper scraped her teeth over her bottom lip. "I hate to miss the last, and potentially most important, hours of your event. But she does seem to have a fever. Let me call my mom right quick."

She got Patricia's voice mail. She was probably in the movie theater. She'd mentioned that morning that she wanted to see something.

As much as she longed to support CJ, Harper had to do what was best for her daughter.

"You go." He gathered her things and returned them to the diaper bag, and the bag to the stroller basket. "Judging isn't until tomorrow anyway."

Hopefully, Emaline would feel better by then or her mom would be willing to stay with her in the hotel, at least for the awards ceremony.

She placed Emaline in her stroller then stood, told CJ she'd be cheering for him from the room, then left to get her little one out of the sun. By the time she'd reached the room, the baby had started crying.

"You uncomfortable, sweet girl?" She texted her mom, asking her to buy ibuprofen for infants, then lifted her daughter from her stroller. Holding Emaline, she paced, gently bounced and repeatedly sang the chorus of a lullaby—all that came to mind.

As Emaline drifted off, Harper grabbed the television remote and inched onto the bed with her back against the headboard. She was halfway through a romantic comedy when her mom burst in carrying numerous bags. One was from a local drugstore. It looked like the others were filled with items purchased from event vendors.

Her mom rummaged around in one, pulled out a small box of medicine, dropped the rest of her items onto the ground and strode to the bed. "Poor little munchkin. Think she caught a virus?"

"A cold maybe. Thankfully, she doesn't seem to be having any breathing trouble or a tummyache."

"Could have an ear infection. You used to get

those all the time." She dropped into the hotel chair. "How's CJ doing?"

"Great. His sculpture is really starting to take shape."

"Any hints as to what it's of?"

"He's still really tight-lipped about it, but it looks like someone kneeling, with their hands outstretched, holding something."

"Interesting."

She nodded. "I know he's worried about having enough time for all the detailed work he wants to do."

"I'm excited to see it once he's done."

"Me, too."

She smiled at the image of him bent over his project, brow furrowed like it always did when he focused on something, jaw muscle clenching and relaxing as he worked. Biceps flexing every time he lifted the chain saw.

Her mom laughed. "Seems someone's finally waking up to her second chance."

Harper's cheeks heated. "What're you talking about?"

"You love him, and you know it."

She shifted, her gaze following the paisley pattern of the comforter. "I told you, I'm not staying."

Patricia closed her eyes and pinched the bridge

of her nose. "You cannot tell me you're going to mess things up. Again. Seems you would've gotten better sense after the first time." She shook her head. "If you think you're going to find a better man in Seattle, or whatever city you go chasing off to, I'm telling you now, you're fooling yourself."

"Maybe I will and maybe I won't. Regardless, at least I'll know I gave my dreams my best shot."

"Even if it means losing CJ?"

She scoffed. "If I stay, and abandon the one thing I was created to do, I'll lose him anyway. Just like what happened with you and Dad."

"What do you mean?"

"You left college for him and ended up resenting him for it." They'd practically destroyed one another. Hearing them fighting, calling each other names and throwing stuff had given her a perpetual bellyache as a kid.

"Your father and I had a lot bigger issues than whether or not I completed my degree. And he wasn't the reason I didn't. The excuse maybe." Her mom stood, got herself a cup of water, then sat back down. "I was flunking anyway—for the second semester in a row. I had a ton of student debt, and didn't see the sense in racking on classes I'd never pass. I just wasn't the school type, you know?"

Harper stared at her, assumptions she'd held for years crashing against this new information and tumbling into a swirl of confusion.

Her mom gulped down her water then tossed the paper cup in a nearby trash. "When your dad told me about his 'high-paying' truck-driving position, it seemed like my way out. Probably the stupidest decision I could've made. We'd only been dating a few months. But we were young, I was desperate, and he was cute." She laughed. "Of course, our time together wasn't a total waste. He gave me you, didn't he?"

Harper grabbed the remote. "Want to watch a movie?"

"In other words, change of subject?"

She gave a slight laugh.

"All right. I hear you. But let me say one more thing. If a dream costs you those you love, it's too expensive."

Her shoulders tensed. "God wouldn't have given me this passion if He didn't want me to use it."

"We both know I'm not much into religion. Still, seems to me Jesus is big enough to give you both—this dream you're chasing and the man who obviously adores you. *And* your daughter. But God might not do things the way you think. Don't go closing doors just because they're opening in places you don't expect."

CJ SPENT THE rest of the afternoon completely absorbed in his project—until the contest facilitator gave the one-hour warning. After that, it felt like a fight not to waste time looking at everyone else's carvings. Every glance, however quick, would cost him more than time. It'd make it even harder for him to get back into "the zone," as Harper called it.

The fact that his muscles were beyond tired wasn't helping. He'd intentionally worked on his endurance while preparing for this event. But clearly not enough.

This type of thinking wasn't helping.

Refocusing on his project, he imagined the larger hands were his father's, those he was supporting were CJ's as a child, and the sapling in the soil was the ash tree they'd planted together after he'd first rode his bicycle without training wheels and fallen. Some might find a wipeout a strange occurrence to commemorate, but through that, CJ had learned a crucial lesson. Failure wasn't something to fear but rather to

be viewed as a courageous step toward tomorrow's success.

Assuming you got back on the bike, of course.

The man next to him let out an angry yell
and CJ turned to see one of the carved antlers
had broken off and was lying on the ground.
Poor guy must have leaned on it or something.
Although he could glue it back on, it might be
heavy enough that he'd need to drill in a dowel
for extra support.

Releasing a breath, CJ grabbed his rotary tool,
fine grinding bit inserted, and started working
on the last details on his hands. He'd managed
to finish all the fingernails except the right pinkie when the final horn blew.

"Tools down and step away." The man's
booming voice was about as intimidating as his
tall, thick frame and sharp scowl.

Some people in the crowd cheered. Others
hooped and hollered, and someone bellowed,
"Moose!"

CJ chuckled. Considering the only large animal he saw resembled an ibex, the guy must've
been rooting for one of the carvers. He shucked
off his protective gear and jiggled his T-shirt in
an attempt to shake off the thick coating of sawdust. A hot shower would feel amazing.

The officiator turned toward the audience. "We invite you all to vote for your favorite carvings, using the QR codes posted at each. You may do so up until 9:00 a.m. tomorrow. The results will account for 25 percent of each contestant's score, which will then be factored in with the judges'. We will announce the winner tomorrow at 11:00 a.m."

Reading that in the contestant notes felt a lot less nerve-racking than hearing it relayed now, knowing he had a good eighteen hours to wait.

CJ scrubbed a hand over his face and shot Harper a text.

She responded immediately, as if she'd been waiting to hear from him. Send me a picture!

Her enthusiasm made him smile. I'd rather show you in person.

When she sent a sad face, he dialed her number.

"Hey." She sounded even more tired than he felt and, based on the way Emaline was wailing on the other end, he could understand why.

"Rough night?"

"How'd you guess? I really want to come down there, but I don't feel right about leaving."

"No, of course. Tomorrow. Will y'all be able to sleep tonight?"

"I feel like I should be asking you that same thing. You anxious?"

"Not enough to override my sheer exhaustion."

She laughed. "Get some rest."

"See you tomorrow."

This conversation reminded him of all the late-night phone calls they'd shared back in high school. Reluctantly saying good-night, knowing they'd reconnect the next day.

Lord, tell me I'm not foolish for feeling that way now. That things will end differently this time.

That they wouldn't end at all.

CJ still had the engagement ring he'd intended to give her. Over the years, he'd told himself he was simply making the wise financial choice by keeping it. After all, he'd worked and saved long and hard to buy that thing. The truth was, he'd not had the heart to part with it.

He'd been unable to acknowledge that before, for fear he was denying reality.

Now he was glad his heart hadn't given up hope.

CHAPTER THIRTEEN

SUNDAY MORNING, THEY arrived at the conference arena to find half of Texas, it felt like, milling about. People were talking about the various designs and accessing the QR codes with their phones.

CJ ran a hand over Emaline's head. "Peanut seems to be doing better. She sleep okay?"

"Once I got her down, yeah."

"And you?"

"Like a rock."

"Me, too."

Harper was surprised. She'd expected him to be wired with anticipation for today's results.

He acted casual and confident, but the way he kept adjusting his cowboy hat and jingling coins in his pocket revealed his anxiety level.

Halted behind a handful of slow-moving voters, she gave his hand a squeeze. Her heart skipped when his gaze, radiating obvious adoration, locked onto hers.

He was so incredibly handsome when his tenderness showed through. Good-looking anytime, but when his more sensitive side emerged especially.

She cleared her throat and shifted Emaline to her other hip.

"What do you think of all this, cutie?" CJ gave the baby's foot a gentle tug. "Would you cast your vote for mine?"

They inched forward, past a carving of various stages of the moon, each raised on a dolly, then one of a tombstone.

Harper regarded it with a raised eyebrow. "So cheery."

"And maybe a bit of inspiration to encourage folks to get to living. Pastor Roger always asks us what we plan to do with the dash between our birth and death dates. Not sure what all the Good Lord will have me do between now and then, but I do plan to excel in one area."

"Which is?"

"Learning to love well." The increased intensity in his eyes suggested he was talking about her.

Not sure what to say, she turned toward an

old-fashioned church steeple with exposed brick peeking through peeling paint. Built, refurbished, and other dates were carved into the siding. "Other than various bouts of remodeling, what do you think this person was trying to convey?"

CJ angled his head. "Maybe all the special moments lived by individuals and families, going back for generations? Weddings, baptisms, first communions and end-of-life celebrations."

An image of Trinity Faith came to mind and the many faces she'd seen within its walls over the years. She'd formed numerous memories in the building, despite her limited time there growing up.

Although, that was changing. She'd made God a promise—if He gave her the hardware job, which He had, then she'd make her faith a bigger priority. She was doing her best to honor that, and had found that she actually enjoyed her Sunday mornings and had even started listening to a daily Bible podcast.

CJ stopped in front of a goatlike animal with large curved horns. "Although I still haven't figured out how this piece represents the passing of time, you've got to admit, the guy's got talent."

Feeling like acknowledgment would almost

be a betrayal, Harper gave a slight nod. "It's interesting to compare everyone's ideas, for sure. But I'm most anxious to see what you chose to make." And through it, to catch a deeper glimpse of the man she was growing to love—again.

Maybe she'd never stopped.

The family of four in front of them veered left, allowing her to see CJ's final project.

"Here it is." He motioned to a carving of a man kneeling, cupped hands extended before him, cradling another pair of hands that held a sapling sprouting from a mound of dirt.

Harper's throat burned. The paternal image pricked the longing she held for Emaline to grow up with a loving father. A man like CJ, who clearly understood the impact of an attentive dad.

She stepped closer. "It's beautiful."

He grinned. "Yeah?"

She nodded. "Tell me about it."

He relayed a story about when he'd first been learning to ride a bike. "I was trying to act brave but, truth is, I would've been content to keep my training wheels on—indefinitely. Only, I wanted to make my dad proud. So, I hopped on and took off like a bullet, pedaling as fast as my five-year-old legs could go. Ended up eating concrete."

"Ouch."

He nodded. "Skinned my knees and hands pretty good. Might've cried a bit. Although I tried my best to fight it. I worried my dad would be disappointed in me. Was mighty confused when he ran up to me, clapping and praising me like I'd just finished the Tour de France."

She frowned. "No offense, but that sounds mean. Like he was celebrating your fall."

"No, but he was celebrating every pedal that led to it. But yeah, maybe my crash and burn, too, so that I wouldn't be devastated when my efforts didn't turn out as I'd hoped."

"He didn't want life's setbacks to paralyze you."

"Right. Which is why we planted that tree in our yard. As a daily reminder of a lesson he reiterated often when I was growing up."

"Your dad's a wise man."

He nodded. "A great role model." He looked at Emaline once again and tickled her under her chin. "Think you and I can plant something one day to celebrate your first wipeout, peanut?"

Harper's heart squeezed. CJ had just inserted himself into Emaline's future. It scared her to realize how much that meant to her. How much she wanted that for her daughter.

Was that what she wanted for herself? Now that it appeared that her choreographer's job wouldn't happen, she was rethinking a lot of things.

But how much of her feelings for CJ were entangled with her desire to give Emaline a father?

She didn't want a plan B romance.

As to the promises Emaline's paternal grandmother had made, she'd been half tempted to text her a snarky "Like mother, like son." Instead, she'd asked about the job, not expecting a response but wanting to demonstrate she wouldn't be easily brushed aside.

Why was she even fretting over that woman or anything she'd said? If she'd been a person of integrity, she never would've driven Harper away in the first place.

Maybe it was time Harper pursued child support. Or rather, past time. She wasn't thrilled with the idea of going to court, but it was something she needed to learn more about.

CJ's stomach rumbled loud enough for her to hear it above the conversations occurring around them.

She laughed. "Hungry?"

"Starved. Ate a bunch of snacks last night for dinner and skipped breakfast this morning." He looked at his phone screen. "Want to grab a bite?"

"Let me call my mom, but yeah." She pulled out her cell and clicked on her mom's contact.

"Hello?"

"Hey." She relayed CJ's question. "Want to join us?" Seemed right to ask, considering this was supposed to be a girls' weekend. While they'd spent a lot of time together in the hotel, they hadn't done much else.

"And be the third wheel?" Her mom scoffed. "No, thank you."

"It wouldn't be like that."

"Don't worry. I'm not offended. I'm thrilled. Like I told you before, it's about time y'all quit mousing about and admit you're in love."

"I'm not—" She clamped her mouth shut, her cheeks heating as her gaze shot to CJ. "If you're sure you don't want to come."

She ended the call, returned her phone to the diaper bag's side pocket, then turned to CJ. "Mind if we swing by the hotel for Emaline's stroller?" She'd left it in her room so she wouldn't have to push it through the crowd.

"No problem."

Hand to the small of her back, he led her through the steady stream of people on the sidewalk.

THEY CHOSE A breakfast place that required a quick drive in his truck to get there. Harper had brought a portable cloth high-chair contraption she secured to a chair. She ordered an egg-white veggie omelet with a cup of fruit. He chose pancakes and bacon with two extra strips, then drenched his food in syrup.

She poured a cream packet into her coffee. "Still haven't lost your football player appetite, I see."

He laughed. "Guess fourteen hours of carving built up an appetite." He couldn't remember the last time his biceps and shoulder muscles had been this sore.

"I imagine. I used to be starving after dance rehearsals."

"Did you all have to watch what you ate?"

She regarded his plate with a raised eyebrow. "I didn't turn my breakfast into a sugary soup, if that's what you mean."

He chuckled. "Hey, now." He took a swig of water. "When you were with that touring company, did you have long days?" He felt torn between wanting to prolong this meal as long as possible and getting back to the competition site. Not that there was much point in that. He wouldn't know anything for a couple more hours.

"Sometimes, yeah. But you also learn to rest on your off days. Otherwise, an injury can take you out for an entire season."

She talked about a typical day from warm-ups, rehearsals and ongoing technical classes, along with some of the places she'd visited. "Once, we did a series of performances in Southern California. Most were back-to-back. But we did get a couple days off to visit the beach. By then, I was so exhausted, I pretty much slept."

Forking a chunk of pancake, he studied her. What he was about to ask could end their pleasant conversation right quick, but he needed to know. "Emaline's dad. He still in the picture?"

Harper stared into her coffee mug, slowly stirring with her spoon. "He's not interested." Her voice was soft, and he wondered what kind of wounds she'd experienced.

"You love him?"

She seemed to flinch. "What? No." Her expression hardened. "He was a jerk who preyed on all the new dancers and got away with it because his mom had pull in the dance world. Or at least made everyone believe she did."

"I'm sorry. That must be hard."

"Sometimes. It'd be nice to have a life partner to talk things through with."

He wanted to tell her he could be that, but not here. Not now. Once they got back to Sage Creek and he had the ring to propose to her proper, then he'd tell her everything—his feelings and his hopes. For all three of them.

After breakfast, they still had time to kill so they decided to meander through San Angelo's historic downtown area. They started at a women's boutique Harper deemed "adorable" with its handwritten chalkboard signs and shelves and displays made from dressers. Ambling down the brick sidewalk, they eventually reached the general store Harper's mom had told her so much about. After purchasing some trip mementos, they headed back.

Harper's mom was waiting for them when they returned to the contest arena.

"There's Nana's sweet muffin." She kissed Emaline's forehead then straightened. "Where y'all been? I was starting to get worried."

Harper relayed their morning.

"Sounds lovely." She turned to CJ and handed him a gift bag she'd been holding. "Here."

He wrinkled his brow. "What's this for?"

"To celebrate your win, goof."

"But they haven't announced that yet. I'm not even confident I'll place."

"Don't underestimate yourself, sugar. You've got as much of a shot as any of the others."

"I appreciate that, ma'am." Not the most encouraging praise he'd heard, but he appreciated the effort. "Talent aside, I've been rethinking their scoring. Seems locals might have a bit of an advantage."

Mrs. Moore angled her head with a frown and glanced around. "Oh. You mean they might've monkeyed with the results by calling in all their buddies and favors?"

He shrugged. "Can't say I'd blame them. If this contest were anywhere near Sage Creek, I'd probably be asking about everyone I knew to come cast votes for me."

"Good point. Harper told me about your and your friend's plans for that building. What're you going to do if you lose?"

"Mom!" Harper's face flushed.

CJ laughed. "It's okay. That's a fair question. I expect the owner will have sold it by the time

I save up my portion. Although, I'd rather see my friend find someone else to go in on it with." Hopefully, he'd still have time to do so, if need be.

"And then?" Mrs. Moore pulled a granola bar from her purse and tore open the package. "You going to go back to working for your parents?"

His gaze shot to Harper, the statement she'd told her friend back in high school, about him lacking ambition, stinging afresh. She'd seemed so proud of him for entering this contest and for carving in general, as if both had changed her previous opinion of him. Would his returning to Nuts and Bolts undo that?

Rubbing the back of his neck, he shifted his weight. "I'll keep plugging away and start looking for another place. Regardless, I *will* open my own business. Even if I have to eat beans and rice for the next couple years to save the cash to make it happen."

"I admire your drive." Harper's eyes radiated warmth.

He couldn't contain his grin. "Thank you."

"Anyway, hope you like the gift I got you." Patricia motioned to the bag. "I was in one of those souvenir stores yesterday. Figured I might as well get you something, just in case." She pulled Emaline from her stroller and, bouncing and swaying, told them about some gag items she'd found when a horn blew, indicating it was time for CJ and the others to stand by their carvings to await the final scores.

His stomach dipped. "Guess this is it."

Harper reached for his hand, gave a squeeze, and, for a moment, their eyes locked.

It felt like the next fifteen minutes dragged on as the officiator explained the scoring categories, specific things the judges were looking for and the cash awards given for the top three placers. Then the man read information each contestant had entered regarding how their carving conveyed the passing of time. CJ had overheard some people complaining about not knowing this prior to casting their votes. He sort of agreed, but he also understood the reasoning. For one, he and the others had only learned of the challenge Friday. Plus, the judges were also probably gauging how clearly the carvers conveyed their ideas to the public.

The man paused and made a visual sweep of the audience. "Y'all ready for the final results?"

Everyone cheered. A few people whistled and, once again, a deep voice somewhere to the right started chanting, "Moose! Moose! Moose!"

The officiator motioned for everyone to quiet down. "In third place, with a score of eight-point-five out of ten, is *The Good Old Days* by Ron Bangle."

The tall, lanky man two projects over gave a whoop and strode forward, bent arms raised, hands fisted.

CJ eyed the wagon holding a ball, floppy baseball mitt and stuffed bear the man had created. He didn't know whether to feel encouraged or discouraged. On the one hand, there were still two open slots. But that also meant he'd need an eight-point-six at a minimum to place. That left little room for error. Not to mention, that man's use of nostalgia had probably grabbed a good number of the older generation's votes.

Jiggling the coins in his pocket, he released a tense breath. He looked at Harper, her big smile and thumbs-up sign motivating him to stand a bit taller.

If he was going to lose this thing, he'd at least look confident doing so.

"In second place..." The man's booming voice made CJ jump. Shifting from one foot to the next, he cracked his neck, first one way then the next.

"With a score of eight-point-nine out of ten, we have *A Man's Legacy* by Christopher James Jenkins."

He blinked, not sure he'd heard right.

"CJ, that's you, boy!" Patricia's voice rose, almost shrill, above the cheering crowd.

He looked her way to see her waving her free arm like she was trying to flag down a plane or something. Beside her, Harper was jumping up and down, hands to her chest.

He froze, vision locked on her.

Man, did he love her. Seeing her response, and her expression of joy, made him believe that she loved him as well.

"Dude."

He turned toward the gravelly voice to his left.

"You gonna go up, or what?"

CJ gave a nervous chuckle, his face hot and his heart so full, it felt ready to burst from his chest. "Oh, right."

Tipping his cowboy hat at the audience, he sauntered to the center of the arena for his trophy and accompanying check. Neither of which meant nearly as much as knowing he'd won Harper's heart.

Again.

This time, he intended to keep it.

He didn't hear much after that, or see much else, except Harper's smiling, sun-kissed face standing amid the crowd.

Once the event ended, he lingered in the arena, chatting with one of the other contestants to give the crowd time to thin out so he wouldn't be thronged by the more energetic and talkative spectators. He'd probably need to learn to deal with these types of situations if he wanted to become a successful carver. But all the attention was more than a little overwhelming.

His newfound friend adjusted his ball cap. "Best get home to the missus." The two shook hands. "If you're ever in the Branson area, make sure to give me a holler."

CJ nodded, knowing the guy was simply being friendly, and followed a few steps behind him.

The moment he stepped from the arena, Harper tackled him in a hug. "I knew you could do it!" She bounced with enough enthusiasm to jiggle his insides.

Relishing the feel of her soft frame pressed against him and the faint pineapple scent of her shampoo, he wrapped his arms around her, reluctant to let go.

"You realize he didn't win, right?"

He laughed at her mom's incredulous tone.

Harper gasped and pulled away.

Patricia looked at her. "What? Was that rude?"

Grinning, he twined his fingers in Harper's. "No offense taken, ma'am. And, yes, I do realize that."

Her mother smiled. "Oh, good. Well, then, how do you intend to celebrate?"

"By asking my friend Oliver to meet me at the Realtor's office so we can make an official offer."

"Yes!" Harper's eyes gleamed. "Can I see it? I mean…is that allowed? I know it's not yours yet."

He smiled. "I'd like that."

CHAPTER FOURTEEN

CJ CALLED OLIVER on his way to settle up with the event consignment store. His friend said he wasn't surprised he'd placed, but his immediate "Yes!" suggested he'd been worried. That was understandable considering the deadline his landlord had given them to make him an offer on the building. Although the man had held off for Oliver's sake, the listing would go live in a few days.

"Nothing like cutting it close to the wire, huh?" CJ parked next to a yellow pickup with plastic taped across a busted window and got out. "I should be leaving here within the hour, which would put me back in Sage Creek by three thirty." Pocketing his keys, he strolled into the busy store.

He recognized a handful of customers from those he'd seen in the audience during the event and assumed that's where most of the others had come from as well. Although, it was fun to think that maybe the local television and radio stations had drawn people out.

"Mr. Jenkins." A woman wearing a brown-and-teal plaid dress that hit a foot above red cowgirl boots greeted him with a smile. "Congrats on receiving second place." Her name tag read Delilah.

He tipped his hat at her. "Thank you, ma'am." The recognition felt odd, but hopefully it had translated to increased sales. Had the spectators purchased much yet?

He glanced through the crowd, pleased to see that some of his items had sold. He was tempted to call Oliver back and suggest they meet later, or even the next day. But he wouldn't do that, not with how excited his friend had been.

Besides, he'd waited long enough.

"Please visit the back checkout counter to receive payment for whatever items you sold." Delilah motioned to a long, rustic counter set against the far wall.

"Appreciate it." He filed in line behind two other competitors. From the sounds of it, the first guy, a fella who hadn't placed, would be leaving with all his pieces and wasn't thrilled. Next up, the man who'd carved the church with exposed brick was walking away with a couple thousand.

When CJ stepped up to the counter, the man behind it flashed him a smile. "Mr. Jenkins. Impressive work today."

"Thank you."

"You were a hit here as well. Sold just shy of half your pieces." He flipped through a stack of papers to his right and pulled out CJ's consignment form. "As you may know, we have a relationship with a local art gallery."

CJ stood a tad taller. "I read something about that on y'all's website."

"Then you may remember that, each year, their dealer selects a handful of carvings to sell in their showroom." He handed CJ a sheet of paper.

He read the terms. "Seventy-thirty split. Not bad. They want them all?"

"Yep."

CJ fought to contain his enthusiastic smile behind a casual smile. "That makes things easy." He took the check for the sold items, thanked the guy and sauntered out, his feet feeling light despite his fatigue from the stressful and physically exhausting weekend.

With nothing besides his tools and gear to

load into his trailer, he made it to Sage Creek earlier than anticipated. Waiting in the Realtor's parking lot, he turned off his radio and looked at the clear blue sky. *Lord, I feel like You have flooded my life with blessings. The contest, the gallery, this business and Harper.*

His throat turned scratchy at the memory of her practically knocking him over with her enthusiastic hug, of how right she'd felt in his arms and the look in her eyes that suggested she felt the same.

God had returned to him the woman he loved. And that was a better gift than all the others CJ had received combined.

Now to make sure he didn't mess things up.

And if another dancing opportunity arose?

He'd simply figure out a way to hold tight to her. He refused to believe God would bring them back together just to take her away from him.

Three quick beeps on a horn alerted CJ to Oliver's arrival. Grinning, his friend pulled in beside him. They jumped out of their vehicles simultaneously and fell into step with one another as they proceeded up the flower-lined walk.

"Dude. Second place, cash money, and on

television, all in the same weekend. What's next, a national tour and book deal?"

CJ laughed. "As long as they'd take a three-page pamphlet, sure."

"Want to grab a burger after this? To celebrate?"

"Rain check? I'm meeting Harper at the building to give her a look-see."

Oliver paused with his hand on the open door. "Really? You two a thing again?" His tone carried a note of concern.

"I wouldn't say that." But they seemed to be heading that direction. He wanted to think she was feeling the same way.

"Hello." Gabrielle came from around the corner. "Come on back."

She led them to a small conference room with powder blue walls decorated with photographs bearing various inspirational quotes. Twenty minutes later, she was walking them out with a promise to call as soon as Oliver's landlord responded to their offer.

"I'm not worried." Oliver initiated a handshake.

CJ did the same, then followed him out and to their vehicles. "Hey, thanks for waiting for me on this."

"Never would've found anyone else foolish enough to share buildings with me."

They both knew that wasn't true.

CJ called Harper as he was leaving.

"That's so exciting." He could picture her radiant smile on the other end. "Text me the address and I'll meet you there. Mind if I bring Emaline?"

"I'd be bummed if you didn't."

She paused. "You're amazing, you know that?"

Warmth swept through him. "Just a mite smitten with that peanut." And her mother.

A shrill chirping sounded from her side. "Ugh! The cookies! I've got to go."

Smiling, he shook his head. Same old Harper. One thing was certain, he wouldn't be marrying her for her kitchen skills.

He *did* plan to marry her. He'd considered proposing to her while they were in San Angelo but worried he'd be too stressed with the contest to think straight, let alone say the words to sweep her off her feet.

Tonight was better, anyway. The perfect end to an amazing weekend, and a relationship he intended to continue investing in until his last breath.

After a quick stop at his house to pick up the engagement ring, he hurried to the building he and Oliver would soon own. The exterior wasn't much to look at now. More of a barnlike structure with an old-fashioned, covered wooden-plank walkway. But they'd get it spruced up soon enough.

When Harper pulled in, he stepped out of his truck and met her at her car. "Hey."

"Hey." She smiled, and his gaze fell to her soft, pink lips.

Lips he planned to kiss soon, assuming she said yes.

She had to. He wasn't sure his heart would recover otherwise.

He moved to the back passenger door. "Mind if I get the munchkin?"

"Not at all. I find it adorable how much you seem to enjoy her."

"Well, she does laugh at all my jokes."

"What jokes?"

"You just proved my point. Sheesh." He rolled his eyes with a grin. "Some people have no sense of humor." He gently tossed Emaline in the air then brought her to his face and nibbled her neck. Her happy squeals made him chuckle. "Come on, peanut. Let's see what I got myself into."

Ascending the sagging step he planned to fix first thing, he motioned with his head for Harper to follow.

The interior was dark and musty and smelled like his grandmother's attic. He flicked on a switch, and a series of light bulbs dangling from beams in the ceiling came on.

"This area belongs to Oliver." He indicated the space spanning the right half of the building and filled with everything from vintage jewelry to antique tools and toys. "This here will be mine." He led the way into the large, open area previously used as a secondhand clothing store.

Unfortunately, the previous tenants had left him a bit of a mess, but nothing he couldn't clean out in a couple of days.

She touched the deeply grooved wooden wall, which matched the floor. "This will be perfect for you!"

"I think it'll fix up nice."

"You have an idea of what you want to do?" Her phone rang. She glanced at the screen, studied it for a moment. "Seattle area code." Her expression tightened. "Maybe I should take this. Sorry."

"Go ahead. Emaline and I will just be planning our renovation strategy, isn't that right, peanut?"

She laughed and, rotating slightly, took a side-step. "Hello, Harper Moore here."

Her eyebrows shot up. "Yes, sir? How can I help you?" The lilt in her voice matched the smile gradually taking form on her face. "I completely understand." Her gaze shot to CJ and lingered, worry lines stretching across her forehead.

Was something wrong? His posture stiffened, his ears perked to her conversation.

"Absolutely. May I check my calendar and get back to you?" She paused and her expression brightened. "Wonderful. Thank you, Mr. Garcia."

She ended the call and turned to face him, her eyes searching his.

Her rapid change in demeanor left his gut unsettled. "Is everything all right?"

She rubbed at her hairline and nodded. "That was the managing director of a theater in Portland, Oregon."

"Okay." This couldn't be good. He wanted to end this conversation before she said more, but he knew that wouldn't change whatever would come next.

He wanted to trust that nothing she'd heard in that call would affect their relationship but, unfortunately, their history said otherwise.

Harper seemed to have difficulty maintaining eye contact as she told him about a promise made, and apparently kept, by Emaline's paternal grandmother.

"Is that what you want? To be a choreographer?" He struggled to get the words out.

"I don't know. But this opportunity…" She released a breath. "I need time to process."

"Fine." Throat tight, he kissed Emaline's temple and handed her over. "Let me know when you've got that figured out." Jaw clenched, he strode toward the door then stopped and turned back around. "I'll lock up behind you."

"CJ, please."

The pain in her eyes stabbed at his heart, but not enough to override the gaping wound reopened within him. He should've known this would happen. He had known, but had convinced himself, beyond common sense, that this time would be different.

That their reconnecting had been orchestrated by God.

She pressed her fingers against her collarbone. "Are you saying you want me to leave?"

"I think that would be best."

HARPER NEEDED TIME to think. Not wanting to sit in an empty house while Emaline napped, she chose to drive out into the country.

With Emaline happily cooing in the back seat, likely moments from falling asleep, Harper allowed her mind to drift as she focused on the scenery around her.

The vibrant roadside flowers and quiet pastures dotted with longhorns, centered by barns, many of them older than her, her mother and her baby combined, soothed her. Bordering the long, winding highway, the landscape emitted a calm, relaxed air that gave her space to untangle everything swirling through her brain and heart.

She loved CJ. She did. Even more than she had when they'd been teenagers. But could she pass up this opportunity that, if handled well, could lead to many more, for a life in Sage Creek, Texas? Or would she always wonder what might've happened, had she followed her dreams?

Yet, if she left the man she loved, who loved her and clearly loved Emaline as well, would she regret it?

She'd never find another CJ. She knew that.

Neither would she find a choreography position like the one Mr. Garcia was trying to fill.

A position that wasn't yet hers. She still had to interview, like everyone else, although he was willing to fly her out next week to do so. That sounded promising.

If only he'd called her a week, or even three days, ago, before San Angelo, the weekend during which CJ had captured the last reserved places in her heart.

Was the timing of his phone call, so quickly after she'd decided to search for a space to open her own dance studio, a sign that God was directing her differently? Or was the fact that the man had reached out *after* she'd finally opened her heart, fully, to remaining in Sage Creek a sign that she should stay?

Tears pricking her eyes, she gazed toward the purple hills stretching across the horizon.

Lord, I don't know what to do. I'm not so great at this listening for Your voice thing yet, or even knowing what that might sound like.

She thought back to what her mom had said about Jesus being big enough to give her both of her dreams—the man she loved and a fabulous dad for Emaline, and a life spent working in her dream career.

Her daughter's deep, rhythmic breathing behind her indicated she'd finally given up her fight to keep her eyes open. After all the excitement she'd experienced over the past cou-

ple of days, she'd probably be out for a good
two hours.

That should give God plenty of time to speak.

Her gas tank, however, wouldn't allow for
that long of a drive.

She pulled onto a long dirt road bordered by
wind-stirred fields and cut the engine.

Closing her eyes, Harper leaned against the
headrest, trying to tune in to the "still small
voice," as Trisha often called it. But all she could
hear were her own thoughts pinging rapidly
through her brain.

At least, she was relatively certain most if not
all of them came from her.

With a huff, she called Trisha.

"Harper. What's up?"

She gave a shortened version of what had happened.

"Oh, wow. Okay." Trisha paused. "Can you
choreograph and teach dance from Sage Creek?"

"You mean open my own studio? I don't
know. I've been thinking about it, only that
takes a lot of money."

"What if you rented space from someone else?"

Harper relayed her concerns regarding sufficient business. "Although, I could maybe supplement through some sort of fitness class." She

told her about her conversation with the ladies from the Little Tykes class.

"Oh! Yes! Little Tykes would be a great space, and that would probably help Julia out a lot."

"What do you mean?"

"I guess she's been struggling some. So much so that she's worried she'll have to shut down."

"That's sad." Harper knew what it was like to feel as if life trampled on your dreams.

"It is, but also potentially good for you in that she might be open to some sort of partnership. You should give her a call—before you make any big, potentially relationship-shattering decisions."

"Okay. That settled, now to the important question. Are you looking for an ice cream buddy tonight?"

She laughed. "Tempting." Was Trisha's mention of Julia God's leading? Or simply a potential idea offered by a friend? "Actually, I was wondering...how do you figure out what God wants you to do?"

"Well, a lot of ways, and I think He probably speaks to us all differently, but first, I pray."

"I did that."

"Yeah?" She sounded impressed. "Good for you."

"Now what?"

"I suggest you take some time to quiet your-self in His presence."

"What does that mean?"

"Ask Him to cleanse your heart of everything that isn't from Him, then take some time to sim-ply praise Him for who He is."

"Like we do at church?"

"Exactly. Then close your eyes and wait."

"For how long?"

It was Trisha's turn to laugh. "That, my friend, is the thousand-dollar question, to which I would say, it depends. He might answer you right then or He might not give you clarity for a week, maybe longer."

"That's a problem."

"Why?"

"Besides the fact that CJ hates me—"

"That man could never hate you."

"Well, he's not exactly happy with me at the moment." Although, she knew her friend was right. He wasn't angry so much as he was hurt. Again. She'd broken his heart again. "And we have to work together."

"You survived before."

Only, this time would feel harder because Harper couldn't convince herself that they'd both moved on. "I also need to call that theater company back. They've already conducted their initial phone interviews and are starting in-person ones next week. Guess they hope to make a decision by month's end."

"Wow. They're not giving you much notice, are they?"

"Apparently, the man told his intern to contact me a month ago. He's not sure what happened but said when he never heard back, that he assumed I wasn't interested. Until he got a call from Chaz's mom."

"I see. Okay. Here's a truth I always find helpful when I want God to answer my prayer like yesterday. I remind myself that He wants me to know His will even more than I do, and He's always right on time. Never late, although He's rarely early, either."

"That's encouraging."

"Actually, it sort of is, once you understand why."

"Which is?"

"Because He wants you to trust Him, so that the next time you find yourself in a situation you're not sure how to handle, you won't freak out so much. This problem you're facing, and every problem you'll face every day after—they're nothing to Him. He's the all-powerful creator of the universe, after all. He holds all your—and Emaline's—tomorrows in His hands."

"Thanks, Trish. That really helps."

"My pleasure. Although you should realize my advice doesn't come free. I bill in ice cream. Chocolate chip, one container, two spoons, and a night of chick flicks with my bestie."

"That, I will gladly pay."

She hung up, did an internet search for Little Tykes's number, then called.

Julia responded to her request to meet with audible skepticism. "Mind if I ask what about?"

Harper released a breath. She would've preferred to hold this conversation in person but assumed that wouldn't occur unless she gave Julia more info. She shared her idea.

"Intriguing." The caution in her tone evaporated. "We certainly have the ceiling for it."

"I remembered your big, strong beams."

"Let me give this some prayer and get back to you."

Harper frowned. "Sure, no problem." What if Julia didn't reply in time?

Trisha had said God was never late or early. Harper would simply have to trust that He would lead her when it was time for her to be led. And that He would make His guidance clear.

Pray, praise, then listen.

With a sigh, she turned on the radio and tapped Search until she found a Christian station. She didn't know the lyrics well enough to sing along, so instead, she turned onto a dirt road and parked beneath the shade of a mature oak.

Leaning against the headrest, she closed her eyes and let the music, which spoke of God's love and faithfulness, fill her mind and soul.

She must've fallen asleep, because she was jolted awake by the ringing of her phone. Sucking in a startled breath, she scanned her surroundings to orient herself. The sun was beginning to set, streaking the sky in gradient hues of pink, purple and red.

Her phone rang again and Emaline started to cry.

"I'm here, sweet pea." Reaching for her cell, she jumped out and slid in beside her daughter's car seat. The way Emaline rubbed her eyes indicated she was just waking up herself.

She answered. "Hello?" Phone sandwiched between her shoulder and ear, she unfastened Emaline and cradled her in her arms.

"Harper, this is Mrs. Jenkins. CJ's had an accident."

"What?" She felt dizzy as an image of CJ and his truck, upside down in some ditch, roof caved in, filled her mind. "What kind of accident?"

"Chain saw. That's all we know. We're headed to the hospital now."

He was alive! *Thank You, Lord Jesus.*

For now. There was no way to know until she arrived just how severe his injuries were. She'd read an article about a guy that had fallen on his blade, slicing it into his neck and shoulder blades, only one-quarter inch from his carotid artery.

She struggled for air.

Stop it. He could easily have cut his hand. She'd seen a guy at the competition who'd been missing two of his fingers, an unpleasant occurrence, no doubt, but certainly not life-threatening.

"I'll meet you there." Ending the call, she returned Emaline to her car seat. The baby immediately began to fuss.

"I know, sweet pea. Just a little longer, I promise." Throwing her car into Reverse, she sped back onto the main country road, tempering her almost uncontrollable desire to speed with the need to drive safe for Emaline's sake.

Please, Lord, let him be okay.

What if he didn't make it? She didn't want their last encounter to be the moment when she should have chosen him but hadn't.

When she arrived at the hospital, CJ's parents, Ken, and about half of Trinity Faith, Trisha included, were already in the waiting room.

Her friend met her with open arms. "I'll take the munchkin."

"Thank you." She rushed to where Nancy was pacing. "Is he okay?"

Mrs. Jenkins looked at her with teary eyes. "The doctor said he cut his femoral artery. He's in surgery now."

"But he got here in time? He's going to be all right?"

Mr. Jenkins came up beside his wife. "He should be. Boy acted quick, made himself a tourniquet using his belt, and called his neighbor." He motioned to an older guy with angular shoulders sitting a few chairs away. "Thank the Good Lord the fella was in and just about to head to town. Said he drove down his potholed dirt road fast enough to knock his teeth out."

Nancy nodded. "If he'd had to call 9-1-1,

the soonest the ambulance would've gotten to him would've been fifteen minutes. That's if they flew."

CJ could've died. If he had, Harper never would've recovered. She knew that now. As for having to choose between him and the open choreography position—there was no question.

She wanted CJ—if he'd still have her.

CHAPTER FIFTEEN

CJ PUSHED UP in the bed, his brain foggy from the pain medication steadily dripping into his IV. His mom was working a crossword puzzle from the chair she'd pulled close, while his dad sat near the window, remote in hand. He'd been flipping through channels for the past ten minutes, evidence of his discomfort remaining stationary.

"You don't have to stay," CJ said.

His dad looked up and shrugged. "Don't got anywhere I need to be just yet."

That couldn't be true considering they'd left Ken to run the store. Then again, Nuts, Bolts and Boards couldn't be that busy given the number of people that had stopped by the hospital to see him today.

None of them Harper.

That hurt more than the wound in his leg. Then again, he hadn't exactly been kind or understanding the day before. Pastor Roger once said that true love always sought the other person's best, even when doing so felt hard and painful.

Based on that definition, if CJ really cared about Harper, he'd want her to chase her dreams. Even if that meant her leaving.

He closed his eyes as a fresh wave of heartache swept over him. *Lord, help me love her like that.* Because he knew there was no way he could do that in his own strength. Not if it meant losing her.

Someone knocked on the open door.

He looked up and struggled to push himself into a more upright position. "Harper."

"Mind if I come in?" Her voice sounded small. Timid.

"Of course."

She greeted his parents with one nod, "Ma'am. Sir," then continued to his bedside, opposite from where his mom sat. She bit her lip, clearly wanting to talk but hesitant to do so.

Had she made her decision? Surely Harper wouldn't tell him now, not with him lying there, attached to machines and tubes.

Then again, he never thought she'd leave him on the night of her graduation, either.

"How are you feeling?" Worry lines stretched across her forehead.

"About like I almost sliced my leg off." He chuckled. "Just kidding. They've got me covered." He lifted his arm with the IV. "How are you?"

"Much better, now that I know you're okay." She blinked quickly, like she used to when she was fighting tears. "I, um…" She glanced first to his mom then his dad, then back to him.

"We were just leaving." His mom stood. "Isn't that right, Johnny?"

He frowned. "Were we going?"

"Come on." She grabbed his arm and pulled him out of the room with a backward wave and a cheery, "We'll be back. Good to see you, Harper."

"Yes, ma'am." She faced CJ again. "I'm really sorry about—"

"What? Getting a phone call? One that you've probably been waiting for since you arrived in Sage Creek?" He shook his head. "I'm the one who needs to apologize." He swallowed past a lump in his throat, not sure he had the strength to say what he knew he needed to. "I don't want to hold you back. I want to be the one person in your life that most encourages you to fly, and if that means moving to Portland, then I'm for that. Because I'm for you."

"That's not what I want." A tear slid down her cheek, and CJ wished he could reach her to wipe it away. To touch her face and run the pad of his thumb across her bottom lip. To feel her mouth on his once again, even if for the last time.

A flicker of hope ignited within him. "What are you saying?"

He was almost afraid to ask, because her answer could shatter him. Or flood his soul with joy he'd worried he might never experience again. Joy he couldn't experience apart from her.

"I don't want that job, or any job, if that means losing you." She grabbed his hand in both of hers. "Oh, CJ, when your mom called, I was so frightened. I worried you might not make it—"

"Death from a leg wound?" The corners of his mouth twitched toward a smile. "It's going to take a lot more than that to wipe me out."

Harper laughed and slapped his arm. "You're horrible. Seriously, CJ, I didn't know how badly you were hurt, and as I drove to the hospital, all I could think about was how empty my life would be without you. And how wonderful it has been to once again have you by my side. Although,

I have to say, that wasn't exactly what I meant when I asked God to make His will clear!"

"What are you talking about?"

"Private joke."

"Between you and the Lord?"

"Something like that. On another, and much more important note, will you forgive me?"

His throat felt tight. "There's nothing to forgive."

Palming away her tears, she gave him a wobbly smile. "Does that mean you'll take me back?"

"Woman, I will hold tight to you for as long as you'll let me, and a thousand years beside." The ring! He still had the engagement ring in his pants.

He glanced around. Where had the hospital put his jeans? They hadn't thrown them away when they'd cut them off him, had they? Yes, he could buy another engagement ring, but it wouldn't be the same. He'd been saving that one—for her. Always for her.

Harper studied him. "What's wrong?"

"Can you hand me my phone?" He motioned to his bedside tray, which the nurse had wheeled out of the way.

"Uh. Sure." She grabbed it and gave it to him. "Did you need me to get you something?"

He shot his mom a text, asking about his clothing. "Nope. I mean, yeah, but...nope." The phone chimed his mom's response. She'd sent him three question marks.

Harper started to speak when his mom burst through the door. "What you needin' your pants for, boy?" She planted a fist on her hip. "If you're thinking about getting up and walking out of here, I'm here to tell you that is not happening. Even if I got to get your dad to strap you to that bed."

Harper looked between them with a perplexed brow. "Pants?"

"Never mind." CJ shot his mom a pointed look.

She crossed her arms. "What?" Then, a look of understanding swept across her face, and she turned to Harper, nudging her toward the door in a similar fashion as she had his father. "I'm sorry, but CJ should probably get some rest. He's had a lot of visitors this morning."

Harper's eyebrows shot up. "Oh. Of course." Fingers rubbing her collarbone, she paused in the doorway to look back at CJ. "I'll call you?"

"Sure."

When she was gone, his mom turned to him with a frown. "What in the blazes was that about?"

"Do you know what happened to my clothes?"

"What clothes?"

"That I was wearing when I came in."

"Those are nothing but scraps, darling. But I can bring you something from your house. When they discharge you."

He told her about the ring.

"And you think this is the time and place to propose?" She swept an arm to indicate the hospital room.

"Seems perfect to me. What better way to celebrate that I'm alive—thank You, Jesus." He cast a glance to the ceiling. "Than grabbing hold of life with both hands?"

"You're afraid she'll change her mind?"

Was he? Maybe a little, but that was just his insecurity talking. "I've been waiting on that woman for going on six years now. Guess I'm tired of waiting. That said, I was hoping you'd help me with the proposal part."

"How so?"

"First, by helping me find the ring. I sure hope they didn't toss it."

"Nope. They gave me and Dad your stuff. It's still in the car. Want me to go get it? And your wallet, too?"

"That'd be great. Mind swinging by Blooming Bouquets for flowers and balloons? Use my credit card."

"Any particular type?"

"Red roses and balloons. Three hundred dollars' worth. Think Arlene would cut us a deal?" The florist and his mom had been friends since middle school.

"If I tell her why I'm buying them, she just might sell everything at cost. The biggest problem might be her not having enough for what you want." She tapped a finger to her chin. "How about I reach out to the Stoughtons?"

"Caden's folks?" They had a bee farm not far out of town. Their property was a kaleidoscope of color.

She nodded. "Bet they'd give us about as many flowers as we can cut."

"That sounds like a lot of work and time."

"Not if I get the Trinity Faith gals to help. I'll shoot Lucy a text." She served on the town's cultural committee. "She'll probably have fifty ladies lined up by the time I reach Arlene's."

"Might want to call the Stoughtons first."

"Duh." She rolled her eyes. But then her expression sobered and tears glistened in her eyes. "I can't believe my son's going to get married."

"She has to say yes first."

She waved a hand. "You know what I mean." She turned to leave, then paused in the doorway. "Keep your phone handy. I'll probably be calling with a bazillion questions."

"I will. Although I'm pretty sure you and Arlene will know the answers before I do."

But there was only one answer he was concerned with, and only Harper could provide that.

HARPER SAT ON her couch, trying to distract herself by playing with a puzzle app, but her thoughts kept replaying her visit with CJ. Why had he acted so strangely? And his mom, too. Had they been talking about her?

She didn't believe what Nancy had said about *CJ being tired*. There had to have been another reason they'd wanted Harper to leave.

Emaline began to fuss from her crib.

Harper stood. "Coming, sweet girl."

She strolled down the hall and into the bedroom.

"Hey, there, sweet girl." Her daughter responded with a toothless smile as Harper slipped her arms under her and picked her up. "You want to snuggle with Mama for a bit?" She kissed her soft forehead, relishing her baby scent.

Diaper changed, she carried her daughter to the rocker purchased at a local garage sale. She loved these post-naptime moments when Emaline was alert and content to simply let Harper hold her.

Rocking, she began to sing the lyrics for a song she vaguely remembered from church, when her phone rang.

Was that CJ?

She stood, carrying Emaline, and hurried to the living room to where she'd left her phone on the coffee table. She didn't recognize the number.

"Hello?"

"Hi, this is Julia from Little Tykes."

"Yes?" A jolt of anticipation shot through her.

"I've been thinking and praying over your offer. I think you've got a great idea and I'm certain we could work together on times."

"You mean…?"

"I'd love to rent you space and, knowing how hard it is to get a new venture off the ground, I won't charge you for the first month."

"Wow. That's so generous, thank you! So, now what?"

"I expect you're going to hire a contractor to set everything up how you want it?"

"Yes, ma'am." CJ could help her with all that.

"Want to meet next week to talk details?"

"I'd love that."

Ending the call, she sank into the couch and bounced Emaline, standing on her thighs. "Grandma was right. Jesus is more than big enough to give me both of my dreams." Tears pricked her eyes. "Thank You, Lord."

She couldn't wait to tell CJ. She clicked to her contacts and hit Call.

"Hey." She could hear the smile in his voice. "I was just thinking about you."

"Yeah? Then why'd you kick me out?"

He chuckled. "I didn't kick you out."

"You kind of did. You going to tell me what all that was about?"

He paused. "Nope."

Why was he being so secretive? "You're making me nervous."

He laughed. "There's nothing to fret about."

"Did you get some rest?"

"I did, thanks. Feeling better by the hour."

"Wonderful. Does that mean you're up for visitors?"

Harper didn't know how to read his pause, especially since she could hear other voices in the background. "This evening, sure. Like, around five?"

"Okay."

She ended the call and sank, holding Emaline, into the couch.

He almost seemed reluctant to see her. He'd said he'd forgiven her, but had he really? Maybe he was more upset than he'd let on. Either that, or maybe his pain medication had started to wear off and his clearer thinking had refueled whatever anger she'd triggered.

Or his accident had simplified things for him, as it had for her; only, unlike her, he'd determined that she wasn't the one. And could she blame him? She didn't exactly have her life together, whereas his was finally taking off.

He'd been on television, won a lucrative award and a place in a prestigious gallery, had purchased building space, and would soon have his own business. One that, with his talent, wisdom and hard work ethic, was sure to succeed.

Tears stung her eyes. "I fear your grandma's warnings may have been right, Ema-bean. I think I may have lost CJ for good this time."

Moping about the house worrying for the next four hours wouldn't help any.

She stood. "How about we distract ourselves

with a blended peppermint mocha and giant chocolate chip cookie from the Literary Sweet Spot and some downtown window-shopping? And maybe a stop at the library for some new bedtime stories for you and a novel for me."

Unfortunately, her desire not to obsess over CJ proved stronger than her ability. After a couple of hours, she gave up and hopped in her car. She arrived at the hospital nearly forty-five minutes earlier than CJ had requested.

She followed behind an older woman she recognized from Trinity Faith pushing a rolling cart of the most beautiful wildflowers in an assortment of vases. She was on the shorter side, with a boxy shape, and had long black hair that hit midback.

As they neared, the sliding glass doors swooshed open, releasing a gust of cold air and the scent of cleaner. When the woman struggled to push her cart over the door seal on the floor, Harper stepped forward.

"Let me help."

"Thank you, my dear. This thingamajig is heavier than it looks."

"I can imagine." Harper wheeled it inside, then stopped, jaw slack, to see so many ladies walking past the main desk, all carrying flowers or balloons. Most, if not all of them, attended Trinity Faith.

"Guess someone is well loved," she said to herself.

Lucy Carr, who'd been hurrying past from the other direction, overheard her and stopped with a grin and dancing eyes. "Oh, yes, I would say so." But then her expression flashed from surprise to concern. "Where are you going?"

"To see a friend."

Lucy's gaze shot down the hall then back to Harper. "Are you in a hurry? Because—"

"Harper!"

She turned at Nancy's alarmed voice, and her pulse immediately spiked. Had something happened to CJ? An unexpected infection or something? "Ma'am. Is everything all right?"

Nancy and Lucy exchanged looks, and neither appeared pleased by her presence. "Yes, of course. But…"

"I was just about to ask Harper if she'd mind helping me." Lucy's tone made it seem as if her words were laden with ulterior meaning.

"Oh, yes." Nancy brightened. "Great idea. I could use some help as well."

Why was everyone acting so strange all of a sudden? "With?"

"I'll show you." She placed a hand in the crook of Harper's arm and gently rotated her back toward the door. "It's in my trunk."

"Mine, too." Lucy came alongside them, both women practically tugging Harper outside, only to seem completely baffled once they reached their vehicles.

But rather than admitting they didn't have whatever items they'd thought they'd brought, they spent the next ten minutes or so searching every inch of each of their vehicles. The back seat and front. The floorboard.

The glove compartment? Surely they could manage whatever could fit there on their own.

When they started talking about driving home to get their items, and it seemed as if they actually wanted Harper to accompany them, she politely excused herself and hurried back toward the hospital.

"Harper, wait." Nancy's footsteps approached quickly from behind.

Once inside, she turned to face her with a smile. "I would love to help you, ma'am. I can stop by your house in a couple hours. Or the store. Wherever."

Nancy released a breath and threw up her hands. "Never mind."

Great. She'd offended the woman. "I'm sorry. I wasn't trying to be rude."

"No, really, it's all right." She glanced at the clock on the wall and then, with a much more relaxed smile, once again placed her hand in the crook of Harper's arm. "Let's go see how my son's doing, shall we?"

"Yes, ma'am."

Other women passed them, eyebrows shooting up upon seeing Harper, as they strolled down the hall. She couldn't help but feel as if they were all sending hidden messages to one another—about something she, apparently, was the only one to know nothing about.

Upon entering CJ's room, she stopped short, eyes wide. Vases, some filled with roses and others with bluebonnets, primroses, daisies, white poppies and other wildflowers, decorated literally every surface space and overflowed onto the floor. Among them were numerous balloons more fitting for Valentine's Day than any get-well sentiments.

CJ sat upright in his bed, cowboy hat on, grinning.

"You're certainly a popular man." Had he always been so, or was this the result of his contest placement and television appearance?

"Oh, I don't know about that."

"Because every hospital room looks like this?" She laughed. "You always did have a way of winning people's hearts."

"There's only one heart I'm interested in."

The women who'd been in the room when she'd arrived deposited their gifts and scurried out.

She shook her head. "Why is everyone acting so strange?"

"Come here." He shifted to make room beside him, his intensified gaze capturing hers.

Harper knew that look. She'd seen it before.

She came closer and sat on the edge of the mattress, angled toward him. She swallowed. "Christopher Jenkins, what are you doing?"

"What I meant to do years ago." He produced a black velvet box from beneath the blanket. "You have done grabbed hold of every last piece of my heart. You're constantly in my thoughts, and you and that adorable daughter of yours have invaded my dreams."

She quirked an eyebrow, her pulse ricocheting against her breastbone. "Invaded, huh?"

He nodded. "Grabbed hold of every last one. Back when we were teens, I thought there was no way I could possibly love you more, but I was wrong. What I felt then, as powerful as that was, pales in comparison to the way I feel about you now. I don't want to spend a single day without you."

A tear slid down her face as CJ opened the box and took out the ring.

He grabbed her trembling hand in his and slipped a gold band with a glimmering diamond bordered by tiny pink sapphires onto her finger. "Harper, will you make me the happiest man alive, from now until I breathe my last, by marrying me?"

"Oh, CJ! Yes!"

His eyes and grin widened. But then his expression sobered as he cupped her face in both his hands, leaned in close and seized her lips in his.

Feeling as if her chest would burst, she grasped the back of his neck, breathing in his smell and his taste as he deepened his kiss.

God had indeed given her both of her dreams.

Behind them came a muffled, "Praise God Almighty!"

Releasing her hold, she glanced back to see the faces of the Trinity Faith ladies pressed up against the hall window and poking through the open door, Nancy's bright eyes among them.

Harper laughed and shook her head. "What's that saying about news traveling fast in small towns?"

CJ shot her the easy grin that always turned her insides to mush. "Guess some things don't change, huh?"

"And I hope they never will."

EPILOGUE

One year later

"Now, DON'T YOU look scrumptious." Harper's mom lifted Emaline, dressed in ballet shoes, a pink leotard with embroidered flowers and a matching tutu, and twirled her about the parish house's living room. "It's really not fair to all the other ballerina flower girls, you're so cute."

Harper laughed. "I'm just glad she's not fighting to take her outfit off. I can't tell you how many times I heard 'Itchy, Mama' when I got her dressed."

"I'm sure seeing the bigger kids in the same getup helped."

"She does want to be grown, that's for sure."

"Reminds me of someone else at her age." Her mom kissed Emaline's cheek then set her down. She turned to Harper. "And you, my girl, look absolutely beautiful." Eyes glistening, she took hold of both of her hands. "Just wait until CJ sees you. He's liable to fall over flat."

"Thank you." Harper turned toward the mirror and ran a hand down the bodice of her formfitting, boho gown. White fabric decorated with cherry blossoms over pink satin formed the silhouette. The tips of her shoes, clear sandals with white flowers, peeked out from beneath the fabric.

"He might fall over before he even gets to that point, with how nervous he's been this morning." Nancy, who'd slipped in with a white basket filled with chilled water bottles, shot Harper a wink. "Can't say I blame him. He's been waiting for this day—for his lady—for an awful long time."

Harper's heart swelled to think of how faithfully he'd loved her, even when she'd spurned his love. "I'm very grateful."

"You realize what that means, right?" Nancy grabbed a tissue and dabbed at her glistening forehead, evidence of all the running around she'd been doing. Everyone had insisted, numerous times, that she relax and simply enjoy the day, but her obvious nervousness wouldn't let her.

"What's that?" Harper fingered her necklace, a crystal teardrop hung on a silver chain.

"He won't let you go, no how, no way."

He'd well proven that.

"Not you or Little Ms. Twinkle Toes." Nancy glanced around. "Where are the other dancers?"

"With Trisha and Julia, getting warmed up. And probably receiving an earful of directions."

A gentle knock sounded on the door and, a moment later, Lucy, who'd worked tirelessly— with the help of her friends—on the decorations, using a plethora of wildflowers donated by the Stoughtons, poked her head inside. "Y'all about ready?"

Harper took a deep breath and nodded. "As ready as I'll ever be."

"And the others?"

"I'll get them." Her mom dashed into the living room, her anxious voice following.

A moment later, half a dozen of Harper's dance students, aged three to five, burst into the kitchen, her mom shooing them forward.

Trisha and Julia trailed behind, radiant in their matching off-the-shoulder bridesmaid dresses, their hair secured by the same beaded pins as Harper's.

With another quick yet firm knock, CJ's dad

entered, wearing a suit, perhaps for the second time in his life, the first being his wedding. Upon seeing Harper, he stopped short then gave a low whistle. "My boy sure snagged him a good one."

His wife slapped his arm.

He laughed and came to Harper's side. "Joking aside, he done did good. You still okay with me walking you down the aisle?"

A lump lodged in her throat. A year ago, she never would've imagined it would be CJ's dad walking her down the aisle. It had touched her deeply when he'd offered, and had helped lessen the ache left by her uninvolved father.

Both of CJ's parents had been amazing, opening their hearts to her as if she were their own daughter. "I wouldn't want anyone else to."

She would've been overjoyed, simply to wed a man like CJ Jenkins. Yet God in His abundance had given her an added gift in allowing her to marry into such a wonderful family.

CJ TOOK A deep breath, his legs jittery, as the music started. It was the instrumental version of a song about a couple reunited after a long separation who remained together through life's ups and downs, wrinkles and gray hair. His chest squeezed with the same intensity as it had when Harper had first played it for him—his thoughts immediately spanning the years that lay before them.

When he'd lost her that first time, he wasn't sure he could go on. The hurt had felt so intense, he'd wanted to close his heart for good. Praise God he hadn't, otherwise he would've missed out on the best gift Christ had ever given him.

Heads turned and people gasped as a handful of girls dressed in leotards and tutus, their hair secured in matching buns, pranced up the aisle on tiptoes, dropping petals as they went. His princess followed, led by the hand by yet another dancer. At eighteen months, she was looking more like her mother every day, and had captured his heart as securely.

God help me do right by that girl. Be the type of dad she needs, and the husband Harper deserves.

Nearing the altar, Emaline noticed CJ, and a wide grin lit her face. "Daddy!" She yanked free from her guide, dropped her petal basket and hurriedly toddled toward him.

He laughed and scooped her up. "Hey, peanut." He kissed her cheek. "What a great dancer you are!"

Expression serious, she nodded. "My toetoes." She pointed to her lifted foot.

"On your tiptoes. I saw." With a gentle squeeze, he placed her in his mother's waiting arms.

The music shifted, this time to the song he'd chosen about a woman so beautiful, inside and out, her man frequently lost his ability to think and speak. A woman whose laugh sounded like the notes from a flute and whose smile lit a room. A woman with an elegant grace and tender touch who made the singer want to be a better man.

A woman like Harper.

His breath caught as she emerged around the corner, looking more gorgeous than he'd ever seen her, in a gown that accentuated her delicate frame. Her hair cascaded over her shoulders, jewels of some sort glimmering throughout the strands.

When she drew near, he noted the shimmer of her lip gloss, the soft pink in her cheeks and the curve of her lashes around her sapphire eyes.

Reaching him, she handed Trisha, her bridesmaid, her bouquet, and faced him with a shy smile that triggered a gut-level protectiveness within him. The part of him that would do anything in his power to make her happy.

Pastor Roger motioned for everyone to sit, thanked them for coming, then talked about a love so deep, it revealed the depth of love Christ had for each of us, which in turn equaled the love the Father and Son had for one another. He then indicated for CJ to say his vows.

He wiped sweaty hands on his pant legs and pulled out his sheet of paper. Unfolding it, he cleared his throat. "Harper Moore, I can still picture the day I first saw you, sitting on my neighbor's back porch, holding a fussing baby in your arms. The way your brow furrowed, and how your wavy hair framed your face. How your eyes lit up a moment later when you laughed at something one of the other kids had said. I knew then that you were a rare treasure worth cherishing."

CJ swallowed, his nervousness giving way to a rush of emotion. "When you left for Seattle, I feared I'd lost you for good. And that I'd never get over you, no matter how hard or long I tried. I was right. I didn't, and I never will. You and that wiggly, giggly, twinkle-toed peanut make life worth living. I thank God each day for bringing you back to me. Now that He has, there's no way I'll ever let you go."

A tear slid down Harper's cheek and she palmed it away. "Nor I you, CJ Jenkins. That girl who left all those years ago was a fool. Because if she'd had a clue as to the gift she'd been given— the type of person you are—she would've realized no dream is worth losing you. You're a man of integrity, of gentleness and strength, who's the first to give, the first to help, and the first—and last—to capture my heart, which I freely give, without hesitation or reservation."

Her words reached the deepest place within him where a hint of insecurity still resided, not because of anything she'd done, but rather because he knew how far out of his league she was.

"You've both spoken powerful words I have no doubt you'll live out in the years to come," Pastor Roger said before directing them to exchange rings. "And now, by the power vested in me by the State of Texas, I pronounce you husband and wife. Christopher James Jenkins, you may now kiss your bride."

A grin exploded across his face then evaporated as his eyes locked onto hers. Cupping her cheeks in his hands, he brought his lips to hers, almost heady with the realization that he'd be kissing this beautiful woman a thousand times a day for the rest of his life.

★ ★ ★ ★ ★

The Cowboy's Return
Danica Favorite

MILLS & BOON

Danica Favorite loves the adventure of living a creative life. She loves to explore the depths of human nature and follow people on the journey to happily-ever-after. Though the journey is often bumpy, those bumps refine imperfect characters as they live the lives God created them for. Oops, that just spoiled the endings of Danica's stories. Then again, getting there is all the fun. Find her at danicafavorite.com.

But as for you, ye thought evil against me;
but God meant it unto good, to bring to pass,
as it is this day, to save much people alive.
                        —*Genesis* 50:20

DEDICATION

For the real Luke and Stolley Bear.
Both gone too soon. We miss you.

CHAPTER ONE

MADDIE ANTERE HELD back the urge to let out a squeal and give a fist pump as she walked out of her supervisor's office. Claire McCabe had been her supervisor for as long as Maddie had worked at the Shady Peaks Senior Center, from the time Maddie had found herself unexpectedly pregnant with her now eighteen-year-old daughter, Kayla. Claire had given Maddie a job when no one else would, and had helped Maddie navigate the ins and outs of the necessary schooling to do more than be a simple aide, so she could have more responsibilities and make more money.

And now…in just a few short weeks, as long as Maddie passed the review with the board of directors, when Claire retired, Maddie would be taking over Claire's job as the director of the center.

It seemed almost unreal.

For years, people had turned their noses up at Maddie, first because of the family she'd grown up in, and then becoming a single mom, and last but not least, all the mistakes she'd made on her own along the way. Maddie had told everyone that Brady King was Kayla's father despite it not being true, effectively ruining his life. Even though he had forgiven her and continued to prioritize her and Kayla as members of the family when the truth came out, Maddie had always felt like she'd never earned her place in this world. Sure, she helped out at Shepherd's Creek Stables and had even created a program for the seniors to be active there so they had more to do than some boring old crafts printed off the internet. But sometimes, she suspected her place there was given to her because they felt sorry for her, and, of course, for Kayla's sake.

But this…this was something Maddie had finally earned—through her own talents, abilities, and hard work.

All she had to do was keep up the good work she'd been doing all these years for one more month, and the recognition of being worthy based on her efforts was finally hers.

With a little spring of hopefulness in her step,

she went into Ida Mae Christianson's room to begin her rounds for the day.

"Good morning, Ida Mae. Did you have a good breakfast?"

She didn't need to ask, since she knew that Ida Mae would likely complain about some aspect of the breakfast, and then launch into a long diatribe of how she could have a much better meal if she were allowed to go home and fix it herself.

But that was Ida Mae, and like all her residents, Maddie always took the time to listen and understand what the older woman was going through, because it was hard on people, not being in the homes they loved and were used to.

However, when Maddie stepped further into the room, she was greeted by the sight of a giant hulk of a man leaning over Ida Mae, brushing her hair with the soft hairbrush she loved tenderly.

"I sure did," Ida Mae said. "My grandson is finally here to visit, and he even brought me McDonald's for breakfast."

Maddie gave Ida Mae an indulgent smile. Though she did have a special preapproved menu to manage her health issues, even the dietician wouldn't be upset at a small treat once in a while. But she'd have to pull the grandson

aside at some point to let him know this couldn't
be a regular occurrence.

"That's so nice," Maddie said, smiling at the
man. "I'm Maddie Antere, and I've been helping your grandmother. You must be the famous
Luke I've heard so much about."

He stopped brushing his grandmother's hair
to glance at Maddie, his warm brown eyes familiar, even though Maddie had never met this
mysterious grandson. While Maddie had grown
up knowing Ida Mae and most of her family,
she'd never met Luke, whose father was in the
military, so they'd always been traveling from
post to post. From what Ida Mae had told Maddie, Luke had followed in his father's footsteps,
so his visits to his grandmother were few and
far between.

"It's nice to meet you," he said. "Granny
speaks highly of you. I think if it weren't for
you, she'd have burned the place down by now."

"I don't belong in here," Ida Mae said, sitting
up straight in her chair "I'm not sick."

They also had this argument every day, but
still Maddie smiled at her. "I know you're not.
But the doctor says you have to stay here until
your hip is fully healed so you don't end up here

again. You know I love you, but I hope I never see you back here."

"You and me both," Ida Mae said, turning her attention to her grandson. "Maybe now that Luke is here, I can go home."

"Absolutely not."

Maddie turned to the sound of the voice behind her, trying not to groan. Briana Smith, Ida Mae's granddaughter who lived in town, who'd grown up with Maddie, and had often been a thorn in Maddie's side. The problem with having a troubled past in a small town was that people like Briana never let you forget.

She'd grown to dislike Briana's visits just as much as she'd disliked having classes with her in school. Briana always thought she was better than everyone else, and now, as the mayor's wife, the woman was even more intolerable. Every time Briana came, she found some fault in how Ida Mae was being cared for.

Hopefully, Luke wouldn't be as bad.

"Briana. Nice to see you," Luke said, stepping around the chair Ida Mae was in to greet his cousin.

But while he went in for the hug, Briana sidestepped him, giving him a dirty look.

"You should have let us know you were

coming. Granny has a routine that shouldn't be disturbed."

"Yeah, a snooze fest," Ida Mae said. "Luke coming home is the best thing that's happened in years. He said he's staying for a while, so I can go home and he'll look after me."

Briana's eyes lit on the remains of the Mc-Donald's breakfast. "I'm assuming he's the one who brought you that."

The smile on Ida Mae's face was brighter than any expression Maddie had ever seen on the older woman.

"My favorite."

"It's not on your diet," Briana said, then turned to Maddie. "Did you let this happen? I have made my expectations very clear in terms of my grandmother's care, and if you are falling short, I will have no choice but to speak to your supervisor."

Not only did Maddie receive this threat on a regular basis, but Briana had followed through multiple times. Every slight, real or imagined, got reported to Maddie's supervisor. Most of the time, Claire laughed it off and said it was no big deal, but with the promotion on the line, an official write up could put that in jeopardy.

"I only just arrived before you. We had just

gotten through introductions, and then I was going to explain to Luke that while bringing your grandmother breakfast was a nice gesture, it's important to check with the dietician on any special treats he brings in."

Hopefully it would be enough to calm Briana down. When it came to her grandmother's care, Briana ran things with an iron fist. No wonder poor Ida Mae just wanted to go home. At least there, she didn't have to deal with Briana's nonsense all the time. But none of this was Maddie's business. She did her best to take care of Ida Mae while appeasing Briana.

"Who even let him in?" Briana asked.

Oh-kay... Maddie had heard that Luke was something of a black sheep. Prior to joining the military, he'd been in a lot of trouble, and even though it was years ago, Briana liked to remind everyone that she was the good grandchild and Luke was the worthless one. Especially when Ida Mae got sentimental about her grandchildren.

"Anyone can visit any of the residents at any time during visiting hours, provided they meet the health requirements," Maddie said.

Briana turned her icy gaze to Luke, and Maddie felt a bit bad for him, because even though it got her out of the firing range, from what Maddie could tell, he was a loving grandson, so he didn't deserve this.

"Have you had all of your shots? I've heard the flu is going around," Briana asked.

Maddie forced herself not to giggle. It was like the other woman was talking about a dog going to a kennel.

"And then some," Luke said, squaring up against her. "With all the military travel I've done, I'm vaccinated against more things than you can possibly imagine, and I was given a clean bill of health before my discharge. I can assure you, you're likely more of a health risk to her than I am."

For a moment, Maddie stared at him for having the audacity to talk to Briana like that. Judging from Briana's indrawn breath, Briana couldn't believe it either. She was used to pushing everyone around and getting her way, no matter what the cost.

Luke winked at Maddie, and she couldn't help smiling. Handsome and charming, plus standing up to Briana? A lethal combination, except that Maddie had sworn off dating a long time ago. In terms of men, Maddie had the worst judgment ever. In high school, she'd had a bad reputation with boys, even though she hadn't done anything with any of them until that fateful party when she'd gotten pregnant by some guy who'd given her a fake name and disappeared the morning after. Then, when she carried out the farce of trying to be with Brady to give Kayla a father, she'd only proven how inept she was at having a relationship with someone who was honestly trying to make things work, despite being in love with someone else. After that, she'd gone on a few dates, but all anyone ever saw was her reputation for being easy that she'd never actually earned.

No one would ever believe that she had only been with one person, one time, and it wasn't even that great. Actually, it was pretty terrible, but men just expected sex from her, so she said no thank you to it all. If all that garbage was what love and romance was about, you could count Maddie out.

Actually, she knew from observing her Shepherd's Creek family that there was a lot more to a lasting relationship than that, but with the way people in town looked at her, she wasn't sure it would ever happen for her.

Still, Luke was pretty cute, and he didn't know those things about her, so maybe…

Maddie shook her head. He was the grandson

of a patient, and Briana's cousin, so that made it all completely inappropriate.

"We need to set some boundaries," Briana said.

Maddie felt her face heat, as if Briana had known her train of thought.

But then Briana continued, "I understand that you want to spend time with Granny while you're on leave. But it's very important that we keep to her schedule and make sure that there are no interruptions to her care that could bring on a setback. Your junk food treat could be harmful to her."

"I'm here to stay," Luke said. "They offered me a nice retirement package, and my friend Ken has a consulting business for veterans that he's asked me to join, so I'm taking his offer once I get Granny settled. I know you're busy with your son and your life, and I never had the chance to do any of that with all my travel, so when Granny broke her hip again when I got my offer, it was a no-brainer. It's time I fulfilled my family obligations. You can't take care of Granny, but I can."

Maddie had taken Kayla to Yellowstone once, and the expression on Briana's face was like a geyser about to go off. It was actually pretty funny, watching someone stand up to her, especially because in this case, there was nothing Briana could do.

"That's a lot of too little, too late," Briana said. "You haven't been involved in our lives in years. Now suddenly you appear? Given all your troubles over the years, I'm wondering what your motives really are and if your story is even true."

Ida Mae straightened in her chair and pounded on her table. "He video chats me every Sunday night, except for when he's doing secret work he can't tell me about."

That part, Maddie knew was true, because she'd helped Ida Mae get her tablet set up so she could chat with her grandson. Though Maddie had only heard "grandson" and had assumed that since Ida Mae hated the "great" reference, it was Drake, Briana's son who was in Kayla's class at school. And like his mother had done to Maddie, constantly tormented Kayla.

The joys of small-town living.

Where grudges ran long and deep. Which was why getting this promotion would finally prove that Maddie could break free of the past that everyone held against her.

"Like I said, I'm here to stay," Luke said. He

pushed up his sleeves, like he was gearing up for battle, which was when Maddie noticed the tattoo on his forearm.

A snake, wrapped around a dagger, and the dagger's point was stuck inside an intricate heart.

She'd only ever seen one tattoo like it.

"Maddie, a word outside if you please," Briana said.

Maddie could barely process the thought as she nodded, her eyes still on the tattoo as she backed out of the room to listen to whatever nonsense Briana would go on about.

At the moment, Maddie felt like her heart was caving in. Just when she thought everything in her world was finally going right, the one thing that could destroy it all was happening.

Only one man had that same tattoo. Maddie had lovingly traced it the night of the party where Kayla had been conceived. He'd told her his name was Snake, like his tattoo, and he was only here to appease his family before going off to boot camp, but he was going to get out as soon as he could, and run away from their controlling ways, and make a life for himself.

Something about what he'd said had called out to her, and okay, they were both more than a little drunk. Maddie had thought it was something special, but he was gone the next morning, and she hadn't known where to find him. When she'd found out she was pregnant, she'd blamed Brady.

She'd always known Brady wasn't Kayla's father.

But for the first time, she knew who Kayla's father really was.

Luke Christianson, grandson of her favorite patient, and cousin of her nemesis.

As MADDIE STEPPED out into the hall to receive the tongue-lashing Briana was going to give her, Luke felt bad for the woman who was just trying to do her job and was now caught between a rock and a hard place. It wasn't Maddie's fault that he and Briana had bad history.

Briana had hated him her entire life because she was jealous of him being the grandkid who lived far away and got spoiled whenever he came to visit. And then, of course, there was the night she never let him live down. His father had sent him to stay with his grandparents for the summer before he went off to boot camp, hoping that being in the small ranching community would keep him from doing anything stupid that would get him kicked out before he began.

He'd gotten in some minor trouble back home, and his father was terrified he'd do something that would disqualify him from the army.

But one night, he'd had enough of the boredom, taken Briana's car, gone to a party, and gotten drunk. On the way home, he'd crashed the car into the ditch in front of their house and totaled it. Okay, there was way more to his side of the story than that, but that's all Briana knew, all she'd ever know, and all she cared about. Even though her dad had been angry, he'd also been pretty decent about the whole thing and not called the police. His dad had paid for the damages, then shipped him back home and pulled some strings to get him into boot camp early so he didn't do anything else to jeopardize his future.

To Briana, it was the worst betrayal, because in her eyes, Luke had gotten away with it. But the truth was, he hadn't. He'd sent every paycheck back to his dad until he'd paid off his debt, living in base housing, and doing everything as cheaply as possible to make up for what he'd done. Yes, he could have gotten arrested and put in jail for a DUI, which was still something Briana brought up as him deserving every time she could, but his dad had been right. Luke had never wanted to join the military, but it had done more to straighten Luke out than jail ever would.

He just wished he'd been able to thank Briana's dad for understanding that as well, but he'd died shortly after, and Luke had been deployed overseas and couldn't make it back for the funeral. Another thing Briana hated him for. He'd missed every major family event over the years. As a single man, he took the hazardous assignments that had him traveling the world so that the men with families didn't have to. Plus, he'd liked the connection to his family by saying he was a member of the cavalry division. His grandfather had served in the cavalry before becoming a rancher. While they only used horses for ceremonial purposes these days, he loved the pride in Granny's eyes when he'd say anything about being cavalry.

Unfortunately, Luke hadn't realized the cost to his extended family, especially his grandmother. Phone and video calls weren't enough to make up for his missing presence. Though he didn't like Briana's attitude toward him, she was right. He should have been here to help Granny.

The only reason Granny was in the senior center was that this was her second broken hip in a year, and both times she'd broken it because she was home alone, trying to do things she should have asked for help with. But now that Luke was out, he could be here for her, helping her so she didn't have to stay in this miserable place.

Okay, it really wasn't that miserable. Every time he talked to Granny, she went on and on about the nice people here, especially Maddie, but she hated having her days planned out, her meals tightly controlled, and constantly being pecked at by Briana. Granny had always been there for him, even when other family members had written him off. The least he could do was be there for her now.

"I do hope she's not being too hard on Maddie," Granny said, staring at the closed door. "Every time I break a rule and Briana finds out, she gets Maddie in trouble. One of these days, she's going to get that poor girl fired. I try to be good, but it's so hard following all the rules. I just want to go home."

That plaintive sigh killed him every time he spoke to her.

Though he wanted to believe that Granny would live forever, he had to be honest that she only had so many years left. The least he could do was spend those years making up for the ones he wasn't around. Granted, there were things he couldn't make up for, but he could do his best.

"I know, Granny, and when Maddie comes back, I'll ask her who I need to talk to so we can get the ball rolling. You're right, she seems really nice."

"And pretty," Granny added.

Not that again. Luke tried not to groan, but the expression on Granny's face told him she saw right through it.

"You've still got plenty of years left in you," she said. "Now you can get married and start a family. If you marry Maddie, you'll get a daughter, too, and Kayla is the sweetest thing. She comes to visit sometimes."

Luke shook his head. "I told you, no matchmaking. I'm perfectly happy with my life as it is, and I don't want your interference."

After all these years of being single, he was comfortable admitting that he was definitely not relationship material. The women he'd dated had complained about his military life, and that he could never share details on all the things he was doing. He might not be traveling now, but he still wasn't the type to give women the depth of emotion and whatnot that they all seemed to want from him. After being trained to stay closed for so long, he didn't know how to open up. Truthfully, he wasn't sure he wanted to. It seemed like every time he thought he was trusting someone, he got stabbed in the back.

He'd thought he was in love once. But all it took was a six-week deployment for him to come back to her messing around with someone else. Or that German woman he'd started dating, only to find out that what she really wanted from him was his money and a green card. If that was what romance was about, he'd pass.

"You just need to find the love of a good woman," Granny said, twisting her wedding rings on her finger. "Your grandfather and I had forty-seven years, and I still miss him every single day."

It didn't do him any good to remind her that these days, relationships like that were a rarity. His parents might have been married for almost thirty years before his dad had passed, but he didn't have a lot of happy memories of his parents' marriage, since they were always fighting. His mom was remarried, but he didn't think much of his stepdad. It seemed more like she didn't want to be alone, as opposed to her finding someone she loved, who loved her back.

But nothing he said would satisfy Granny, so he patted her hand instead. "I wish all marriages were like what you had."

The door opened, and Maddie stepped into the room. "Sorry about that," she said. "Briana is talking to the director now."

The flat tone to Maddie's voice didn't encourage him. "Should I go have a word?" he asked.

She shook her head. "I'd wait until Briana leaves. She's got a nail appointment in an hour that she's stressed about getting to, so you can go then."

Then Maddie looked over her shoulder and back at him. "But please don't tell her I said so."

The bright, cheerful woman he'd met earlier had turned into a mouse. Despite telling Granny he had no interest in romance, he'd definitely agree with her assessment that Maddie was pretty. And Granny liked her, so that was a bonus as well. But he was definitely not interested in her, so he couldn't let his mind wander like this.

That said, he did feel bad that his presence was now causing trouble for her. Briana never seemed to care who she hurt, as long as she got her own way. And when she didn't, as in the case of Luke not going to jail for wrecking her car, she held the grudge forever.

"I do want to make sure that your boss knows none of this is your fault," he said. He glanced over at Granny, then added, "And I would like the information from the dietician so I can make sure that none of my treats are a threat to her health. I want to contribute to her care, not cause Granny harm."

The smile Maddie gave him warmed his heart, but he noticed it didn't fill her eyes, like she was still troubled about the situation.

"Seriously," he said. "None of this has anything to do with you. Briana has held a grudge against me for years, and she's taking it out on you. I'm truly sorry, and I will make sure that you don't face any repercussions."

His words didn't seem to make her feel any better. In fact, she looked even more agitated.

Finally, she said, "I know this is going to sound weird, but could I talk to you privately for a moment?"

So she was in trouble. Why did Briana have to be such a pain? But if she was going to make waves, then he'd do what he could to make things better for an innocent victim.

"Sure."

He followed her into the hallway, where she led him into a small conference room and closed the door behind them.

"Okay," he said. "You're scaring me. Granny isn't dying, is she?"

Maddie shook her head. "No. This is personal."

He stared at her. How could there be anything personal when they'd just met?

"Do you remember when you came home that summer before boot camp?"

Luke nodded. "Yeah. I take it Briana told you what I did?"

"No." Maddie wrung her hands in front of her. "Sorry. I didn't ever expect to have to do this."

"Do what?"

This woman was seriously weird. But something was clearly bothering her, and whatever it was, he'd hear her out.

"Do you remember going to a party?" She looked at the ground, shaking her head. "Sorry, you probably went to a lot of parties."

She didn't look up as she continued. "Anyway, there was this one party, and I met you, and…"

"I only went to one party," he said quietly. She didn't have to continue the story. He knew what she was trying to say. He'd met this great girl, they'd connected, and they'd…

"We did things I regret," she said really quickly, like she hadn't wanted to admit it, but felt that she needed closure. "And I ended up pregnant, which I don't regret, only I did other things I regret, but I promised myself and my daughter that if I ever saw her father, I'd find out his name, and I would tell her so that she would know who her father is."

Even though she spoke about a mile a minute, the words processed very slowly in his mind, almost like they were taking forever to form and didn't make sense.

And then it hit him.

"I'm her father?"

Maddie nodded, and tears filled her eyes. "I'm sorry. I gave you my number, but you never called, and you told me your name was Snake, and no one knew a Snake, and then I told a bunch of lies, so I didn't think it mattered, but then they all came out, so I promised that when I finally found out the truth, I'd tell the truth."

She looked at him, wide-eyed. "So I'm telling the truth. I have a daughter, her name is Kayla, and you are her father. So now I have to keep my promise."

A father. The one thing Luke had always said he'd never be, because he didn't know what kind of father he'd be.

"Are you sure?" he asked.

"I've only ever been with one person, but I'm willing to take a test if you want."

He believed her. He didn't need a test to do so.

"I remember that night," Luke said. "I always meant to call you, but I got into some trouble, and I couldn't. I'm sorry."

Now his mistakes of that night seemed even worse than he'd ever thought.

A child.

He had a child.

Kayla.

"How did you realize it was me?"

Maddie gestured at his tattoo. "You said you designed it yourself. It was your eighteenth birthday present to yourself, and you were really proud of it."

His heart thudded to the pit of his stomach. In all his earlier thoughts about opening up to women, he'd failed to include Maddie. The truth was, he'd opened up to her as well. That night, they'd connected in a very deep way. He'd shared things with her he'd never shared with anyone, and they'd been up most of the night, mostly talking. He'd thought it was something special.

But in the aftermath of his accident and everyone in the family being upset, he hadn't had time to call her. He'd asked Briana if she knew a girl named Maddie, and Briana had laughed and said the only Maddie she knew was no one worth knowing. Since Maddie was a common name, it hadn't occurred to him that all along, the Maddie he remembered was the Maddie they all had been talking about.

All this time.

She was right in front of him, and he hadn't known.

Worse, they had a child, who, based on when this had all happened, was essentially an adult now.

"She's what? Eighteen?"

Maddie nodded. "I don't want money or anything from you. We've done okay. I honestly never thought I'd see you again. But now, I have to do the right thing. My lies have cost me too much, and even though it might cost me even more, I need to tell the truth."

The woman was practically shaking, and while he was still reeling from the knowledge that he had a daughter, he wanted to reach out to her and tell her it was okay and comfort her somehow.

Yes, she'd made a mistake by having sex with him, but then, so had he. Somehow, they had to figure a way forward. Together.

CHAPTER TWO

MADDIE COULDN'T BELIEVE she'd done it. Even though she'd come clean about Brady not being Kayla's father a few years ago, it still felt like she'd had part of her lie hanging over her head because she hadn't been able to provide Kayla with her father's name. After watching the rest of the Shepherd's Creek family create their own versions of what family meant to them, which included bringing Maddie and Kayla into the fold despite Maddie's lies and having no blood connection to the family, she'd always felt guilty that she could never identify Kayla's biological father.

But why did it have to be Briana's hated cousin? Worse, her son Drake hated Kayla as much as Briana hated Maddie. And now they were family?

And here Maddie thought her life couldn't

get any more complicated. Just once, she'd like God to make these lessons easy for a change.

She tilted her head heavenward and said silently, *Please?*

"I'm sorry to throw this all on you," Maddie said, looking at Luke again. "But I couldn't let this fester, not when it's been hidden so long. Because of my promise to Kayla, I have to tell her when she gets done with school."

Luke nodded. "She's a senior?"

"Yes. Already accepted to college. She's going to be a pediatrician because she loves kids."

A small smile lit up Luke's face. "So she's smart in addition to being a good kid who's nice to Granny."

She liked that Luke immediately picked up on Kayla's good qualities, as a proud father would do. "Yes. When she was little, I had to bring her to work sometimes because I didn't have childcare and didn't want to bug Brady, so they let me bring her as long as she didn't get in the way. She's always liked visiting the residents. Even as she got older, she liked to visit and entertain them."

Once again, he smiled, seemingly happy to have this insight into Kayla's positive qualities. It was probably good he learned these things about her before experiencing her bratty side, because she was still a teenager. And even the best teenagers could be trying at times.

"Who's Brady?"

Right. More facing her past.

"I was not a very good person back then," Maddie said, knowing that accepting this part of her was just as healing as anything else—at least, that's what her counselor told her. "I had a grudge with Junior, that is, Josie Shepherd, now King, and her boyfriend was there, and he was really drunk. I thought it would be funny to take pictures that made it look like we'd been intimate to cause problems between them. And then I discovered I was pregnant, and you were nowhere to be found, so I lied and said the baby was his. No one asked for proof, so everyone, including Brady, believed he was Kayla's father until she was almost fifteen."

Luke nodded slowly, and unlike everyone else who heard that story, he didn't look like he was judging her. "How did the truth come out? She wasn't sick or anything, was she?"

Again, Maddie had to give him credit for caring about a child he'd just found out was his. But it only made her feel worse, admitting what a despicable person she'd been.

"No, she's fine. Perfectly healthy." Maddie took a deep breath, then said, "Josie came back to town. She'd left because of my pregnancy and a falling out with her father, but he died, and he left the stables and his entire estate to her, so she came back. We had a fight, and the truth came out. I behaved very badly. Everyone seems to have forgiven me, but sometimes, I don't know if I can forgive myself. I hurt a lot of people."

All this time, Maddie had never thought much about what it would be like to face Kayla's father. She'd written him off as some guy at a party, without considering how he'd feel if he ever found out the truth. Granted, she hadn't known how to get in touch with Luke, or even know who he was, but the guilt was still there.

"I've done a lot of unforgiveable things, too," Luke said. "That's why I'm back. To make amends. I guess I have more amends to make than I thought. I should have called you. But I left you on your own to raise a baby and tell a lot of lies to cover up what we did. I'm just as responsible as you are."

He looked thoughtful for a moment, then said, "But Granny and I have been talking a lot about God, and what forgiveness means. Granny keeps telling me that God forgives me, so I should forgive myself. I guess we both need to learn that, so maybe we start by introducing me to our daughter, and facing those consequences."

It might be dumb to find comfort in his words, but all this time, part of her had been angry with him for abandoning her like that. And then she'd been angry with herself for being angry over him not being there for her because he didn't know, and she should have done more to figure out who he was. Why hadn't she been able to connect the dots that Ida Mae had a grandson visiting at the time? Probably because back then, she wouldn't have cared about some old lady and her visiting grandson. Unlike Kayla, who had an abundance of compassion, Maddie had not been that caring a person as a teenager.

Kayla was a reminder of the things Maddie had done right.

Funny how her daughter's example was what made Maddie want to do better and be a better person.

"If it's okay with you, I'd like to do this as a family for Kayla. After the truth came out, Brady and Josie insisted we be part of their family, and Kayla is very close to them. We're supposed to have dinner tonight as a family anyway, so maybe you could come, and I could tell everyone then?"

Even though she'd made it about Kayla, and it was true that Kayla would need their support, the truth also was, Maddie needed their support as well. Though Josie had once been Maddie's biggest nemesis, she was now one of Maddie's closest friends, as were Josie's cousins Abigail and Laura. Fortunately, Abigail and her husband were visiting from Minnesota, so it truly would be a family affair.

"Sure," Luke said. "Let me give you my number, and you can call with the details."

Though Maddie had a hard time seeing the rifts between her and Briana and Kayla and Drake mending, maybe this would heal their relationships as well.

But then Maddie looked out the window of the conference room she'd pulled Luke into. She saw Briana storming in their direction, Claire trailing helplessly behind her, and she wondered if it might take pigs flying first.

Briana threw open the conference room door. "What are you two doing in here?"

The last thing Maddie wanted was to have to tell Briana that Luke was Kayla's father before

Kayla found out. As soon as Briana found out, the rumor mill would be hopping within minutes. Kayla didn't deserve that until she'd had time to process the news. Even then, she didn't deserve it, but it was inevitable.

That was the trouble with one lie. You think it's one little lie, but then it snowballs until it gains the power to hurt more and more people. And, in this case, the person Maddie least wanted to hurt in the world kept being the one hurt the most.

"We were discussing something private," Maddie said, hoping it was enough to calm Briana down long enough for her to come up with an excuse that wouldn't be a lie, but wouldn't share information she wasn't ready to share.

That was the other problem. Maddie had promised not to lie again, and so far, she'd kept that promise.

"This is highly inappropriate," Briana said, turning to Claire.

"Simmer down," Luke said. "This has nothing to do with Granny. Maddie thought she recognized my tattoo from all those years ago, and because she didn't want to get Granny excited with all her matchmaking nonsense, she wanted to ask me privately if I was the person she remembered."

Briana looked at them both suspiciously. "When would Maddie have met you?"

The expression on Luke's face was a lot like how Maddie felt. At least Luke could stand up to Briana without repercussions.

"The summer I wrecked your car. I was coming home from a party, which is where I met Maddie. We connected on a deep level. I'd promised to call her, and I never did, because of the car thing."

Instead of looking happy that they weren't conspiring about something having to do with Ida Mae, Briana glared at Maddie.

"So instead of taking care of my grandmother, which is your job, you decided to confront my cousin about ghosting you."

Briana turned to Claire. "And this is who you want taking your place?"

Maddie wanted to cry in frustration. But the few times she'd allowed tears to fall in front of Briana, Briana had weaponized them against her.

"Stop it," Luke said. "It's nothing like that. She was simply curious if I was the same guy or not. If you've been listening to Granny at all, you'd hear that she keeps telling me about every single woman she knows because she's desperate for me to settle down. I'm sure Maddie is getting the same, so it only makes sense to talk discreetly so no one gets Granny's hopes up. Unless you want Granny trying to set us up."

The shocked look on Briana's face both relieved and terrified Maddie. Clearly, Briana didn't want Maddie in the family anytime soon. But what was she going to do when she found out that Maddie's daughter was, in fact, Briana's family?

"We were about to go back to Granny," Luke continued. "So do you want to continue making a case out of nothing, or do you want to take care of her?"

"Fine." Briana gestured at the door. "After you."

As Luke stepped out of the room, Briana followed, but Claire hung back, motioning for Maddie to stay, then closed the door behind her.

"Look," Claire said. "I know that whatever private conversation you had with Luke was completely innocent. But you need to be on your guard right now. No more being alone with him or doing anything to give Briana the impression that you might be on his side. She thinks he's a danger to Ida Mae."

Maddie stared at her boss. "That's ridiculous. Luke isn't a danger to her. He loves her. She talks about him constantly."

"We need to stay out of their personal squabbles. And you need to stay away from Luke. Briana has the power to make both of our lives miserable, and she knows enough members of the board that she can keep you from getting this promotion."

Maddie knew Claire wasn't exaggerating. She had never seen such a grim look on her boss's face.

"But that's not fair to Ida Mae. I've never seen her so happy. We don't have the authority to interfere in that relationship without evidence he's harming her."

Claire shrugged. "He did bring her fast food, which is against her dietary restrictions."

Which people did for patients all the time, and they had meetings about it, and it was usually easily resolved.

"Luke asked me to set up a meeting with the dietician so he could understand Ida Mae's needs to make sure it doesn't happen again."

Maddie had followed protocol on this, and it

seemed like Luke was willing to do the same, so it all should be a non-issue, except for Claire's concern.

Claire glanced at her watch. "I've got a meeting to get to, and you need to finish your rounds. We can talk later."

As they exited the conference room, Maddie felt like she had to throw up. She finally had the chance to make things right with her daughter, and tell the truth, but it might cost Maddie everything else she'd been working for.

Worse, a sweet old woman was being caught in the middle, and that didn't seem fair either.

So what was Maddie supposed to do? Any show of support for Luke, and she could lose her job. Even though the job itself was important to Maddie, there were also the people like Ida Mae that she genuinely cared for. If she got fired, she couldn't help them at all.

But all of that might be a moot point as soon as Briana found out that Luke was Maddie's father.

Whoever said that the truth would set you free had no idea just how rocky the path to freedom was.

LUKE FOLLOWED BRIANA into their grandmother's room, where Granny was watching a cop show and knitting one of her projects. All the years in the army, Granny would knit him things and send them to him, and when he'd mentioned his friends liked them, she'd started knitting random things for soldiers who didn't have anyone back home.

"What is this trash you're watching?" Briana asked.

"It's her favorite show," Luke said. Briana might take him to task for not being there, but at least he knew that their grandmother loved cop shows.

Briana glared at him.

"You are ruining our routine," Briana said. "We are supposed to go get our nails done. We have an appointment."

The frustration in her voice made him feel bad. Even though he did think she was being way over the top with her need to control, he hadn't thought about the plans she might already have that he was interfering with. He already knew that Briana wasn't his biggest fan, so he needed to tread lightly and give her space to accept that he was a different person now.

Maybe, if he eased her into the idea that he just wanted to be there for Granny, and even help lighten the load, they could come to a place of forgiveness.

"I'm sorry," Luke said, pulling out his wallet. "I didn't think about what plans you might have with her. Let me give you some money to cover the nails. Maybe take her out to a nice lunch, since you know what she can have. I know you probably have enough to cover it all, but let me do this for you as a way of saying I'm sorry."

At first, he didn't think she'd take it, but she grudgingly accepted the bills he handed her.

"Thank you," she said. "But don't think you can buy my affections."

He shrugged. "Not at all. I genuinely feel bad for not giving you warning and taking the time to work with your schedule. I was just excited to surprise Granny. Why don't you give me a call later today and we can work out plans so I can spend time with her without stepping on your toes? I'm here to stay, so let's figure out a way to work together."

Especially now that he knew he had a daughter here, leaving was the last thing he was going to do.

A daughter.

He had a daughter.

Even though he'd hoped to spend a good part of the day with Granny, maybe it was better that she and Briana had plans. He was still reeling from this new information, and he had to figure out what he was supposed to do.

What did you do when you found out you had a daughter after eighteen years? It wasn't like he could jump in and be a father. She was old enough that she didn't need parenting, so what was his role in her life?

He'd driven straight to the senior center to see Granny, and had planned on just staying at Granny's house, doing some of the work on it to make it more livable for Granny to come home. He was torn about getting a hotel so he didn't annoy Briana further by staying at the house. Now that he had a child, even an adult child, it seemed important to have a real home.

And then there was the complication of Maddie…

Granny had been pushing him a lot in that direction. What would she do when she found out that he and Maddie had a child together? At least Granny already knew and liked Kayla.

Kayla.

It was a nice name. What was her middle name? How had Maddie chosen it? Had she and Brady chosen the name together? The more questions he thought of, the more he wanted to know. This was his daughter, and it seemed almost surreal to think of himself as a father.

As he pulled up to Granny's house, it looked shabbier than he remembered. Gramps had been gone a long time, but surely Briana's husband, Corey, helped with the maintenance.

Still, he felt guilty because he should have been here more to help. It was just easier to take another overseas assignment than to come home and face the consequences of the things he'd done.

It wasn't just the car. It was everything. The disrespect. The alcohol use. Stealing things from his family here and there to pay for it.

He'd thought that by following in his father's footsteps and joining the army, he'd finally make everyone proud, and it would make up for all the bad things he'd done. Granny was happy to see him, but Briana hated him. Luke's father was gone, but he'd died before Luke could ever hear the words, "I'm proud of you, son." His mother was remarried to some guy who preferred not to be reminded that she'd been married before.

So what else did Luke have?

A daughter.

In spite of all the things he'd done wrong, he had a daughter.

Who, by all accounts, seemed like a pretty great human being. He hadn't contributed to her life, other than some genetic material, but he was glad to know that at least she'd been raised well.

As he let himself into the house, he was horrified by the mess and disrepair. Granny had always been a meticulous housekeeper, but as he saw how things had gone unkempt, he could understand why everyone wanted her at the senior center so she could heal.

This was a way he could give back. Luke could clean up the house and fix all the things necessary for her to come home. He peeked into the main bathroom, which hadn't been updated since he'd left, and thought about how he could add some of those safety bars and things for older people. And as he passed from the kitchen to the dining room, he could see the step she'd tripped on while carrying a large box of junk and fallen and broken her hip. All of this, he could make safer for her so that when he talked to the doctor about her coming home, the doctor wouldn't be as concerned about her safety.

Maybe it would make Briana feel better as well.

He and his cousin didn't use to hate each

other. Prior to that summer, they'd been the best of friends. But he'd hit his rebellion stage, and she'd remained Miss Perfect, and they forgot all the things they'd had in common.

Luke went into the room he'd stayed in when he'd visited. Still exactly the same as when he'd left. It wasn't like it was a special childhood room with his mementos, since it was just a basic guest room, but they hadn't changed anything in it.

He went to the floorboard where he'd created a hiding place and pulled it up, smiling as he saw the old box he'd hidden there. He opened it to find a half-empty bottle of vodka, which could go in the trash, a couple of crumpled dollar bills, and a folded piece of paper that brought back more memories.

He didn't have to examine it further. It was the paper Maddie had given him with her number. Funny that he still had it after all these years. Except it made him feel even worse that he had left her to cope with a pregnancy all alone.

But he'd been a hot mess back then, and according to her, she hadn't been that great of a person, either. Maybe it had been for the best, but it was hard to say.

His phone rang, and he didn't recognize the

number, but he answered it anyway, in case it was one of Granny's doctors.

"Hi, it's Maddie."

Duh. Of course it was Maddie. He'd given her his number. And, unlike him, she was calling him to follow up.

"Family dinner is tonight at seven. Do you remember where Shepherd's Creek Stables is?"

"I do. You can't miss it driving out of town."

"Cool."

She sounded nervous, which was cute, but he hoped that the talk earlier of making sure no one thought there was anything romantic between them had gotten through. Wrangling his current life situation was hard enough as it was without having to throw in strange romantic feelings.

"Well, it's at the main house, so just show up and we'll see you then."

She hung up, but once again, it struck him how weird she sounded. He thought about Granny's matchmaking attempts. And then he realized how silly it was for him to automatically assume that bringing him into their lives would be easy. Of course she was nervous. She was about to tell her family and their daughter who he was. Anyone would be nervous.

Hadn't he already been stressing out about

what he was supposed to do as Kayla's new-found father?

Should he bring a gift? If she was younger, he might get her a teddy bear or something, but even then, did kids even like stuffed animals these days?

He felt like he was failing at this father stuff already, and he'd only known he had a kid for a few hours.

The sight of flashing lights in front of the house interrupted his train of thought. Obviously, a neighbor had seen someone in the house and called the police.

Okay, then. Time to face that music, and then he'd figure out what to do with the rest of his life.

CHAPTER THREE

MADDIE'S STOMACH WAS a ball of nerves when she opened the door to let Luke into the house. The rest of the family was gathered in the living room, chatting as they always did.

"You okay?" he asked, looking into her eyes, like they'd been friends forever and had only reconnected today. Aside from that one night, they'd hardly known each other at all.

And yet, something about having him here with her felt right, and that his concern for her gave her the strength she needed to nod.

"Yes. I'll feel better when it's over."

He reached forward and gave her a quick squeeze on the shoulder. "I know we barely know each other, but Granny constantly sings your praises, so I know that despite all your mistakes, you're still a good person. We have a child together, so no matter what, I'm going to be here for you to support whatever is best for her. I may not have been much of a father thus far, but going forward, I'm going to do whatever she needs."

His words brought tears to her eyes. As much as she'd been struggling all day, this small show of support gave her a tiny boost that made her believe things might turn out okay after all.

As they entered the room, conversation stopped. The family all turned to look at Luke.

"Hi, everyone. I want you to meet Luke."

Before she could continue, Kayla jumped up. "Mom! You finally have a boyfriend!"

Ouch. Kayla had been obsessed with the idea of Maddie finding someone, especially lately with the rest of their Shepherd's Creek family finding love. Maddie probably should have better prepared her daughter for this, but she wasn't sure how she was supposed to accomplish that.

"No." Luke stepped forward. "I'm your father."

Maddie cringed at the forwardness. She and Luke probably should have talked about how they were going to share the information rather than blurting it out like that. But at least the bandage was ripped off, so to speak.

If only her daughter didn't look like she'd been punched in the gut.

The silence of the others in the room told her that maybe she should have done a better job of preparing everyone.

Before Maddie could speak, Kayla said, "Well, then. Am I supposed to jump up and down for joy? What did you think would happen? I'd get all excited that finally my father is here?"

Kayla turned, like she was going to leave in a huff, but Maddie stopped her.

"Kayla!" Maddie turned to Luke. "I'm sorry. She's usually not this rude."

Some of the family murmured in the background, but Maddie was too focused on her daughter to hear what they were saying.

"She's entitled," he said quietly. "After all, where have I been her whole life?"

Remaining in her fighter stance, Kayla said, "You already know my questions, so why bother having a conversation? I don't need your answers."

"Kayla Mae," Brady said, gesturing at the couch. "Sit down and listen to what your father has to say."

"Which one?" she grumbled, doing as she was asked.

"You have every right to be angry," Luke said. "The truth is, I was a poor excuse for a human being when I met your mother. We had met at a party, she gave me her number, and I never called. There were extenuating circumstances, and I was off to basic training a couple days later, but that's no excuse. A decent man would have called. I am truly sorry for my actions. I should have been there for you and your mother, and I wasn't."

The humility in Luke's voice made Maddie want to reach out to him. But that would likely only stir Kayla up further.

"Mom says you gave her a fake name. Is that true?" Kayla asked.

Luke shrugged. "Yes and no. I had given myself the nickname of Snake, because I thought it sounded cool. I didn't realize until later that it was dumb."

"You said you went to basic training? How long were you in the military?" Kayla's stare remained hostile, and Maddie wished she could take her little girl in her arms and make it all better. But at some point in this conversation, that hostility would be directed at her as well.

"I just got out. My grandmother is in the care center your mom works at, so I came to visit her. Your mom recognized me, and she told me about you, then said she promised you that if she ever found me, she would tell you. So here I am."

Kayla looked thoughtful for a moment, then turned to Maddie. The pain in Maddie's stomach intensified as she hoped that she hadn't made a terrible mistake. "How did you recognize him?"

Maddie swallowed. An easy question at least. "His tattoo. He'd just gotten it when I met him, and he'd said he'd designed it himself."

As if he knew Kayla was going to ask, Luke rolled up his sleeve. "See?"

"So what am I supposed to do now?" Kayla asked.

Maddie sighed. "I don't know. But I'm keeping my promise to you. You get to do whatever you want with the information. I thought it would be easier to introduce him if the family was here to support you."

Judging from the way they all looked at her like she was crazy, Maddie wondered if she should have talked to the therapist they'd seen when the truth about Brady came out or something. But the weight of all the years of lies was heavy on her, and she'd thought this would be easier. Maybe that was where Maddie was still needing to grow. She'd thought about how it weighed on her, but not on Kayla.

"You don't have to call me Dad or anything," Luke said. "From what I understand, you already have a great dad. I don't want to take away from that or interfere. But I would like to get to know you, if that's okay."

Brady stood and held a hand out to Luke. "You are very welcome here. I don't know if Maddie told you, but we do family different from most."

He gestured at Josie. "This is my wife, Josie. Though I'm not biologically Kayla's father, I'm still Dad, and Josie is a bonus mom, but Kayla calls her Josie. Kayla calls our daughter, Shana, her sister."

The warmth in Brady's voice reassured Maddie and made her feel like everything was going to work out. He'd become the head of their strange family, and even though she'd initially gone about it the wrong way, she was grateful to have him in their lives.

"Let me introduce you to the rest of the family," Brady said. Then he gestured at Wyatt and Laura. "Laura is Josie's cousin, but they were raised as sisters."

For a moment, he hesitated, then said, "We

don't make a big deal of it here, but I want to explain it so you understand that for us, family is much deeper than what most families are. Wyatt is Laura's second husband, and while the twins were technically fathered by her late husband, they're his boys, and they call him Dad. They named their baby boy Cash after her late husband."

Finally, he gestured at Abigail and Isaac. "Abigail is Laura's sister, and she raised both Josie and Laura. She's married to Isaac, and they live in Minnesota now. They're in the process of getting certified to adopt a kid from the foster care system. Who knows what that kid will call them, but regardless, he or she will be family."

Listening to Brady describe their family warmed Maddie's heart. Sometimes it was easy to forget how they were all connected, and she welcomed the reminder that family looked however it looked, as long as it was full of love.

Brady turned to her, and she appreciated the way he looked at her—as a friend, and even after all this time, an equal partner in parenting Kayla.

"As for Maddie," Brady added, "yeah, she came to our family in an unusual way, but without her, Kayla would not be part of this family, so we choose to love and accept her as our family. Whoever she chooses to add to the family, they become our family, too."

Brady had given her this speech a few times, but it still never failed to bring tears to Maddie's eyes. Though she never loved him in a romantic way, he and Josie provided an example of what she hoped for in finding love for herself. And, if Maddie were honest, she'd come to love Brady as a trusted brother and friend. Even though this was news to everyone else here, Maddie had called Brady and told him what was going on. Though he must have been feeling a wide variety of emotions now that Kayla's biological father was in the picture, Brady was handling the situation with the same kindness and ease he did everything.

Then Brady looked Luke in the eye. "You are Kayla's biological father, and therefore, you are family now, too. Sure, we have stuff to work out. But when she's not upset at having new information thrown at her, Kayla's a pretty good kid, and you'll enjoy getting to know her."

Josie tugged at Brady's hand. He looked down at her, grinned, then addressed the group. "And, since we have everyone together, and so we can take some pressure off Kayla, we might as well let you all know, we're expecting another baby."

As the room burst into excited chatter, Maddie felt the tension leave her body. Doing this as a family had been the right decision, because Brady had managed to make it easier on everyone.

Maddie turned to Luke. "Well, welcome to the family. Now come help me finish getting dinner on the table."

As they all made their way into the kitchen, Maddie noticed Brady pushing Kayla in Luke's direction. The poor guy looked overwhelmed and nervous as all get-out, but fortunately, Kayla noticed, too.

She held out a hand to Luke. "Hi," Kayla said. "I'm Kayla, and I'm kind of a jerk sometimes, but my dad says I'll eventually grow out of it. Mostly, though, I try to be nice."

Maddie laughed, and Josie put an arm around her. "It's going to be okay. He and Kayla will be friends in no time."

Maddie gave Josie a squeeze. "I hope so. Ida Mae thinks the world of him, so I have to trust that I didn't make a mistake in bringing him into Kayla's life. And look at you! Another baby! Congrats!"

Josie gave a weak smile. "Thanks. I have way more morning sickness this time, so I don't yet have the energy to be excited, but the doctor says everyone is healthy, so I can't ask for more."

"Healthy is all we care about," Maddie said, smiling.

"Did you say that he's Ida Mae's grandson?" Abigail asked, joining them. "I heard that he was back and creating a stir. I guess we're about to add to the pot."

Luke obviously overheard and hung his head, and Maddie felt bad for him. After today's mess at the senior center, and his comments about wanting to make up for past mistakes, he was probably feeling overwhelmed. At least that was something Maddie could relate to. She'd spent so much of her life being the outcast that she understood his pain.

Which put Maddie in an even more precarious position. This man was the father of her child, so she owed it to them all to have a good relationship with him. Given their similarities in having compassion for Granny, she could see where it would be easy to work with him as a co-parent. The trouble was, getting close to him could mean endangering the career she'd worked so hard for, if Briana had anything to say about it.

On one hand, it should be easy enough to choose family over career. On the other, why should she have to choose?

And yet, seeing the pain and regret on Luke's face told Maddie that this wasn't going to be an easy road.

"I forgot how fast gossip travels in small towns," Luke said. "For those who haven't heard, Briana had me arrested for breaking into Granny's house today."

Maddie knew that Briana was cold, but that seemed a bit too cold, even for her. "What happened?" she asked.

Everyone was looking at Luke, who shook his head slowly. "I went to the house to see what I could do to fix it up to get Granny home eventually, and Briana saw me there and called the cops to say someone was breaking into the house. Thankfully, Granny was able to corroborate that she'd given me the key, but they cuffed me and everything. I'm pretty sure Briana took photos to frame."

"She is so difficult," Abigail said sympathetically. "I'm sorry you went through that. Is everything okay now?"

Luke nodded. "Yes, and it makes me more determined to fix up the house so Granny can come home. No offense to the senior center, but it seems like they're doing everything they can to make sure I get as little time as possible with Granny."

He looked over at Maddie as he spoke, and Maddie wanted to crawl under the table. "I'm sorry," she said quietly. "Briana met with my boss, and she's determined to cause trouble for you. I don't know why she's so threatened by you. Your grandmother constantly talks about you and how much she loves you."

"Wait a second," Kayla said. "I love Ida Mae. Sometimes I go in there and she tries to teach me how to knit, but I'm terrible at it. That's so cool that she's actually my grandmother. I always thought it was neat that we had the same middle name. Now it's even more special."

"Great-grandmother," Luke corrected her. Then he turned his attention back to Maddie. "I had wondered where her name came from. I love that she has Granny's same middle name, even though it was unintentional."

Before Maddie answered, Kayla said, "Mom and Dad both liked the name Kayla, and Mae was for Mom's grandmother, Mae, who Mom said loved her the best of anyone in her family. I like that I'm named after both of my great-grandmothers, since they both have the same name."

And just like that, the ice between her daughter and Luke was finally broken. They started chattering about Ida Mae, and Kayla's excitement at being related to her, and it seemed like everything would be okay between them.

Though Maddie had a million reasons why it was a bad idea, she couldn't help thinking how attractive Luke was, smiling and talking animatedly with her daughter. That was the other reason Maddie had never dated much. Since she was born, Kayla was the most important thing to Maddie, and she'd never found a man who was willing to connect with her daughter the way Luke was doing now.

But even if Maddie was open to dating, Luke needed this time to focus on his relationship with Kayla, not start something with Maddie.

By the end of the evening, Maddie was feeling better about the situation. Her daughter knew the truth, had met her father, and aside from a few snarky comments, it had been mostly smooth sailing.

Maddie had offered to do the dishes so the

people with little ones could get them home and to bed, and so Luke and Kayla could have time together. As she was putting the last of the dishes away, Kayla came into the room.

"Luke is getting ready to leave, so I thought I'd let you know if you wanted to say goodbye."

Maddie wiped her hands on a dish towel. "Thanks. I hope you had a good chat with him."

Kayla shrugged. "He seems nice. But gross, that means I'm related to the Smiths. That's going to be fun when Drake finds out we're related."

Then she smiled. "Luke said he'd meet up with me after school tomorrow, and we can tell Granny together that we're related."

Just like that, the bubble of hope was burst. While telling Ida Mae about Kayla was the right thing to do, it also meant Briana would find out. Which meant that Maddie had until Kayla got out of school tomorrow to figure out a way to let this news be known without it destroying everything she'd ever worked for.

God, I know I've made a lot of mistakes, and I don't deserve the kindness I've been given. But please, help us get through this without me losing my job.

As far as prayers went, it wasn't the best or most elegant. But Maddie wasn't known for her wisdom and talent when it came to communicating with God. She could only hope that God could see how truly sorry she was for all the bad things she had done, and that she was desperately trying to make them right. Maybe God could give her a break here. Not just for her sake, but for Kayla's, Luke's, and even Ida Mae's.

LUKE FELT MORE confident the next day as he entered Granny's room. He'd called a lawyer about the situation in the senior center, and they'd told him that legally, Briana didn't have the right to exclude him from seeing Granny. The center could not prevent him from seeing her, either. Unless they had a legal reason for denying him access, or Granny did not want him there, blocking him from seeing her was against the law.

Granny was sitting in her favorite chair, knitting as she watched her favorite police show. However, when she heard Luke, she abruptly shut it off and turned to him, then laughed.

"Sorry, I thought you were Briana."

Luke laughed with her. "Why do you care about Briana's disapproval of your television shows? They make you happy."

The crestfallen look on Granny's face made Luke go over to her and take her hand.

"It's just easier to agree with her. She's always been a disagreeable person, and she and her family are the only family I have left."

Luke gave her hand a squeeze. "That isn't true anymore. I'm here for you, and this time, I'm not going anywhere."

As Granny smiled at him, Luke was once again relieved that he'd made the decision to come here. It also strengthened his resolve to fix up Granny's house so she could come home. She'd had a good, long life, and she deserved to spend all the days she had left enjoying it.

"You remind me so much of your father," she said. "The trouble with him was that he had a devotion to his country that his family couldn't compete with. I'm glad that you've seen the importance of family before it's too late."

Her words struck a chord he hadn't expected. He'd spent so much of his life trying to prove himself worthy of his father that it seemed funny to hear how much like him he was. He thought his actions had come out of devotion to his family, but now he could see that it was more of a devotion to his insecurity than anything else.

But that only made telling Granny that he

had a long-lost child more nerve-racking. Family was everything to her, so how was she going to react to being denied this for so long? His palms were sweating as he waited for Maddie and Kayla to arrive.

"What's going on?" Granny asked. "You're acting mighty suspicious."

He'd never been able to hide much from Granny, which was why it was funny he thought he'd gotten away with so much as a teenager. Maybe that was why it was important to him to make things right with her. She'd always been the one who had loved him unconditionally, even when he'd done stupid things.

He shook his head and chuckled to himself as he remembered the time he'd found her stash of cash she'd been saving. He'd planned on using it to take a bus to get out of there, but when he'd tried to sneak out in the middle of the night, Granny was sitting there in her chair, calmly knitting a blanket, and told him that if he needed more money, her purse was on the table.

He hadn't been able to go through with it. He'd come up with some lie he couldn't even remember now and gone back to his bedroom. The next chance he'd gotten, he'd returned all the money he'd taken. So now when she gave him the same look she'd given him that night, he wanted to tell her everything.

"I promise, Granny, it's good news. I just need a little more time to tell you, so please be patient."

Granny grinned. "I've still got it, don't I? I can still sniff out subterfuge."

He laughed. "You sure do."

Then she gave him a conspiratorial look. "Did you bring me any chocolate?"

Luke shook his head. "I'm not going to fall for that this time," he said. "I met with your dietitian to find out what you are and aren't allowed to have."

Granny scowled. "I knew I shouldn't have signed those forms to give you permission to look at my private stuff. It's bad enough I've got to be stuck in this place, but everyone's conspiring against me to not have any of the good things in life."

Luke tried not to laugh, and shook his head at her instead. "We're only doing this because we love you."

Granny snorted. "If you love me, then break me out of this prison."

Just then Maddie walked in, and Granny looked even more perturbed. "No offense to you. You're not that bad. You should bring that daughter of yours to come visit me."

Which was when Kayla entered the room. The scowl left Granny's face.

"Finally something good is happening today," Granny said.

Luke looked over at Maddie. "She's upset with me because I didn't bring her any chocolate. Now that I know what her dietary restrictions are, she's annoyed at me because I'm not breaking the rules."

He loved the way Maddie smiled at him, then at Granny. She was such a wonderful woman. He was really grateful that as the sins of his past caught up with him, she was the mother of his child.

"Ida Mae, I've told you that there are alternatives that taste just as good. I'll get you some tonight and bring them over to you tomorrow."

Granny scowled at her. "That stuff tastes like cow manure. All the fake sweeteners and all that supposedly healthy stuff tastes like garbage. What's wrong with a potato chip?"

Maddie gave her another gentle smile. "Even the low-sodium ones have too much salt. If you'd gone to our healthy snack class, you would have

seen the demonstration of how we can use a dehydrator and turn vegetables into a crunchy chip."

Luke tried not to laugh at the disgusted look
on Granny's face.

"No one is ever going to convince me that
kale is a delicious snack."

Maddie shrugged. "You might think so, but
when I make my kale chips, Kayla and all of her
friends eat them as soon as I get them out of my
dehydrator."

Granny looked over Kayla. "If you break me
out of this joint, I promise, we will have the biggest junk food feast of your life, and you'll see
what you've been missing out on."

Kayla shrugged. "I know it makes me a
weirdo, but I like my mom's healthy snacks.
I've never been into sweets, so as much as I hate
to say it, you're not getting any help from me."

While Granny was seemingly looking for a
new retort, Luke chose to take this as his opportunity to speak.

"Remember you said that you thought I was
hiding something from you?"

Granny glared at him. "Oh, I know what
you're doing. You're just distracting me from
finding out what Kayla's weakness is to use to

bribe her to bring me snacks." Then she grinned. "But I'll allow it. I do love a good secret."

Luke took a deep breath, then gestured at Kayla. "Granny, Kayla is my daughter."

Granny made a face and stared at him. "Oh, come on. I might be an old fool, but I wasn't born yesterday. Your attempt at a practical joke isn't going to trick me."

Maddie stepped forward and gave Kayla a little nudge in Granny's direction. "It's true," she said. "Kayla is Luke's daughter."

The shock on Granny's face was quickly replaced with curiosity, and maybe a touch of happiness. It always bothered her that Luke never married and had children and that Briana had only chosen to have one.

"Why didn't you tell me about this before?" Granny asked.

Maddie shrugged, then laughed. "Because I didn't know before. When I met Luke, he told me his name was Snake. We'd only met once before he disappeared."

Luke swallowed as he looked at Granny. He'd have to bring up that horrible night, but it was the right thing to do. So Granny understood they weren't deliberately keeping secrets from her.

"It was the night that I stole Briana's car and went to that party. I met Maddie, and, well, you know what happened after I got home. It wasn't like I could stay in touch with her."

Granny nodded thoughtfully. "I've never seen your father and grandfather so angry. And Briana's father. It wasn't even that great of a car."

Trust Granny to tell it like it was. Then she stared at Maddie. "How did you figure out Luke was the father?"

Maddie gestured at Luke's forearm. "His tattoo. He said he designed it himself. I knew it was unique. When I met him yesterday, I recognized it immediately."

Granny made a noise. "That ugly thing. I always said there was no reason for a person to mark up a perfectly good body like that."

Then she looked over Kayla. "But I suppose, since it has finally brought my great-granddaughter to me, that ugly thing wasn't so bad after all."

Then Granny held out her arms. "Now come here and give me some love. I've hugged you before, but it was before I knew we were family. So that means I've got a lot of hugging to make up for. I do hope you're a hugger."

Maddie leaned into him and whispered,

"Kayla is actually not a hugger, so the fact that she's hugging your grandmother right now is a really big deal."

Kayla must've heard her mother, because she looked up at her and said, "Yeah, so get used to it. I'll give her hugs instead of drugs in the form of sugar and junk food."

They all laughed at Kayla's pronouncement. He'd known that Granny would accept Kayla, but he'd been afraid that she might get really angry with him.

Once Kayla finished hugging Granny, Granny said, "So, that's it? That's what had you all nervous?"

Luke nodded. "I know I did a lot of things during that time of my life that I am not proud of, and I came here hoping I could make up for it, but it feels like I just keep being presented with more and more of my mistakes."

Granny gestured at Kayla. "I would never call this beautiful girl a mistake. While I would've liked to have been part of her life sooner, I've at least had the privilege of getting to know her over the years, and I couldn't be more thrilled to find out we're related."

Granny smiled at Kayla, then said, "Even if you are one of those health food weirdos."

Granny adjusted herself in her chair. "Now get me my cell phone. I need to call my lawyer and get him to change my will."

Luke glanced over at Maddie to see if she understood what a big deal this was. Granny hated her cell phone, and she also hated parting with her money. So for that to be Granny's first response after accepting Kayla, it truly did mean everything was going to be okay.

The frustration on Maddie's face was obvious, and Luke could understand why. He'd been dealing with Briana and her suspicions about him trying to take Granny's money, and it was offensive. He had plenty of money of his own. Even with his plans to fix up her house, he was going to use his money, not Granny's.

"That's very kind of you," Maddie said. "But please don't make any rash decisions. Kayla and I are fine, and we don't need anything from you, other than a relationship."

The sincerity in her voice brought even more comfort to Luke. She'd told him the same thing, yet he did feel like he needed to contribute to Kayla somehow. But that was a conversation for a later time.

"I have more money than I know what to do with," Granny said. "I can't take any of it with me to the grave, so why not give some of it to Kayla?"

The stubborn set to Granny's jaw told him that Granny was going to do this whether Maddie agreed or not.

Granny looked at Kayla. "What are your plans for college?"

Kayla shrugged. "I've gotten accepted to a few, so I'm applying for scholarships."

Granny looked over at Maddie. "What's in her college fund?"

The distressed look on Maddie's face made him feel bad for her. There likely wasn't a college fund, and when they had a private moment, he would make sure Maddie understood he would contribute his share. Actually, more than his share, because Maddie had supported their daughter her whole life. It was his turn to step up.

Before Maddie could answer, Kayla said, "My parents have worked hard their whole lives just to keep a roof over my head. That's why I'm applying for some scholarships. I've studied hard to get good grades and done all the things scholarship people look for in a worthy recipient."

Granny looked at Kayla, then at Maddie, then back to Kayla. "You keep me posted on those scholarships. When the time comes, I'll make sure you've got enough money to go where you want, because this is your future we're talking about."

"What are you saying?" Briana asked, bursting into the room. "Why would you give this child your money for college?"

Then she looked over at Maddie. "This is your doing, isn't it? That's the real reason your daughter has been coming here to interact with all the seniors. It's not to keep them company. It's to take their money."

"Now, wait just a minute," Luke said, feeling the heat in his face rising as he watched his daughter shrink back uncomfortably. "How dare you walk into the middle of the conversation and make wild accusations? I've barely met them, and I know they have more integrity than to do something like that."

Briana glared at him. "And yet here we are."

Maddie held out her hands. "Whoa. Let's get something straight. First of all, I have never asked anyone, least of all Ida Mae, for money for college or anything else. You just walked in on Ida Mae offering, too soon to hear me refuse, but here I am, refusing."

Maddie looked over at Ida Mae and gave her a

warm but firm smile. "That is very kind of you to think of Kayla, but I'm afraid we will have to turn down your generous offer. It wouldn't be appropriate."

Instead of appeasing Briana, she only glared at Maddie. "So you say. I'm going to be watching my grandmother's finances just to make sure you aren't getting anything."

Maddie looked distraught at her words, and Luke didn't blame her. After all, Maddie had never done or said anything to give any indication that she would do something like that, especially since she'd already been insistent that she didn't want anything from him financially, and he was Kayla's father.

Maddie squared her shoulders. "You are welcome to do so. You won't find anything wrong. In fact, because there are so many safeguards preventing employees of senior care facilities from accessing their residents' finances, there's a better chance of me embezzling from the federal government than accessing any of your grandmother's money. I don't want her money or anything else from her, other than her friendship."

Given that Luke wanted to wring his cousin's neck, he had to give Maddie double credit for being so kind to Briana. But again, rather than acting appeased about the situation, Briana marched over to the nurse call button and pressed it.

"What are you doing?" Maddie asked. "I'm right here. What do you need for your grandmother? I'll take care of it."

"I want the supervisor," Briana said. "It's very clear that you should not be anywhere near my grandmother, and even though I was assured yesterday that you would not be a problem, it's clear that you *are*. I told you to stay away and not to interfere, so now you will face the consequences."

The fear on Maddie's face made Luke wish he could do more for her. His cousin was a bully, always had been, and this wasn't right. He could tell by the way Kayla hovered close to her mother that this was upsetting for her as well. Unfortunately, since he barely knew his daughter, he wasn't sure how to reassure her.

One of the nursing assistants entered the room, appearing a bit frazzled. "What can I help you with?"

"Get the director," Briana said.

The aide looked over at Maddie, seeming confused.

"I know you're really busy," Maddie said,

"but Briana isn't going to be happy until Claire has been brought into the situation. Can you please get her?"

The aide nodded, giving Briana a terrified glance, and it occurred to Luke that Briana probably terrified all the staff here. Not just Maddie. He already talked to a lawyer to make sure that his rights were protected, but maybe it wouldn't be a bad idea to get some advice on making sure that Granny was also protected. Not that he thought Briana would do anything malicious to Granny, but he had to wonder if Granny was getting the best care from people if his cousin was constantly bullying the staff. One more reason for him to get her house ready for her as soon as possible.

Briana glared at Maddie. "That was brave of you, asking for your boss. You realize that you're going to be fired, right?"

Maddie looked defeated. Luke wished he had the kind of relationship with her that he could give her a hug and tell her it was going to be okay. He didn't even know that for sure, but he did know that Maddie had done nothing wrong, and it wasn't fair that his cousin was treating her like this.

Even though he hadn't discussed with Maddie or Kayla who else was going to know about their relationship, he said, "Stop this. There is a very good reason why Granny was offering money for Kayla's college."

Then he looked over Granny. "But it won't be necessary, not because I'm bothered by Briana's threats, but because she is my daughter, and I will be paying for it."

As petty as it was, he wished he'd had a video of Briana's gasp and stunned expression.

"That's not true," Briana said.

"It is true," Luke said. "Kayla is my daughter, conceived the night I went to that party and wrecked your car."

It was so worth it to see the shock on Briana's face. But she quickly recovered, then said, "Maddie has already lied about who fathered her baby, so she's probably lying to you, to get her hands on your money and Granny's. Maddie keeps telling everyone she's changed and she's a Christian and she's working to make up for all the bad things she's done. But here she is, lying about her child's father, yet again, to get money out of a helpless old woman."

"I'm not lying," Maddie said. "I know you have every reason not to believe me, but this is the truth. And if Kayla and Luke are in agreement, I am happy to have a paternity test done. I know who her father is, and it's Luke."

She looked like she was ready to cry, and Luke wanted to put his arms around her, but then her supervisor came into the room. "What's going on in here?"

Briana glared at Maddie. "I demand that you fire this woman," she said. "She's trying to take advantage of my grandmother by lying and saying that Kayla is Luke's daughter. I want her gone."

Claire appeared calm, then said, "Maddie, can you please explain?"

A tear rolled down Maddie's face. Then she crossed her arms over her chest and said, "I realize this is a strange situation, but after meeting Luke yesterday, I realized that he is Kayla's father. I didn't intend for it to come out this way, but it was important for Luke to let his grandmother know who Kayla was. I just want to tell the truth."

"And take all of Granny's money," Briana said.

"Stop!" Kayla said, tears running down her face. "Why won't you listen to my mom?"

Granny, who had been watching the whole scene with interest, grabbed her cane and pounded the table with it. "That's enough. Maddie says that Luke is Kayla's father, and based on the circumstances that are known to me, I believe her. Maddie did not ask for money. I offered."

Then Granny pointed her cane at Maddie. "And she refused, but it's my great-grandchild, and I'll do what I want."

A tender look crossed her face as she brought her gaze to Kayla. "I don't want you worrying about all this adult nonsense. You are my family, and I love you, and that is that."

Luke's heart felt lighter as his daughter wiped the tears from her face with her sleeve and nodded.

Maddie turned to Claire, looking anxious. "I promise, I did not ask for anything, and I will refuse anything that is offered. I don't want her money. I didn't tell Luke about Kayla because I wanted his money. I just want the truth to be known."

Claire nodded. "All right, then." She looked over at Granny. "I don't want to have to keep dealing with these scenes, and I'm doing the best I can in the situation. I understand that you have just received some interesting news. However, with your heart condition, it's also good for you to not get so excited. I'm going to have one of the nurses come in and make sure that you haven't suffered any ill effects from this newfound knowledge."

Then she turned her attention to Luke. "As I told you yesterday, your grandmother's health and safety is my primary concern. I know you want the best for her, but since you've come, there's been more excitement in her life than she needs. So you, me, Maddie, and Briana are going to have a little chat in my office, and we're going to figure out how to create the best environment for Ida Mae's healing."

Then she glanced at Kayla. "I know you're a regular visitor here, and everyone loves having you. But for today, I'd like you to go home while we figure out the situation."

Granny scowled. "Don't I get a say in all this?"

The director smiled at Granny. "Yes, you do. However, with the way everyone has been acting, and since I was called in here to deal with the situation, I need them all on the same page. Then you and I will talk about how to make this work for you."

Luke smiled at the director. Ultimately, he wanted what was best for Granny, and he appreciated that the director was going to be considering Granny's needs and desires.

"Good." Granny stared at the director. "Can we also discuss giving me some food with flavor?"

Everyone in the room except for Briana laughed.

"I can't change your diet," Claire said. "But I will talk to the dietitian about trying some new things with you that might make you feel better."

Then Claire looked at each of them. "But for now, I'm going to sit everyone down and we're going to figure out what's going on, and come up with a plan to move forward."

Even though he felt a lot like he was being called into the principal's office, Luke meekly followed her out of the room. He knew Granny was going to be okay, but after some of the things Briana said, Luke was now concerned about Maddie and her job.

CHAPTER FOUR

Maddie took a sip from the steaming coffee as she sat in her truck, waiting for Luke and Granny to arrive at the stables. Since finding out that she was related to Granny, Kayla had been to the nursing home to visit her father and great-grandmother every day. Now that Kayla and Granny knew about their relationship, both wanted to be more active in each other's lives.

Though Granny had seen Kayla ride countless times before at community events, she'd never done so with the knowledge that Kayla was her great-granddaughter. So today, Luke was bringing Granny out to watch her practice, after having obtained permission from Granny's doctors to allow her to leave. At this point, her stay at the senior center was largely due to safety concerns. While a home nurse could theoretically check in on Granny and she could be driven to and from her PT appointments, Granny's house still wasn't safe enough for her to stay in, even with Luke's help. Hopefully, soon, with the renovations he was doing, she could go home.

And then, they could put all the mess with Maddie's job behind them. Maddie took another sip of her coffee. She was exhausted from having to be at work all night, and had only had a couple hours' sleep before coming to the stables to watch Kayla ride.

In order to keep the peace, Maddie's shift had been changed to nights so that she would avoid any unpleasant encounters with Briana. It felt incredibly unfair having to move her life around like this. But as Claire reminded her, Maddie had to keep her eye on the prize and do what was necessary to get through the next couple of months as the board reviewed qualified candidates to take Claire's position.

Though Briana didn't have the legal right to control who did and didn't get to see Granny, Claire had suggested that it would be best for everyone involved, especially given the spotlight on Maddie, for Maddie to lay low for the time being. And, despite the fact that they all knew there had been no wrongdoing, Claire wanted to protect Maddie.

When Luke's black SUV pulled up, Maddie

stepped out of the truck and waved them over. As much as she had been trying to fight her attraction to Luke, she couldn't help noticing how good he looked today, wearing simple jeans and a T-shirt. Nothing special, but it was the way he held himself. Every day that passed since finding out that Kayla was his daughter, he stood a little taller and walked with more of a spring in his step. The way he went over to Granny's side of the car and helped her out and got her situated with her walker made Maddie's heart skip a beat. Even though she'd call him handsome, her attraction to him was more about him being kind.

In all her years at the senior center, Maddie hadn't met many doting grandsons who cared for their grandmothers the way Luke did. Briana might think that Luke had ulterior motives or was trying to get something out of Granny, but Maddie had run into a number of those people in her time, and there was no way she could believe that Luke was one of them.

"Dad!" Kayla came running out of the stables with a smile on her face. "Granny!"

Kayla hadn't started calling Luke "Dad" until she'd talked to Brady and made sure it wouldn't hurt his feelings. Brady would always be Kayla's dad, and now she had another one.

"Hey, kiddo," Luke said, holding out his arms and receiving a big hug from his daughter.

The crunch of boots on the gravel behind Maddie made her turn. Brady.

"Hey," she said.

He nodded at her. "Hey."

She couldn't read the expression on his face, but she could tell he was watching Kayla and Luke intently.

"You sure you're okay with this?" she asked.

Brady nodded. "From day one, we both said that we wanted the best for our daughter. I told you, even when the truth came out, I wasn't going back on that promise. From everything I can tell, Luke is a good man, and he loves her. Our daughter is quite blessed to have so many people in her life who care about her."

Once again, Maddie was thankful she had called off her wedding to Brady before they'd hurt each other even more. Having him as a friend was a huge blessing in her life that she thanked God for daily.

"How is Josie doing?" Maddie asked, changing the subject to give Brady some breathing room.

Brady shook his head. "Not feeling great, but Laura took Shana for the day so Josie could rest."

Maddie would've never imagined having such a deep love for the woman who had once been her childhood nemesis. But the concern on Brady's face also brought the same feeling to Maddie's heart.

"Let me know if there's anything I can do," Maddie said.

Brady nodded. "People have been bringing us meals and helping Josie with Shana, so we just need to wait for the morning sickness to pass." Then Brady chuckled. "Whoever called that morning sickness sure doesn't know how long the morning is supposed to last."

Maddie had always considered herself fortunate that she had a relatively easy pregnancy with Kayla. Her heart warmed as she remembered that was one of the questions Luke had been concerned about. Even though she'd had Brady, Luke had been very worried that he hadn't been there to help her during that time.

Just one more reason why Maddie couldn't help liking him.

Brady walked over to Luke and Granny. "Luke." He held his hand out to the other man, and Luke took it. Brady always made the extra effort to make Luke feel comfortable, and it made her happy to see the men getting along. They both understood that the most important person in this equation was Kayla, and no matter how many times Maddie saw this interaction, she would never cease to be grateful.

Maddie joined the group, greeting Luke and Granny. But when she gave Granny a hug, Granny seemed to cling a little tighter than usual.

"I've missed you," Granny said.

"I check in on you every night when I come to work," Maddie said.

Maddie's new shift didn't start until after visiting hours were over, and one of the aides always made sure that Briana's car wasn't in the parking lot.

"I know, I know," Granny said. "But I'm usually asleep by the time you're done with your report, so I never get to see you."

Maddie smiled. "I always leave you a little something so you know I've been by."

Maddie had talked to the dietitian, who'd found some sugar-free chocolate that Granny could have in moderation. It wasn't much, but every night, Maddie left one at Granny's bedside.

Granny gave half a smile. "Just to mess with

her, I told Briana those chocolates were from my boyfriend."

Luke laughed. "It has been pretty funny watching Briana try to figure out who Granny's boyfriend is and whether or not he's after her money."

Kayla laughed with them. "I even brought flowers one day, and we told her it was from her boyfriend."

Maddie laughed as she shook her head. "You shouldn't tell tales like that."

"And Briana shouldn't be causing so much trouble," Granny said. "I have a mind to take her out of my will if she doesn't start behaving."

"No," they all said together, then laughed.

Maddie looked at Granny. "Given that Briana is already afraid you're being taken advantage of financially, that would be a terrible thing to do."

Granny straightened. "And it would serve her right since she cares more about my money than my happiness." Then she smiled over at Luke and Kayla. "And it's been a long time since I've been this happy. Not since my Gerald died."

Her eyes got misty, as they always did when she talked about her late husband. Then she looked from Maddie to Luke and back at Maddie again. "You know, the greatest gift I've ever had in my life was the love of my Gerald. You two had something once, so maybe you should find out if there's still a spark."

Maddie tried not to groan. "No offense to Luke, but my romance days are over. I've made so many mistakes, and I'm not willing to make a mistake with Kayla's father. I wouldn't do anything to hurt our relationship."

Granny stared at her. "Well, it seems to me you've already gone and made one big mistake." Then her voice softened. "But you know, we shouldn't allow our mistakes to control us. We all have made mistakes. What matters is not the mistakes you make, but getting up and trying again. Don't give up on love just because it's never worked out for you."

Maddie had been given that advice before, and it wasn't that she disagreed, but given all her mistakes, sometimes she thought that it was her punishment for all the people she hurt in her life. Maybe she didn't deserve that kind of love.

Luke caught her eye, as if to say he understood what she meant and where she was coming from. "No offense taken," he said. "Granny, you know I love you, but I'm with Maddie on this one. My focus right now is building a relationship with my daughter, not trying to do a romantic reconciliation of my past. Like Maddie, I've made more than my share of mistakes, including how I treated her back then. Right now, what Maddie and I both need is to be friends so that we can learn how to be good co-parents to our daughter and not let all that other stuff interfere."

While Maddie was grateful to be on the same page as Luke, she felt a small pang of regret at his "just friends" comment. It wasn't that he was wrong, but a tiny part of her did wish for something more. When she said that she'd made so many mistakes dating, she had been telling the truth. But she hadn't met anyone with Luke's character, either.

"I need to go finish getting my horse ready," Kayla said. "You guys can sit in the stands and wait."

Then she grinned, smiling over at Granny before looking back at them. "Mom and Dad, you should sit together."

It was obvious what she was trying to do, and Brady, bless him, grinned. "That is such a great idea," he said. "I'm glad I don't need to be in the arena today. I get to watch. It will be nice sitting and talking to your mom about your riding."

Kayla scowled. "That's not who I meant, Dad,

and you know it. But maybe I need to come up with different nicknames for you guys so that when I say 'Dad,' you know which one of you I'm talking about."

With that, she turned and headed back toward where the horses were kept. Brady clapped Luke on the back. "I do need to go supervise, and I'd like to say that we raised her better than that. But the truth is that she is exactly what we raised her to be. A strong woman who knows her mind and isn't afraid to speak it. It can be annoying parenting her sometimes, but I think it will serve her well as she goes out into the world."

"I agree," Luke said. "So many kids I see these days act entitled, so I think the two of you have done a fine job turning our daughter into an exceptional young woman."

It was strange seeing the genuine way these men complemented each other. Although Maddie believed in the idea of confessing her sins and obtaining forgiveness, sometimes it was hard to reconcile that idea with the fact that she couldn't entirely regret her actions. Her sins had led to her daughter having these two great fathers. Maddie would have never been able to raise Kayla so well on her own, and it was weird living in that tension. The only thing she could cling to was God and the fact that things intended for harm could be used to glorify God. She had to believe that's what happened here.

Though Maddie wanted to sit as far away as possible from Luke just to spite her daughter, given that this was the first time Luke had gotten to see Kayla ride, Maddie wanted to be near him to explain everything. Or at least that's what she told herself. She would be lying if she said that she didn't breathe in Luke's cologne a little more deeply than was proper. She tried telling herself that it wasn't her fault he smelled like the air after a summer's rain.

When Kayla and the other riders entered the arena, Granny immediately pointed her out. "There she is," Granny said, sounding excited.

Granny's happiness made Maddie glad they had told her the truth as soon as possible. Granny's joy at seeing Kayla brought renewed attention and regret to Maddie that Granny had been denied this experience for so long.

Luke reached over and took Maddie's hand. "Don't do that to yourself," he said.

Maddie looked over at him. "What?"

He shrugged. "The regret. I know that look in your eyes. It's the same one that haunted me for so long and kept me from coming home. You can blame yourself all you want, but the truth is, we both made mistakes. And I haven't seen you hating on me the way you hate on yourself over it."

Wow. How did he know all that about her? She wanted to ask, but then she noticed that Granny was looking over at them with a twinkle in her eye, which meant she had seen him take her hand. Maddie quickly pulled her hand away and shoved her hands in her pockets.

"I saw that," Granny said. "You don't have to hide your feelings from me."

Luke glanced at Granny and rolled his eyes. "Stop. We've already told you that our focus is on Kayla, not each other. You keep up your antics, and I'm going to make you go to Drake's birthday party tomorrow by yourself."

The look of horror on Granny's face made Maddie laugh. "You wouldn't."

Though there was a twinkle in Luke's eyes, he said, "Oh, I would. Just think. You, stuck at Briana's house all day, all by yourself, with no one to protect you from her incessant nagging."

"At least there will be decent food," Granny grumbled as they all laughed.

Then Luke said, "Come on, you know I

wouldn't really do that to you. You asked me to go with you, and I said I would, so I am. I even got Drake a present."

Granny relaxed slightly, and Luke added, "I mean it, though. You stay out of my business. We do not want or need your help with our love life."

"Fine," Granny said. "But I'd like to point out that the two of you aren't getting any younger, and you're still young enough to give me more great-grandchildren, so hurry up."

Ouch. Granny was pushing the timeline on things, and the thought unsettled her. Something stirred within her as she imagined doing it all over again with Luke, raising their child together. Luke could experience all the things he missed with Kayla. But she quickly realized those thoughts were inappropriate.

Besides, jumping into something too soon was what had gotten her into this mess. If anything were to happen romantically for Maddie, it would take time, consideration, and careful thought. She'd have to be even more cautious with Luke, given that if anything happened between them and it didn't work out, the person who'd be the most hurt was Kayla.

But as Luke adjusted the collar on Granny's

coat and she saw the tender way they looked at each other, Maddie was reminded that if she were to pursue a romantic relationship, Luke was the kind of man she would want to date.

WHAT HAD GRANNY been thinking, making such an insensitive comment about babies? Luke could see the uncomfortable look on Maddie's face, just as he noticed all the ways she'd reacted to everything else today.

He tried keeping his eyes on his daughter as she was riding around the edge of the arena, but it was hard to pay attention when his thoughts kept drifting to Maddie.

"They're just warming up the horses right now," Maddie said, leaning over him and toward Granny.

The brush of her sleeve against his was accidental, but it reminded him of how briefly he held her hand, and that he liked her touch. He thought he'd given her some comfort, too, at least until Granny ruined it.

But how was he supposed to fault her? He knew that all of Granny's remarks came from a place of love. She wanted to see them both happy, and even before Luke and Maddie had officially met, Granny had long been telling him about the nice woman in the senior center that she thought would be a good match for him. He now knew she'd been talking about Maddie. He'd always shrugged off her suggestion, but obviously, Granny knew something they didn't.

Kayla rode over to the edge of the arena. "I'm going to be leading today," she said, a wide grin on her face.

"That's great," Maddie said. "It'll be easy for everyone to spot you."

Maddie gave a wave, and then Kayla turned and rode off, lining up her horse with the other horses in the arena.

Maddie turned to them. "What Kayla is doing today is called a drill. Basically, they ride the horses in different formations to make patterns in time with the music. It's quite beautiful to watch, but it requires a lot of talent and precision on the part of the riders to make sure that everyone is in the right place in the arena at the right time, or someone could get seriously hurt."

Granny snorted. "It's not as if I haven't been watching drills for most of my life. I know what she's doing. And it's great that she gets to lead."

Maddie laughed. "I know, but I wasn't sure what Luke knew."

Luke turned to Maddie and smiled, appreciative that she took the time to include him. "Not much," he admitted. "I can ride, and I love being around horses, but this is a foreign world to me."

When he was a kid, summers with Briana here had been some of his favorite times. He was a city boy, and the country life was completely new and different to him. Sometimes he wished he could travel back to that one summer and make things right between Maddie and him, as well as fix Briana's view of him. But like he'd said to Maddie, there was no sense dwelling on what could have been. They had to accept the situation they were in now and make the most of it going forward.

Trying to ignore the warmth of the woman next to him, Luke focused his attention on the arena, where they had begun the drill.

After a few minutes, Granny clapped her hands, then gestured. "They're setting themselves up for a pass-through, aren't they?"

He glanced at Maddie to see the smile on her face. "They sure are. It's one of my favorite maneuvers." She pointed at the arena and said to Luke, "Horses don't naturally like to charge toward one another, so it takes a lot of skill and talent to get the horses to run toward each other and sustain momentum as they pass. It also requires a great deal of precision in their spacing so that no one crashes into each other."

Luke held his breath as he watched his daughter and her horse charge in their group toward another group of riders and horses. Sure enough, they passed right through each other, ending up on the other side.

"That was spectacular," Luke said. "My heart skipped a beat there for a second. You must be a nervous wreck watching her sometimes."

Even though Granny's scrutiny earlier had made them uncomfortable, Maddie took his hand and gave it a squeeze before letting it go. "And to think you haven't seen her ride trick. I'm pretty sure every single one of these premature grays on my head is from her."

A soft smile filled her face, and it was hard not to remark on how beautiful she looked in that moment.

"But just look at her. Look at that grin. Kayla loves what she's doing, and even though I get nervous, having done it myself, I know that she's got the necessary skills, as well as instructors who are focused on her safety at all times."

He'd forgotten that Maddie had been a trick rider herself. "That's right," he said. "I remember you talking about that the night we met. You were so mad about someone named Junior taking your spot."

Maddie groaned. "Thanks for that reminder. I was such a mess back then. I hated Junior because I thought she had everything handed to her, and she was taking what I deserved."

A dark look crossed Maddie's face, and Luke wanted to reach out to her again as she wrestled with one more regret from her past.

"Junior goes by Josie now," Maddie continued. "You might remember her as Brady's wife. I did a lot of horrible things, but thankfully, God gave us another chance, and now she is one of my dearest friends."

Luke nodded slowly, realizing just what an amazing environment Kayla had grown up in. He was glad his daughter had been raised with such love and Christlike examples. He knew that if he said that to Maddie, she would argue with him, but what he was learning about the love of God was that no one was perfect all the time, but was loved just the same. And that love was what helped other people to emulate that same behavior. Even though they wanted to be like God, they couldn't do it right all the time, and that was okay.

Instead, he said, "Yeah, well, just remember, I wasn't much of a prince then either. But I was just thinking how grateful I am that God can still redeem us for mistakes. It's really neat that you and Josie were able to become friends."

He was rewarded with another beautiful smile. "Funny, I had the same train of thought earlier. In spite of everything I've done wrong, God has chosen to bless us richly."

"Maybe someday we can find that kind of forgiveness with Briana," Luke said.

"That harpy?" Granny asked. "She's always been a spoiled petulant child."

Luke shook his head. "That's not true. She was one of my best friends when we were kids. I had so much fun the summers I came out to visit. Earlier, I was thinking how much I wished we could somehow regain that relationship."

Granny snorted. "That was before she discovered popularity and all that nonsense. These days, all Briana cares about is what other people think. Her house has to be perfect, she has to drive the nicest car, go to the salon all the time, and everything else she thinks will make people notice her. I find it nauseating. She wasn't raised that way."

A weird pang of sympathy hit Luke's heart.

"Does it matter? Granted, I've just recently come back to Christ and the church, but Jesus loves her, too."

Even with the horses going at full speed in front of them, Granny's indrawn breath could clearly be heard.

"I suppose you're right," she said. "I haven't been much of a Christian to her lately because she's been so annoying."

Luke looked at Granny's hand and gave it the same comforting squeeze he'd given Maddie. "We both know that the Bible doesn't say love one another except for when the other person is being annoying. I also know it's hard, and I haven't done a very good job either, so why don't we all just resolve to do better? Sure, we won't be perfect, but we should at least try."

The tears forming in Granny's eyes made it hard for Luke to get those last words out. "God surely did give me the greatest gift when we brought you home," she said.

If he spoke now, he was liable to say something stupid, mostly because his head was filled with so many regrets and wishes for having done better, despite all of his earlier thoughts that it was pointless to do so. Instead, he sat in silence with the others as they continued watching Kayla ride the drill.

He had to agree with Maddie. Their daughter was magnificent. Her wide smile and bright eyes told him that she was in her happy place.

When the ride was over, Luke started to help Granny out of her seat, but she was already pushing him away, and in doing so, she started to lose her balance. He grabbed her by the wrist to keep her from falling all the way down, but she still banged her knee on the side of the bleachers.

"Granny, are you okay?" Maddie asked.

"Get your paws off me," Granny said. "I'm fine. I just stumbled a bit, and suddenly everyone's acting like the world is ending."

"It's only because we care," Luke said. "Besides, if you want to be home again, the last thing we need is for you to fall and break your hip even worse."

He got her walker situated and set it in front of her. "Now, no complaints about the walker this time, you hear?"

Granny mumbled something under her breath that he couldn't hear, but he knew she was frustrated that he was right. They made their way out of the stands, and Maddie directed them through a large lobby and into another area where the horses were kept.

"Kayla will be a few minutes getting her horse unsaddled, so I thought I would show you around. I know Granny is already familiar with everything, but Luke might want to see where Kayla spends most of her time."

Walking through the stables, Luke was reminded of visiting his grandparents as a child. Obviously, it was nothing elaborate like Shepherd's Creek, but the smell of hay and animals brought him back. Granny paused at one of the stalls.

"That looks just like Caramello, the first horse your grandfather bought me," Granny said.

Maddie paused at the stall and turned to them. "That's Stolley Bear, and if I remember correctly, Shepherd's Creek bought a bunch of horses from you and your husband back when you were breeding. It's possible he might come from that stock."

Granny's eyes filled with tears, and her voice quivered as she said, "Wouldn't that be something? You sell off your horses, but you never know what ends up happening to them. I'm pretty sure Gerald did sell some to Big Joe, but like you, I would have to look at the records to be sure."

Even though she wasn't close enough to touch Stolley Bear, Granny reached her hand toward him.

Maddie held her arm out to Granny. "Let me move you closer so you can pet him. He's one of the sweetest horses you'll ever meet."

Luke watched with gratitude as Maddie helped Granny get closer to the horse. Stolley Bear lowered his head as if he knew Granny wanted to pet him, and Granny gently stroked the horse's nose.

The simple gesture made his grandmother so happy, and Luke loved the way Maddie gave such care and attention to Granny, helping her with the horse, and also giving her a steadying hand that didn't seem to bother Granny. The rich brown of the horse did indeed look like caramel.

Granny sighed a couple of times, saying, "Ah, Caramello."

He didn't know how long she stood there, petting the horse. The look of gratitude he gave Maddie was a silent acknowledgment that he appreciated she wasn't rushing them through or pushing them to the next activity.

He had intentionally kept the day free so they could all do whatever they wanted.

Before long, Kayla came bounding over. "What did you think of my ride?" she asked.

Granny never took her eyes off Stolley Bear but said, "It was wonderful. Did you know that this horse looks just like a horse I once had, Caramello?"

Just like her mother, Kayla smiled indulgently. "Oh, that's great. Maybe you could find a picture of her or something, and we can compare."

Granny nodded. "As soon as I get out of that death trap they have me locked up in."

Maddie shook her head. "It's not a death trap. The senior center has one of the highest quality and safety ratings in the state. It's so highly rated that we have people from all over trying to get in."

Granny turned and scowled at Maddie. "They can have my spot. Why can't I just go home when I have Luke able to stay there and take care of me?"

Luke watched the exasperated expression flit across Maddie's face before she smiled and said, "We've already been through this. Your doctor hasn't cleared you to do so. But keep working on your physical therapy exercises and following all of your other instructions, and I promise, you'll be home before you know it."

He appreciated that she didn't mention he hadn't completed the necessary renovations to Granny's house. It seemed like every simple project had turned into a bigger project. When he peeled back the carpet to fix one broken step, he'd realized the entire staircase needed replacing.

As frustrating as it was for Granny to have to wait, he wanted her house to be safe so she wouldn't have any more falls or other injuries that would prevent her from living at home permanently.

Maddie held her hand out to Granny. "How about we go get some lunch now, and we'll walk by Brady's office and see if he can look up any information on Stolley Bear's parentage?"

Though Granny looked reluctant, she nodded. "As long as you're not going to make me eat that health garbage."

Maddie laughed. "Actually, since you're missing pizza day at the senior center, I was thinking we could go out for pizza."

Granny's eyes widened. "Pizza? Like from Giorgio's?"

Maddie grinned. "Is there any other pizza place in town?"

"Mom and I always go to Giorgio's on Saturdays for lunch. It's our thing," Kayla said, smiling at her mom.

Luke didn't know why, but tears stung the back of his eyes at the thought. He was being included in their family traditions. Sure, they had made it clear that he was part of the family, but something about being included in their routine solidified his place with them. As they walked back to the stables, Granny kept turning backward to look at Stolley Bear.

"On your next visit, we can allow for some extra time for you to get to know him better," Kayla offered. "And even help you ride him. Stolley Bear is gentle enough that we often use him for some of the other seniors as well as small children and people with disabilities."

While Granny's face lit up, Maddie shook her head. "That won't be for a while. We need to check with her doctor to make sure she is healed properly and he thinks it's safe. They're working hard to get Granny off her walker, so maybe we can use this as incentive for her to actually do her physical therapy exercises instead of spending half of her session complaining at her therapist."

Granny scowled, but then she said, "Really? You'll let me ride?"

Maddie nodded. "You know I am a big believer in people being as active as they can be. It's what keeps us young, healthy, and vibrant. But like I said, we need your doctor's approval first. Where you're at in your physical therapy, he is not going to give it. So, do we have a deal? Are you going to give your all in physical therapy so that you can get well enough to ride the horse?"

Even though Luke felt like they'd been having the conversation over and over about Granny's desire to go home, the expression on her face told him that this might just be the ticket. He loved the way Maddie was always creative about how she dealt with Granny. So many times, he saw how Briana just forced issues and bossed Granny around. Then Granny would get cranky because she didn't like having someone tell her what to do.

Once again, Luke was grateful that Granny had Maddie in her life. Even though Maddie had been moved to the night shift, when Luke visited Granny during the day, he noticed how so many of Granny's friends often threw something about what Maddie said or did into the conversation. She was well-loved by the residents, and Luke could see why.

Moments like these made it hard for Luke

to resist Granny's matchmaking efforts. Maddie was everything he could want in a woman, and more, but not only had she made it clear she wasn't interested in being anything more than friends, she was right to say so.

CHAPTER FIVE

HAVING TO COME in early for her Sunday evening shift was never a good sign, especially if it was her boss texting her to report directly to her office when she got there. When Maddie showed up in Claire's office, Claire looked like she wanted to rip her hair out, except that Briana was standing next to her, fuming, and Luke looked about ready to cry.

"What's going on here?" Maddie asked.

"I want you fired, that's what's going on," Briana said. "And I'm filing charges of elder abuse against Luke. The police are on their way."

Looking exasperated, Claire said, "The police are not on their way. The doctor is examining Ida Mae now, and the social worker is there as well. They will decide whether or not the police are necessary."

Instead of being happy that Granny was getting the best of care, the bright red shade of

Briana's face only intensified. "She'll just lie to protect them. Granny is so happy to have Luke home and a so-called new granddaughter that she's going to lie to hide the truth. She's always wanted more great-grandchildren, so she's going to do whatever it takes to not risk it. I'm still not convinced that Kayla is Luke's."

Luke glared at his cousin. "I have all the proof I need, but just so people like you will shut up, we took a paternity test, and the results are being processed. But regardless, it's none of your business, so you need to let it go."

"I'm not letting it go," Briana said. "You are taking advantage of an old woman, and I won't allow it to happen."

Because Maddie knew she was already on thin ice, she remained silent at the cousins' bickering choosing to take a wait and see approach, since she'd find out the details soon enough. She wanted to tell Briana that it was ridiculous the way she was standing in the way of an old woman's happiness, and if she really wanted what was best for Granny, she would do what she could to be a partner in the situation and not an adversary.

"That's part of why the social worker is there," Claire said. "Given that we have two family members fighting over the situation with Ida Mae, Eva will not only check on these abuse allegations, but she will also be looking out for Ida Mae to make sure that her best interests are being taken care of. I know both of you are coming from a place of caring about Ida Mae, but since you can't agree, Eva will be a neutral party to make sure that we are serving Ida Mae's best interests."

Even though having to bring in a social worker meant paperwork and hassle, in this case, Maddie was grateful they had the option. While Maddie was certain that Eva wouldn't find any evidence of abuse, it would be reassuring to all parties to know that Granny was getting the best care possible.

"And what about Maddie?" Briana demanded. "I gave specific instructions that she was to have no contact with Granny, and yet that direction was ignored."

Claire pressed her fingers to her temples. Maddie felt sorry for the woman, who had been brought in on her day off to deal with this nonsense.

"As I have explained to you, Maddie is a trusted employee who has done nothing wrong. Given that we're in a small town where everyone knows each other, there's no way we can dictate who talks to who outside of the center. I can't dictate what Maddie does during her time off. Luke took your grandmother on an outing as approved by her doctor, and I have no control over whether or not they see Maddie there."

While Claire had explained all this before, it still felt to Maddie like she was being punished. But as Claire had privately told Maddie, they needed to do whatever they could to keep negative attention off Maddie while they were searching for Claire's replacement.

"You still haven't addressed Maddie's involvement," Briana screeched. "Is she responsible for those bruises that I saw on Granny? I have a hard time believing that Granny simply stumbled."

Bruises? Maddie looked at Luke and then over at Claire. "What's this about Granny having bruises? Clearly, I'm missing something."

Claire's face remained stoic. "Earlier today at her son's birthday party, Briana noticed that Ida Mae had a limp and some bruising on her arm. Though Ida Mae said it was an accident that happened while at Shepherd's Creek Stables, we are doing our due diligence to make sure."

At first, Maddie was confused, because there had been no accident. Then she remembered.

"Wait, you mean when she had a hard time getting out of her seat in the stands? I was there. She started to fall, and Luke tried to help her, but she didn't want help."

Claire looked at her notes and wrote something down. "That's what I have been told," Claire said. "But that's also why we have Ida Mae alone with the doctor and the social worker, to make sure."

By the tension in Claire's voice, Maddie knew Claire thought this whole thing was ridiculous. But because they took every accusation of elder abuse seriously, they would have to do a full investigation. It hadn't occurred to Maddie that Granny would have any bruising or even a limp afterward, but she'd forgotten how delicate the elderly woman's skin could be, so it was possible that there might be some bruising.

"I'm sure they got together and concocted a story," Briana said.

"And as I told you," Claire said, "our doctors and social workers are trained to look for signs of abuse as well as signs that the abused party is lying to protect their abuser. I realize that this is new to you, but our team is very experienced in investigating elder abuse. Please let everyone do their jobs, and I promise, everything will be done to make sure that Ida Mae is safe. Her needs are the most important thing here."

Were Maddie not under suspicion, she would go and grab some chocolate out of the hidden stash in her desk to make Claire feel better. But Briana would likely use it against her in some way. Briana wasn't the first overbearing family member that Maddie had to deal with, far from it. But it had never hit home so personally before.

A knock sounded at the door, and Dr. Reynolds came in. "I've finished examining Ida Mae, and everything's fine. The bruise looks much worse than it actually is. She's limping because she's been neglecting her physical therapy exercises, and she overexerted herself. She just needs to stay on top of her physical therapy, regain her strength, and I'm fully convinced that she'll be running laps around us in no time."

Briana looked over at the doctor, a disdainful expression on her face. "But you admit they pushed her beyond her limits. I think we need some very strong boundaries about Granny's physical limitations, and they shouldn't be taking her to such an unsafe place as horse stables."

The doctor gave her a firm but compassionate look. "I disagree," he said. "The only reason I said Ida Mae overexerted herself is that she hasn't been doing her exercises. The truth is, someone in her stage of recovery should be able to participate in all of that without feeling adverse effects. I'm hoping this is the wake-up call she needs to realize that her exercises are for her own good."

Then he looked over at Luke. "As for taking her to the stables, I think it's good for her to be out in the fresh air. She loves animals, and this is a great way to get her interacting with them. More importantly, it's a reminder of the life she misses, and motivation to get her on the road to recovery. Most of what's wrong with your grandmother isn't about her injury, but about her attitude and motivation to get well. I think you might've hit on just the thing she needs."

"But she got hurt," Briana said.

Dr. Reynolds shrugged. "When you have a small child, do you keep them from playing on the playground because of a skinned knee? That's really what we're talking about here, or at least the same principle. While I would like for Luke to talk to her physical therapist about additional ways to help Ida Mae, both in keeping her safe and helping her push her limits in safe ways, I think more outings just like this are exactly what she needs."

Though in many ways, this was a victory for Luke, he still looked dejected. Maddie wished she could give him a hug or even squeeze his hand or something. That was the trouble with having such blurred lines between personal and professional life. Anything she did that seemed to be in support of Luke, especially in front of Briana, would only set Briana off and give credence to her accusations of bias. As it was, not only was Maddie's job on thin ice, but everything she had worked for professionally was so close to falling apart.

"Thank you, Dr. Reynolds," Claire said. "I believe you've put all of our minds at ease."

The doctor nodded. "Of course. As I said, I hope this motivates her to take her recovery seriously."

Claire made another note in her file, then looked up at them. "You both can go see Ida Mae now," she said. "The social worker will be in touch with each of you to set up an appointment to talk about your individual concerns. You'll both have a chance to speak with her, and the social worker will investigate."

"And what about Maddie?" Briana asked.

Claire closed her file and stood up. "We have zero evidence that Maddie has done anything wrong. Though we did switch her shift to accommodate you, you have to remember that your grandmother is not our only patient. There will be times when Maddie is needed to take care of her, and I have full confidence in her ability to do so."

Then Claire looked over at Luke. "If Luke wishes to interact with Maddie outside of the nursing home while your grandmother is present, there is nothing wrong with that. Unless you have real evidence, I will no longer entertain your complaints against one of my best employees."

Tears welled up in Maddie's eyes at Claire's defense. All this time, she'd been afraid of losing her job, but it was clear that Claire firmly had her back.

"Fine," Briana said. "But I will be watching. There is nothing more important to me than my grandmother's safety and health. So do not think that you can lull me into complacency simply because you can't do your job."

Without waiting for a response, Briana got up and walked out of the office. Luke remained seated, still looking worried.

"Give it to me straight," he said quietly. "I love Granny, and I truly do want what's best for her. How do I handle this and protect my grandmother?"

It was the right question to ask. Judging from the sympathetic look on Claire's face, she thought so, too. "Just keep doing what you're doing. I know Briana is upset, but Ida Mae is happier and making progress, so I have to believe that you are having a positive effect. Of course, the social worker will make the final decision, but as long as you are following the instructions of her doctors and caregivers, you are doing all the right things."

Luke nodded slowly. "Okay," he said. "But please know, I'm willing to do whatever it takes to help my grandmother."

Maddie wished she could reach out to him and tell him how much she admired him. Although Claire had stuck up for her, Maddie still needed to be careful about what she said and did at the Senior Center.

When Luke left, Maddie turned to Claire. "What are we supposed to do about Briana? I'm trying to do the right thing, but it's hard when she wants to have me fired."

Claire shook her head. "Honestly, I don't

know. This is all new territory for me. I believe in you and your integrity, and I know that everything Briana is saying is false. But as the director of the center, you know I have to do my due diligence."

Maddie nodded. "I know. It just seems so unfair, the way Briana is attacking us, and no one's done anything wrong."

Claire nodded. "I agree. But we promised our residents that we would do our best for them, so here we are. Honestly, I'm glad that Briana made an official allegation of abuse because that means the social worker who has been brought in will do a thorough investigation, clearing both you and Luke of all wrongdoing. Once that happens, she can't complain anymore. And hopefully, then Ida Mae will return to her own house, and we can all get back to business. Briana won't like it, but I think Ida Mae will be happier, and it will be easier on everyone."

As Maddie turned to leave, Claire added, "That said, we do need to talk about your involvement with Luke."

Maddie froze with her hand on the doorknob.

"What do you mean?"

A compassionate look filled Claire's face. "I know you two share a child, so you have to interact. But a person would have to be blind to miss the fact that you and Luke have chemistry. There's nothing in the employee handbook prohibiting a romance between the two of you, but I'm thinking of the optics here. Briana has a big mouth, and while I can disprove her allegations about Ida Mae, don't give her a reason to start rumors about you and Luke."

Closing her eyes briefly, Maddie took a deep breath. "We're just friends."

"With chemistry," Claire said. "Look, I'm on your side, and personally, I would be thrilled for you to finally meet Mr. Right. But Briana is out to get you, and if she can't get you fired for mistreating Ida Mae, she'll find some other way to hurt you."

Maddie hated that Claire was right. Not about the chemistry part, though. "Like I said, we're just friends."

"Fine." Claire gave her an exasperated look. "Just watch your back. And don't do anything with Luke that she can twist into making you look bad."

Well, it was too late for that, since Maddie had already had a child with him, but she got Claire's point.

"Okay," Maddie said. "Message received."

Claire sighed. "I didn't mean it like that. I know I'm your boss, but I'm speaking as a friend who wants to see you succeed. You've worked so hard to get where you're at. I don't want someone like Briana ruining it for you. In a few months, this will all be over, and then you and Luke can pursue whatever it is between you."

Even though Maddie knew Claire was trying to encourage her, it didn't help to have one more person pointing out things between her and Luke. "Luke and I are clear on the fact that we're just friends. We won't be pursuing anything, now, or in a few months."

Though Maddie spoke with conviction, her heart hurt at the words. Claire was right that Maddie had worked hard to get where she was at, not just with her career, but in being seen as a respectable part of society after everything she'd been through. If her reputation could be ruined so easily by Briana's accusations, then had Maddie really accomplished anything?

"Thanks for the support," Maddie said, opening the door. "I'll do my best to make sure I'm not upsetting Briana in any way."

And make sure people stopped talking about Maddie and Luke. Since Maddie hadn't done anything wrong in her interaction with him, there was only one solution: to avoid him as much as possible.

LUKE WATCHED WITH pride as Granny took a few steps without her walker in her physical therapy session. Ever since their visit to the stables a couple weeks ago, Granny had become more determined to take her physical therapy seriously and was focused on going home. Even though the social worker had said it wasn't necessary, Luke was doing everything in his power to ensure that he was an active participant in Granny's care and that everyone knew he was there for her. There was nothing more important in his life than taking care of Granny and helping her come home.

His phone beeped with an incoming text message, and when he opened it, Luke smiled. Kayla was the other reason he was doing everything he could for his family. He would have never imagined just how much becoming a father would mean to him, and he was so grateful for this chance to be in her life. Kayla had made arrangements for an extra practice today, and wanted to know if he and Granny could come along. That was more than he had expected: just how much his daughter and the rest of her family wanted him to be part of her life.

When Granny and her physical therapist stopped for a brief rest, Luke asked, "Kayla invited us to go see her ride again today. Do you want to go?"

They'd been back to the stables a few times now, so he knew Granny would be excited at the opportunity. For him, that was an even bigger joy: seeing Granny so happy. As much as he had hated the feeling of letting her down by not accepting responsibility for his actions all those years ago, it was clear that Granny was taking this in stride. If you asked him, Kayla was also a huge reason for all the progress Granny was making.

"Of course I do," Granny said. "One of these days, I'm going to get back on a horse."

The physical therapist chuckled as she shook her head. "Keep up with your exercises, and I think you'll be able to do it eventually."

Luke had seen a lot of beautiful things in his time, but the way Granny's face lit up at the physical therapist's encouragement had to be one of the most dazzling sights he'd ever seen. Back in the day, his grandmother had been one of the beauties of the area, and when she smiled like that, he could see why. Sometimes he thought he saw a bit of Granny in his daughter, and he liked the idea of having been able to pass down something so remarkable.

He responded to Kayla's text, then observed as Granny finished up her routine. After which, Luke escorted his grandmother back to her room to get ready for the outing. Before they left, he paused at the nurses' station to give them an update on the plan. Even though he knew it wasn't yet time for Maddie's shift, Luke glanced around wistfully, hoping to get a glimpse of her. Sometimes she came in early for meetings, and even though she'd told him that for professional reasons, she had to keep her distance from both him and Granny at the senior center, he couldn't help looking.

"She's got the night off," the nurse at the station said.

"Who?" he asked, trying to sound innocent. Maddie had asked him to not add fuel to the fire when it came to people's interest in their relationship, so hopefully this would throw them off the scent. It seemed like everywhere he went, Briana had spies, and the last thing he needed was for someone to gossip about him to her.

The nurse grinned. "We're not blind, you

know. You like Maddie. She likes you. It's really a shame that Briana is so difficult."

Luke didn't want to agree with her, just in case. "It's not like that," he said. "We share a child, so of course we care about each other. We want the best for our daughter."

The nurse nodded. "You can say that, but it's obvious to everyone. Mark my words, this time next year, you two will be married."

Before he could answer, the nurse walked over to the board where they kept notes about their patients and made a note about Granny leaving with him. Maddie had told them that they usually didn't make such a big deal of all of this, but with Briana's accusations, they over-documented everything, just in case.

He'd get to see Maddie without the prying eyes of the staff, and his steps felt a little lighter as he headed back to make sure that Granny was ready to go.

When he got to Granny's room, Briana was sitting in Briana's usual spot.

"Granny says you're taking her to the stables again," Briana said.

Luke pasted a smile on his face. "Yes. We go to all of Kayla's practices. We've both missed out on so much of her life that we don't want to miss a second more."

Briana glared at him. "My son has a band concert tonight."

Right. If it wasn't concern over Granny's health, it was some way that he was interfering with Briana's family.

"I know," he said. "I have it all planned out. We're going to watch Kayla ride, grab a quick dinner, and then we'll be at the school in time for the concert."

His reassuring words didn't erase the scowl off Briana's face. "You know Granny can't have fast food. I hope you don't make a habit of this."

"It's a good thing I have a healthy soup in the crockpot," he said, grinning. "I agree on fast food. I never liked it much. As soon as I learned about Granny's special diet, I got a list of recipes from the dietitian so I can make foods she can eat."

Briana looked down her nose at him. "You cook?"

Luke laughed as he patted his belly. "Do I look like I spent my life starving to death? I enjoy cooking, and it's always given me comfort, no matter where I am. When I remember the slop the military gave me to eat, it makes me all the more thankful that I can cook."

"And he's a good cook, too," Granny said.

"Unlike in this place, healthy doesn't taste 0like garbage."

He shook his head at Granny. "I told you, it's all in the seasoning. They can't use these spices in the food here because there are too many dietary restrictions. But at home, we can add as many spices that are on the list as we like."

Briana still scowled, but he gestured at the little jar on Granny's dresser. "Hasn't the food here been better since I gave you your own set of spices to add to the food?"

He looked over at Briana and smiled, hoping to soften her a bit. "I really have to give you credit for doing such a good job taking care of her when she's so cranky. I know Granny isn't used to so many different spices, and she's turned up her nose at some of the names of things, but it's been really interesting to see how she has taken to the variety of new flavors."

Granny turned her attention to Briana. "I've even been eating that turmeric stuff that you told me was so good. I never liked the look or the sound of it, but Luke put it in some of my food, and I have to admit, it improved the flavor."

For once, Briana didn't look angry. She actually looked, dare he say, interested.

"Really? What did you make her?"

"It was one of those chicken recipes from the dietitian. I could see why Granny thinks the food is boring. If you add spices, turmeric being one of the primary ones, it can really enhance the flavor. If you like, I'll write it down for you."

Briana smiled. "That would be nice, thank you. Turmeric is one of my favorite spices."

Could his relationship with Briana finally be turning a corner?

This was the longest civil conversation he had had with Briana since coming back, and he saw a softness in her that made him realize how human she was. Maybe instead of fighting with her constantly, they could find ways like this to get along.

Granny banged her walker on the floor. "Can we finish playing Susie Homemaker and get on the road? I'd like to get to Kayla's ride early so I can get a good seat."

Luke grinned. Granny always said that, and she always sat in the same place. In all the times they had gone to the stables, no one was ever in that seat. But, getting there early meant he might have a few minutes to talk to Maddie.

They said goodbye to Briana and then headed out to the stables.

It was a beautiful spring day, and the sun was shining. The weather was warm enough that instead of wearing her sweater, Granny had put it in the little pouch in her walker. Some of the horses were out grazing, and a few were close to the fence.

"Can we go see the horses?" Granny asked.

"Of course," he said. "We've got plenty of time before Kayla's ride starts."

He had already glanced around the parking lot and hadn't seen signs of Maddie's truck yet. Maybe she'd join them by the horses. The more he got to know her, the more he realized that Maddie was a hard worker dedicated to her job and her daughter. She didn't often take a moment to pet the horses, so to speak. He admired that quality in her, but having led a similar life, dedicated to his job, not so much the family, he hoped she'd take advantage of his presence in Kayla's life to take some time for herself.

A lump formed in his throat at the thought of how seldom Maddie took a break. How long had Maddie been sacrificing her own personal happiness? Probably ever since Kayla came into the picture, and he hadn't been there to help her.

Sure enough, Maddie pulled in just as they got to the horses. He turned and waved at her, and she waved back. His heart did a tiny little somersault, and he felt like the teenage boy who'd seen her at that party and thought she was the prettiest girl there. Funny how some things never changed.

"I like that paint," Granny said, pointing to one of the horses. "Your grandfather and I used to look at them the way some people look to clouds, trying to find the patterns on their body and what they might be."

She gestured at a spot on the horse's back. "That one looks just like a hot dog," Granny said. "It's been ages since I've had a hot dog, but I've always loved them."

"And it will be ages until you get another one, if at all," Maddie said, coming up behind them. "They are terrible and contain way too much sodium. Your biggest problem right now is that you like too many salty and sweet things."

"A little salt never hurt anyone," Granny said, looking grumpy.

"I agree," Maddie said, smiling. "But too much salt is terrible for your heart and blood pressure."

He had to give Maddie credit. She really did try when it came to making sure that Granny's best interests were taken care of. He hoped that some of the things he was doing to help her would also be seen that way. Granny's insistence on salt being necessary to give food flavor was part of why he had begun his spice experiment with her. While it was true that you did need some salt in cooking, Granny had been the kind of person who would liberally dump salt from the saltshaker all over her food before even tasting it.

Now she was learning another way, and hopefully this would remain a good method for getting her to eat healthier.

"What's the name of the horse?" Granny asked, looking eager to change the subject.

Maddie stepped closer to the fence and held her hand out to the paint. "This guy is called Rascal," she said. "I've ridden him a time or two, and he lives up to his name."

Granny came closer and patted his neck. "That's real fine," she said. "A horse with a hot dog on his back has to be a rascal. I like him."

If Luke could pick the thing he loved the most about Maddie, it was the genuine way she smiled and her eyes lit up when Granny said something that amused her. She'd never taken on the patronizing attitude of so many others in the senior center who interacted with her. You could tell she genuinely liked Granny. That was how Maddie treated everyone—with the same kindness, dignity, and respect. No wonder she'd raised such a great daughter.

They spent a few minutes petting the horse. Then Maddie said, "We need to get moving. Kayla's ride starts in a few minutes."

It was probably for the best, considering he'd caught himself staring at Maddie and her beauty a little longer than was appropriate. Even though he intellectually knew that putting their daughter first and not getting caught up in all of this personal stuff was the right thing to do, his heart seemed to disagree, and he was constantly pulling it back in alignment with his mind.

But as he watched Maddie lean in and say something to Granny, Luke couldn't help wondering what it would be like to have Maddie as more than just his friend.

CHAPTER SIX

MADDIE WAS IMPRESSED with Luke for how quickly he had stepped up to be there for Kayla since finding out he was Kayla's father. He had come to every one of Kayla's practices, every school event, and whenever they invited him to something, he always said yes. Many of those times, Granny was with him. Maddie couldn't have asked for a better situation for their daughter.

The trouble was, the more time she spent with him, the more she found him attractive. It wasn't just the way he had gingerly helped Granny across the uneven ground, but it was the look of compassion and tenderness as he did so. Just as importantly, she saw the way he engaged with their daughter. He was genuinely interested in Kayla's activities, and it warmed her heart to see the way Kayla responded.

As they met Kayla at the stables, she was standing with Brady, probably going over today's practice. When Luke got to her, he asked her, "How was your day?"

Usually, if either she or Brady asked Kayla that question, Kayla would roll her eyes and tell them that it was fine. But Kayla, too, appeared to be trying, because she said, "It was great. And I didn't have to deal with Drake."

Both Luke and Brady laughed, but concern filled Maddie. She knew that tone in her daughter's voice, and it meant that Drake was picking on her. She hoped that Briana would have kept her feud to herself, but she supposed that was a bit too much to expect.

"Such an ill-mannered child," Granny said. "But I will give him credit. Ever since you came into the picture, he's been coming around more."

Granny snickered. "The spoiled brat is finally learning that he can't take me for granted. But I am sorry that he's not being nice to you. I just wish people understood that there is enough of everything to go around."

Maddie looked over at her daughter. "How bad is it?"

Kayla glanced over at Luke, and they exchanged a look before she shrugged. "Nothing I can't handle. Hopefully, as he gets used to the idea, things will be better. It's just harder because he never liked me anyway."

And that really was the trouble. Things might be different if Maddie and Briana had gotten along, and Kayla and Drake had gotten along. But they'd been at odds for as long as Maddie could remember.

Kayla seemed to sense the direction of Maddie's thoughts. "Mom, it's fine. Like I said, nothing I can't handle. He is just being a jerk because he's jealous. I didn't do anything wrong. I'm not gonna let him make me feel bad for it. I love Granny, always have, and now that she's my actual Granny. I'm going to enjoy it, and no one can take that away from me."

She sent another look over to her father, and Maddie knew that the strength in her daughter had come from him. It kind of stung for Maddie. Kayla hadn't confided all this to her, and for a moment, she was a little bit envious. Which was silly, considering she had Kayla her whole life, and now it was Luke's turn to be there for their daughter. And it wasn't like Kayla was choosing sides or trying to make Maddie feel bad. She just had the opportunity to connect with her father on something important.

Kayla gave them all a quick hug, then dashed

off to finish getting ready for her ride. This was another one of the sweet changes that had happened. Before Granny started coming to her practices, Maddie never got these few moments before practice. Kayla would be so busy with all her stuff, and if Maddie interrupted, she would get mad.

So even though it was hard, watching her daughter bond with someone else on such a deep level, she also had to be grateful because it was getting her a little time back as well.

As they walked into the stands, Luke put his hand on her arm. "I'm sorry if that felt like an intrusion," he said. "Kayla ran into him the other day at the nursing home, he made a couple of snide remarks about her, and I could tell it really upset her. So we spent a lot of time talking. I guess I should've told you about it."

There was so much sincerity in his voice that it was hard for her to feel bad. She could only feel grateful that he'd been there in that time of need.

"It's okay," she said. "I don't expect you to tell me everything. I just wish I'd known that he was giving her a hard time, that's all."

Luke nodded slowly. "I'm still learning how to do this parenting thing. You've got eighteen years on me, and I don't always know what to do. She made me promise not to tell you, but I guess that her saying that should have been my clue that it was something I should've told you."

Then he blew out a breath. "I just wanted her to trust me, you know? Like if she thought that I was going to you for everything, maybe she wouldn't tell me some stuff anymore. I guess I feel like I need to earn that trust by keeping her secrets."

The torment on his face made her feel even worse about the situation.

"No, it's fine. You're right. You should have your relationship with her. Kayla tells Brady a lot of things she doesn't share with me. But he ends up sharing most of it with me anyway. It's a delicate balance."

Luke nodded but looked confused. "Well, that was clear as mud," he said, shaking his head. "But you two had all this time to figure it out, so I imagine you probably messed things up a lot in the beginning."

Brady came up to them, cracking up. "In the beginning? We still mess things up. I got in trouble with Maddie the other day for giving Kayla some money. She asked for it because I didn't know Maddie had already told her no."

Even though Maddie had been really angry with Brady that day, she laughed with him. "We agreed that before either of us gives her money for anything, we talk about it. Otherwise, she'd play us all. She wanted a bunch of new clothes, and I told her she couldn't have any until she got rid of some of the stuff in her closet. Which she hasn't done, but she's now spending the money that you gave her to buy more clothes anyway."

Brady held his hands up like he was under arrest. "I know, and I'm sorry. Sometimes I just can't tell her no."

Then he put his hands down and looked over at Luke. "You see? We still don't have it figured out, but we do try to talk about it and work through whatever it is. Once I found out what Kayla did, I gave her a bunch of extra chores to pay me back."

Maddie shook her head. "But that doesn't change the fact that it looks like a bomb went off in her bedroom."

A guilty look crossed Luke's face. "Then I guess I should fess up that when we took Granny to the mall, I let Kayla buy a few things."

Then they all laughed, including Granny. "You see? They're all just a bunch of con artists," Granny said, chortling. Then she looked over at Maddie. "I did tell him that he should ask you before letting Kayla buy clothes. One of those shirts she picked out was scandalous."

They all laughed again. Kayla wasn't the sort to wear clothing that Maddie would consider scandalous, and she was dying to know what Granny thought was.

Maddie turned to Luke. "So, clearly we do need to have a conversation about this. At this point, I think we can all agree that Kayla does not need any new clothes. Except for a prom dress, and last year, she went shopping with her girlfriends and sent pictures to both me and Brady. We all decided together what we thought was appropriate. We'll just make sure she loops you in."

Another guilty look crossed Luke's face. "So I shouldn't have ordered her the one that she told me she really liked?"

Granny howled with laughter. "You all. This is more fun than making Briana think I have a boyfriend."

Brady groaned. "Well, we can only hope that it's not too ugly. I mean, she has modest taste, so it really can't be that bad. But the stuff that's in style right now is just awful."

Maddie appreciated the way Brady was taking this in stride. In truth, Brady was the one who cared the most about the kinds of dresses his daughter wore.

Maddie shrugged. "Well, she is eighteen, so I guess at some point we do have to let her grow up and make decisions for herself. But I hope this shows us all how important it is to communicate."

She looked over at Brady, who looked a little glum, but nodded. "I will add Luke to our group text. I guess we should've done it sooner."

All this time, Maddie had been feeling bad about how she felt her role had been taken over by Luke, but she couldn't imagine how Brady must feel, with another father in the picture.

Brady gestured at the stands. "You better get settled because we'll be starting in a few minutes."

He started walking to the entrance to the arena so he could start instructing them, but Maddie ran to catch up with him.

"Thank you for what you did back there for Luke," she said. "I know this has to be hard on you, having to share her all of a sudden."

Brady shrugged. "It's okay. You know, I feel bad for you, remembering how everything happened with me and Josie. I kept thinking to myself that you were ridiculous for being so jealous. But now I get it. I see how strongly they're bonding, and I wonder if she'll still call me Daddy. Then I remember I'm being silly because that's just one more person to love her and take care of her."

He reached out and took her by the hand. "I'm really sorry for any of the things that me and Josie did that made you feel bad when she came back into our lives. Though we've been through a ton of therapy on this, and you said you're good, but I now understand on a deeper level, so I want to apologize to you again."

Maddie shook her head. "You don't owe me any apologies. If anyone should be apologizing, it's me. I was horrible to you back then, and I hurt Kayla in the process. So let's just keep it all firmly in the past, accept that we forgive one another, and ultimately, what we all want is what's best for our daughter. As I told you, you will always be her father. She is just fortunate enough to have another one."

Brady stepped forward and wrapped his arms around her, giving her a big hug. "Thank you," he said. "I hope you realize that I have completely forgiven you for all of the stuff that happened."

He pulled away, looked deep into her eyes.

"And I know you, so I know that you are still feeling very guilty over everything with Luke. Don't. We were all just a bunch of dumb kids, doing the best we could, and now you have a wonderful man, doing what he can to make things right. Don't let your bad feelings from the past keep you from moving forward in the future."

Somewhere in the back, someone was calling Brady's name, and he shook his head. "Gotta love impatient teenagers. But take my advice, let go of all the pain from the past. Obviously, we all have a lot of work to do to get our heads right, but our hearts are all in the right place."

He hesitated for a moment, and said, "Though it's none of my business, I see the way you look at each other when you think no one else is looking. Give him a chance. Since you've been working nights, you're not getting as much time with Kayla, but think about maybe taking one of those nights off and going on a date or something with Luke."

Maddie stared at him. "That's a big stretch," she said. "I'm sure you mean well, but we don't have that kind of relationship."

She looked back over to the bleachers, where Luke was helping Granny get settled. "Our priority is Kayla, and what's best for her. So don't act like her and Granny and get any ideas about the two of us."

Brady laughed. "If there are three of us trying to get you together, there might be something there. As you mentioned earlier, Kayla is eighteen and an adult. Her life isn't going to end if you and Luke start dating. She could be your biggest cheerleader."

Maddie shrugged. "And if it doesn't work out? Right now, Luke is at our family gatherings, and we can all be a family together. How awkward is that going to be if he and I have a bad breakup and we don't get along anymore?"

Brady shook his head. "The same way we figured it out when we had our share of fights. We all want what's best for Kayla, so even if we don't get along, we will find a way to at least be nice for the sake of our daughter."

"He is not wrong," Luke said, coming up behind her. "The cat's out of the bag, and it's obvious that there's something here. So why don't we try to figure it out to make it work?"

Maddie turned to look at him. "Because of what I just said. I've put Kayla through enough fighting with one of her fathers. I can't do that to her again. I'm sorry."

One of the girls yelled for Brady again, so he turned and grinned at them. "I'm in trouble now," he said. "But seriously, give it some thought. I'd like to think that you're both mature enough that if things don't work out for you romantically, you'll still figure out how to make it work for our daughter."

A tender look crossed Brady's face. "Seriously, Maddie. You deserve a chance at happiness."

Before Maddie could answer, he turned and jogged back toward where the kids were lining up with their horses.

As she turned to make her way back to the stands, Luke stopped her. "Wait."

"I meant what I said," Maddie said.

"I know," he said. "But I also agree with Brady. We are both mature adults who have already agreed that our daughter's needs come first. She keeps dropping hints to me about everything you love and nice things I can do for you. I think she's in favor of the idea, too."

Maddie groaned. "I get it. But you also haven't had eighteen years of your daughter wanting to be like the rest of the kids and having a mommy and daddy who were married, living in the same house as her. It's just a leftover childish fantasy. Don't read more into it than what it is."

This time, when she turned to walk away, he let her. But before she'd taken more than a step, he said, "I don't think this is about the best interests of our daughter. This is more about you and whatever it is that you are afraid of, and having a real relationship. Kayla has already told me that you've never had a serious relationship and only been on a few dates. Maybe, instead of using your excuse, you need to take a long, hard look at what your real motivations are."

Maddie's face burned the entire way to her seat. Who was he to talk to her like that? He didn't even know her. He was just mad because he was interested in her, and she basically turned him down. It was the same thing with every man she tried to date. People told her that she was closed off to romance, but that wasn't true. Her daughter was her most important priority. Her second was her career. She couldn't just push either of those aside for every charming, handsome man who came her way.

Hadn't she grown up with that? Hadn't she experienced the very real pain of being a latchkey kid without a father and a mother who was out every night with a different guy? It was one of the reasons she had been so jealous of Josie. Sure, Josie didn't have a mom, but Josie had

had what seemed like the perfect family. Now, of course, Maddie knew that Josie's family was messed up in its own way, and there was no such thing as a perfect family.

Regardless, Maddie understood well enough the damage that having a selfish parent focused on their own happiness could do to a child. She wasn't doing that to her daughter. Maybe in a few years, after Kayla was settled in college, and Maddie was comfortable in her new job, they could think about what a dating relationship would look like.

She glanced over at Luke, who had followed her back to the stands, but was sitting further away from her, closer to his grandmother. But she could tell that whatever Granny had said to him hadn't been encouraging. A dark look covered his face, and Granny looked like the cat who had eaten the canary.

Everyone thought Maddie was resistant to the idea of Luke, but it wasn't true. It was just really bad timing, just like when they first met. It wasn't fair for her to ask him to wait, especially when he pretty much seemed to be champing at the bit. He had only been a father for a few weeks, so he didn't understand the importance of sacrificing for your children.

But as Granny nudged him and said something that brought a smile back to his expression, Maddie wished she had been the one to do that. She wished she could go and sit next to him, but she couldn't afford to cause any more talk about them. Obviously, she needed to work on holding herself more aloof.

WHAT HAD LUKE been thinking, doing something so stupid as to try to get Maddie to see him in a different light? Even days later, Maddie was avoiding him at every turn. He stopped off at the hardware store to pick up a few things he needed for working on Granny's house. Granny's physical therapist didn't feel comfortable releasing her unless the house was made more handicapped-accessible. Not that you could say the *H* word in front of Granny. Even though she was recovering well, she would still need things like safety bars in the shower, and better handrails around the stairs.

And the more he worked on the house, the more he realized just how badly it had fallen into disrepair. At some point, the toilet in the bathroom Granny used the most had developed a leak. It went unnoticed and had rotted the floor. Which was what he was doing here now.

Since he had to replace both the floor and the subfloor in the bathroom, he decided to just go ahead and get everything redone. However, they had to special order the parts to create the new bath/shower combo, which had finally come in.

As he watched the employee go to the back to get the bath/shower combo, Luke realized just how badly he had miscalculated things. There was no way it would fit in his SUV.

Just as he was about to tell the employee that he wouldn't be able to get it today, and he'd have to arrange for alternative transportation, Brady and Wyatt walked up to them.

"Hey, how's it going?" Brady said. "You remember Wyatt, don't you?"

Luke nodded. "Sure do. Good to see you again. I think Kayla is going over to your house to babysit tonight."

Wyatt grinned. "Yes. We got tickets to the Cattlemen's Ball, and I'm excited for me and Laura to get out for a change."

Brady groaned. "I forgot that was tonight. Not only did I not arrange for someone to watch Shana, but Josie is still feeling terrible."

Then he looked over at Luke. "You want to use my tickets? Take Maddie. She loves going, but—"

Wyatt grinned. "That is a great idea. Maddie was a little miffed that we booked Kayla tonight, because she forgot to buy herself a ticket before they sold out, so she was planning on a girls' night watching movies."

It didn't take a rocket scientist to figure out what these two were doing. The hardware store employee came out with his bathtub combo.

"Oh no. I got caught up talking, and I forgot to come in and tell you that I'm not going to be able to take it home today. It won't fit in my SUV, so I need to find someone with a truck who can help me get home. I hate to make you drag it all the way back in, and I'm really sorry."

Wyatt and Brady slapped him on the back.

"No problem, friend," Brady said. "We're just picking up a couple of parts, so you can save everyone a trip, and we'll just load it up in there."

Wyatt looked over at the clerk. "Cody, you know my truck. I'll pull it up here. We'll get it loaded."

Once again, Luke was struck by the way this family all jumped in to help each other out. He hadn't known how he was going to get someone's truck. But here Brady was, volunteering to take care of it anyway.

"Thank you," Luke said. "Now I don't have

to deal with Maddie. Things are weird between us. She's the only one I know with a truck."

Both men laughed and jostled each other. "You're not getting off that easy," Brady said. "As payment for the use of the truck, you have to take us up on that offer for the Cattlemen's Ball."

Luke laughed, shaking his head. "Of course there are strings. Ha ha, you got me. But even if I say yes, it doesn't mean Maddie will."

"Yes, she will," Brady said. "Maddie's favorite event of the year is the Cattlemen's Ball. She wouldn't miss it for the world. And you won't be the one doing the asking, I'm going to call her up and tell her I can't use my ticket."

Luke shook his head. "No offense, but Maddie is already uncomfortable with everyone's attempts at setting us up. So much so that she's been avoiding me. I can't do that to her."

Brady looked over at Wyatt. "You see? I told you he was the salt of the earth. He's the kind of man that we have been praying Maddie would find."

Luke tried not to groan at Brady's pronouncement, but he couldn't help saying, "I appreciate all the prayers, fellas, but nothing is going to happen between me and Maddie. We're both clear on that. Our priority is our daughter."

Even though he didn't like the way Maddie was using her own personal baggage as an excuse to not be with him, the truth was, Luke had enough baggage of his own. How many women had dated him simply because he was a military man, or in the case of his ex-fiancée, because her general daddy told her that he'd make a great husband? He didn't want Maddie to date him because she felt obligated to or because everyone kept pushing them together; he wanted her to date him because she liked him and wanted to be with him.

If anything was going to happen between him and Maddie, it would have to develop on its own time. Though he had moments of attraction to her, and he hated the way she was avoiding him, he wasn't willing to add more drama to their already drama-filled lives.

"All right then, I'll think of a way to get you both to the Cattlemen's Ball," Wyatt said. "I'll grab my truck real quick."

As he walked off, Maddie came toward them. "Hey, guys," she said. "What's this? A family reunion?"

Brady laughed. "Well, you know what they

say: the exciting stuff in a small town happens at the hardware store."

Maddie laughed. "Don't forget the ice cream place," she said, smiling. "I'm headed there next to get some sustenance for tonight's project."

Brady grinned. "Yeah, I hear Wyatt stole your date for the night."

Maddie shrugged. "It's okay. I've been wanting to watch that movie for a while, but you know our daughter. She will jump at any chance to make an extra dollar or two. And good for her. I appreciate her go-getter spirit. Just no fun watching romantic comedies by myself."

Luke watched the interplay between Maddie and Brady, and he could tell that Brady was setting her up to go to the Cattlemen's Ball. At least he was here to make sure it was clear he would be taking the other ticket.

"So, you go to the hardware store instead?" Brady asked.

"Yes," Maddie said. "One of the shelves in Kayla's closet is broken, which is one of the reasons her clothes are everywhere, so I'm picking up a few things to fix it and maybe find another organizer or something. Now she won."

Brady's grin told Luke exactly how this was going to play out.

"I have a better idea," Brady said. "Josie isn't feeling well enough to go to the Cattlemen's Ball tonight, so instead of letting our tickets go to waste, what if you go?"

Excitement lit up Maddie's face. "You know I would love to go! It's been ages since I've been to the Cattlemen's Ball! Tickets sell out so fast, and with everything that's been going on, I didn't get the chance to get mine."

"Great," Brady said. "You can ride with Wyatt and Laura. They'll pick you up after they've picked up Luke."

And there it was. The crestfallen look on Maddie's face. Maybe he had been imagining the attraction between the two of them. It made him feel even worse about his words to her the other day. Everyone was pressuring her, and all she wanted was to go about her life.

"You have got to be kidding me," Maddie said. "Your offer wasn't even subtle at all."

Exactly how Luke had seen it. But he hadn't been as wounded by the offer as Maddie clearly was. No wonder she'd been avoiding him.

Brady shrugged. "I know you want to go."

Maddie shook her head. "But you're making it into a date."

Luke could hear the frustration in her voice. He supposed that as wonderful as it could be to have a family to help out, it was tough when they meddled in your business.

Luke smiled at Maddie. "Look, it doesn't have to be a date. We'd be going as a group of friends and to be honest, I'm not even sure I should go. I don't have anything to wear to a ball, except my mess dress."

At least it got a laugh out of Maddie. "It's not like a ball on TV," she said. "It's the annual fundraiser for our Cattlemen's Association, and while it does give us all a chance to dress up, for the men, it can range from a suit to a nice pair of jeans, a dress shirt, and a Western hat. If I remember correctly, mess dress is your fancy military uniform, and I've seen plenty of people in those."

That was one of the many things he liked about Maddie. Even though she obviously didn't want to go with him, she was still trying to help him feel comfortable if he chose to go.

"Does that mean it's okay if we go together?" He saw the hesitation on her face, so he quickly added, "As friends, of course."

Maddie rewarded him with a smile. "I guess. Miles Jeffries always does the best smoked brisket, and all of his sides are on point. You have to go for the food alone. You definitely haven't lived until you've tried the amazing food at this event."

Wyatt pulled up in his truck. He called out the window, "Let's get you loaded up." Then he noticed Maddie. "Did you talk to her about tonight?"

Brady puffed out his chest like he'd won a major event. "She's in," he said.

The other men might think it was a victory, but he could tell from the expression on Maddie's face that this was likely going to make things even more difficult between the two of them.

"Were you in on this?" she asked, looking at Luke.

"I was ambushed just like you," he told her honestly. "And I told them you weren't going to appreciate the interference. I meant what I said. If this is going to make things difficult for you, then I won't go. Unlike you, I don't know what I'm missing."

Maddie's shoulders rose and fell like she was letting out a long sigh. "I must seem like I'm being overly sensitive, but I've worked hard to get where I am and to repair my reputation. I thought I was finally there, but all this stuff with Briana…"

Her voice trailed off, and she didn't need to finish the sentence. Despite his gains with Briana over Granny's diet and sharing recipes, she still seemed eager to find fault with everything, and made snide comments about Maddie every chance she got.

"I get it," he said. "Just remember that everyone else is being supportive, and as I've heard your boss say multiple times, you've done nothing wrong. I promise I'll do everything I can tonight to keep tongues from wagging. Let's just go have a good time."

Maddie nodded slowly, then smiled. "It really is good brisket."

She gestured at the men getting ready to load the tub fixture in the truck. "You should probably go help them. I'll see you tonight."

Even though she said going to the Cattlemen's Ball with him was no big deal, she said she'd see him tonight with all the enthusiasm of someone headed to get a root canal.

Hopefully, they'd find a way to have a good

time. At the very least, as Maddie said, he'd be in for a good meal.

But there was a part of him that was disappointed it wasn't something more.

CHAPTER SEVEN

WHY DID MADDIE feel so giddy at the idea of going to the Cattlemen's Association Ball? She'd been to the event many times before, and it was always the same thing: mingle with their friends and have hors d'oeuvres when they arrived, then go to their tables, where they'd be served a nice dinner—no, a feast—catered by the J Bar W Ranch and their prime beef. Everyone looked forward to that meal. It was probably the best meal she'd have all year, so her nerves weren't about that. Instead, she was standing in front of the mirror, fussing over her appearance for another reason.

"Please tell me you're not wearing that ugly old thing," Kayla said.

Maddie turned and looked at her daughter. "What's wrong with this? It's my best dress."

Kayla groaned. "Exactly. You've worn that dress for as long as I can remember."

Maddie shrugged. "Well, it's all I have. I'm not like you, with my closets overflowing."

Kayla gave the usual teenage eye roll. Maddie was used to it. "Not really, considering you made me give away a bunch of stuff."

Then Kayla's face brightened. "Hey, wait a second. In those dresses I tossed into the give-away box, there's one I ordered off the internet. It was too big, and they wouldn't take it back. It'll fit you."

Before Maddie could answer, Kayla dashed off, then returned with a flowing pink princess dress. Maddie remembered that one all right. She'd told Kayla no because it was too fancy, and that if she wanted the dress, Kayla would have to buy it herself. Maddie had also said no because it was from an online retailer. She had warned Kayla that many of those places were often scams.

Kayla had insisted, and Maddie told her that it was fine, as long as Kayla spent her own money and was prepared to be disappointed. Her daughter had cried that day when the dress arrived, a couple sizes too big, and Maddie had consoled her, saying that they could probably get it taken in somewhere, but then one of Kayla's friends had offered her a different dress, so it had languished in the back of Kayla's closet instead.

"It's perfect for you," Kayla said.

Maddie looked at her suspiciously. "No offense, but that's not really my style, and it's way too fancy."

Kayla snorted. "I'm on the same social media as you. I know what other people wear to the Cattlemen's Ball. This dress will fit in nicely. And it's far better than your usual ugly black thing."

In truth, Maddie hadn't loved the idea of wearing the same tired black dress she wore to every function. But it wasn't like she had the time or extra money to get something else. All her money went to caring for her daughter, which meant there wasn't anything left to buy fancy dresses she'd wear maybe once a year.

With nothing to lose, Maddie took the dress to the bathroom to try on. She didn't think of herself as much of a pink person, but this shade of pink looked good against Maddie's skin, and even though Maddie had thought it was not really her style, she had to admit she couldn't remember the last time she'd worn such a flowing gown.

"Mom!"

Maddie grudgingly came out of the bathroom, knowing she was going to hear Kayla say, "I told you so."

But instead, her daughter's eyes widened. "Wow," she said. "Mom, you're..."

The surprise in her daughter's voice made Maddie laugh. At one time, Maddie might have wanted to think she was hot, but now she was just a woman approaching middle age, hoping that maybe she might look nice.

"We have got to do the whole thing," Kayla said. "We don't need to leave for Wyatt's for another thirty minutes. I can get you even more glammed up."

Maddie gave her daughter a look. She wasn't sure she wanted Kayla's idea of glammed up, but before she could protest, Kayla said, "Have you ever seen me wear makeup that you didn't like on me? Just because you don't do yourself up often doesn't mean you shouldn't once in a while."

As much as Maddie hated to admit it, Kayla was right. She couldn't recall a time when her daughter had walked out of the house with hair and makeup that she thought was inappropriate. Everyone always complimented Kayla on her appearance, so it wasn't really what Maddie was nervous about.

"People will think I'm trying too hard," Maddie said.

"So what? You're the one who always tells me not to care about what other people think. As long as you're acting with integrity, who cares?"

Fine time for her daughter to use her words against her. But there was a huge difference between what people thought of Kayla, and how they'd always treated Maddie. What if Briana was there, and saw Maddie dressed to the nines? And then there was Luke...

"Wait till Dad gets a load of this."

"Exactly." Maddie pulled away from Kayla's ministrations.

"Stay still," Kayla said firmly.

Maddie took a deep breath. They had to address this. "Honey, I know you and Granny are trying to get me and your dad together, but neither of us are ready for a relationship right now. So if you're doing this in hopes that your father will look at me and fall in love, just stop. We're just using Brady and Josie's extra tickets. Going as friends, with friends. Just like you do for your school dances."

Kayla groaned. "That's only because I can

never get a date. And because if I did get a date, Dad would totally freak out."

Maddie grinned. Brady definitely had strong opinions on what kind of boy his daughter was allowed to be around, even if she was eighteen. But he only wanted what was best for his daughter, so Maddie had always told Kayla to give him a little grace.

"Mom, you never go out on dates. If you worry that it's going to upset me, don't. I'm worried about what you're going to do when I go to college. I would feel a lot better about going away to school if you had someone to keep you company."

Her daughter's heart was in the right place, and even though it wasn't Kayla's job to worry about whether or not Maddie was lonely when she went off to college, it was so sweet.

But dating now, and especially Luke...this was the wrong time to be thinking about such things.

"I promise," Maddie said. "As soon as you go off to school, I'll join one of those dating apps."

Kayla tugged at her hair a little too hard with the brush. "Ow!"

"Sorry," Kayla said. "Why would you need to sign up for one of those apps when you have a perfectly good man staring you in the face? Not that I'm supposed to notice anything, but my dad is pretty cute for being a dad."

Her daughter was impossible.

"That may be so, but I don't want to pick a date based on how good they look. I need a chance to get to know a person and find out about their character first. Luke is a good enough guy, but just because he's good as a father doesn't necessarily make him a good romantic partner. After all, that's why Brady and I never worked out."

Kayla stepped back from her. "Yeah, but you and Brady Dad never had any kind of sparks. I've never seen him look at you the way Luke Dad looks at you."

Busted. But this wasn't an appropriate conversation to have with her daughter. Especially since Kayla had too many romantic notions in her head to understand the level of sacrifice a real relationship took.

"I think you're trying to see things that aren't there because you want so badly for us all to be a family. I'm not ready to be in a relationship right now, and I need you to accept that."

As always with her daughter when they disagreed, the fight shone in Kayla's eyes.

"Why should I?" Kayla said. "Look, you always sacrificed for me. I remember times when I was younger, and someone would ask you out to dinner or a movie or something, and you'd always say something like, 'Oh, sorry, I have Kayla.'"

For a moment, Kayla looked genuinely upset. Then she said, "But maybe the real reason you told all those people that is because there was a part of you that always loved my father. Please give him a chance."

How was Maddie supposed to tell her daughter that this romantic notion she'd built up over Maddie and Luke loving each other all these years was just a fantasy?

Kayla held up a mirror to Maddie's face. "There you go. All finished."

Maddie almost didn't recognize herself in the mirror. Even though she'd known that Kayla wasn't going to turn her into a painted lady, she hadn't expected the subtle but artful way the makeup had been applied to her face.

Her eyes were highlighted in the stylish way for teenagers, but didn't make her look like an adult who was trying too hard. The rest of her makeup was subtle, classy, and made Maddie think she was staring at a younger woman in the mirror. Kayla had also found some shoes that matched Maddie's dress. If Maddie had chosen a look for herself, this is what she'd have chosen. Maybe her daughter knew her after all.

"I look amazing. Thank you." Maddie smiled at her daughter, then held her arms out. "You think I can have a hug?"

Kayla grumbled. "I suppose, since I know you'll just pout, like you do when I hug Granny and my dad."

"Why should they get hugs and not me?"

"You've been hugging me my whole life, and they need to catch up."

But then Kayla came and gave her a hug. A real hug, and even though Maddie had been mourning the loss of her little girl, seeing the woman she was becoming brought a new feeling of joy to her heart.

The alarm on Kayla's phone beeped. "That's my reminder," Kayla said. "We need to get over to Wyatt's so I can babysit, and you can ride with them to the ball."

They had all agreed that it would be easier for everyone to meet at Wyatt's and ride together. Parking at the Cattlemen's Ball was always at a premium, so carpooling made sense.

"I can't wait to see the look on Dad's face when he sees you."

As much as Maddie wanted to remind her daughter once again that this was not happening, they just had such a beautiful moment that she couldn't spoil it.

When they got to Wyatt and Laura's, Maddie began to feel self-conscious. Sure, Kayla had said she looked good, but that was the opinion of a teenage girl. Had she overdone it? She didn't want to be one of those older women trying to look young.

But when she walked through the door, Laura's face lit up. "Wow, you look incredible."

"Yeah," Wyatt said. "You look nice. If we hadn't already lined up a date for you, I'd say you're going to have all kinds of heads turning."

"We only want Dad to notice her," Kayla said emphatically.

"Stop, both of you," Maddie said. "This is not a real date. Don't put ideas into people's heads that don't belong there. Luke and I are just co-parents, and maybe friends."

Kayla gave another annoyed groan. "I'm going to check on the little ones," she said. "They're being awfully quiet, and the last time that happened when I was over here, they had just painted the bathroom mirror with Laura's new lipstick."

As everyone laughed, Kayla started for the back of the house where the kids were, but then she paused. "You just keep working on her about my dad. Mom is getting on my nerves with how stubborn she is."

"Kayla," Maddie said. "You're really crossing the line into being disrespectful today."

Kayla grinned. "I'm only speaking the truth in love."

Before Maddie could chastise her daughter again, Kayla had skipped off into the bedrooms.

"I need to check something in the kitchen for a minute," Laura said. "Come with me."

As Maddie followed Laura into the kitchen, she said, "I know Wyatt isn't going to be any help, but I really needed to be supported here. I don't want a romantic relationship with Luke."

The doorbell rang, and Wyatt went to answer it. Laura looked at Maddie. "Why not? Wyatt keeps commenting that there's obviously something between you two. Everyone else sees it. Maybe you should stop fighting it and just see where it goes?"

"Come on, Laura. You know why. I can't risk hurting my daughter again. She's happy and excited now, but what if we do get together? Then we break up, and it's going to hurt her."

"Can we stop with that?" Luke said, entering the room. "You're using fear to not allow yourself a chance at happiness based on a lot of what-ifs, and you have no evidence of what will actually happen. I thought you were a woman of faith. But that isn't how a woman of faith talks. I was willing to give this a try. The more I hear you argue against it, the more I'm not sure I would want to date someone who lives her life in so much fear."

Then he looked her up and down. "I'm supposed to tell you how beautiful you look tonight because I understand Kayla went to a lot of trouble. And I'll tell her that. I'll tell you that. But I hope you know, you've always been beautiful to me, no matter what you wear."

He turned his attention to Wyatt. "So, when does the shindig start anyway? I'm starving."

Even though she had been telling herself all night that Luke's opinion didn't matter to her, his easy dismissal of her stung. This is what she wanted. For her Luke to be just friends.

The cold way he'd just spoken to her about her faith made her heart hurt, and it felt like there was a greater distance between them than there had ever been. But if this was the price she had to pay, then she'd pay it. Everyone might think she was acting out of fear, but she was no longer that reckless girl who thrived on taking risks. Her daughter was everything to her, and Maddie was never going to do something that would harm her daughter.

She'd already done that once, by revealing the truth about Kayla's paternity in a moment of anger. Though they had worked through it as a family, and Maddie knew Kayla had forgiven her, Maddie would never forget the lesson she'd learned.

Even though Luke had questioned Maddie's faith, Maddie closed her eyes and prayed that God would give her the strength to handle the situation. She'd cried out to God so many times over the years, and it seemed like now, with everyone pushing her in a direction that could cause more pain, she needed His strength even more.

MAYBE HE SHOULDN'T have said that about her faith. Luke was painfully aware of how stiffly she stood next to him at the Cattlemen's Ball. He just didn't understand why this woman who seemed to have everything going for her would be so afraid to take a chance on love.

But maybe it was better this way. He'd thought things would be easier once he got out of the army and women weren't afraid of his dangerous job. Yet here he was, attracted to a woman who'd made it quite clear she wasn't interested in him. Even though he'd called her out on her excuses, it didn't matter what the excuses were. The bottom line was that she didn't want to date him, and he needed to leave it alone.

He stole another glance at Maddie. He had not been lying when he told her that he thought she was beautiful. She looked like the belle of the ball. He kinda liked her better in her scrubs. She always found something fun to wear and used her outfits as another way of keeping people's spirits up. He liked that about her. But he couldn't express that to her. He wanted to say a lot of the things to her, but because he'd already messed things up, he felt like he couldn't. Still, he should've been more complimentary about the dress.

"You look really nice tonight," he said. "I should've made a bigger deal about it than I did because I know it's special."

She gave him a funny look, like she wasn't sure why he was bothering now.

"And I'm sorry about what I said about your fear and your faith. That was out of line. Your reasons are your reasons, and I need to respect them, just like everyone else should."

Maddie gave a small smile. "Thank you."

Finally. Progress. At least her posture had softened, and she didn't look like she wanted to run as far away as possible from an event she'd been looking forward to.

"It's not you, you know," she said slowly. "I'm sure you'd be a great person to date. It's just not where I'm at in my life right now."

The firmness in her voice made him realize just how hard it was on her to have everyone pushing her to date. All she really wanted was for people to respect her and her wishes. He'd messed that up tonight.

"I get it," he said. "In all honesty, I should probably figure out my own life priorities first as well. In just a few short weeks, it seems like my whole life has changed."

She gave him a tender smile. "And you're doing great managing it."

For a moment, it looked like she wanted to

say something else, but a woman came up to them and greeted Maddie warmly.

"I'm so glad to see you here," she said. "I feel like it's been ages since I've seen you at the senior center. It's always fun catching up with you when you pop in to check on Mom."

Though Maddie smiled, it didn't light up her eyes the way her smiles usually did. Probably because the reason she hadn't seen her friend was due to all the trouble Briana had caused. "It's great to see you, too, Sadie."

Then Maddie gestured at Luke. "Have you met Luke? He's Ida Mae's grandson, freshly out of the army. Luke, this is my friend Sadie."

Sadie smiled and held out her hand. "It's a pleasure to meet you. Ida Mae is one of Mom's crafting buddies. I can't tell you how happy it has made your grandmother to have you home."

Then she looked slyly over at Maddie before turning her attention back to him. "And to think you've been Kayla's father all along. What a great blessing for everyone. From what your grandmother tells my mom, I hear we may be dancing at a wedding soon. The Cattlemen's Ball is a great place to practice."

This was definitely not what Luke wanted to hear, especially after he and Maddie had seemingly made their peace over the match-making issue.

"Well, I'm sure we'll all be happy to see who the bride and groom are," Luke said, smiling. "But if Granny is trying to match me up with someone, she's in for a rude awakening. I'm afraid getting married, or even dating, isn't part of my plan right now. I have two priorities: my daughter and getting the house fixed up so Granny can come home."

Though he'd been telling himself those were his priorities all along, saying that to a would-be matchmaker made Luke feel even better about his conversation with Maddie. This wasn't the best time for him to be thinking about dating.

Sadie looked puzzled, then glanced over at Maddie. "I thought you two had gotten back together."

Maddie shook her head. "I'm afraid that's just wishful thinking on Ida Mae's part. Like Luke, my priority is my daughter, and the next priority is my job. Between the two, I'm afraid I don't have much time for romance."

Sadie laughed. "Oh, trust me. I get it. My mom gives my name and number to every handsome man who comes into the senior center to visit a relative. I know our families just want us to be happy, but they need to let us make our own paths."

"Hear, hear," Luke said as enthusiastically as he could. He wanted Maddie to know he was on her side.

"I know you're not on the market, but the band is getting ready to play a few songs. Do you think we could dance?" Sadie asked.

Even though Maddie had told him vehemently how much she didn't want to date him, he couldn't help noticing the way she flinched at the question.

"I'm afraid I've got two left feet," Luke said. "That's the other reason why there won't be anyone dancing at my wedding anytime soon."

As Sadie turned away, Maddie said quietly, "You don't need to turn anyone down on my account. We're just here as friends, so you can dance with whoever you like."

Luke shrugged. "There's only one woman here I want to dance with," he said. "And not only has she made her feelings about me painfully clear, but given the talk that's already happening, and how uncomfortable it makes her, I wouldn't want to give any more reason for people's tongues to wag."

Her expression softened slightly. "Like I said,

it's not personal." She gestured at the crowded room. "It's just life in this town. All these people have looked down on me for one reason or another. First it was because my mom was such a mess and I didn't have a dad. Then I got pregnant as a teenager, and became the typical statistic."

His stomach churned at the pregnancy reference. She always seemed to blame herself, yet he was equally to blame.

But he didn't want to interrupt her as she continued, "I was the horrible woman who ruined Brady's life, and created drama when Josie came home. And then, just when I was finally feeling like I was getting past all the bad things people said about me, you arrive, and it's back to square one."

Wow. He hadn't considered how everything they were going through now had brought up so much of Maddie's past.

The band began playing a lively song, and even though it didn't match Luke's and Maddie's moods, everyone else moved toward the stage, giving them a little more privacy in the crowded room. Still, he took her by the arm and led her to a more secluded corner to get away from the noise, and allow Maddie to get this off her chest.

Maddie's eyes filled with tears as she said, "I finally have my chance at redemption and proving them all wrong. My daughter is ready to graduate high school and go to college and be successful despite everything everyone ever said about how I'd never raise a good child as a single mom. I'm hopeful about getting the promotion at my job that I've always dreamed of. I'm making a real difference in people's lives. I can't afford to have anything mess that up."

That was probably the most real thing she had said to him about why she couldn't date him. Sure, she'd given her reasons about Kayla, and he believed that was one of her concerns. But as he saw the pain on her face, he understood that it was about so much more.

Luke could relate. Hadn't he spent his whole life trying to prove himself worthy to his family? The weight of all the medals adorning his mess dress pressed against his chest. He'd thought that all the decorations and medals would be enough. Even his second purple heart hadn't gotten his father to say, "I'm proud of you."

His dad was long gone, but as soon as Luke came home, he was still the black sheep who had ruined everyone's lives.

No, not everyone's. Just Briana's. No matter

what he did, it seemed she would always hate him. Sure, they'd come to some level of detente, and he was doing his best work on their relationship. But he still felt the weight of her disapproving glare whenever they were in Granny's room.

"I get it," he said. "Maybe you should tell that to Granny and Kayla."

Maddie shook her head. "I can't. Sometimes kids at school pick on Kayla, so I'm constantly telling her not to worry about what others think."

"Then why don't you take your own advice?"

Luke stopped a passing waiter to grab a bottle of water for each of them. They could both use the distraction of a drink, and he was parched.

Maddie accepted the water with a smile, took a long drink, then sighed. "Because unlike Kayla, I have done a lot of things wrong. I don't deserve all the things people have said about me over the years, but let's be honest. Some of them I did deserve. I've been trying to be a better person, but I can never seem to escape my past."

If only they weren't in a room full of the people Maddie was so afraid of judging her. Luke wanted to hug her and let her know he understood.

He hadn't been a good person back when he'd

first met Maddie, either. It seemed like they had both worked so hard to move past those old identities. The Bible said they were all new creations in Christ.

So why, if both he and Maddie had changed, couldn't others see that in them?

Instead, he said softly, "I know how that feels. After all, you've seen how Briana still treats me over all the mistakes I've made."

Maddie nodded sympathetically. "So you see why I have to do everything right. I've worked too hard to ruin it now."

He could tell she was on the verge of tears, so he gestured at the door. "Why don't we go outside and get some fresh air?"

Maddie nodded, and they walked out into a courtyard decorated with twinkling lights. Part of him wished things were different so he could comment on how romantic it was and share a special moment with her. But he couldn't be that for her; he could only be a friend.

They found a secluded area decorated with hay bales arranged as seating for guests. A breeze picked up, and Maddie shivered, so Luke shrugged out of his jacket. "Here. Put this on."

Maddie looked up at him as if to remind him that it would only give people something to talk about.

"I'd rather people talk than you freeze. Put it on," Luke said firmly.

A soft smile lit up Maddie's face. "Am I that obvious?"

Luke shrugged. "Maybe. But like you said, I get it. I keep thinking about Briana and how angry she is with me over the past. How much longer do I have to pay for something I did as a kid? What is the timeline for how long someone should pay for their sins?"

Maddie shrugged. "I don't know. It feels like forever."

Luke looked down at the ground, thinking about the verse that had come to him earlier about being a new creation in Christ. "It does, but then I wonder about God and Jesus, and how our sins were forgiven on the cross. How long does the Bible say we're supposed to pay for what we've done?"

Maddie rewarded him with a gentle laugh. "You know, I've never quite thought about that. What we're taught in churches is that we're forgiven once and for all."

"Yeah," he said, looking down at the ground, wondering why he didn't just accept that forgiveness. Why neither of them could. Here he was, trying to give good advice to Maddie, but he needed to take it as well.

"I guess it's easier said than done," he finally said. "It makes it a lot harder when people are constantly rubbing your nose in your past."

The understanding expression on Maddie's face gave him hope. "Exactly. I just want prove to all the people who said I was a good-for-nothing and I'd come to a bad end that they were wrong about me."

"And who are those people?" Luke asked.

Maddie shrugged. "I'd like to say no one that matters, but I guess I let them matter."

"For what it's worth," he said, "it seems to me that the people in your life who matter, like Brady and his family, and Kayla, they don't seem to hold it against you."

Maddie appeared to be processing his words, nodding slowly, and then he said, "You should also know that I've never held your mistakes against you, either. You did what you had to do, and I'm really grateful that thanks to everything you've done, we have a really amazing daughter."

Maddie rewarded him with another smile. "I've always been grateful that in spite of my mistakes, God has chosen to bless me so richly."

Even though Luke had been using this conversation to make Maddie feel better, he was actually starting to see how much it was helping him. All this time, he'd been angry with himself and blamed himself for his mistakes. Yet despite everything he'd done wrong, the most important person in his life, his Granny, thought the world of him. And somehow, he'd also ended up with a wonderful daughter who loved him. Those were the people who mattered most in his life, and they didn't hold anything against him.

In fact, God loved him on an even deeper level. For the first time since coming home, Luke felt the weight of all his sins fall off him. He had nothing to prove to anyone, especially not God, and it was God's opinion that mattered the most.

Before he could share this revelation with Maddie, Briana walked up.

"Well, well, well. If it isn't two little lovebirds who say they aren't lovebirds."

Luke glanced between himself and Maddie. They might be sitting next to each other, but there was plenty of space between them, and save the fact that Maddie was wearing his jacket, no one would have thought anything of it.

"Why don't you mind your own business?" he

said. "We came out for a bit of air, and Maddie was chilly, so I did what any gentleman would do, and I offered her my jacket."

Briana looked Maddie up and down. "Shouldn't you be at work? I thought they moved you to nights."

Maddie glared at Briana. "If you were so familiar with my schedule, you'd know that tonight is my normal night off."

Unfortunately, her words didn't sway Briana at all. "And I thought it had been made perfectly clear that you aren't supposed to be fraternizing with patients' families."

Pulling Luke's jacket around her, Maddie stood. "That is not true. There is nothing in the employee handbook that says I can't talk to Luke outside of work. Both me and Claire made sure of that."

This was beyond ridiculous. They shouldn't have to deal with Briana's harassment like this, especially since this had nothing to do with Granny.

"Look," Luke said. "I know I hurt you in the past. I'm sorry for everything I've done. You were my best friend when we were kids. I can't change what happened, but we can change how we treat each other in the future."

He expected Briana to make a smart comment, but she remained silent, so he continued. "We both want what's best for Granny. So does Maddie. I don't know why you don't like Maddie. She's been nothing but good to Granny, and that's what should matter."

"You don't know her like I do," Briana said.

He could feel Maddie stiffen beside him.

"What did she ever do to you?" Luke asked.

Briana shrugged. "She has a terrible reputation."

That wasn't an answer, and they all knew it. But it only confirmed the fears Maddie had confessed to him earlier.

"Until I came home, did you have any complaints about how Maddie cared for Granny?"

Briana didn't answer.

"And has anyone at the senior center ever complained about how Maddie helps others?"

Again, no answer.

Luke squared his shoulders and looked at Maddie, then back at Briana. "I realize I haven't been here very long, and I don't know all the history. But what I do know is that every person I talk to in this town tells me what a great job Maddie does at the senior center and how she's helped someone they know, including Granny.

So stop with the personal attacks and the attacks on her competency. This isn't what your treatment of Maddie is about, and it's time you stopped bullying her."

Briana looked like Luke had just thrown a bucket of ice water on her, and he was glad. He didn't know why it had taken so long to stand up to her, but this was the first time they'd encountered Briana outside the senior center. Maddie probably would have stopped him had he done so there.

Briana's husband, Corey, walked up to them. "There you are. Luke, good to see you again. Nice night, isn't it?"

He placed a kiss on his wife's cheek, then seemed to notice the tension.

"Fighting about Granny again?" he asked.

Briana sent Luke a glare, then said, "I have a headache. I want to go home."

"Of course." Corey held his arm out to Briana.

Once Briana and Corey were out of earshot, Maddie said, "Thank you. You shouldn't have said that, because I'm sure it will cause trouble later, but it was nice to have someone stand up for me. Not many people have been willing to do that."

Maddie didn't often show this vulnerable side,

and he could see how it had taken a lot of courage and trust for her to share as deeply with him as she had tonight.

"No," he said. "I should have said it to her sooner. I meant what I said. You said earlier that Kayla hadn't done anything to deserve it when people were mean to her. You've done nothing to deserve how Briana treats you."

All this time, Maddie had been working to encourage their daughter, because Kayla was a good kid who didn't deserve to be picked on. Maddie thought she deserved it because of her past mistakes, but as far as Luke could tell, she'd already made up for them.

"It doesn't matter," Maddie said. "In Briana's eyes, I'll always be the worthless girl who got pregnant out of wedlock and ruins people's lives because of it. I may not have done anything to her, but now she sees me and my daughter as a threat to her relationship with Granny."

Unfortunately, that part was true. But as the lights shone in Maddie's tear-filled eyes, there was one thing Luke could disagree with.

"You aren't a worthless girl. Never have been. Never will be. Surely you know that."

Maddie looked at the ground. "I want to believe it. But at what point will people stop treating me like I am?"

"When you stop letting them." He took her by the hand. "When you stop thinking that you somehow deserve it."

He thought about the wisdom from the Bible and the forgiveness of sins that he'd wanted to share with her earlier.

"Do you believe God forgives you?" he asked.

"Of course." A peaceful look crossed Maddie's face. "My faith is all I've had to cling to at times."

The breeze kicked up, and even Luke was getting a bit chilly. But before he suggested going back inside, he said, "Then who cares what they think? If you're living for God's approval, that's all that matters."

She looked like she was going to argue, but he shook his head. "Yes, I know, Briana is trying to get you fired. And I promise, I'll do everything I can to prevent that. I promise, I will stand up for you."

The tears that had been shining in her eyes started to roll down her cheeks.

Luke reached forward and brushed them aside. "But you have to promise me something."

"What?"

"No more avoiding me. We're not doing anything wrong. And for the sake of our daughter, we need to communicate and spend time together."

Maddie looked doubtful. "But the matchmaking…"

"I'll help you make it clear that people need to stop. I humored everyone, but I can see now that you needed me to back you up more strongly."

More tears fell, and Luke pulled a handkerchief out of his pocket and handed it to her.

"Let's move forward, Maddie. Together."

She dabbed at her eyes and nodded. "Okay."

Once again, he'd have liked to hug her. Instead, he squeezed her hand and said, "I'm here for you. I can't change the past, but I'm here for you now."

The warmth he felt from Maddie told him that he'd finally gotten through to her. It didn't solve the problem of Briana, but at least now, Maddie wouldn't be avoiding him, and whatever came their way, they'd figure out together.

CHAPTER EIGHT

THIS WAS MORE like it. Maddie sat back on the porch swing at the main ranch house at Shepherd's Creek, sipping her lemonade. Sometimes Maddie marveled at how easily they could all be family, considering everything in the past. Funny how all those years, Maddie had envied Josie for her family, and now Maddie was a part of it. In that spirit, they were including Luke and his family as well.

Maddie grinned as she saw the little ones crawling all over Granny. She knew that Granny's dearest wish had always been to have more grandchildren and great-grandchildren to spoil. While she definitely wasn't going to be giving in to Granny's pressure to have more children, it was nice to see that Granny could fulfill her need for children in a different way. In fact, Granny was probably getting an overload with

Wyatt and Laura's three toddler boys, and Josie's toddler daughter.

Luke sat beside her. "Every time I think it's not possible for Granny to be any happier, something happens to surprise me. Maybe this will get her off our backs about giving her more great-grandchildren."

Maddie laughed. "Funny, I was thinking the same thing."

He gestured at Laura handing Granny a glass of lemonade. "Should she be having that? I know we're supposed to be watching her sugar intake."

Maddie shrugged. "It's fine. The family has always been conscious of healthy eating and minimizing the amount of sugar in things."

She watched as Granny took a deep, appreciative sip of the drink. "Besides, you can't control everything she does."

Luke nodded. "I know. I just want her home so bad. And I'm afraid of anything that would mess that up for her. I'm not faulting the care that she gets at the senior center. If I had to be in a place like that, I'd want to be in one you run. But I can't stand seeing her so unhappy, and if this is what it will take to get her home, I'm willing to do it."

Maddie appreciated Luke's dedication. But before she could comment on it, Brady came toward them from the barn, and the kids ran to him.

"Ride?" they all shouted in unison.

Brady's loud laugh made her giggle. "All right," he said. "We've got Stolley Bear saddled for you, and we'll all take turns."

Maddie looked at Luke. "Even though they have all these horses, it's actually a rare treat to let the little ones ride. It's too much work to keep them all corralled and out of mischief."

Maddie brought her attention to Granny. "You want to go with us? I know how much you love Stolley Bear, especially now that we found out he's related to Caramello."

Granny grinned. "Do you think I could ride, too?"

Maddie hesitated. Though Granny was making great strides in her physical therapy, she hadn't heard that Granny was cleared to ride.

"I'm not sure about that, Granny," Luke said. "I know that technically your hip is healed, but you're still supposed to take it easy."

Then he gestured at her cane. "We got you out of your walker, but you're still not fully getting around on your own. I'm not sure how safe it would be for you."

Brady joined them. "We could do like we do with the little ones. She can sit on the saddle, and one of us will lead her around the arena."

Granny looked at them both wistfully. "Please? You know how much I've been wanting to ride."

Maddie wanted to tell the old woman yes. They had a stool that would help her mount, and all she would need to do was sit in the saddle. But if something happened and Briana found out, Maddie's job would be on the line for sure.

"I think I need to bow out of this decision," Maddie said, taking a step back. "I can't say yes, and I can't say no."

She could feel the weight of Granny's disappointment, and even Luke was looking at her funny, but then he nodded like he understood.

"Granny, you know that if anything happens and Briana finds out, she's going to get Maddie in trouble. Maybe even me. Can't you see that we all are trying to get you home? Once that happens, I promise I will take you here anytime you want as long as they're willing to help you ride. But not for now."

Granny's eyes filled with tears. "What if I don't get to go home?"

"Of course you will," Maddie said. "The staff is doing a great job helping you, and you're working so hard to do all the things you're supposed to. And Luke, too. Everyone's doing their part, so you just have to have a little more faith."

"Please," Granny said.

Brady looked at Granny with tenderness and love in his eyes. "Ida Mae, I have known you my whole life. While I believe that you are completely safe, I also know that these two are just trying to do their best for you. I give you my word that once you are released to go, I will drop everything and I will take you for a ride."

Maddie smiled at Granny. "We can plan a family trail ride."

The disappointment on Granny's face was real, but she nodded slowly.

"I don't want to make any trouble. I know how hard everyone is working to get me home. I don't know why Briana is being so mean, but if she gets you fired, I will cut her out of my will."

Maddie shook her head. "Don't you dare. Her insecurity is what's causing her to act like this, so let's instead think about ways we can make Briana feel more secure. It would go a long way if you told her that you had the opportunity to ride, and we told you no."

"Fine," Granny said. "I guess it won't hurt me to wait a little while longer. Let's go watch those kids. I do love the sound of a child's laughter on a horse."

Garrett, one of the twins, ran up to Luke and extended his arms. "Ride."

Luke grinned. "Yes, we're going to the barn now."

The little boy shook his head gestured up at Luke. "Ride."

Maddie held her arms out to the little boy. "I can give you a piggyback ride," she said.

"Well, if that's what you wanted," Luke said, "I'm happy to oblige." He bent down and let the little boy climb onto his back.

Even though Maddie was used to this kind of behavior, and she'd seen the different men at Shepherd's Creek giving dozens of piggyback rides, she'd never seen Luke have the opportunity to interact with the little ones. As they all went to the barn, Maddie couldn't help noticing the way the boy on Luke's shoulders chattered to him, and Luke seemed to be responding.

She had no idea what they were talking about, but it made her heart melt. A pang of regret hit her as she realized that Luke had never gotten to experience this with Kayla, but maybe someday when Kayla married and had children of her own, he could at least be a grandfather to her kids.

Even though Granny still walked with a cane, there was an extra spring in her step as she kept up with everyone headed to the barn. Being here at the stables probably did more for Granny's rehabilitation than the hours in the gym.

That was the thing about Maddie's dreams of being director at the senior center. It wasn't just the idea of upward mobility in her career, but the fact that she truly loved her job, and she was invested in the lives of the people who came through their doors. Granny was special to her, not just because she was Kayla's great-grandmother, but because Maddie enjoyed her as a person.

When they got to the barn, they all went out behind it to the round pen. Brady and Wyatt had set everything up for the kids to ride. When it came time for the twin that Luke had on his shoulders, as he lifted the eager little boy off, the boy kicked him in the face, causing Luke's nose to bleed.

Someone handed him a napkin, and Maddie

grabbed him by the arm. "Let's get you into the first aid room and we'll get you taken care of."

Maddie led him into the first aid room in the barn, which was kept fully stocked in case of minor injuries. "Why don't you come in here and sit down for a moment so we can get the bleeding to stop."

Luke groaned. "I'm not hurt that badly," he said. "It's just a bloody nose."

Maddie shook her head. "He kicked you pretty hard. And I can see that it's already starting to swell. Humor me and sit here with an ice pack on it for a little bit. Here's a cloth to catch the blood. If you give me a hard time, I'll make you go to urgent care."

For a moment, he got the same argumentative look on his face that Granny did when Maddie tried to advise her to do something for her own good, but as Luke stood, the fight went out of him. Yes, he was injured worse than he was giving himself credit for. This wasn't Maddie's first rodeo, and if she wasn't mistaken, Luke would have quite the shiner tomorrow.

Maddie opened the freezer and grabbed an ice pack, then handed it to him.

With kids, horses, and all sorts of other animals and dangers, they had everything they needed for a nosebleed.

"Who knew your nursing skills could be used on someone other than the elderly," Luke said, giving a small laugh.

"Oh, you'd be surprised. We have a team of volunteer first-aid personnel at the stables watching every ride, just in case. We take safety very seriously here and are prepared for just about everything." Then she gestured toward the outer walls. "And, for the rare occasion, the ambulance isn't that far away."

Luke removed the cloth from his nose and stared at it for a moment. "I think the bleeding has stopped."

A lock of hair had fallen over his forehead, and though she'd overheard him complaining to Kayla that he needed to get it cut and was asking for recommendations of where to do that, Maddie personally liked it. There was a vulnerability to him that she found quite attractive. She probably shouldn't be thinking such things about him, especially since he was hurt.

She couldn't deny that there was something between them, not after the night at the Cattlemen's Ball, and certainly not now.

He gestured at the empty spot next to him.

"Sit. I know you're supposed to watch me to make sure everything's okay, but I'd feel better if you weren't hovering over me."

Maddie shrugged as she joined him on the long padded bench they used as an examining table. "Occupational hazard," she said. "I'm not supposed to get so familiar with the patients, you know."

And, in spite of the very serious situation that was plaguing them, she gave a small, self-deprecating laugh. "As I'm sure you are well aware. Can you imagine the trouble I'd get into right now, cozying up to the patient like this?"

Luke scooted closer. "Well, if they talk, let's give them something to talk about." His voice was husky and warm, flowing over her body so gently and smoothly that it brought a warmth to her that she hadn't experienced in a long time.

"Now, now," she said. "I think you had a head injury, and it's affecting your judgment."

She hoped her tone was light and flirty, as she was trying to be. After all, she was out of practice with this flirting thing. They'd agreed to handle this. Maybe they should date like mature adults and talk about boundaries and how to handle it as a family at their next family therapy session. Here she was, alone with Luke, and she couldn't deny the chemistry between them.

Luke must've been thinking the same thing, because he leaned forward, brushed a tendril of hair away from her face, and said, "Maddie, you are still the most beautiful woman I've ever seen. I know we said we need to figure this out as a family, but I want nothing more, right now, than to kiss you."

Even though the rational part of her brain told her she shouldn't, Maddie nodded. "I want that, too," she said.

As Luke leaned in closer, she leaned in to meet him, their lips joining in a tender embrace.

She couldn't remember the last time she'd been kissed by anyone like this, and she'd certainly never experienced anything so wonderful. As their lips came together, Maddie finally felt like she'd come home.

But just as briefly as their lips touched, footsteps sounded, and Kayla called out loudly, "Mom! Dad! Granny is riding a horse!"

They jumped apart, but not before Maddie realized that Kayla had seen them kissing.

Luke stood. "What do you mean Granny is riding a horse? We told her no. Everyone knew we didn't want Granny riding."

Maddie got to her feet, and they followed Kayla out.

"Yes," Maddie said. "We all agreed."

"I know." Kayla sounded annoyed. "One of the neighbors showed up with a puppy, and the twins went bonkers and ran after it. When everyone was busy chasing the twins, Granny climbed the steps next to where Stolley Bear was tied. And now she's riding him."

Of course, Granny took advantage of the moment. Because that's what Granny did. They should've watched her more carefully, or at least assigned someone to make sure she didn't go and do something stupid.

But when Maddie went to take care of Luke, how could they have predicted this?

"I'm sure she's fine," Luke said. "Everyone's watching her now, so we'll let her finish her ride, get her off the horse, and remind everyone of safety."

Maddie nodded. "As long as she doesn't get bucked off or something before we get there."

Kayla snorted. "When has Stolley Bear ever bucked?"

Maddie shrugged. "Well, never that I know of, but there's always a first time. Look at how everything is already not going according to plan."

Kayla gave her a sly grin. "You mean like you and Dad kissing?"

Oh boy. This was exactly what she didn't want to happen. That's why they had agreed that they were going to talk about this together as a family with a therapist before they did anything rash.

"That was a private moment between your mother and me," Luke said. "And while we are planning on having a family meeting with our counselor to make sure that we are all handling this appropriately, it doesn't give you the right to pry into our personal business. My relationship with your mom is my relationship with your mom. No meddling."

Maddie watched as Kayla gave a little sniff and flounced. "Fine by me. Just don't take so long about it. As Granny says, you two aren't getting any younger for getting me a sibling."

Maddie blanched at Kayla's words. What was Kayla thinking, making jokes like that? She was too angry to respond to her daughter, and held back. As Kayla ran ahead, Luke reached over and grabbed Maddie's hand. "It's okay," he said. "I know. We'll address that later together."

As they rounded the corner, Luke let go of her hand, as if by some unspoken agreement that even though Kayla had just caught them kissing, neither of them was ready to face their families' questions or Granny's eager gaze.

Besides, they had bigger fish to fry. As they got to the round pen, Granny was on the horse, grinning like a fool.

"Yeehaw," Granny shouted. She had one hand on the reins, and one in the air like she was riding a bucking bronco, even though Stolley Bear was at a walk.

Even at her age, Granny still sat in the saddle in perfect form. Though it had been years since she'd been on a horse, her body remembered.

Brady was leading the horse, his hand on the reins by the horse's mouth so that even though Granny was holding the ends of the reins, he still had firm control. She also noticed that while they were trying not to make a big deal of it, Wyatt was walking along one side of the horse, constantly checking to make sure nothing went wrong.

Even though Maddie was concerned about Granny, and frustrated that Granny had gone against their instructions, at least everyone else had stepped up to make sure that Granny was safe.

Maddie opened the gate and entered the

round pen. "Granny," she said. "Looks like you're riding a horse."

She kept her tone gentle but firm. She still hadn't figured out how to handle the situation. How do you chastise a grown woman for something like this? If Granny had been a child, Maddie knew exactly what she would say as she got the kid off the horse and gave her a stern talking-to about safety. But despite her extensive experience working with the elderly, Maddie had no words for this. The problem with how people like Briana treated Granny was that she was a grown woman, with a great deal of worldly experience, and she didn't need to be shamed like a child for her behavior. Oftentimes, the shame was what caused people like Granny to act out. So what did Maddie say here?

She glanced at Brady, who mouthed, "I'm sorry," and she understood. From what Kayla said, Granny had gotten on the horse when they'd all been distracted by the kids, so Brady had done the best he could to keep Granny from getting hurt.

Now the challenge was to get her off the horse just as safely.

Brady led the horse back to where they had been helping everyone get on and off, but then

Granny started to cry. "Please. I'm not ready to get off."

Maddie went over to Granny and gently placed her hand on Granny's leg. "I know you don't want to, and I understand. But we need to get back to the house so everyone can eat."

At this point, making Granny feel bad about riding didn't seem like the right thing to do, especially since she didn't want to get off the horse. Maddie could always redirect Granny's attention for now, and later, when it was appropriate, they could have a conversation with Granny about the situation.

But as the men helped Granny off the horse, the older woman looked so heartbroken that Maddie sincerely felt bad. Though Stolley Bear had acted perfectly, and nothing had gone wrong, Granny had the stiff walk of someone who hadn't been on a horse in years. She'd be even worse tomorrow, which meant they'd have to come up with an explanation to keep Briana from crying foul.

Which was probably an exercise in futility, but hopefully they would get past it as they'd done with all of the other incidents involving Granny.

Even though Maddie genuinely prayed that

Granny would be able to go home soon because Granny would be much happier there, it would also ease the sense of foreboding that followed Maddie around, making her wonder if the latest snag in the plans would be the one to finally cost her the job she'd been working so hard for.

LUKE HATED THE brokenhearted expression on Granny's face as they helped her off the horse. He wished he could get her to understand that they were doing this out of love for her, not because they were trying to be mean to her.

His head throbbed from being kicked in the face, but at least the nosebleed had stopped. Who would've thought that giving a kid a piggyback ride would have caused so much trouble?

But when the toddler ran up to him and hugged his legs, saying, "I sowwy, Wuke," how could Luke be mad?

He ruffled Garrett's hair. "It's okay, buddy. Accidents happen."

Maddie caught his eye, and he returned her smile. They should probably treat this incident with Granny the same, but her actions were no accident.

Did she understand the risk she'd just taken?

Before following Maddie out of the round

pen, Granny made another beeline back for the horse.

"Oh, Caramello," she said. "You're my best friend."

Then Granny wrapped her arms around the horse's neck, giving it a big hug.

Tears streamed down her face when she let go of the horse and turned back to them. "This has been the best day of my life," she said.

Then a mischievous grin filled her face. "Aside from the day that Gerald made me his bride."

Though he was concerned about his grandmother, and how they were going to deal with the fallout once Granny started telling everyone she'd ridden the horse, Luke couldn't help smiling at Granny's pronouncement. He could give all the excuses for why he hadn't married and settled down, but the truth was, no one had ever loved him like that, and he had never felt like that about anyone else.

As they started back to the house, Kayla ran up to Granny and put her arm around her. "Granny, that was fantastic. I can't wait until you're fully recovered and we can go on a trail ride together."

Then she looked over her shoulder at Luke

and said, "Actually, I think we should all go on a family trail ride. After all, a former cavalry soldier is good with horses."

Luke laughed. "I keep telling you, they don't use horses for that purpose anymore. It's just ceremonial."

Kayla stuck her tongue out at him. "Yes, but I know you know how to ride a horse."

They had this discussion multiple times before, and while Luke eventually would go horseback riding with his daughter, it felt like a low priority compared to all the other things he needed to get done. Besides, it seemed incredibly unfair to go riding when Granny wasn't yet able to.

Still, he appreciated that everyone had kept the mood light after Granny's ride. Things had been tense for a while because they were all concerned for Granny's safety, but now that she was off the horse, everyone could breathe a little easier.

They could at least enjoy the rest of the day before heading back to reality and figuring out how they were going to keep Briana from blowing a gasket when Granny told her she'd ridden a horse.

When they got back to the house, they all

gathered for the family meal, and Luke was grateful when Maddie sidled up to him and said, "Don't worry, everything here is allowed on Granny's diet. We specifically chose what she can eat because we didn't want to make her feel bad that she couldn't have what everyone else was having."

It was wrong of him to think so, but all he really wanted to do was pull Maddie back into his arms, hold her tight, and kiss her. The kiss they'd shared had only been a taste of what he hoped would be between them, and the deep level at which she loved his grandmother made her that much more attractive. But he caught Kayla's watchful eyes on him, as did Maddie. They stepped away.

"Who's hungry?" Maddie asked.

"Don't think I didn't just see that," Kayla said. "For two people I just caught kissing, you're bad liars about nothing going on between you two."

"That's enough," Luke said. "Didn't we just have this discussion? What's between me and your mother is none of your business right now."

Then he turned and looked at everyone in the room who was staring at him. Now that they knew about the kiss, they, too, seemed to think it solved everything between him and Maddie.

He'd felt guilty for not standing up for her before, so now was his chance.

"That goes for the lot of you," he said. "Look, I know you all mean well, but all this matchmaking is putting undue pressure on our relationship, and if you don't let things just happen naturally between the two of us, you're only going to drive us further apart."

He stole a glance at Maddie, to see if any of this was helping. He didn't want that first kiss to be their last. But he knew that if everyone kept pressuring them, it would only confirm all of Maddie's fears about the relationship. He'd been miserable when she was avoiding him, so the last thing he wanted was to push her away again.

"This chicken looks fantastic," Brady said.

Even though it was obvious to everyone that Brady was deliberately changing the subject, Luke appreciated it. He didn't want or need anyone else weighing in on this.

As Luke went to fill his plate, he saw Brady lean in and say something to Kayla, who stiffened like she was being chastised. Since Luke and Maddie had already had their words with Kayla, he hoped whatever Brady had to say would get through to her. But he also knew how he had been at that age.

Even though he'd followed in his father's footsteps by joining the army, he'd intentionally chosen a job that would take him as far away from his family as possible, putting him in danger. This made it clear to his father that while he was technically doing what his father wanted him to, he was going to do it his own way.

Certainly, he had his share of regrets over that decision, especially because it meant he'd missed out on watching his little girl grow up. But he also knew that his time in the army and the experiences he had had shaped him into the man he was today. He wasn't sure the young man he'd been when Kayla was conceived would have been that good of a father.

But his rebellion felt different from Kayla meddling in their lives. She didn't understand what was at stake.

When he got his plate and sat down next to Granny, she smiled at him. "I'm so glad you and Maddie are getting married," Granny said.

Great. This was why he should have been firmer in telling Kayla not to say anything about the kiss. Now that Granny knew, it was going to put so many big ideas in her head. How could he let her down?

"Granny, people kiss all the time, and they don't necessarily get married."

Saying it out loud made him feel like he was cheapening the experience he'd shared with Maddie.

But he couldn't express how much that one kiss meant to him. Not now, not in front of all these people who didn't understand. It was easy to play off their encounter all those years ago as just being a couple of drunk kids. But the truth was, he felt something for her then, and he felt something now.

But how was he supposed to explore those feelings with everyone trying to push them in a certain direction? As he looked at Granny's dejected face, he finally understood why Maddie was hesitant in getting involved with him.

What if they gave the relationship a chance, and for one reason or another, things just didn't work out?

He had dated enough women where that was the case. It wasn't that any of them had done anything wrong or they'd hurt one another, but there just wasn't that spark. Or the spark had faded over time.

Luke could see them going through the motions for longer than they needed to, simply because they didn't want to disappoint their families by telling them it was over. Even now, looking at the crushed expression on Granny's face made Luke's heart hurt.

How devastated would she be if, after a time, they'd been dating, and things ended? He looked over at Maddie, but she quickly turned away. Apparently, it was now too dangerous for them to even look at each other.

Like her husband, Josie seemed to understand the tension in the room and turned to Granny with a smile. "Ida Mae, I know that this is my second baby and all, but I was wondering if we could get together sometime and you could help me with my baby quilt? The ladies at church made a beautiful one for Shana, and I'd like this baby to have something as well."

Granny used to run the sewing circle at church, and she lit up at Josie's invitation. It was the perfect subject to distract Granny's attention, and Luke relaxed into his chair and joined in some of the other conversations happening at the table.

When he thought about his childhood and coming here to Granny's ranch, this was the sort of thing he remembered. Family gathered at the table, talking about a million different things, and sharing life together. He hated that he couldn't have that with Briana anymore. The times they'd gone over to her house, it was always stilted and uncomfortable, like Briana was still trying to punish Luke for his past and find evidence to keep him away from Granny.

Even though they had made strides in their relationship, Luke wondered if he and Briana would ever get beyond coexisting, and have a real relationship.

As they started clearing the plates, Granny looked around with a question on her face. "Where's Gerald? Has he gotten to eat yet?"

Everyone glanced around, their gazes landing on Maddie. After all, she was the expert in dealing with situations like this.

Luke's stomach knotted. Granny had never had a lapse in memory before. His grandfather had been dead for nearly ten years, so why was she asking for him now? They'd all been working so hard to get Granny home, thinking it was just a matter of her regaining physical strength. But what if it was something more?

"What do you mean, Granny?" Maddie asked.

Granny looked around the room again. "I can't believe that we had supper without Gerald.

He's going to be mighty disappointed when he finds out that we ate without him."

Maddie smiled at Granny and held out her hand. "Why don't we have a seat in the living room and relax while we figure out what's going on?" Granny nodded, and as she got out of her chair to follow Maddie, she stopped and looked at Luke.

"Charles? Are you home? I thought you were at Fort Meade."

Luke swallowed the lump in his throat. Charles was his father, and he'd been stationed at Fort Meade when Luke was so small he barely remembered that time.

"Granny, I'm Luke, Charles's son."

Granny gave him a strange look and shook her head. "I don't know what kind of game you're playing, but when I tell Gerald, you will all have a lot to answer for."

Maddie held her hand out to Granny again. "Come on, let's go to the living room. I think you'll be pleased to see how they've redecorated since you were here last. I'll let you get cozy on the sofa, and I'll bring you some coffee and dessert."

Instead of looking pleased at Maddie's offer,

Granny frowned. "I should be helping with the dishes."

Maddie shook her head. "Oh, I wouldn't hear of it. In fact, young Kayla over there has volunteered to do all the cleanup today as part of a service project for her family to make up for sassing her parents."

At Kayla's groan, Luke bit back a laugh, in spite of his concern for Granny. He had to hand it to Maddie, she was one smart cookie who knew how to put her daughter in her place.

"Oh." Granny turned to Kayla. "I don't know who you are, young lady, but I suggest you start respecting your elders."

"But…" Kayla stared at Granny, obviously confused.

Granny put her hands on Kayla's shoulder and turned her toward the kitchen. Luke could tell by the expression on Kayla's face that she didn't understand why Granny just said that, but hopefully, in the kitchen, out of earshot of Granny, Brady could help their daughter.

Luke and Maddie got Granny settled with a slice of low-sugar apple crumble, and after chatting for a few moments, Granny dozed off.

When they finally took the empty dishes to the kitchen, Maddie said, "Granny fell asleep.

But I think when she wakes up, we need to have her seen by a doctor. I know it's strange and scary that Granny is acting like she's in the past and doesn't remember things, but we need to be calm and loving toward her because if she sees us panicking, she's going to panic, too."

Kayla looked at her mom, a worried expression on her face. "She didn't know who I was."

Their daughter usually resisted her mom's hugs, but when Maddie opened her arms to Kayla, she ran right in and clung to her for dear life. "I know Granny's old, but I just got her."

Maddie squeezed her daughter tight. "It's going to be okay, I promise."

Maddie looked at everyone in the room and said, "It's unusual for a lapse of memory to come on this quickly. As we were in there talking, I tried to observe for signs of any other medical issue, and I don't think that's what's going on. But we'll let her rest, and then when she's ready, let the doctor give her an exam so that we can all make sure she's getting the best treatment possible."

Luke didn't know what he would've done if Granny had an episode like this and Maddie wasn't there. Once again, he was grateful for her, and he hoped that this latest setback wasn't going to create a deeper rift between them when Briana found out.

Even though his greatest concern was for Granny, he also knew that this was going to create even more issues with Briana. But he prayed that they could find a way to come together as a family to do what was best for Granny, as impossible as it seemed.

CHAPTER NINE

MADDIE FELT HER heart pounding as she and Luke brought Granny through the emergency room, trying to maintain the air of calm she'd held since Granny had started acting strangely.

Even though Maddie had been reassuring everyone, the truth was, she was nervous, because Granny's sudden onset of forgetfulness wasn't normal, nor was it something she'd encountered before.

"Where am I?" Granny mumbled, her eyes wide and unfocused. "This isn't my house."

"Granny, it's okay. You're in the hospital," Maddie reassured her, trying to keep the fear from seeping into her voice. She knew how important it was for Granny to feel safe right now.

"Who are you people?" Granny asked, her gaze shifting between Maddie and Luke, a hint of panic flickering behind her blue eyes. "Oh.

Charles. What are you doing home? Where is your father?"

Then a look of pained understanding filled Granny's face. "Oh. Something's happened to Gerald, hasn't it?"

Maddie didn't know what was worse, Granny thinking they were at the hospital because something was wrong with her beloved husband, or that they would have to eventually tell her that he had died ten years ago.

This was a catastrophe.

"It's going to be okay," Maddie reassured Granny.

On the way to the hospital, Luke had texted Briana, and judging by the worried expression on his face, she was finally responding.

Maddie couldn't help but shiver as she watched the medical staff bustling around Granny, their faces etched with concern. They, too, were trying to act like everything was fine, giving Granny comfort and reassurance in her confusion. But Maddie's own training caught all the signs that this was a serious situation they weren't taking lightly.

She felt Luke's hand on her arm, offering a silent reassurance that they were in this together.

"Sir?" A nurse approached them, clipboard in

hand. "We're going to need some information about your grandmother."

"Of course," Luke replied.

As the nurse scribbled down the answers, Maddie glanced back at Granny, who was now being wheeled away for more tests. Her heart ached at the sight of the elderly woman, so disoriented and vulnerable.

Maddie had already placed a call to Granny's social worker, and Eva came bustling through the doors.

"Did they already bring her back?" Eva asked.

"Yes," Maddie said. "Just through there, but I told them to expect you."

Even though it pained Maddie that she and Luke weren't by Granny's side in this moment, Granny didn't recognize Maddie, and she thought Luke was his late father. They would be less useful to Granny than the social worker, who would be able to document that everything had been done properly so Briana couldn't use any of this against them.

It felt incredibly unfair that this is what things had come to, but they had to keep their focus on the bigger picture, and what was best for Granny, and not just what they wanted.

"Thank you," Eva said, giving Maddie a

warm smile before heading back to where they had Granny. They'd worked together on other cases, and Maddie knew that Eva's compassionate nature would help Granny.

Luke shifted in the chair next to her. "I hate that we have to sit here and do nothing. How long until you think they'll let us back there?"

Before Maddie could respond, Briana appeared at their side, her face a mask of barely contained fury. "What happened?" she demanded, her eyes darting between them. "Why is Granny here?"

"Granny got confused and disoriented," Maddie explained, trying to keep her voice steady. "We don't know what caused it yet, but they're running tests."

Briana crossed her arms, her gaze drifting from Maddie to Luke. "You'd better hope it's nothing serious," she told them coldly. "Because if anything happens to her while she's under your care, I'll make sure everyone knows it's your fault."

"Enough, Briana," Luke snapped, his anger flaring. "This isn't the time for your petty accusations. We're all worried about Granny here, so let's just focus on that."

"Fine," Briana huffed, taking a seat nearby,

but not before shooting Luke one last venom-
ous glare.

"Try to ignore her," Maddie whispered,
reaching for Luke's hand and giving him a reassuring squeeze. "We need to stay strong for
Granny, and that means sticking together."

Even though she could feel Briana's angry
gaze on her drifting to the hand Maddie held,
Maddie didn't let go. Luke needed her right
now, even if that meant subjecting her to more
of Briana's abuse.

Why did doing the right thing have to be so
hard?

THE WARMTH OF Maddie's hand in his gave Luke
more comfort than she could possibly know. It
meant even more to him, feeling the weight of
Briana's glare on them, suspecting she was judging Maddie, which Maddie was likely aware of
as well.

After Maddie's confession about her insecurities over her reputation, Luke had promised
himself to do whatever it took to protect her,
even denying his own feelings.

It had to mean something that Maddie was
willing to take this risk for him.

"Another health scare," Briana muttered under

her breath, glaring at Luke and Maddie. "Always seems to happen when you two are around."

"Can we not do this right now?" Luke pleaded, trying to keep his voice level despite his rising frustration. "Granny needs our support, not petty arguments."

"Petty?" Briana scoffed, her gaze narrowing as she stood up and approached them. "I don't think it's petty to be concerned about my grandmother's well-being."

"Of course it isn't," Luke said, his tone even. "We're all worried about Granny, Briana. That's why we brought her here—because we care about her. So let's save the family drama."

"Family drama?" Briana challenged, folding her arms across her chest. "Or are you deflecting so you have time to make up lies to cover up your wrongdoings?"

Luke's jaw clenched, and he tightened his grip on Maddie's hand. She gave him a squeeze back.

"Are you really suggesting that I'm deliberately harming Granny?" Luke asked, speaking quietly.

"You said it, not me," Briana snapped, her eyes glistening with unshed tears. "All I know is that my family's falling apart, and you're at the center of it."

Luke's heart ached as he looked at Briana—not just for himself and Maddie, but for the woman standing before them, consumed by jealousy and fear.

"Listen, Briana," he said softly, his voice gentle but firm. "We all want what's best for Granny, but tearing each other apart isn't going to help her. I'm sorry you feel like your family is falling apart. That's the last thing I wanted when I came home."

For once, Briana actually seemed like she was listening, so Luke took a deep breath and continued, "Please. Let's see what we're dealing with, and find out what's happening with Granny. Then we can figure out the best way to work together for Granny's sake."

Briana pursed her lips, looking unconvinced, but before she could respond, they were interrupted by the arrival of Granny's doctor.

"Good evening," he greeted them, his gaze moving between the three concerned faces. "I have an update about your grandmother's condition."

"Please," Luke urged, his voice wavering slightly. "Tell us what's going on with Granny."

The doctor nodded, taking a deep breath before he began. "Your grandmother has been diagnosed with transient global amnesia. It's a sudden, temporary episode of memory loss that can't be attributed to any known cause."

Luke's chest tightened at the news, his mind racing as he tried to process what this meant for Granny.

"Is it serious?" Briana asked, her voice barely audible as she clutched her hands together in her lap.

"Thankfully, it typically resolves itself within twenty-four hours, and most people who experience it have no lasting effects." the doctor replied, his tone reassuring. "However, we'd like to keep her here overnight for observation, just to be on the safe side."

Luke let out a soft sigh of relief, and he could feel Maddie's body relax beside him.

"Thank you, Doctor," Maddie said. "When can we see her?"

He smiled. "Soon. They're just getting her settled in a room, and then Eva will be down to talk to you all and bring you up."

As soon as the doctor left, Maddie squeezed his hand tight. "This is great news. I'm so glad Granny is going to be okay."

"Me too." Luke wanted to pull her in his

arms, but he knew he was already pushing Maddie's boundaries with the hand-holding.

Briana, however, didn't seem to share their optimism. Her face twisted into a scowl as she glared at Maddie and Luke, her eyes dark with accusation. "If you two hadn't been so focused on playing house, this never would have happened," she spat, her voice trembling with anger.

"Excuse me?" Maddie replied indignantly, taking her hand out of Luke's.

"Granny needed us, and we were there for her," Luke shot back, his voice firm yet controlled. He wasn't about to let Briana's misplaced anger get the better of him.

"Really?" Briana sneered. "Because it seems like every time she's left alone with you two, something goes wrong. What exactly do you two do when you're at the stables? Are you really watching Granny?"

Luke's gut twisted at the accusation. He'd never admit it to Briana, but this time at least, Granny had gotten into trouble when their backs had been turned. But it hadn't been nearly as sordid as Briana was making it out to be.

"Transient global amnesia isn't caused by anyone, Briana," Maddie interjected, looking like she was doing her best to remain calm despite the hurtful accusations being thrown their way. "The doctor explained that there isn't any known cause. Based on what I know of it, the medical community doesn't have any clear answers as to why it happens."

"If you know so much," Briana said, her tone sharp and biting, "then why did you bring her into the emergency room?"

Eva joined their group. "Because the symptoms Ida Mae presented could have been a number of things, and Maddie was wise to seek medical attention to rule out anything more serious."

Though Maddie appreciated Eva's defense, it didn't take the scowl off of Briana's face.

"And why were you called in? If they have nothing to hide, why was your presence necessary?"

The expression on Eva's face didn't change as she said, "Precisely for this reason. You're questioning the care Ida Mae received under Luke and Maddie's supervision, and I'm here to make sure that everything was done properly, which it was. Remember, I'm here as an advocate for Ida Mae. Your interests are immaterial to me, because my responsibility is to her."

It would have been completely inappropriate

for Luke to do a fist pump at this point, but he wanted to. What was it going to take for Briana to understand that their focus should be on Granny?

"Anyway," Eva said, "Ida Mae is resting right now, and while I'm happy for all of you to go see her, I really must caution you against upsetting her. She still doesn't remember what's going on, so please be gentle and don't force any issues with her. If you must continue your family squabbles, please do so outside of her presence."

Luke felt bad that he was part of the family squabble even though he had been doing his best to avoid it.

Eva gave them the information for Granny's room, and when Luke, Maddie, and Briana were alone in the elevator, Briana said, "There might not be a known cause, but it sure is convenient that it happened when you two were in charge."

Luke clenched his jaw, trying to swallow the angry retort that threatened to spill out. He knew that arguing with Briana would only make matters worse, but it was difficult to hold his tongue when faced with such baseless accusations.

"Enough," Luke said firmly, his voice cutting through the tension like a knife. "We all love Granny, and right now, playing the blame game isn't helping."

"Fine," Briana muttered, crossing her arms tightly over her chest. "But don't think for a second that I'm going to let you two off the hook."

When they got to Granny's room, she was asleep, snoring softly. She looked so peaceful, and Luke was hopeful that tomorrow, things would seem better.

If only resolving things with Briana would come as easy.

The flickering fluorescent light above them cast an eerie glow as Briana's gaze bore into him, her voice low and cold. "I don't think either of you is capable of taking care of Granny properly. She's had too many coincidental mishaps."

"All easily explainable," Luke said. They stepped out into the hall, and he tried to remain calm as he closed Granny's door firmly behind them. Eva asked them to not fight in front of Granny, and the last thing he wanted was for her to wake up to them arguing.

"I don't want to hear your excuses," Briana said, her voice dripping with venom. "It's clear that no one here is taking my concerns about Granny seriously, so I'm looking into having Granny transferred to a facility in Denver.

Maybe there she'll receive better care and be away from your influence."

Briana's eyes were filled with conviction, making it clear that she was serious about her intentions.

"Granny is family, Briana," Luke said, his voice strained as he tried to maintain control of his emotions. "We love her and want what's best for her. Taking her away from her home and everyone she knows isn't the answer. Her house is almost ready. Maybe you and Corey could come by sometime and help with the final details."

"Granny isn't capable of living on her own," Briana said, her tone sharp as a knife. "You haven't been here like I have. I tried helping her, but she wouldn't let me. I'm sure you looked at the house and thought we must be neglecting her. That's far from the truth, and you'd know it if you'd have been here."

Tears rolled down Briana's face, and for the first time, it hit him how hard this must all be on her. He'd been so focused on Granny that he hadn't given much thought to what it had been like for Briana.

"You're right," he said softly. "I'm sorry. Since Granny is sleeping, let's go get some coffee or something, and we can talk. For real this time."

Briana shook her head. "It's too little, too late. I'll be talking to the place in Denver to see how soon they can get her in. This was the last straw."

Luke watched as Briana stormed away, her heels clicking angrily on the hospital floor.

"Luke," Maddie said softly, placing her hand on his arm. "What are you thinking?"

He sighed, running a hand through his short-cropped hair. "I'm worried about Granny, obviously," he admitted, his voice strained. "But I'm also... I can't help but wonder if maybe Briana has a point."

Maddie stared at him. "You don't really think we're hurting Granny, do you?"

"No, of course not," Luke replied quickly, reaching out to take Maddie's hand. "Maybe it would be better for Granny to be at a facility without any personal connection to us. That way, there would be no bias in her care, and your job wouldn't be at risk."

Then he sighed, not wanting to face the truth. "Maybe we're being too optimistic that Granny can come home. People who don't know her might do a better job of evaluating her readiness."

"I don't believe that for a second," Maddie

said. "No offense to Briana, but she's too harsh with Granny. I know Briana means well. But she treats Granny like a child instead of a full-grown adult. We just all need to find a way to work together."

Did Maddie realize that she'd just said "we" in terms of working together?

Luke probably shouldn't be thinking these thoughts, even though their kiss today had given him more hope for their future than he'd had since discovering their connection. But it felt good to realize that even with Briana's attacks, Maddie wasn't pulling away from him.

Still, would it be enough to fix all the things falling apart around them?

CHAPTER TEN

MADDIE STEPPED INTO Granny's hospital room, the delicate scent of herbal tea wafting from the travel mug she carefully carried in one hand. In her other hand was a container of freshly baked muffins, made with ingredients that adhered to Granny's strict dietary requirements.

Granny was sitting in her bed, looking as she always did when Maddie checked in on her the mornings she was at the senior center. It was hard to believe she'd spent the night in the hospital, except for all the equipment monitoring her condition.

"Good morning, Granny," Maddie said gently, setting the items on the small table beside the hospital bed. "I know hospital food is worse than what you get at the senior center, so I brought you a little treat."

A twinkle shone in her eyes. "I suppose they're made with the healthy garbage you like. You didn't put kale in it, did you?"

Maddie laughed. "No kale, I promise. Just lots of healthy super fruits and all sorts of yummy goodness."

She opened the container and held a muffin out to Granny, who sniffed it suspiciously. "Is there chocolate in it?"

"What do you think?" Maddie asked, grinning.

Despite her concerns, Granny took a bite. "Hey, this isn't bad!"

"Now have some tea," Maddie urged. "It's the blend I bring you at the senior center. No caffeine, so I know you can have it."

Granny frowned. "Yeah, they said I couldn't have coffee. I really wanted a cup."

Maddie took a deep breath. Though Granny was in the hospital because of her amnesia episode, the doctors had found some concerning things in her blood work. "I know. And we need to talk about that, because it seems to me that someone isn't sticking to her diet."

Giving an exaggerated sigh, Granny said, "Even the Bible says people need salt."

Great. Now Maddie was going to have to debate the theology of nutrition with Granny. The old woman knew her Bible better than anyone else Maddie was acquainted with, so the last thing she wanted was to get into this discussion.

"Not in excess," Maddie said. "Your blood work shows it's been in excess. What I don't understand is that with the care we're taking to monitor your diet, how are you getting all this sodium? When we get you back to the center, we'll schedule an appointment with your doctor to find out what's going on."

Thankfully, Granny didn't look like she wanted to argue further, mostly because she knew she'd been caught. Maddie wasn't naive enough to believe that Granny hadn't been getting secret treats somehow, because there was no other reason for her levels to change so drastically.

"These muffins are so delicious," Granny said, taking another bite.

Busted.

"See? Healthy food doesn't have to taste bad," Maddie said.

Granny swallowed, still looking cranky. "It could have used more sugar."

Maddie shook her head. "You're impossible. I just wish you could understand that we're trying to get you home. We're not being mean for the sake of torturing you. This is for your own good."

"Speaking of home," Granny said, wiping a

crumb from her mouth, "I feel so much better now. When can I go back?"

Glancing at the open door, Maddie said, "As soon as the doctor comes in and gives you a final all-clear, we'll bring you back to the senior center."

"I don't know what all this fuss is about," Granny said. "I still don't understand why I'm even here."

Maddie hesitated for a moment, not wanting to upset Granny with the details of the previous day. "You don't remember what happened yesterday, do you?"

Granny shook her head, her brow furrowing in confusion. "No. But I think there was a barbecue at the stables." The furrow in her brow got even deeper. "Why can't I remember? What happened yesterday?"

They hadn't talked about how they were going to tell Granny about the previous day. But the worry on Granny's face made Maddie feel like she ought to say something.

"There was a lot of excitement for you yesterday at the stables."

Before Maddie could answer, Kayla came bounding in the room.

"Granny! Are you feeling better?"

"I'd be better if I was sleeping in my own bed, instead of having these people wake me up every time I got into the dream zone."

Kayla gave a perfect teenager groan. "I hate that. My alarm does that to me every morning."

Granny made a face. "This is worse than an alarm. I still don't understand why everyone is making such a fuss."

"You were acting really funny yesterday, Granny," Kayla said, plopping into the chair next to the bed. "You didn't even know who I was."

Maddie wished she could take the expression of pain from Granny's face.

"What else happened yesterday?" Granny asked.

Kayla's face lit up. "You rode Stolley Bear!" Then she frowned. "But you weren't supposed to, and Mom and Dad were really upset with you."

"Did I really?" Granny asked, her voice filled with surprise.

Maddie nodded, swallowing the lump in her throat. "Yes, but you shouldn't have, and we were all worried about you. Then you started talking like we were in the past, so we thought it best to bring you here. Did the doctor explain any of this to you?"

Granny's face fell, and she looked down at her hands, clearly saddened by Maddie's words. "He said something about some kind of temporary amnesia. I'm sorry for causing everyone so much trouble. I wish I could remember it, though."

Then she looked over at Kayla. "Especially the part about riding Stolley Bear. That must have been something!"

"Oh, it was," Kayla said, the grin returning to her face. "I took some videos if you want to see."

Maddie didn't really want to relive the day, and she needed to have a word with the nurses anyway.

"Okay, you two. I'm going to go talk to the nurses, so I'll let Kayla show you the videos. Just remember that you weren't supposed to be riding Stolley Bear, and we're not letting you do it again until the doctor says it's okay."

Kayla sighed, taking Granny's hand in hers and giving it a reassuring squeeze. "You did really good, Granny. But everyone was upset because you could have gotten hurt. Once the doctor says it's okay, though, I promise to take you on an even better ride. We'll go as a family."

The tears in Granny's eyes made Maddie's heart melt. Even though everything was so

messed up right now, she couldn't regret the relationship she'd given both Maddie and Granny.

"Thank you, Kayla," Granny said. "That
means the world to me."

Maddie stepped out, giving them some alone
time to share their moment, and went in search
of the nurse in charge of Granny's case. It was
unusual that Briana hadn't shown up yet, but it
was also nice to have a break.

At the nurses' station, Maddie saw that the
person she needed to speak to was on the phone,
so she patiently waited for her to finish. It was
strange, being on the other end of the care con-
tinuum, but it was a good reminder on how to
have empathy for her patients and their families. And as she was kept waiting longer than she
would have liked, it felt good to have patience
for the harried woman who was just trying to
do her job at what seemed like an extremely
busy time.

Once she talked to the nurse about getting
Granny's discharge instructions and coordinat-
ing with the senior center, she went back to
Granny's room. Granny and Kayla were giggling
together like schoolgirls, their heads close as they
whispered something that Maddie couldn't quite

make out. The sight warmed her heart, and she couldn't help but smile as she approached them.

"All right, ladies," she said playfully, "What's going on? What am I missing here?"

"Ah, Maddie," Granny said, still giggling as she wiped away a tear. "It's just a little secret between me and Kayla here."

Kayla nodded in agreement, her eyes dancing with mischief. "Yep, just us girls, Mom."

"I see how it is," Maddie teased, feigning offense. "I'll remember this the next time I have a secret." She winked at them both, happy to see their spirits lifted.

"Anyway," Kayla said, standing up and smoothing her skirt. "I've got to go. I promised Dad and Josie I'd come over for a bit today." She leaned down to Granny for a quick peck on the cheek and then gave Maddie her usual wave before heading out.

"Okay, Granny," Maddie said, settling into the chair next to Granny's bed. "Now that it's just us, are you going to tell me what all the giggling was about?"

"Nice try, Maddie," Granny replied, chuckling softly. "But a secret's a secret. You'll just have to wait and see what it's about."

"Fine," Maddie said. "I talked to the nurse,

and they're working on the paperwork to get you back to the senior center and to coordinate the doctor information."

"I thought my amnesia was temporary," Granny said, looking worried.

Maddie took Granny's hand. "It was. But they are worried about the results of your blood work, and the doctors are talking to see what we're going to do moving forward. Honestly, I'm kind of glad this happened, because they did a lot of tests to see what's going on. Now we know that you're not sticking to your diet, so the doctors need to determine the next plan of action."

As Maddie talked, Granny looked more downcast. "You're really mad at me, aren't you?"

Maddie shrugged. "As I've been telling everyone, you're a grown woman who can make decisions for herself. I just wish you'd understand that no one is trying to be mean to you. We all love you and want the best for you, so somehow we've got to figure out a way to make this work for everyone."

Granny nodded slowly, like she understood what Maddie was saying and didn't like it. But it was up to Granny to make the decision about her health. Maddie couldn't do it for her.

"I'll try to do better," Granny said, patting her hand affectionately. Then her eyes twinkled with mischief, and she raised an eyebrow. "But speaking of secrets… Kayla did tell me about something else."

"Oh?" Maddie asked, knowing Granny was trying to change the subject. She'd let her, because Granny was likely to get a very stern talking-to from Briana, and she didn't want to add to Granny's stress.

"Indeed," Granny continued, a teasing smile playing at the corners of her mouth. "She mentioned something about you and Luke sharing a little…kiss?"

Maddie felt her face heat, and she looked away, unable to meet Granny's gaze. She'd definitely be having words with Kayla later.

"Oh, that," she mumbled, wishing she had a better answer. "It was just a mistake."

"A mistake?" Granny echoed, her smile fading as she regarded Maddie with concern. "Why do you say that?"

"Because…" Maddie began, struggling to find the right words. "That moment took our focus off of what was important. We should have been making sure you were safe and shielding Kayla from any potential disappointment.

Instead, we let ourselves get caught up in our own emotions."

Granny listened silently for a moment, her expression thoughtful as she squeezed Maddie's hand reassuringly. "My dear," she started gently, "you are allowed to have moments of happiness, too. You don't always have to put everyone else first."

The others had been telling her that as well, but they didn't understand what Maddie's mistakes had cost her. She didn't regret having Kayla for a second, but no one understood what it was like to be under constant scrutiny for having made that mistake.

"Granny, I appreciate your concern," Maddie said softly. "But I've made so many mistakes in my life that I need to be sure no one else is harmed by my actions. If that means giving up a chance at romance with Luke, then that's a sacrifice I'm willing to make."

"You're too hard on yourself," Granny replied, her voice firm but gentle. "You can't keep everyone safe all the time. I'm a grown woman, and while I don't remember what happened yesterday, looking after me isn't your responsibility. And Kayla is practically an adult. You need to trust that she can handle herself."

Hadn't everyone else been telling her the same thing?

And yet, because Maddie had that private moment with Luke, Granny had gotten on the horse. While they couldn't say what had caused Granny's amnesia, Maddie had read enough about it to see that one of the suspected causes was the person having a highly emotional experience.

Riding Stolley Bear was definitely a highly emotional experience. Had Maddie's momentary lapse caused Granny's setback?

Maddie sighed, staring down at her fingers intertwined with Granny's. "I know, and I'm trying. It's just not as simple as everyone seems to think."

"Sometimes, letting go and trusting in others is the best way to show your love," Granny advised, her eyes warm and understanding. "And perhaps, in allowing yourself a chance at happiness with Luke, you'll find that your love for each other can only strengthen the bonds between all of us."

Maddie considered Granny's words, feeling a mixture of hope and fear tug at her heart. Could she really allow herself to be with Luke, without risking harm to those she cared about?

Maybe, but the middle of a family crisis and so close to Kayla finishing school wasn't the time to test that theory. Once Kayla was settled in college, and Granny was thriving back at home, then she could consider it.

"Close your eyes, dear," Granny instructed softly. Maddie hesitated for a moment, then complied. She felt Granny gently sliding rings onto Maddie's fingers, one by one. The rings fit perfectly, as if they had been made just for her. Maddie opened her eyes in surprise, looking down at the golden bands now adorning her hand.

"Granny, what are you doing?" she asked, her voice barely above a whisper.

"Those rings were blessed by the Lord when Gerald and I exchanged our vows," Granny explained quietly, her gaze locked on Maddie's hand. "And I believe, with all my heart, that you and Luke are meant to be together. Someday, those rings will be yours."

Maddie stared at the rings, feeling their weight on her fingers, and the significance of Granny's gesture weighed heavily on her heart.

Maddie looked into Granny's eyes, seeing the love and conviction that filled them. But as much as she appreciated Granny's faith in her and Luke, she couldn't bring herself to let Granny think they had a future.

"Granny," Maddie said softly, taking off the rings and placing them back into Granny's hand. "I'm so grateful for your love and support, but you can't promise these to me. They belong to you, and they're a symbol of the beautiful life you and Gerald shared."

She closed Granny's fingers around the rings, feeling the warmth of their connection through their touch. "Luke and I are just friends, and that's how it has to be. I know your heart is in the right place, but I need you to accept my decision."

Granny studied Maddie's face for a moment, her expression thoughtful. Finally, she sighed and nodded. "Fine. I won't push you anymore. But promise me one thing."

"Anything, Granny," Maddie replied, her voice laced with relief.

Granny's eyes bore deep into Maddie, almost desperately. "Please don't write off being with Luke simply because you're afraid of what others think. You have to stop living your life chasing after the good opinion of other people. The ones who matter will love you no matter what."

Hadn't Maddie and Luke had a similar conversation at the Cattleman's Ball? It felt like a lifetime ago.

Back when Maddie's scandals erupted, it felt like the world was closing in on her, with no one there to support her. Could it be different this time?

Maybe.

But Maddie also wasn't sure she had the strength to face having her life fall apart again.

LUKE WANDERED THE empty stables, looking for Kayla. She'd left her bag in his SUV the other day when they'd taken Granny to the hospital, and she'd asked him to meet her here so she could get it back.

Maddie came around the corner, then stopped when she saw him. "Hey. What are you doing here? Kayla doesn't ride today."

Holding up the bag, Luke said, "I was given the impression that Kayla needed this urgently."

"Right." Maddie groaned. "Even though she agreed to back off on the thought of our romance after witnessing our kiss, I think she's still trying to play matchmaker. She knew I was coming over here to drop off some of the things the sewing circle made."

Luke sighed, shaking his head. "I should've

known she was up to something when she asked if I was busy and then said she needed her bag. Why hasn't she needed it sooner?"

Then he chuckled in spite of the situation. "You and Brady warned me that she could be sneaky. I guess it was my turn to be on the receiving end."

Maddie's warm laugh filled him with peace. It was the sound of two people who were in it together.

"I know we didn't really talk about the kiss, or us, since everything got so chaotic that day," Luke said, hating the words that were going to come next, but feeling like he had to say them.

Shrugging, Maddie said, "We have way more important things to worry about than a poorly timed kiss. Don't stress about it."

She'd just put everything he'd been feeling into words, and yet it felt empty hearing them from her. Part of him wished she cared enough about him to fight for their relationship, but logic told him that she was also right about it being bad timing.

After all, had it not been for them getting distracted, Granny wouldn't have gotten on that horse, and maybe this whole thing wouldn't have happened.

Because it wasn't just about the kiss. It was about how he'd spent that whole day, mooning over Maddie, falling in love with her family, and being grateful to be part of it. The Shepherd's Creek family was everything he'd always wanted in a family, but he hadn't known he'd wanted it until he'd gotten to experience it.

The little boy had kicked Luke in the face because Luke was too busy staring at Maddie like a lovesick teenager. He hadn't been paying attention.

Which led to Granny riding the horse, then having her amnesia episode, and everything falling apart with Briana.

As soon as Briana found out that Granny had gotten on a horse, even though they had plenty of people to back Luke and Maddie up about it being Granny's choice to break the rules, it gave Briana reason to move Granny to a facility in Denver, where it would be harder to take Granny out on excursions like what had happened the other day.

"You're right," Luke finally told Maddie. "We don't need the distraction in our lives right now."

At least she looked as pained to hear it as it felt to say it.

"Maybe someday," Maddie said. "I know Kayla wants us to be together more than anything, but I don't think she realizes how much it's costing us."

"What is wrong with you people?" Kayla demanded, stepping out from one of the stalls. "You have the kind of true love that's better than any movie, and even though everyone is telling you to be together, you're making a bunch of dumb excuses."

Was this what Maddie had to live with constantly?

"I don't like your tone of voice," Luke said. "This is beyond disrespectful. We're trying to do the right thing here, and it's not your place to interfere or judge."

Instead of backing down, Kayla squared her shoulders. "The right thing is to be there for your daughter as a family. This is all I've wanted my whole life, and you're both being too stubborn to be good parents."

Whoa. Maddie looked like Kayla had just slapped her, and the gut punch was nothing like what Luke had expected.

"You're a child. You don't know anything about being good parents," he said.

"Mom was my age when she had me," Kayla

retorted. "And I make way better choices than the two of you did."

Before Luke could process Kayla's hurtful comments, Kayla turned and looked at her mother. "You tell everyone you do all this stuff for me, but when it comes down to it, you're really just selfish. You don't care about what I need at all."

Maddie had looked like she'd been slapped in the face before, but now her expression turned to anguish, like she'd been stabbed in the gut.

Luke glared at Kayla. His daughter or no, Maddie didn't deserve this. "Don't talk to your mother like that."

"I'm technically an adult. I can say what I want." Kayla put her hands on her hips, trying to look tough, but Luke could see her for the scared little girl that she was.

"Maybe in age," Luke said quietly. "But you've still got a lot of maturing to do before I'll consider you an adult. You're acting like a child, and this needs to stop."

He stole a glance at Maddie, who looked like she was doing everything she could to hold it together. She'd lived with the shame of her actions for so long, and now her own daughter was judging her. No wonder she'd been fighting their attraction. If only Luke had done a better job doing the same.

"You barely came back into my life, so you have no right to tell me anything."

Maddie took a step forward. "Enough. Kayla, this level of disrespect is completely unacceptable. I don't care how old you are. You don't get to talk to people like this."

"Fine," Kayla said, glaring at them both. "I'm going to my real dad's, where I know he actually cares about what I want. It's his day anyway, so you can't stop me."

Turning on her heel, Kayla stomped off.

Even though Kayla was right about Luke barely being back in her life, it didn't stop the deep pain in Luke's heart at hearing Brady referred to as Kayla's real dad. Until now, he hadn't realized how much it hurt to know how he hadn't been there for his little girl.

Maddie stepped beside him and took his hand. "I know. It hurts. I've been through this before with her, only in that case, I was in the wrong. We're not wrong here, and Kayla has to learn to accept that when it comes to other people's hearts, it's not her place to dictate."

Even though he'd been telling himself all this

time that he didn't need Maddie, her hand in his was the only thing keeping him steady right now.

"But I hurt her," he said quietly.

Maddie squeezed his hand. "We've been telling her all along that this wasn't happening. Maybe she'll finally see the truth."

Was it the truth? Yes, they'd agreed not to have a relationship, but if they were talking about the truth here, Luke *did* want a relationship with Maddie. He just didn't want to pay the price of losing everything else.

He closed his eyes as he realized this was how Maddie had been living ever since she'd found out she was pregnant. All along, he'd felt bad about the sacrifices she'd made, giving up her own personal happiness for Kayla's sake.

But as Maddie had been saying all along, things were way more complicated than simply being willing to give their relationship a try.

God, please help us. I've only been a parent for a couple of months, and I'm clearly not doing it right. I've lost the woman I love, and I'm not doing a great job of helping my grandmother or my daughter. Show me the way, because I don't know what else to do.

CHAPTER ELEVEN

MADDIE SURVEYED THE activity in Granny's room as Luke and Briana were working to pack things up. Things had been tense in the week that followed their confrontation in the barn with Kayla, and Kayla was still not speaking to her. Their family therapist had encouraged Maddie to give Kayla some space, so Maddie was doing her best to respect that.

The past week had been harder than Maddie could have imagined. This had been the longest Maddie had gone without spending time with her daughter, and she'd been missing Luke as well.

Worse, Briana had convinced Luke and Granny that the best place for Granny was some nursing home in Denver.

As Maddie stole a glance at Luke, he seemed like a shell of the man she'd first met when he'd come here. Part of her wanted to pull him aside and ask him what he'd been thinking, but with the way Briana kept glancing in Maddie's direction, Maddie didn't dare.

When Claire had stoically informed Maddie of Granny's decision to move, it had come with the subtle reminder that Maddie needed to stay out of the situation. All Maddie had to do was get through today without incident, and tomorrow, she'd have her final interview with the board of directors about taking Claire's place.

Easy peasy.

Except none of it felt like a victory.

In fact, Maddie felt sick to her stomach, watching what felt like a travesty.

No one in the room, save Briana, looked happy.

Kayla entered the room, then stopped short as her eyes lit on Maddie, then on Luke. Brady had told Maddie that he'd spoken with Kayla and said she was being unreasonable and needed to apologize, but so far, not a peep.

"I can't believe you're really moving. This is so unfair," Kayla said, obviously having learned nothing about not being so blunt. But at least she'd said what everyone besides Briana had been thinking.

Granny looked at Kayla sadly. "I know, but maybe it'll finally stop all the fighting."

Would it?

Maddie had her doubts, but it wasn't her place to say so. That's why they had the social worker advocating for Granny, and somehow Eva had agreed to it.

Briana walked over to the small table where they kept Granny's teas and other treats. As she started putting the things in a box, she lifted the bowl of spices Luke had made. "I'm not sure what to do with this. It's going to spill in the box."

She held up the bowl and dipped a finger in it. "What's in it, anyway?"

As quickly as Briana put her finger in her mouth, she made a face. "Salt! What is the meaning of this? I thought we were controlling your salt. No wonder your blood work was so bad."

"That's not possible," Luke said, taking the bowl from Briana, then tasting it himself. He also made a face.

"Granny! What happened to the spice mixture I made you?"

Instead of backing Luke up, Briana glared at him. "Nice fake surprise. I should have looked into this sooner."

Things might not be good between Luke and

Maddie, but Maddie believed him. He looked genuinely distressed that what he'd been trying to help Granny with had become something that had harmed her. And this was causing yet another conflict with Briana.

"Oh, stop, you harpy," Granny said. "Luke's mixture didn't have any salt. I added some to give it more flavor. You can't control everything I do."

Maddie bit back the urge to laugh. Though Briana had won this round, Granny wasn't going down without a fight. And at least Granny had defended Luke. Not that Briana looked like she believed it.

"You'll say anything to protect him. Just like all those times he caused trouble as a teenager. You let him get away with it then, and you're letting him get away with it now."

The fury on Briana's face was evident, and Maddie said a silent prayer that God would help Briana find comfort and forgiveness. The bitterness she was carrying over a grudge that was nearly twenty years old was tearing her family apart, and Briana needed the hand of God more than anything to help her.

"What do you want from me?" Luke asked.

"How long do you need me to pay for my sins before they're forgiven?"

Then he gestured at Maddie. "How long does she need to pay?"

Maddie shrank back, trying not to be part of this. She was too close to getting what she'd dreamed of to have it ruined now.

Luke returned his attention to Briana. "We go to the same church. Tell me where it says in the Bible how long we are to be punished before our sins can be let go of?"

Even though it was a mostly rhetorical question, Maddie had hoped Briana would give some kind of answer. Instead, Briana put a few more things into the box she'd been packing.

"Granny's stuff isn't going to pack itself."

Maybe Luke's speech didn't have an impact on Briana, but Kayla had stepped closer to Maddie, almost to the point of touching. At least Kayla was taking Luke's words to heart.

Briana picked up the small box Granny kept her rings in, and frowned. Then she opened the lid.

"Granny? Where are your rings?"

Granny looked puzzled. "They should be in the box. My fingers have been swollen lately, so I put them away."

The expression on Briana's face darkened. "They're not here."

A hush fell over the room as everyone looked up in shock. Granny frowned, her eyes searching the room for any sign of the missing belongings.

"I know I put them in the box," Granny said.

"What about on your nightstand by your lotion?" Maddie suggested. "I know you often set them there when you put on your hand cream."

As she spoke, she looked over at the empty nightstand. It had already been cleared of Granny's belongings.

"You seem to know an awful lot about Granny's rings," Briana said. "I saw you in the hospital, trying them on. Though you gave them back to Granny, perhaps you wanted them for yourself, after all. You probably didn't think anyone would notice them missing in the bustle of the packing."

Maddie's heart dropped as she felt the weight of Briana's accusation. She could feel the eyes of everyone in the room on her, their gazes filled with varying degrees of shock and disbelief.

"Briana, you've misunderstood what happened…" Maddie began, but her voice trailed off as she realized that defending herself would be an uphill battle against Briana's determination to discredit her.

She didn't take the rings, so she had nothing to worry about. But they had to find them, and fast, to ease the sting of Briana's accusation.

"Maddie would never take my rings." Granny said. Her eyes filled with love and concern. "It's true I gave them to her in the hospital to try on, but she wouldn't accept them, even though I still want her to have them."

Granny's defense of her only lifted Maddie's spirits slightly. Briana was looking at Maddie like she'd committed an unpardonable sin, and both Luke and Kayla wore expressions Maddie couldn't read.

"Let's just clear this up right now," Briana said, her voice dripping with false sweetness. "If you didn't take them, then you have no problem showing us what's in your bag."

That gave Maddie an even greater sense of security. Her bag was safely in her locker in the employee break room. There was no way Granny's rings would be there.

"I believe we need Claire to witness this," Briana said, pulling out her cell phone. Claire had given Briana her cell phone number because it was wearing thin on the staff to constantly call her in response to Briana's demands.

When Claire arrived, Briana explained the situation to her. Even though Maddie could see the doubt and frustration in Claire's eyes, Maddie knew that Claire had to follow policy.

"We'll have security go with Maddie to her locker, and we can look at things there."

"No," Briana said stiffly. "I want her to bring them here so we can all see for ourselves that she's a lying thief."

"I have nothing to be afraid of," Maddie said. "We can get my things and search them here."

Though it was humiliating for Maddie to let Claire call security, then have them walk her to her locker to get her bag, she held her head high, knowing she did nothing wrong.

When they got back to the room, Maddie handed her bag to Claire, trying to maintain her composure as her boss searched through the contents.

A heavy silence settled over the room, punctuated only by the sounds of items being moved around in the bag. The tension was palpable, each second feeling like an eternity. And then, Claire's eyes widened as she pulled something out of Maddie's bag.

"Is this what you're looking for?" Claire asked, holding up the rings, her voice a mixture of disappointment and disbelief.

Maddie stared at the rings in shock, unable to comprehend how they had ended up in her possession. Her mouth opened and closed, but no words came forth. Her heart ached, knowing that the people she cared about most now questioned her integrity.

"Maddie, I'm sorry to have to do this," Claire said softly, her voice laced with sadness. "You're fired."

The room spun as Claire's words echoed in Maddie's head. *Fired*.

"Wait, this isn't right!" Maddie exclaimed, her voice cracking with emotion as she stared at the rings in Claire's hand. "I didn't take those. I would never do that!"

Her eyes welled up with tears, and she desperately tried to blink them away. It was hard enough having her integrity questioned, but the thought of losing everything she had worked so hard for was almost unbearable.

She looked over at Luke, but he wouldn't meet her gaze.

As she glanced around the room at the shocked expressions, Maddie realized that she had zero support. How could she, when the rings had been found in her possession?

Briana looked satisfied, at least. This is what the other woman had wanted all along, so why shouldn't she be happy?

Even though Maddie hated for her daughter to witness this, she turned to Kayla. She was never going to forgive Maddie now.

"Mom didn't take those rings!" Kayla said, stepping forward. Her gaze locked onto Briana, a fire smoldering in her eyes. "You did it, didn't you, Briana? You're just trying to sabotage my mom's relationship with Luke and Granny!"

Briana rolled her eyes at the accusation. "Why on earth would I do something like that?"

It was obvious Briana had something to do with the rings being in Maddie's bag. But Maddie had no way of proving it. Nor did she know how the rings would have ended up in her bag.

Granny, who had worn an unreadable expression on her face, finally spoke up.

"Everyone, please," she said, raising her hands to quiet the room. "Let's try to find a reasonable explanation for all this. I know Maddie, and I can't believe she would do something like this. If she'd wanted the rings, all she had to do was ask. I'd already offered them to her."

Maddie felt her heart swell with gratitude for Granny's unwavering faith in her, even in the face of the evidence. But she could see the doubt in Luke's eyes.

"See?" Kayla said. "Mom didn't have to steal anything. But everyone knows Briana hates her and would do anything to get rid of her."

"Kayla," Luke began hesitantly, his gaze shifting between Maddie and Kayla. "As much as I don't want to admit it, I don't think Briana could have planted them. She arrived after Maddie did."

"Luke's right," Briana chimed in. "I wasn't even here when Maddie could have taken those rings. How could I have possibly set her up?"

The room was silent, everyone absorbing the weight of Briana's words. It was true. Briana had come in after Maddie, griping about Drake needing her to do something for him. And although it pained her to realize, Maddie had no way to prove her innocence.

"Luke?" Maddie whispered, still unable to believe he hadn't defended her. She searched his eyes, desperately seeking understanding or reassurance, but found only uncertainty.

"You know I would never do something like this."

Luke hesitated, his own confusion plain on

his face. "I… I want to believe you, Maddie," he said softly, his gaze flicking toward Briana for a moment. "But the evidence…"

Maddie felt as if an icy hand had closed around her heart, squeezing tightly. The betrayal stung like nothing she had ever experienced before. Of all the people in the room, she thought Luke would be the one to stand by her.

"Fine," she choked out, tears streaming down her cheeks as she turned away from him. "If you don't believe me, then there's nothing more I can say."

"Enough of this," Briana snapped, her voice dripping with disdain. "Claire, I demand that this thief be escorted off the premises immediately."

"Very well," Claire conceded, her expression grave as she motioned for security to approach. "Maddie, I'm sorry, but you'll have to leave."

"Wait," Kayla cried, rushing forward as the guards escorted Maddie toward the door. "Mom, I believe you! I know you didn't steal those things!"

"Thank you," Maddie whispered, her voice cracking with emotion. "I love you."

"I love you too, Mom," Kayla replied, her own eyes shining with tears. "I'm sorry about the other day. I've been a real brat."

"It's okay," Maddie said, putting her arm around her daughter as they continued toward the door. "We'll figure it out."

But as the door closed behind her with a resounding click, Maddie had no idea how any of this was going to work out. She'd lost Luke, her job, and any hope of being able to hold her head up high in town.

At least things were looking better with Kayla. While Maddie could consider it a victory, it was bittersweet, considering everything else she'd lost.

LUKE'S BOOTS CRUNCHED against the gravel as he walked up to the family ranch house, his heart heavy with guilt and frustration. He couldn't get the image out of his mind of how Maddie had looked at him, begging for his help, and he hadn't been able to come up with anything.

Did he think Maddie capable of stealing? No.

But he also had no reasonable explanation for how the rings could have gotten in Maddie's bag. He'd seen Granny take them off the night before, which was after Briana had left for the night. Briana hadn't returned until after Maddie arrived that morning, so there was no way she could have planted the rings.

"Lord, help me through this," he whispered.

When Luke pushed open the door, a sound coming from upstairs drew his attention.

The house had been locked, and no one should have been in there. Using his military training, he did a quick sweep of the downstairs, making sure no one was there. A few more noises came from above, so he made his way up the stairs, grateful he'd fixed the broken steps so he could move silently.

At the top of the stairs, Granny's bedroom door was ajar. From his vantage point, Luke could see that Granny's jewelry box lay open on her vanity, empty and abandoned, surrounded by a sea of trinkets and keepsakes. And there, kneeling on the floor amidst the chaos, was Drake, Briana's son.

"Drake," Luke called out softly, not wanting to startle the young man. "What are you doing here?"

The boy looked up with wide eyes, a mixture of guilt and fear playing across his features. He tried to hide whatever he was holding behind his back, but it was too late—Luke had seen enough.

"Nothing," Drake stammered, attempting to sound casual. "I was just…looking for something."

"Looking for something?" Luke repeated gently but firmly. "In Granny's things?"

"Yeah," Drake mumbled, avoiding eye contact. "I thought maybe she would want some of her stuff to go with her to the new place."

Given that they'd all been talking to Granny about reducing her belongings to go with her to the nursing home, Luke knew it was a lie.

"Drake," Luke said, taking a step closer to the boy, his tone steady and firm. "Whatever you're hiding, I need you to show it to me. It's important."

"Really, it's nothing," Drake insisted, his face turning a deep shade of crimson. "Just an old ring. I thought… Granny…would like it."

Another lie, because everyone knew that Granny hated all rings, except her wedding rings.

"Please, Drake," Luke implored, his eyes searching the young man's face for any sign of honesty. "I need to know why you're going through Granny's things. It's not like you."

"Fine," Drake conceded, finally revealing the ring he'd been clutching. "But it doesn't matter. It's just a stupid ring. I was just trying to be nice."

"Drake," Luke began, his voice quiet but

firm. "I can tell just by looking at it that this ring is too small for Granny. But it looks pretty valuable. Tell me what's really going on. Are you in some kind of trouble?"

Drake's expression shifted to one of panic, his eyes darting between Luke and the door.

"Please," he said. "My mom is already mad at me."

Putting two and two together, Luke asked, "Did you take Granny's wedding rings?"

Tears filled the boy's eyes. "I already gave them back to my mom."

"Why?" Luke asked, trying to keep his own emotions in check as he sought to understand the boy's actions. He'd been right in thinking that Briana hadn't taken the rings, but was it possible that instead of returning them to Granny, she'd slipped them in Maddie's bag to blame her?

"Because..." Drake hesitated, swallowing hard. "Please don't tell my mom and dad. I know you did bad things at my age, so maybe you won't be mad at me the way they will."

Luke felt a rush of sympathy for the young man before him. Whatever trouble the boy was in, he had to be terrified.

"Drake," he said, placing a hand on the boy's shoulder. "I know things have been difficult for all of us lately. But stealing from Granny isn't going to fix anything. How can I help?"

Drake nodded slowly, his eyes filling with tears. "I'm sorry, Luke," he whispered. "Hannah, my girlfriend, is pregnant. I just want to do the right thing, you know? I gotta give her a ring."

The air rushed out of Luke's lungs as he understood what this boy was saying. He'd met Hannah on a number of occasions, and she was a sweet girl. All the things Luke had done wrong, and Drake had the chance to do them right.

"I get it," Luke said. "I know you know about me and Maddie, and..."

Drake nodded. "My mom always says nasty things about her. I don't know what she's going to do when she finds out about Hannah."

Luke held his arms out to the boy. "She's going to love Hannah, and the baby. And we're going to figure this out as a family, okay?"

Even though Drake had never seemed like an affectionate kid, he hugged Luke tight, like he was hanging on for dear life.

From what he'd heard about Brady and his family, they'd accepted Maddie with open arms and given her the support she'd needed for Kayla. Here was Drake, trying to do the same thing.

When they pulled apart, Drake held up the ring. "You think Granny would mind if I gave this to Hannah? Mom used to always say that Granny's rings were for my future wife, but then I heard her yelling about how she overheard Granny telling Maddie that she wanted Maddie to have them when you two got married."

Luke blew out a breath. Maddie. His stomach clenched at the knowledge that he'd been so wrong in not standing up for her. Isn't that what had been their problem to begin with?

He had so much to make up for, but right now, he had to help his cousin's son.

"How about we ask Granny? It's a nice enough ring, but maybe she'll have something else in mind."

Drake's face fell. "She's gonna be mad at me, too. And here I've been trying to butter her up so she'll give us money for the baby by bringing her treats and things she likes."

One more mystery explained. "You know those treats are making her sick, right?"

Drake looked away, his face flushed with shame. "I... I didn't think it would hurt her," he stammered.

"Granny's health is delicate, and by giving her those things, you're putting her at risk,"

Luke said. "If you had just talked to her, she'd have understood."

"I just wanted her to love me," Drake whispered, tears welling up in his eyes. "I didn't want her to take away my inheritance and give it to Kayla instead. I'm trying to find a job, but babies are expensive."

Luke sighed, feeling a wave of sympathy for the young man standing before him. How would he have handled it, had he known Maddie was pregnant?

"Listen, Drake," he began softly, placing a hand on the boy's shoulder. "I get it. I'm probably the best person you could have confided in. I promise, no matter what, I'm here for you."

Drake nodded. "Thank you. I'm sorry for trying to steal from Granny. I guess I'm not that good at it. I just hope she can forgive me."

Laughing, Luke said, "Oh, she will. Trust me. Did you ever hear the story about the time I tried to steal from her?"

"No." Drake's eyes widened. "Mom always said you were the black sheep, so I'm surprised she didn't."

"I'll tell you in the car on the way to talk to Granny. Maddie was fired because she was accused of stealing Granny's rings, and you need to make things right. That, and it sounds like we've got a baby to plan for."

Luke put his arm around Drake and began telling him the tale of his own mixed-up youth. Though Luke may have made a mess of his own life, he had hope that he could help someone avoid making the same mistakes. Fixing Drake's damage would be easy enough, but he wasn't so sure he could fix the damage to his relationship with Maddie and Kayla.

CHAPTER TWELVE

MADDIE TOOK A deep breath as she stood outside the senior center, her heart pounding in her chest. Claire had texted her, asking her to come in for an urgent meeting, and she couldn't help but assume it was to sign the final papers for her dismissal. A knot settled in her stomach at the thought.

Upon reaching the meeting room, she hesitated for a moment before entering, her heart racing. Maddie's gaze swept over the room, taking in the familiar faces of Luke, Briana, Drake, Kayla, Claire, Eva, and Granny. Her heart ached at the sight of Granny, who looked so small and fragile sitting in her chair.

Even though Maddie had been feeling sorry for herself, she'd been worried about how all of this stress was affecting Granny.

"I'm glad you could join us," Claire said, nodding toward an empty chair beside Granny. "Please have a seat."

Maddie nodded, trying to keep her composure as she sat down. The air in the room was thick with tension, and she couldn't help but wonder what had brought them all together like this.

"Thank you for joining us, everyone," Luke began, his voice steady but firm. "There's something important we need to discuss."

He paused, then looked at Drake. "I caught Drake stealing from Granny's house, and in our discussion, he admitted to taking the rings Maddie was accused of stealing."

Maddie's eyes widened, and she looked at Drake, who shifted uncomfortably in his seat.

"Drake, what happened to the rings after you took them?" Luke asked, his tone gentle despite the gravity of the situation.

Drake hesitated, his eyes filled with shame. "I… I gave them to my mom," he admitted quietly, his voice cracking.

Maddie felt a mixture of relief and sympathy wash over her, realizing that she'd been called to this meeting because Luke had found a way to exonerate her. And that it had been as she and Kayla had suspected all along.

Briana had set her up.

Briana's face paled at Drake's admission, her

eyes darting around the room as if searching for an escape. "That's not true," she stammered, her voice trembling. "I don't know what he's talking about."

"Mom, don't lie!" Drake cried out, his eyes filling with tears. "We all make mistakes, and we have to own them and try to do better. I also was the one who sneaked Granny all those unhealthy things. I was afraid she was going to replace me with Kayla."

Maddie glanced at Granny, who looked genuinely upset at Drake's words. She'd had a lot of harsh things to say about Drake in the past, but hopefully this was making her realize that Drake was simply a boy who needed his Granny's love.

"No one could ever replace you," Granny said. "I keep telling everyone there's enough of me—and my money—to go around."

Maddie reached for Granny's hand, took it and squeezed. Hopefully, this would finally get through to everyone that they didn't need to go to such extreme measures.

"Now it's your turn, Briana," Luke said, giving his cousin a firm look. "Can you please tell everyone what happened?"

Briana stiffened in the chair. "Fine. Drake did take the rings. I was going to return them to

Granny, but then I saw Maddie's bag sitting on top of the nurses' station. I was tired of people not listening to me about Maddie's ineptitude, so I...helped things along."

Maddie closed her eyes and said a quick prayer for patience. Even after all this, Briana was still going on about Maddie.

But that'll serve her right for not taking it directly to her locker. She hadn't intended to leave it unattended, but there was a crisis when she'd arrived, and then she'd gotten distracted, so she had left her bag out for too long.

Luke shook his head. "We need to have this out, once and for all. Maddie has had the patience of a saint dealing with you. Other than not giving you your way, has Maddie ever acted negligently?"

Briana stared at him, openmouthed.

Without letting her answer, he turned his attention to Eva and Claire. "Have any of Briana's complaints against Maddie had any credibility?"

Eva and Claire looked at each other, then shook their heads.

"Until the theft accusation, Maddie's record has been impeccable. Unfortunately, theft is grounds for immediate dismissal," Claire admitted.

The expression on Luke's face could have

made him a lawyer. "So since it's been proven that she didn't steal the rings, I'm assuming she has her job back."

Claire nodded. "If she wants it. I feel awful about what happened. I should have done a better investigation."

She turned to Maddie. "I am so sorry. I was a terrible boss, and an even worse friend. Can you forgive me?"

Tears filled Maddie's eyes at the way Claire's voice caught. She didn't know what she'd have done in Claire's position, but she was grateful the truth was out.

"Of course," Maddie said. "And yes, I do want my job back. And the chance to interview for the promotion, if that hasn't already been spoiled."

Luke made a sound. "For what you've been through the past couple of months, you deserve the promotion and more."

Laughing, Claire said, "Agreed. But it's out of my hands, and I will be sure the hiring committee understands that not only were you set up, but you handled the situation with the kind of grace and aplomb that a director should have."

Relief filled Maddie at the idea that her dream might not be out of reach after all.

As Maddie watched the scene unfold before her, a wave of relief washed over her. The truth had finally come to light, exonerating her from any wrongdoing. At the same time, her heart ached for Drake, who had been so desperate for love and attention that he had resorted to such drastic measures.

"Drake," she began, her voice full of compassion. "I'm so sorry we didn't see how much you were hurting. We were all so focused on Kayla and her well-being that we didn't think about how this might be affecting you, too."

Shrugging, Drake said, "I guess I didn't make it easy, either. The truth is, I'm going through some of my own stuff, and I guess I was a little desperate."

Kayla straightened. Then her gaze met Drake's, and she said gently, "Drake, we've never really talked much at school or been friends, but I'd like to change that. We're family now, and it'll be nice to have a cousin my age."

The compassion in Kayla's voice reminded Maddie of how great her daughter could be. They'd talked briefly after Maddie was fired, and though Kayla had apologized, they'd also agreed there was still some work to be done to heal the relationship.

"Maybe," Drake said. "But maybe you'll be embarrassed about me when you find out what I'm going through."

"What could you possibly going through?" Briana scoffed. "You have the perfect life."

Drake shook his head. "No, Mom, I don't. Hannah is pregnant, and I already told her that I'm marrying her and stepping up to be a good father to our baby."

He looked over at Granny. "I'm sorry, Granny. That's why I stole your rings. I was trying to give Hannah something nice. Luke caught me going through your things to find her a different one, and he said I should just talk to you."

Maddie glanced at Briana, who wore an expression of shock. This probably wasn't what she'd imagined as her son having the perfect life.

"I'm not embarrassed to be friends with you," Kayla said. "It sounds like you're trying to do the right thing and be a father to your baby, like Brady Dad did for me, and like I know Luke Dad would have if he'd known."

Maddie felt a swell of pride as she watched her daughter, sensing the bravery it took for Kayla to reach out to Drake in this difficult moment. Especially because she saw how her daughter's eyes searched for Luke's, like she knew that she had some amends to make there.

"I don't know what to say," Briana finally said.

"I do." Granny stood and went to Drake. "I'm sorry you felt you had to sneak around to do something nice for your future wife. You wouldn't have found anything good at the house, though. I keep all the good stuff in the safety deposit box. We'll make plans to meet there, and you can pick something nice."

She reached forward and hugged her great-grandson. "A baby! We're going to love that baby, and it's going to grow up with family. I hope you know we're here for you."

Maddie teared up at Granny's words. She'd longed to hear those words from her mother, who'd scoffed at her and told her it was her funeral. Having Kayla was the best thing to ever happen to Maddie, even if it had been hard.

Then Granny said, "I only agreed to go to Denver because I wanted to stop all the fighting. But now I want to stay here at the senior center until I'm released to go home. Drake and Hannah need family around them more than ever, so I'm staying."

Eva, who had been silently observing the confrontation, finally cleared her throat. "I must say that I'm disappointed in both of you," she said, looking at Briana and Drake with a stern expression. "But I support Granny's decision to stay at the senior center. It's important for her health and well-being, as well as for the healing of this family."

As the tension in the room seemed to lessen, Briana's posture slumped. "Granny, Maddie, Luke… I'm so sorry," Briana choked out, tears streaming down her cheeks. "I let my jealousy and resentment cloud my judgment, and I acted maliciously. I never meant for any of this to happen."

Then she turned to her son. "I'll admit that being a grandmother so young was never in my plans. But neither was a lot of things, and here we are. Of course we'll be here for you, Hannah, and the baby. I'm sorry I made it so hard for you to tell me."

Maddie reached out and placed a gentle hand on Briana's arm, hoping the warmth of her touch conveyed empathy. "Briana," she began softly, "I understand better than most what it's like to do things you're not proud of."

She hesitated for a moment, feeling the weight of her past actions bearing down on her as she continued, "I lied about who Kayla's father was, and I hurt so many people along the way, but I've come to learn that acting out of fear only brings more trouble into our lives."

As Maddie spoke, Briana's tear-filled eyes met hers, revealing a shared pain. It reminded her a lot of how she and Josie had to work to overcome their painful past, but in the end, they'd figured it out.

Maybe now, Maddie and Briana could move forward in their relationship.

LUKE'S HEART HAMMERED in his chest as he watched Maddie and Briana make peace. He was no stranger to fear—after all, he'd faced it countless times during his military career. But this time, the stakes felt higher, more personal. This wasn't about risking his own life; it was about his relationship with Maddie.

"Since we're all doing the apology thing here," he said, "Maddie, I'm sorry I didn't do more to defend you against Briana's allegations. I knew in my heart that you couldn't have done it, but with the evidence staring us in the face, I didn't know what to say."

He looked over at Kayla. "Even though you still need to learn to do a better job of not blurting out every little thing, I'm glad you stuck up for your mom. I should have done the same."

He gestured at the doorway. "So now that we've gotten all this worked out, let's get Granny to her room so we can unpack and help her settle back in."

As everyone filed out, he stopped Briana. "All that forgiveness stuff, I want to work on that between us, too. We didn't use to hate each other, so let's see if we can find that again."

Briana gave a jerky nod. "I guess maybe I've taken my grudge-holding a little too far. For what it's worth, Corey keeps telling me that, and I suppose I should start listening to him."

The last person out was Maddie, and Luke wanted to believe that perhaps the reason she'd hung back was to talk to him.

"I'm really sorry, Maddie," he said. "I hope someday you can forgive me. I keep using the excuse that I'm new at this, but I feel like it's going to be one of those things I'm constantly trying to get right."

Her smile warmed him all the way to his toes. "I'm pretty sure that's called life. We're all just trying to get it right. I forgive you."

She leaned in and gave him a hug, flooding him with a feeling of safety and comfort.

"I'm so afraid of messing everything up," he admitted. "I've faced death countless times in the army, and I was never so afraid as I am now. I have so much to lose."

Maddie pulled away from their hug and looked up at him. "I'm scared, too. I nearly lost everything, and yet it all worked out. I have to believe that God has had His hand on our lives, guiding us, especially when things look the bleakest."

"So what you're saying is we'll figure it out."

Smiling at him, she said, "It hasn't failed me yet."

Though he'd thought Kayla had left, she came around the corner and said, "If you two are serious about facing your fears, then maybe it's time to work on the fears you have about each other and your relationship."

He recognized the look of irritation on Maddie's face. And this time, he had it covered.

"You trying to tell us what to do didn't end well for the three of us the last time. Just like we have to trust in God and each other to work through things, you have to trust that your mom and I are going to figure that out, too."

Kayla's shoulders slumped slightly. "Is it so wrong to want you two to be happy?"

"That's on us, not you," Maddie said gently. "We both get it. Now you need to stop."

For the first time, Kayla looked contrite. "I'm sorry. Brady Dad also said I was out of line. I'll try to do better."

"Kayla's right," Granny piped up. "You two belong together. I've seen the way you care for each other and how you both light up when you're around one another. There's something special between you, and it would be a shame not to give it a chance."

"Maybe you're both right," Maddie said, her gaze shifting between Luke, Kayla, and Granny. "We've been so focused on our own fears and insecurities that we haven't given our relationship the opportunity it deserves."

For a moment, all was quiet in the hallway as the weight of their daughter's words settled over them. Luke took a deep breath, realizing that as much as he'd thought he had at stake, they did have family members who also wanted to see them happy.

"Yes, but this is our relationship," Luke emphasized. "You two have to let us figure it out ourselves. No more meddling. Got it?"

Even though Kayla and Granny exchanged conspiratorial looks before nodding, Luke would accept that as a yes.

Then he looked up at Maddie, her eyes shining. She'd never looked so beautiful, and even though the nursing home was not the most romantic spot for their first official kiss as a couple, he pulled her back into the now-empty conference room, closing the door so Granny and Kayla couldn't see in.

"What is this about?" Maddie asked.

"Just that I want to seal our newfound relationship with a kiss, and I don't want those two nosy Nellies spying on us."

Maddie nodded, her eyes full of light as she gazed back at him. And somehow, in that moment, all Luke's fears dissipated.

Slowly, Luke leaned down and captured Maddie's lips with his own. The kiss was sweet and tender, speaking to the promise of the future together as a very large and unusual family. But family, nonetheless. And he was so grateful to Maddie for showing him that family truly was what you made it.

EPILOGUE

MADDIE COULDN'T HELP but smile as she looked around the table in Granny's newly fixed-up house, her heart swelling with gratitude and love for everyone gathered there.

"Thank you all so much," Granny began, her voice thick with emotion. "I can't tell you how wonderful it is to be back in my own home, surrounded by my family. Your support during my recovery has meant the world to me."

Maddie felt tears prick at the corners of her eyes as she listened to Granny's heartfelt words. She knew just how important this moment was—not only for Granny but for every person sitting around that table. They'd all worked so hard to get her home.

As the meal came to an end, laughter and lighthearted chatter filled the air while they all helped clear the table, everyone rushing a little more than usual. Granny had finally been cleared by her doctor to ride again, and they were all looking forward to going to the stables so they could have a family horseback ride.

Ordinarily, they'd have had the family meal at Shepherd's Creek, but given that this was their first meal with Granny being released, they wanted to do it at her house.

"Granny, I can't wait to see you back in the saddle," Maddie said, glad she could finally encourage Granny in her passion.

Luke's eyes met Maddie's from across the room, a warm smile playing on his lips. Their gazes held for a moment longer than necessary, hinting at the connection between them.

The best part about waiting so long to have a romance was that she felt they both were committed to doing things right, which strengthened their bond.

"Are you all ready to head out?" Brady asked, addressing the group. The excitement in his voice was contagious as he glanced back at Maddie, who couldn't help but grin back at him.

Once more, she was so grateful that they'd been able to have such a deep friendship in spite of their past.

"Yes!" Kayla chimed in, her eyes sparkling

with anticipation. "I've been waiting for this day forever!"

They all loaded into their respective vehicles for the short drive to the stables. It was a little inconvenient, but it was well worth it to give Granny the chance to have her first family meal in her own home.

Once they arrived at the stables, Maddie noticed Briana and her husband, Corey, along with Drake and Hannah, lingering behind. They appeared hesitant, their eyes darting back and forth between the group and the horses. Maddie knew they weren't as familiar or comfortable with the animals as the rest of them were.

"Hey, guys," Kayla called out, a friendly smile on her face. "You should join us. It's going to be so much fun!"

Hannah patted her growing belly. "I'm going to sit this one out. Josie and I are due around the same time, and she was going to give me some tips on what else I need for the baby."

It warmed Maddie's heart that the young girl had someone who could be a mentor to her as she navigated these changes in her life. Maddie hadn't had that, and in a way, having the family be there to support Drake and Hannah felt like a redemption of her own story.

"What about you? Come on, Briana! Drake! Corey!" Kayla's encouragement made Maddie smile.

"Thanks, Kayla," Briana responded hesitantly, glancing at her husband and son. "But we're not really...horse people."

"Aw, don't worry about it," Kayla reassured them, her voice sweet and encouraging. "We can all help you. I promise, it's not as scary as it seems."

Drake's face lit up as he walked over to Kayla. "Honestly, I've always wanted to learn more about horses."

"Me, too," Corey said, joining them. "Funny how you live in the country, and you're surrounded by animals you don't know much about."

Having Briana and her family join theirs seemed like a natural progression of the Shepherd's Creek group. Somehow, they'd all managed to make everything fit together, and it was working better than Maddie could have imagined.

"What about you, Briana?" Kayla asked.

"Thank you," Briana said, her voice softening. "But I think I'll just stick to taking pictures for now. I want to capture all these beautiful memories for Granny."

As the laughter and chatter continued around them, Maddie caught Luke's gaze from across the yard. The warmth emanating from his eyes sent shivers down her spine, and she couldn't possibly imagine herself loving anyone more.

Loving Luke had been worth the wait.

"Hey, Maddie," Luke called out to her, walking closer with a soft smile playing on his lips. He looked around at their gathered family, then back at her.

"You act like you're up to something," she said. "If this is another one of Wyatt's water balloon fights, I will get you all. Kayla did my hair so nice for today."

Now that Kayla had agreed to let Maddie and Luke's relationship be what it needed to be, mother and daughter had found a new closeness. Today, Kayla had even offered to do Maddie's hair, saying it would be fun to dress up for Granny's special dinner.

Of course, they'd all soon be covered in dust, but Maddie wasn't going to have it ruined by the guys and one of their silly pranks.

"And it does look beautiful," Luke said. "But you know I think you're beautiful no matter how your hair looks."

She smiled at him, feeling so loved by this

man. Now that everyone had given them a little space to explore their relationship, she was learning to feel secure in his love.

"So you might notice that everyone is here for Granny, but they're also here for another occasion."

Maddie looked around, noticing that everyone had gathered in a sort of semicircle.

"Oh? What's the occasion?"

Luke grinned and bent on one knee, holding out an engagement ring. "Will you marry me, Maddie?"

Tears welled up in Maddie's eyes as she processed the enormity of his question. Sure, she'd known they were eventually going to get to this place, but having him ask her, here, in front of everyone they'd loved, it seemed almost too much to process.

The people gathered represented so much of their lives, the past they regretted, the things they'd done wrong and made right, but also a present, where they'd learned to support each other. More importantly, as she felt the love from everyone gathered, she saw the hope of the future, and was secure in the knowledge that together, with God's help, they could get through anything.

"Yes," Maddie said.

As Luke rose and kissed her, she could hear Kayla in the background.

"Finally!" she exclaimed. "I knew you two were meant for each other. We're going to be a real family now!"

Maddie and Luke exchanged a tender smile as laughter bubbled up from everyone around them.

"It's about time," Granny said as they pulled apart. "We've got a wedding to plan!"

"Wait, wait!" Briana called out, holding up her phone. "I got it all on video! I can't wait to share our family's happy news with everyone."

"Thank you, Briana," Maddie said, touched by the sincerity of her words. She wouldn't call Briana her best friend, but at least they'd finally become friends.

"Let's come together," Luke encouraged them, spreading his arms wide to invite everyone into a group hug. They all stepped closer, wrapping their arms around one another, symbolizing the bond they now shared despite their past mistakes and misunderstandings.

Maddie would have never imagined, as the little girl who loved being here at the stables, but always felt like she didn't belong, that this was now her home, and this was now her family.

And she'd found a love in Luke that she'd never dreamed possible, but with God's hand on them all, was hers to cherish.

WESTERN

Rugged men looking for love...

Available Next Month

The Maverick's Thirty-Day Marriage Rochelle Alers
A Cowboy For The Twins Melinda Curtis

....

Fortune's Lone Star Twins Teri Wilson
Her Temporary Cowboy Tanya Agler

....

 LOVE INSPIRED

Safe Haven Ranch Louise M. Gouge
A Cowgirl's Homecoming Julia Ruth

Keep reading for an excerpt of a new title
from the Medical series,
AN ER NURSE TO REDEEM HIM by Traci Douglass

CHAPTER ONE

Tate Griffin jerked upright in bed, breath seizing in his chest as jagged lightning bolted across the sky. Sweating and trembling, he scrubbed his hands over his face, then shoved off the covers. The chilly night air, made chillier by the rare, raging mid-October nor'easter outside, cooled his heated skin. He fought the urge to fall back to sleep because if he did, he'd be right back there again, smack in the middle of the nightmare that had dogged him for four years now. But as he stared into the rain-lashed darkness the memories returned anyway.

"We can't get any lower!" the pilot yelled as the UH-60 Black Hawk tilted precariously above the churning Indian Ocean. "It's too dangerous!"

Three stranded airmen depended on his team to rescue them.

"We can't leave them!" Tate shouted back. "No one else will get here in time!"

Ten seconds later, lightning cracked and towering waves slashed the bottom of the helicopter, causing it to shake violently. Close. Too close. A sharp blast of light, followed by intense heat and excruciating pain, then...

Nothing...

Tate stared over at his window as raindrops pelted the glass and forced himself to take a deep, shaky breath. He wasn't trapped in the burning wreckage of that downed chopper anymore, choking on seawater and the horrible knowledge he was the only survivor.

He hadn't saved a single soul that night. In fact, his fateful decision to even go on the mission had cost the lives of his team as well.

Back then, he'd been young and cocky. They all were. Tommy and Brad were pararescue like him, eager to save the world. Kelly was pararescue too, one of a small, elite group of women to graduate from an Air Force Special Warfare pipeline, qualifying as an STO—special tactics officer—by passing the grueling Apprentice Course at the service's Combat Control School at Pope Army Airfield. She'd done it in two attempts. It had taken Tate and the other guys at least three.

Kelly had been a force to be reckoned with, both on duty and off. She and Tate had even dated for a while, but in the end, they'd made better friends than lovers. He still missed her and the others on his crew every single day. Each time he boarded the helicopter at Wyckford General, he said a silent prayer for them. Then another for himself. That maybe someday he could atone for his failures.

Tonight, with the storm raging and his tension high, all the horrors of the accident seemed far too close to the peaceful, tiny tourist town of Wyckford, Massachusetts. He'd come here on extended leave from the Air Force after additional surgery on his leg to remove some scar tissue because he'd thought it might give him a chance to rest and heal, both mentally and physically. But he'd quickly gotten bored just sitting around on his butt and had ended up taking a temporary job as an EMT on the hospital's new flight crew, doing his level best to put one foot in front of the other and not get lost in the guilt and grief and shame living in his soul now because of the accident. Because in Tate's mind at least, it was his fault all those people were dead. And at night, when he was alone, there was too much space to think about everything he'd done wrong on that last mission and the burden he'd carried every day since.

The next streak of lightning and crack of thunder had him jumping out of his own skin again.

Christ.

Angry at his own weakness, Tate got up. No more eating lobster rolls before bed.

But if he was honest with himself, he knew it wasn't food that brought on those nightmares.

It was his PTSD from the accident. Another reason why staying busy was the best idea for him. When his friend Mark Bates—a firefighter in Wyckford—had first mentioned the flight EMT job, Tate had been skeptical and more than a little worried it might be too much for him. But when the past started haunting him more and more in the quiet, uneventful days, Tate had decided helping others was the least he could do to keep those ghosts at bay. Plus, working in the private sector turned out to be a nice change of pace from his usual highly regimented existence in the military.

Standing, Tate winced as he stretched his stiff leg, then pulled on a pair of jeans and tugged on his shirt from earlier before pulling on his socks and shoes. He'd rented this ranch-style house when he'd first arrived but hadn't really done much with it yet. He went into the living room and turned on the emergency scanner in the corner, figuring if he was up, he might as well make himself useful. Medical emergencies happened 24/7, regardless of the weather or location, so there was a good chance the flight crew could use an extra set of hands tonight.

In fact, maybe he'd just drive into town anyway. Stop at that little diner with the funny-looking bird on the sign on the way, if they were still open in the storm, and get some coffee to fully wake him up before going in.

Tate grabbed his jacket, then walked into the attached garage. As he flipped on the lights the smells of motor oil, well-greased tools and rubber tires welcomed him. In the center of the space sat his baby, his restored 1970 Chevelle SS454. The one luxury he afforded himself, his car brought back fond memories of working on vehicles together with his dad when Tate was growing up. Both his parents were gone now, so the car felt like a little piece of home.

He grabbed the keys from a peg on the wall and slid behind the wheel. The garage door lifted as the engine purred, and Tate backed out into the tempest, eager to outpace his past and pay his debt to all those lives lost on that fateful night four years ago.

The nor'easter raged as Madison Scott ran the short distance from her Mini Cooper to the front door of the Buzzy Bird Café. Thunder shook the ground, and the wind nearly blew her over. She'd forgotten an umbrella that morning because of course she had, but it was just as well—in these gales she'd probably have taken off like Mary Poppins anyway.

A bright bolt of lightning cleaved the ominous clouds, and Madi gasped as everything around her glowed like daytime for an instant: the parking lot, Buzzards Bay across the road full of angry roaring whitecaps and the menacing sky above.

Everything went dark again as she burst into the café, feeling like the hounds of hell were on her very tired heels. Her rubber-soled white nurse's shoes squeaked on the linoleum floor as she stood near the entrance to catch her breath.

The tiny seaside town of Wyckford tended to shut down after 10 p.m., and the diner was deserted except for Madi's best friend, Luna Norton, behind the counter. Luna's parents owned the café and Luna filled in part-time when needed and when it didn't interfere with her regular full-time job as a physical therapist for the hospital. She'd always reminded Madi of a fashion model, tall and leggy, not exactly beautiful, but with an interesting face that made you want to learn more about her. She was also a fantastic artist and had a fearless, kick-ass attitude to life in general. Tonight, her short black pixie cut was tousled and her gray eyes amused as she watched Madi make her way over to the counter.

"Nasty out there," Luna said. "Like a Stephen King novel or something."

Madi nodded as she shook off the icy rain from her scrubs. She'd forgotten a jacket too, having been on the go since dawn and in a perpetual rush for the whole day. One incredibly long ER shift and seventeen hours later, her clothes were now stuck to her like a second skin.

Another gale howled against the building and something heavy lashed the windows. Madi frowned, squinting back at the glass door. No. It couldn't be. Not five minutes ago it had been raining and now… *Snow.* Coming down fast and furious. "This weather's nuts. It's only October."

"That's New England for you," Luna said, her expression disgusted. "Sixty degrees this morning, thirty now. I never know how to dress this time of year."

Speaking of clothes, Madi really needed to change. She bit her lip and glanced out the door again. Maybe if she left now, she'd be okay.

As if reading her mind, Luna said, "Wait it out. This storm will blow over quick enough."

Madi knew better, but it was her own fault. She'd ignored the forecast ever since last week, when the weather guy had promised seventy-degree temps and the day hadn't gotten above fifty, leaving her to spend a long day frozen in the ER. Man, all she really wanted to do was to go home and go to sleep. "My house isn't far. I can make it, I think. I just need to pick up something for dinner first."

"Sorry." Luna hiked her thumb at the pass-through window showing a darkness beyond. "Grill's closed. I can make you a PB&J if you want."

Madi exhaled slow. Dead on her feet, she'd only stopped because she didn't want to cook that night. Or ever. She was horrible in the kitchen and could burn water. "Sounds good."

She took a seat at the counter while Luna gathered the ingredients and made sandwiches.

More lightning flashed, followed immediately by a thundering boom. Great. Now they had thundersnow. The entire diner shuddered under the blast of frigid winds. Then glass shattered as an ear-splitting crack sounded. A giant tree limb now waved at them through the new opening where the front door and windows had been moments before. Then the lights flickered and went out as another hard gust of wind sent more sharp shards tinkling to the floor.

Madi scurried to join Luna, who was crouched behind the counter. "We're safest right here, away from flying debris."

Luna swallowed audibly. "Maybe we should both leave now."

"No." Madi shook her head, staring through the shadows at the blocked entrance of the café. "It's not safe. Let's call for help though." She slapped her scrub pockets. "Damn. I left my phone in the car."

"I forgot mine at my apartment earlier when I changed," Luna said.

Huddled together in the dark, illuminated only by the battery-powered green exit sign over the back door in the kitchen, Madi said, "Too bad we don't have a big, strong hero who'll come looking for us."

Luna snorted. "Don't need one. I do my own heavy lifting."

Madi glanced at her friend's camo cargo mini-skirt, butt-kicking combat boots and snug long-sleeved tee. All topped by a bright pink apron with a cartoon buzzard on the front and the words Buzzy Bird Café emblazoned below it with their web address. One of Luna's designs, because on top of being a physical therapist and filling in as a waitress when needed, Luna was also a great artist. Madi would've been jealous if she didn't love her best friend so much.

She peeked over the counter again, hoping the snow had lightened up outside. It hadn't. In fact, the flakes were blowing sideways now, a constant icy bombardment against the remaining windows and flying in through the broken ones. Maybe if she went out through the rear exit, she could make her way around the building to get to her car. Madi peered up at the pass-through into the pitch-black space. Going through the obstacle course of the kitchen in the dark posed its own set of issues, but what else could she do? They couldn't just sit there all night and freeze to death.

Decision made, Madi climbed to her feet and started toward the swinging door into the back, only to halt as the sound of the two windows over the sink smashing echoed. Her heart stumbled. She sat back down beside Luna as the tree branch in the front entrance continued to wave at them tauntingly. Another escape attempt foiled.

The temperature inside the diner was dropping fast now as wind and snow gusted from two directions. Despite the situation, Madi was still starving. Her stomach growled, and Luna grabbed the sandwiches off the counter above them, handing one to her. They ate like it was their last meal, unnerved by the storm, huddled close to share body heat.

Eventually, Luna said, "If we survive this—"

"Hey." Madi scowled in concern. "We're going to be okay. As soon as the storm lets up, I'll get to my car and call for help, and—"

Luna shifted her weight. "Well, even so, once we get out of here, I'm going to change things. Live my life instead of letting it live me. I suck at that."

"Me too." Madi sighed. Growing up, she'd always been the stable one, the only child in her family who never caused drama, who always followed the rules, who didn't color outside the lines, who supported everyone else. And she did do all those things. She had her reasons, of course, but sometimes—like now—she wished she'd loosened a little, stopped worrying about being the glue at work, in her family. But seeing as how changing the world's perceptions of her would take a lot more than wishing and hoping, Madi decided to go with a more realistic request. "I'd just be happy with a date to the free clinic fundraiser next weekend. I'm the only nurse in the ER without one."

"Okay then." Luna pulled her order pad and

a pen from her apron pocket. "We're stuck here right now, so let's make a list of possible dates for you. And promise me you won't write off anyone too fast, even if he seems like Mr. Wrong."

Luna held out her pinkie for a swear. They'd done that since they were kids. Madi hooked little fingers with her bestie. "I promise—"

A loud thump sounded on one of the walls.

They went still, staring at each other with wide eyes.

"That wasn't a branch." A bad feeling came over Madi, the same one she got sometimes right before they got a serious incoming case. "It's a fist."

She rose to her knees and peered through the dim greenish light toward the direction where the sound had come from near the entrance. A snow drift now blocked the area. Incredible for this early in the season, but big, fat, round snowflakes the size of dinner plates piled up fast she supposed.

The thump came again, along with a moan. A pained one.

Madi stood. "Someone's out there and they're hurt."

"It's too dangerous to go out there right now," Luna pleaded.

"I can't just ignore them." She sidled around the tree branches clogging the front door, arms wrapped around herself. Someone was in trouble, and it was her duty to help. The nurse's curse.

Glass crunched beneath her shoes, and snow blasted her in the face, making her shiver. Amazingly, the aluminum doorframe had withstood the impact, and she was able to shove her way outside. She peered into the parking lot but saw nothing.

"Hello?" Madi called, inching farther out into the night. "Is anyone—"

A hand grabbed her ankle, and she screamed as she fell into the darkness.

NEW RELEASES!

Four sisters. One surprise will. One year to wed.

Don't miss these two volumes of
Wed In The Outback!

When Holt Waverly leaves his flourishing outback estate to his four daughters, it comes to pass that without an eldest son to inherit, the farm will be entailed to someone else…unless all his daughters are married within the year!

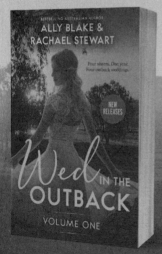

Subscribe and fall in love with a Mills & Boon series today!

You'll be among the first to read stories delivered to your door monthly and enjoy great savings.